Distant Gardens

Distant Gardens

TEN STORIES OF EXPLORATION, BIODIVERSITY, AND FOUND FAMILY

Edited by J.S. Fields & Heather Tracy

CONTENTS

Introduction

Five friends.
One critique group.
Far, far too much time in lockdown.

I joined an online critique group back in 2017, after getting an R&R on the first Ardulum book and needing some fresh eyes on the work. Fast forward to 2021 and the core group found our work increasingly coalescing in theme and tone—to the point where someone (I'm not naming names) got it into their head that we could probably write an anthology.

But what kind of anthology? Turned out my love of lesfic, especially SFF lesfic, had become a weird, unifying force. We talked about lesbian culture a lot, from teasing out chapstick lesbian from lipstick lesbian, to nail lengths, to nail polishes, to the uniquely subverted patriarchal-tinged pick-up lines women sometimes use on each other. All those conversations, including having read through my past five books, we felt ready—as a group—to write a collection of stories. Plus, having me edit the collection ensured we didn't fall into any 'her breasts breasted boobily' traps. Not that our readers would likely mind extensive breast bouncing scenes but, you know, I wanted this anthology to be at least slightly higher brow.

We wanted more than just a collection of otherworldly lesbians, however. We wanted to write for lesfic and wlw readers, while holding true to our shared SFF roots (especially the tropes in those roots). 'Distant Gardens' spans deadly plants, space fungi, stolen planets, and terraformed worlds. There are superheroes (in very tight pants), monster real estate agents, koalas, interstellar corporations, and exploding faeries. We have also used the broadest possible definition of 'lesbian' to include bisexual and pansexual women, trans women, and nonbinary and intersex folx who find themselves at home under the lesbian flag. This anthology is f/f in the very best sense— inclusive and exploratory and unabashedly anti-TERF.

Each author here has included two stories—one from a completely new world, and another based on characters from their already established books. It's my hope that if you've come here following

your favorite author, you might also find a window into an entirely
new series or genre. If you're new to us all, then double welcome!
From Atalant and Emn's long-awaited engagement story, to a trans
mycologist and her very friendly mercenary, to a woman who loses
control of her car and finds herself hanging from a tree in fairyland, I
hope you enjoy this weird, wild, eclectic collection of wayward
planets, plants, and fungi, and the lesbians who battle (and sometimes
love) them.

- J. S. Fields, May 2021

A NOTE ON THE STORIES CONTAINED HEREIN:

Each tale is marked on the title page with what sapphic representation is involved, as well as any content warnings. There is also a "Heat Level" if you wish to read or not read particular sexual content. The scale is as follows:

Low/None: There may be talk of sex, holding hands, or possibly kissing.

Medium: Mention of body parts, touching, and make-out sessions, but all scenes are "fade to black."

Hot!: Has at least one full sex scene, start to finish. You have been warned (or encouraged...).

Radiant

N.L. Bates

Sapphic Representation: Lesbian, Bi/Pan
Heat Level: Medium
Content Warnings: Coarse Language, Violence

There were plenty of superheroes who could handle your standard foil-the-villain, defeat-the-doomsday-device, save-the-child-from-the-burning-building type situation.

Annalise Warren, glorified garbage collector, wasn't one of them.

True, the garbage she collected for a day job happened to be radioactive. Which was kind of neat, sure. But mostly being immune to radiation meant having to 'out' herself as a super constantly. Like when her dentist asked for an X-ray. Or explaining to her OBGYN that science had yet to discover a way to give her a mammogram.

Still, Anna *did* enjoy ordinary things. Gardening. Manicures with color-changing nail polish. Deconstructing old toasters into suits of armor. When CAPER's priority ringtone startled her out of her garden on a Saturday afternoon, Anna—more intrigued than annoyed—answered on the first ring. It wasn't like she had plans with her girlfriend. Ex-girlfriend. Pauline. Whatever.

"Code name Radiant," her boss said. "It's Eleanor. I need you for a waste retrieval. I'm afraid it's urgent."

Unlike chasing after supervillains, nuclear waste cleanup was predictable, urgent or not. And overtime pay never hurt. She could probably finish today, make enough to pay this month's rent, and be back in time to watch karaoke at her favorite dive bar. "All right," Anna said. "Where am I heading?"

"Vancouver Island."

"What?" Christ, she hoped this wasn't a tanker spill or something. "There aren't any nuclear facilities on the island."

"Correct," Eleanor said. "You'll be recovering material that was improperly released into the Pacific by Torgen Technologies. They were unlawfully using it to power their 'Omen' Project."

"Shit," Anna breathed. "Didn't they *just* have an inspection of their power generation facilities? They asked me to consult on it but I passed because Pauline...I mean she...we had a thing."

Eleanor, mercifully, ignored the last part of Anna's sentence. "The authorities didn't find anything. We now know why. They decided to dump the evidence in lieu of paying a fine."

"I guess that nice waterfront property makes the ocean an easy dumping ground," Anna said. They were using *nuclear fuel* to power that quantum computing thing they were building—the Optimized

ElectroMagnetic Network (pronounced 'omen,' not OEMN, because of course it was). "Idiots."

"Yes," Eleanor said, in a tone that suggested there were many more words where that one had come from. "Ambient radiation levels have been rising since the initial detection, signature consistent with uranium-235. A runaway reaction is unlikely, but we need to act quickly. The salt in the water can form particularly dangerous contaminants that could have disastrous consequences for the marine life."

"Right." Anna had never done an underwater retrieval before. The trip to the island had been one of the reasons Pauline hadn't wanted her to take the consulting job. Also because they'd just had a big fight over Anna's long working hours and growing pile of dismantled toasters. "Do you have an exact location?"

"Not yet. There's a map in your dossier," Eleanor said. Anna's phone buzzed in her hand. She tapped the screen and brought up the document.

Eleanor continued, "We've identified an area of interest, approximately twelve kilometers across. It's an ecologically sensitive area. The kelp forest there still has healthy biomarkers, however. For that reason, we assume the uranium has landed in the deeper waters beyond the kelp forest's borders."

That was good news, at least, that the forest was intact. Working in the Environmental Remediation and Recovery Department of CAPER, the Canadian Agency of Powered and Extra-ordinary Regulation, had taught her that kelp forests were immensely important to biodiversity and carbon sequestration—which humanity had realized almost too late. After the predictable climate apocalypse, what was left of the international community had undertaken the single greatest geoengineering effort in human memory, re-seeding and re-wilding vast swathes of land and sea. It had worked, mostly, but just recently, there'd been a human-started fire that was going to set the region's hard-won climate equilibrium back by years.

Dumping nuclear waste in the ocean could do a lot more damage than a brush fire.

"Your requisitioned submarine is radiation-spec and has sufficient space for the amount of nuclear waste we expect you will recover,"

Eleanor said, "but you'll need to conduct the retrieval manually. The scuba gear and the Atmospheric Diving Suit do not have radiation shielding, which is why I need you."

Anna cleared her throat. "I, um, don't actually know how to *use* any of that."

"Your partner for this assignment does," Eleanor said, with such perfect assurance that Anna almost laughed. Of course Eleanor was way ahead of her. "She's a diving enthusiast, and will be able to train you on the equipment. I also have permission to divulge that she has advanced capabilities which should help you locate the uranium once you're on-site."

'Advanced capabilities,' of course, was office code for superpowers.

"You may have met before, actually," Eleanor added. "Chris Carlysle?"

At first, Anna couldn't place the name, but scrolling through the dossier she found a staff photo of a woman she recognized: tousled brunette pixie cut, complexion as sandy as the beach they'd met on, and an easy, confident smile that drew Anna in like a tide to the shore.

"The dossier includes your travel itinerary," Eleanor added.

"Itinerary," Anna mumbled. Chris's dimples reminded her, fleetingly, of Pauline. She'd always been a sucker for dimples.

"Annalise? Is something the matter?"

Anna should have been planting tulips in her garden, trying to forget all about women. And Chris probably didn't even remember her. This did not have to be a big deal.

"Nothing," she replied. She flicked a clump of dirt from her knee, cleared her mind of all ex-girlfriend-related baggage, and said, "I'll get ready to go."

Just a totally ordinary waste retrieval, under the ocean, with equipment she didn't know how to use and a woman she'd once had a crush on. Not that she cared about crushes. She'd broken up with Pauline less than a month ago. No, there was nothing the matter at all.

* * *

Anna had met Chris—two years ago? three?—at one of CAPER's "how to be a superhero" workshops. She'd always thought the events were a waste of time, since she wasn't really a superhero. But they were mandatory, because you never knew when you might be in the right place at the right time to save the world. And they were held at CAPER's main headquarters on Vancouver Island, so Anna wasn't going to complain. Saltwater spa. World-class fish tacos. It gave her an opportunity to explore the island's many resort spots, which was how she'd wound up on a quiet beach in Tofino that weekend.

There was laughter from a nearby lodge, hidden by the treeline. She'd heard birdsong. And the waves. The taste of lime-dressed halibut lingered in her mouth. Anna sat with her feet in the water, watching the waves trace patterns of lace across a surface of mirrored turquoise.

"Nice, isn't it?"

When Anna retold the story in her head, she hadn't jumped at the sound of another voice. She definitely hadn't squeaked.

The speaker was a tall brunette in a black wetsuit. Her face was distorted by a snorkeling mask, but Anna remembered that distinctive hourglass shape from the workshops. She'd been wearing a bracelet the same brushed nickel color as Anna's most recent toaster acquisition.

"Nice? Yes," Anna said. And then, trying to find a response that wasn't completely silly, she added, "Lots of beautiful things out here. Like your bracelet. And you."

She'd promptly covered her mouth with her hand.

The brunette smirked. "I'm glad you think so." She walked past Anna and into the water, untucking a pair of flippers from under her arm. "Name's Chris, by the way."

"Uh. Anna." She got to her feet, suddenly conscious of her soggy shorts.

Chris glanced up from her flippers as Anna brushed clumps of sand from her legs, and grinned. "Might want to go for a swim and rinse everything off. That sand gets *every*where, trust me." And then, before Anna could come up with a clever response, she winked and turned toward the sea.

At the time, Anna had found the comment a bit crass. But in the hotel shower that night, scrubbing sand from the inconvenient crevices between her thighs, she had to admit Chris had had a point. And an incandescent smile.

The steady stream from the showerhead felt cold against the sudden warmth of her body. Anna reached for the soap. Flirting was one thing. Lusting after coworkers quite so *avidly* seemed like another. She should focus on the bracelet. The smile. Ignore the hips and...everything that went along with them.

But for the rest of the trip, every time she had to shake sand out of her underwear, she found herself thinking about Chris.

* * *

Anna had wondered a few times if she should've made more of an effort to reconnect. She'd even looked Chris up in the staff directory once, but chickened out. Too creepy, she'd told herself.

She'd met Pauline not long after, so she hadn't regretted it much. Until Pauline had thrown out half her toasters. Until Pauline had made the rule about wire clippers in the bedroom. Until Pauline had left and now...

"You're overthinking it, Anna," she murmured. Time for a distraction. She set her phone to read her the news as she boarded the ferry that would take her to Vancouver Island.

"Today is the fifth anniversary of the 'hurricane hacker' ransomware attack," her phone chirped. "The attack deactivated an entire fleet of StormAI rescue vehicles during Hurricane Malia, resulting in eleven deaths. While perpetrator Samantha Siimes was imprisoned after the attack, her accomplices were never discovered."

"Annalise, right?" said a familiar voice behind her. A voice that conjured up images of sand, and underwear, and that amazing lime dressing.

"...may be behind the most recent copycat attack," her phone continued. "Recently, a cyberattacker calling themselves the 'Tropical Trojan—'"

Anna swiped at the pause button. "Hi. Yes. It's me. You're, uh. Not wearing the bracelet."

Chris smiled and didn't even look at her wrist. "It's good to see you again, too."

Anna couldn't help but smile back. "You too," she said, and followed Chris down to the private room CAPER had reserved below deck. A tiny, closet-like room where Anna couldn't avoid staring. Chris's hair was a little longer than Anna remembered, but it still stuck out every which way. She had a hook nose and a strong jaw. She wore fashionably understated lip gloss and leggings that showed off far more than the wetsuit had.

No lusting after coworkers, Anna.

Anna turned to Chris as the door closed behind them. "I guess you're driving the submarine?"

"That's right. I am your underwater field guide for this adventure," Chris said. "I know you have an ADS, but I'll show you how to use the scuba gear."

"ADS?"

"Atmospheric Diving Suit," Chris said. "It's a pain in the ass, but it'll keep you from getting the bends." She frowned. "But it won't protect you from radiation exposure."

"Oh, I don't need to worry about that," Anna said, trying to sound casual. "I'm immune."

Chris's face lit up. "Oh! You're Radiant! I've heard of your work."

"You have?" Okay, Anna had been bragging, but she hadn't actually expected it to work. "I mean...Mostly I pick up heavy things and put them down somewhere else. It isn't that big of a deal."

So much for bragging. She sure wasn't going to impress the girls that way. Not that she was trying to impress anyone.

"You pick up *radioactive* things."

"I just do what the drones can't get close enough to handle," Anna said. "Too much radiation makes them bug out. Does this ADS have a computer system?"

"Communications and propulsion," Chris said. "But you can walk in it. Think of it like a really bulky hazmat suit."

It was impossible to look cool in a hazmat suit. Anna made a face. "Maybe we should stick with the scuba gear."

"In that case!" Chris gestured to a set of scuba tanks that had been laid out in one corner. The ferry's horn blared. "Let me show you how it works. We can practice on the ride over...You know how to lift, I bet, so let's focus on how to get this on you." She hefted one of the tanks and shrugged it on, pointing out the various straps and carabiners. Then she gestured to the other tank. Anna lifted and slid the harness over her shoulders.

The horn sounded again. "Not bad," Chris said.

The boat jostled. Anna stumbled.

Chris caught her by the shoulder. "All right?" she asked.

The suave superhero that Anna wanted to be would have said "of course," and said it with a roguish grin. The real Anna mumbled "fine, thanks," and fumbled with her carabiners.

Chris swallowed a sound in between a hiccup and a cough. "You also need to practice taking this stuff off. It's harder than you'd think. Let me know if you need help with that." Which was a perfectly professional thing to say under the circumstances.

Anna started unclipping everything she'd just clipped.

The ferry lurched again, more violently this time, and so did Anna. She might have fallen if Chris, half-crouched to set her own scuba gear on the deck, hadn't caught her waist. Her hand braced Anna's hip. Steady. Professional. Much more intimate than Anna had been prepared for.

Anna's cheeks heated.

She needed to say something.

The gentle pressure of Chris's hand vanished from her hip, and Chris said, "You forgot to undo this strap here." Her fingers lingered just below Anna's belly button, as if they might dip a little bit lower. "Sorry I didn't wear the bracelet. I didn't know you liked it so much."

Anna swallowed.

"Right," she said, and set the scuba gear back on the deck.

* * *

CAPER chartered a truck, with a brand-new, green hydrogen engine that the driver would not shut up about, that got Anna, Chris, and the submarine to the west coast of Vancouver Island by early evening.

The submarine was cigar-shaped, with a fin that looked like a chimney and a mottled paint job that was probably supposed to be camouflage. Not a swatch of silver anywhere, which was a downright shame. Anna did breathe a sigh of relief when she saw the Red Sea

Rescue logo splashed along one side. One of the new vehicles, thank God. CAPER still had a few StormAI vehicles in rotation, but Anna did not want to drive a vehicle that had been hacked by a supervillain like Siimes. Sure, the submarine probably wouldn't manage to kill eleven people if it went haywire, but that was a complication she did *not* need while underwater and playing with nuclear waste.

The submarine looked even smaller from the inside. The back was closed off: engine, water desalination, oxygen generation, and power, in the form of a tiny, gen-eight nuclear reactor. Halogen lights glared against stainless steel walls. There was only one window, a small, round one near the submarine's nose. Chris, whose hair brushed the ceiling when she stood straight, informed her that most submarines didn't have windows at all. There was a fold-out table bolted to the wall and a bathroom so tiny it didn't bear thinking about. All their mission-critical items were stowed in the compartment below their feet, which would also, Chris said gleefully, spit them out if they needed to go for a swim.

The remainder of the sub was control panels and displays: area maps, periscope output, sonar, radar. Another screen showed aggregate readouts from the Ucluelet kelp forest, reported by dozens of sensors grown into the kelp itself: growth and death rates, water pH and temperature, other indicators Anna couldn't make much sense of. Radiation in the kelp forest still appeared to be within normal range.

"Make yourself comfortable," Chris said. "Our target's at least a couple hours away, depending on exactly where it landed."

"How do we find that out?" Anna asked.

"That's why I'm here," Chris said. "I helped develop the detection tech we're using. Based on, you know." She waved a hand vaguely at herself.

"I don't, actually," Anna said. They'd never really talked in Tofino. Or they had, and Anna had just been busy staring at Chris's...bracelet. "Eleanor didn't share."

"Oh!" Chris flexed one arm in an exaggerated 'we can do it!' pose. The result was definitely impressive. "I am the Mighty Magnetron!"

"Magnetron? Like what they use in microwaves?" *Oh my God, Anna, shut up.*

But Chris laughed, a delighted, delightful tenor. "Same principle, different application. I can magnetize metals, generate EMPs, that sort of thing."

"You're with Community Safety?" Anna guessed. The Community Safety department did most of the traditional superheroing: rescue services and law enforcement contracts. The code names starting with "Mighty" in that department took up three pages of search results in CAPER's staff directory.

Chris laughed again. "Everyone thinks that! I'm actually in Research and Development. If I want adrenaline, I go diving. Less paperwork."

Anna had to smile. "Well, you're with me, and I work for Environment. There'll be *some* paperwork."

"But you'll do it for me, right?" Chris winked. "What if I, oh!" She fished in her pocket and pulled out a silver ring with a line of inset blue stones. "Forgot to take it off this morning and it's been riding in my pocket since." She slid the ring on her pinkie finger, then pressed her pinkie to her cheek. "What about now? Shiny enough?"

Early stage flirting was not the time to discuss her toaster problem. To change the topic, Anna asked, "How does that help us find the uranium?"

Chris shrugged and dropped her hand. "I can read magnetic fields." She then launched into an explanation about radiation and charged particles that Anna could barely follow. "It'll come down to a visual search in the end. But I should be able to cut the area we're searching at least in half."

"That's a relief," Anna said. Manually searching twelve kilometers of kelp forest did not sound like a good time.

"Don't thank me yet," Chris said. "The currents will make precision a lot harder. We could be out here a couple more days if we're not lucky."

"That doesn't sound so bad," Anna said, without thinking. But Chris smiled at her, flashed her ring, and Anna wasn't about to take the words back.

* * *

The plan was simple: Find where the radiation was strongest in their twelve-kilometer zone, locate the uranium, and stuff it into a radiation-rated barrel where it couldn't contaminate the marine life. Then haul it back to shore for processing. Easy.

"Anna," Chris said. "The radiation readings are getting stronger the farther west we go, and there's a magnetic field near the peak. It's probably a product of the radiation. Take a look."

Anna leaned in for a better look. Chris's body radiated heat. A superpower, or something else? Was it a faux pas to ask a coworker on a date while you were still on the job?

"Focus," Chris whispered in her ear.

Anna focused. The map showed green lines and navy ones—kelp forests and currents, maybe?—and some shifting black lines that Anna didn't understand. One set of numbers immediately caught her attention: the radiation in some spots was almost double what it had been an hour ago. Geographic indicators stained the blue ocean an ominous purple.

"Is this real-time data?" Anna asked.

"Pretty close." Chris blew out a sigh and leaned back. "This is probably our target, but let's be sure. Any chance it could be naturally occurring?"

"Not if it's uranium-235," Anna said. "There wouldn't be nearly this much of it." She looked at the readouts again and shook her head. "We're in trouble. It shouldn't be decaying this quickly."

Chris's eyebrows twitched. "Will it...explode?"

"Maybe. The trick is to walk away *before* something explodes," Anna said.

She'd meant it as a joke, but Chris looked at her like she'd actually said something impressive. Anna shrugged. "The radiation can't hurt me, so..."

"You do have a neat bag of tricks," Chris remarked.

"Aheh," was the best that Anna could manage.

Chris fiddled with her ring. "I'm struggling with this. I'm doing my PhD in electromagnetism. Water is a coolant. It should make the uranium *less* reactive."

"The uranium could be in a waterproof casing," Anna suggested. "We'll just have to go and look for ourselves."

"I thought you said it might explode? I'd rather not get blown up."

"We aren't going to get blown up," Anna said. "I've just never done an underwater cleanup before."

"You're not helping."

Anna tapped the navigation and redirected the submarine toward the radiation peak, which was in the middle of a kelp forest—a forest returning no abnormal readings whatsoever from the planted 'trees.' The radiation might have been hard on the fish, but the kelp appeared to be flourishing. "We should hurry. The ecosystem won't withstand that level of radiation for very long...although I really can't explain the kelp. Maybe it's broken firmware in the kelp sensors? But the last readout is from just a few seconds ago."

"On it," Chris said. She walked away from the controls, toward the back of the sub.

Anna turned to ask, "What's our ETA?" but the words dried in her mouth when she saw Chris's clothes discarded on the deck. Belatedly, she realized that Chris was pulling on a wetsuit, a slate blue number that perfectly accentuated her eyes. It accentuated a lot of other things, too—like the curves and lines of her hips, which Anna had to admit she'd been admiring as Chris had walked past her that day in Tofino. Even with the ring and the banter, Anna wasn't sure where casual nudity fell on the 'flirty' spectrum.

"ETA is about twenty minutes," Chris said. Anna tried not to follow the zipper with her eyes as Chris casually secured a flap across her bust. "I know you're doing the dirty work, but I wanted to be ready for a quick deployment. You'll want to get changed too."

"Um."

Chris's right cheek dimpled when she smiled. "You didn't have to look."

For God's sake, say something. Anna blurted: "What if I didn't know how to get into it?"

Maybe not that, idiot.

But Chris's grin broadened, and she winked. "All you had to do was ask."

Anna only managed to stop herself from wondering out loud if that was a double entendre by saying, all in a rush, "It's a good thing we got the good submarine."

"What?" Chris's brow furrowed, but her smirk didn't entirely fade.

"The good submarine. I mean. The ones that can't be hacked. That *weren't* hacked."

"Oh, you mean the Siimes thing?" Chris's expression shifted from bemusement back to just amusement. "Supposedly she needs hardware access to do that stuff. And I doubt they're giving her computer time in jail anymore."

"I...yes. Well. We should hurry."

Her face felt hot enough to boil water. Anna retreated to the bathroom.

* * *

The submarine's tiny storage compartment was too small to hold the radiation barrels, the ADS, and two people. Chris bent over the ADS. Anna pressed herself against the ladder, one hand on the rungs after accidentally brushing against Chris's...glutes. Chris politely ignored it, just like Anna ignored—tried to ignore—the way Chris's elbow kept landing between her thighs. Not hard, just...there.

The ADS was an articulated metal monstrosity, more like a suit of armor than anything Anna associated with watersports, but you didn't have to be an experienced diver to use it. Hoses snaked up from the back of the suit into the tether, which served as tow line, air supply, and fiber optic cable. A small floodlight was mounted on one shoulder.

The top half of the ADS winched up and away as Chris turned the mechanical wheel and opened the suit. Its helmet clonked against the ceiling; inside the submarine, they didn't have room to open it all the way.

Anna unpeeled herself from the wall and swung one leg over the suit's waist.

Chris offered her arm as Anna clambered inside. Anna took it, even though she didn't need the boost. Now for the really fun part: cramming herself into the half-open torso.

Before she could make the attempt, Chris's hand tightened. Anna turned to look at her. Their faces were only inches apart. Why—

"Hey," Chris said. "Good luck out there."

Her breath was hot and fruity. Anna's pulse hammered, and not because she was about to go wandering across the bottom of the ocean. "Thanks."

Chris's hand lingered on her arm.

Anna took a breath.

Chris licked her lips.

Anna experienced a moment of complete, unadulterated panic, leaned back, and wedged herself into the suit.

Chris shrugged, winched the top back down, then took a thick faceplate and popped it in into the helmet. It clicked into place.

Anna banged her forehead against the faceplate, both to test the seal, and to remind herself that canoodling with coworkers was a *really* bad idea.

* * *

The water was dark. Barren. A minute passed while the submarine towed her along, silent except for the rhythmic click of a Geiger counter. Then two. The submarine's floodlights swept across white sand and the corpses of seal pups. A small constellation of tools floated around her, harnessed to the ADS. The radiation barrels, each the size of a small wine cask, strung out behind her like the world's worst charm bracelet.

"Radiation?" Chris asked, hopefully referring to the carnage of seals.

"Better be," Anna murmured.

Something loomed in her vision, dark and sudden.

"Whoa!"

Broad, yellow leaves flattened themselves across her faceplate. She heard the soft brushing of kelp stalks against her suit, and hoped they wouldn't tangle. The mobility of the ADS sucked enough as it was. Then, just like that, they were gone.

The submarine continued to drag her west.

"Magnetron?" Anna said. It was CAPER convention to use codenames on official comms, whether your identity was public or not, because no communication channel was as secure as you thought.

"Was that the canopy?" Now that they'd passed it, she couldn't see anything else.

"No," Chris said, her voice tense. "That was a bunch of dead kelp."

Anna winced. She wasn't an expert in marine biology, but if a lot of the kelp had died off already, they might be too late to stop cascading effects on the ecosystem. Even though their sensors said the kelp was fine.

"This doesn't make sense," she said, more to herself than to Chris. There might be a flaw in one of the sensor suites that explained the faulty radiation reporting. Mass die-off, not so much. She'd have to grab a sample. Maybe someone at CAPER could figure out the problem.

"Canopy!" Chris said, actual excitement in her voice.

The submarine slowed to a crawl.

Anna saw stalks. She saw brown, whipcord stalks that stretched from the seafloor and up, all the way to the surface. Each of those individual...kelps? Plants? Rounded out to a bulb-like tip. The tips opened into fans of fronds that—haloed in the light from a distantly setting sun—were a brown so warm they were almost gold. The kelp undulated lazily against a backdrop too dark to be called blue. The floating sediment looked like stars.

"Radiant?"

There was concern in Chris's voice. Anna realized she hadn't responded.

"It's beautiful," she said.

Chris's voice softened. "Yes. It is."

The water deepened to twilight colors. Kelp fronds caressed the ADS as Chris lowered Anna to the seafloor. Some of those fronds were longer than Anna was tall.

A school of fish swarmed the submarine, glinting silver in the floodlights. A handful of them listed, violently, to the right. Their eyes glazed, their fins shook, and they lay suspended, hanging limply in the water.

The Geiger counter clicked.

The area of interest was only a few kilometers across. This close, any uranium fuel bundles should be easy to spot with a floodlight. Anna covered the area in methodical sweeps, back and forth.

Occasionally she stumbled on rocks, one of which was actually an irate crab. It skittered away, its mandibles opening and closing in reproach. She saw seals, urchins, and an octopus. Living ones, thankfully. At one point, a stalk of kelp broke away from the seafloor by degrees, as roots like short, spindly fingers unclasped a rock one by one.

"Are they supposed to break away like that?" Anna asked. "The roots?"

"They're called 'haptera,' and yes, it's a normal part of the life cycle," Chris said. "If you see it once or twice, it isn't a concern. If it happens a lot, the forest is in trouble."

The haptera clenched together as they floated toward the surface, for all the world like a fist.

Anna refused to be creeped out by seaweed. She kept moving.

Anna glimpsed a silhouette, out of range of the submarine's floodlights. A dune, or whatever you called a hill at the bottom of the ocean. Too big for a fuel bundle, or even an intact nuclear core. She continued her sweep.

Another breakaway happened a few minutes later. The haptera *reached*. Driven by the current, she knew, but she still felt a flash of adrenaline when they trailed across her arm. She shook the kelp—and the feeling—off. "Ugh."

"You all right?" Chris's voice over the intercom, a lifeline.

The Geiger counter picked up speed.

"Fine. It's just some kelp." On second thought, the silhouette at the edge of the floodlights was probably a wreck. She hadn't realized there was wreck remediation still happening in this area. Didn't matter. Not her problem.

She kept searching. More kelp drifted upward, catching on the tether. Its bottom end dangled in front of her faceplate, the haptera waving back and forth like windshield wipers. She brushed them away, bonking the metal of her gauntlets against the metal of her helmet.

The Geiger counter, dangling from her harness, continued to clickclickclick.

Anna snatched for it. It was noisy and annoying. She didn't need to worry about safe radiation thresholds, anyway. The Geiger's display flashed a number in microSieverts as she reached for the off switch.

Anna paused. She read the number again.

If she hadn't been under a hundred feet of ocean, she might have believed this was a runaway nuclear reaction. She'd seen numbers like this exactly once before. She'd been *inside* an active power plant at the time.

The kelp wobbled in the current. Between the stalks, she saw again the cylindrical silhouette, bigger than their submarine. It was too smooth to be a rock formation, too symmetrical to be a wreck. The only irregularity she could see was a protrusion rising from its top, like a chimney. Or a cooling tower.

"Chris—" She almost forgot the embargo on given names, but managed to turn the syllable into a cough. "There's a goddamned nuclear power plant down here."

"*What*? How would someone hide an entire nuclear power plant?"

The sensors in the kelp hadn't been malfunctioning. They'd been hacked.

Seaweed wrapped around her helmet. "Jesus Christ! I can't see!"

"Radiant, what—holy shit! The kelp is...it's everywhere! I can barely see out the window. And our external comms just got cut off—"

Cut off.

Knife.

Somewhere Anna had a knife.

She didn't have to panic. She was wearing a suit of metal armor, for crying out loud. It was just an overgrown plant, right? There wasn't much it could do except cause a nuisance. There wasn't anything to break or pull off except...

A bundle of roots wrapped around her oxygen hose and tugged. Hard.

Shit.

She had a million things attached to her harness. Where was the damned knife?

Her hand found the handle of...something, and she thrashed wildly at the stalk still wrapped around her helmet. The elbow joints on the stupid suit were not designed for 'thrashing.' She bashed the kelp. She sawed at it. "Fucking fuck!"

"Anna, what's *happening*?"

Don't panic. It was *seaweed*, for Christ's sake. It definitely couldn't pull a quarter-inch rubber hose out of a metal grommet.

"I think someone hacked the reporting firmware!" Her foot caught against what she thought was a rock. She had to hit the propulsion to keep the suit from falling over. She *hated* the ADS. "They're using it to manipulate the kelp. It keeps grabbing me."

"To do *what*?" Chris demanded.

The propulsion had upset the sand beneath her. Her field of vision—still 99% seaweed—was briefly overtaken by a swirl of sediment. She still felt the pull on the oxygen hose.

"Take out my life support!" Anna smacked more kelp away. "Maybe blind me?"

"Jesus. Are you okay?"

"I need to get free!" Cutting through the kelp wasn't working. She needed a different tactic. "Hold on. I'll try not to crash into you."

"What the hell—"

Anna piloted the suit straight up.

For a moment, she thought it had worked. Suspended above the seafloor, she could see—she could see again!—the kelp twisting in the eddies she'd created. Stalks dangled where her sudden acceleration had ripped them away from the seafloor. One was still wrapped limply around the oxygen hose. It no longer had any anchor to pull from.

"Can you disconnect the ADS from the submarine?" Anna asked. "I need to get to that power plant." She wasn't sure what she'd do about the person running it, but she knew exactly what to do with nuclear reactors.

"Are you out of your mind?"

The free-floating kelp stalks around her tangled together like a braid. Or a rope.

"Don't you want to find out what's going on in there?" Anna asked. "Besides, we have to get the uranium. That's the whole mission."

The kelp rope reached for her. Anna backed the suit away.

"The mission was to retrieve some *discarded* uranium," Chris said. "Community Safety are the ones who are supposed to deal with villains. Let *them* handle this."

"Community Safety won't be able to get close," Anna said. "Not with radiation levels this high." The kelp kept coming, strands swirling like a gymnast's ribbon. They grasped at her, oddly beautiful. One still clinging to a rocky outcropping tried again to find her oxygen tube. She slapped it away.

"Look, I need to shut that place down," Anna said. She knocked away another reaching kelp stalk. Three more took its place. "It's trying to stop me from getting back to the submarine."

"I'm extracting you," Chris said.

It *was* the knife she'd been holding. Anna swiped at some kelp fronds. They danced away from her in tandem. "You don't have radiation gear, remember?"

"Then aren't I already fucked?" asked Chris.

"Not if you stay inside the sub," Anna said. "It's shielded." She heard muffled swearing in response.

The kelp rippled. Anna slashed, to no effect, and tried not to think about how much of the kelp forest had been re-purposed for...whatever this was. What other tricks did the hacker have up their sleeve?

"We need to get you out of there," Chris said. "Can I leave the submarine at all?"

"Recommended maximum exposure time at these levels without shielding is approximately twenty minutes," Anna said without thinking. "But—"

Her head bounced against the helmet as she was jerked violently downward. Her vision went white, then black. She heard ragged breathing. Someone yelling. Everything hurt.

That was Chris, doing the yelling. She knew she should answer. She kicked uselessly at the kelp. Her head spun as she was pulled upward. She tried to say something, even if it was only Chris's name.

The kelp slammed her into the rocks again. Her ears rang, but the yelling had stopped.

The kelp pulled her down a third time.

"Magnetron!" Anna yelped.

Chris didn't reply, but Anna didn't hit the rocks again, either. The kelp cocooned her, determined to drag her down and smash her to death. But its downward pressure was matched by the slow pull of the tether upward. Chris must be spooling it back in.

Great. She was now the centerpiece in a tug-of-war between a submarine and an entire kelp forest.

Anna took another shaky breath. Even that felt like a struggle. Something was smeared across her faceplate. "Magnetron?"

Chris should be safe in the submarine. Maybe she'd left the intercom to retract the tether? But no, she'd said you could automate that. Anna tried to wipe the water droplets away from her face with her hand. The stupid metal mitten clunked off the helmet.

"Magnetron, status report. *Please.*"

It occurred to her, quite suddenly, that she shouldn't be seeing water droplets when she was already underwater. Then it occurred to her that the droplets she shouldn't be seeing were *inside* her helmet.

She didn't have squished kelp bits on her faceplate. She had a hairline fracture.

"Magnetron," she choked, though it didn't seem like Chris was there. "I think my suit is broken."

The kelp moved up, toward the submarine, folding into a net. It was going to block the hatch.

Of course. All the hacker had to do was keep her in the water long enough for the broken suit to finish her off. Anna stretched shaking fingers over the propulsion controls.

The suit sputtered. Anna wasn't moving any faster than the damn kelp.

The beam of a headlamp appeared between the stalks, resolving into a scuba diver holding a pair of shears that would have seemed comically oversized any other time. They were likely meant for cutting steel cables.

"Chris!" she shouted. "You have to get back to the sub! You're not shielded!" Her voice rattled unpleasantly inside the helmet.

The kelp writhed as Chris swam forward, shears at the ready. She darted away from reaching fronds, cutting down or swatting away stalks that got too close. She was fast, but she wasn't superhuman fast, and the kelp was everywhere.

Anna tried to knock some of the kelp away, but the ADS wasn't responding. She felt like she was swimming through pudding. The kelp surrounded Chris—reaching, tugging, slapping, grasping.

What kind of useless superpower meant you couldn't protect somebody when it mattered?

Chris sheared through a stalk coiled around her ankle, and another grabbed her arm. She jerked away, but the kelp held on.

Chris dropped the shears.

"Chris!" Anna screamed.

Chris lunged. Anna had been sure she would make a last-ditch attempt for the shears, was surprised when Chris grabbed her arm instead. As romantic gestures went, dying together wasn't bad. Maybe Tofino had meant something after all.

Anna braced herself, fumbling in her stupid useless gauntlets for Chris's hand. She couldn't even tell if she was holding it. She wasn't sure what she was bracing for.

The submarine's lights went out.

"Hello?" she said, stupidly. The light mounted to the ADS wasn't working either. All the electronics were shot. Maybe that had been Chris? She'd said she could do EMPs. Was she still there?

The air in the ADS turned hot and stuffy.

A drop of water, ice-cold, landed in her eye.

Chris's face appeared, lit by the beam of a handheld flashlight. Dead kelp, dead fish, dead animals floated past Anna's field of vision. Nothing was attacking them anymore.

Another drop of water hit her cheek. She took a breath of stale air. Chris had reached down to recover the shears. Anna waved, tapped her helmet, wishing they had a way to actually communicate.

Chris's eyes widened as she registered the fractured faceplate. She grabbed something, held it up to the meager beam of the flashlight. A spare regulator. Most scuba tanks had an extra mouthpiece for situations like this.

Well, maybe not exactly like this. Anna nodded vigorously.

Chris tucked the flashlight under her armpit and floated closer, one hand ready to pull the faceplate off, bracing her feet against the torso of the ADS. Her free hand held three fingers in front of Anna's face. Two.

Anna braced herself, and the sea came roiling in.

The cold was enough to make her gasp, but Chris had been ready, pressing the regulator into Anna's mouth. Seawater trickled in from the corners of her lips and she had to close her eyes against the salty sting. But she could breathe. Chris put a steadying hand on the top of her head, and Anna hoped she wouldn't let go.

Water poured in at her waist as Chris opened the ADS and tugged her free of it. Anna was glad Chris had insisted on the wetsuit.

Chris's arm slid down her back, wrapped tightly around Anna's waist. The contact introduced Anna to bruises she hadn't realized she had, but she wouldn't have traded it away. She could breathe again. With her eyes squinched tightly shut, she could almost pretend they were somewhere other than the bottom of the ocean.

Something brushed against Anna's arm, and she shivered. Together, they rose toward the submarine.

* * *

The submarine's systems were down thanks to Chris's EMP. They had only backup oxygen. They still couldn't call for help. All they could do was replace their scuba gear and carry on.

Chris had *insisted* upon coming into the supervillain lair with her. Of course.

It was selfish as hell, but swimming through a nighttime ocean—dead kelp casting long, twisty shadows in the narrow beam of her flashlight—Anna was glad she wasn't going alone.

Anna raised her laser cutter as they approached the power plant, but Chris swam up next to her and laid her hand on the door, palm flat. When she wrenched her arm to the side, the door followed. Metal moaned as Chris pulled the door shut again. That left them in a small antechamber, water pooling around their ankles, a similar door ahead. Chris opened that one too.

They were in a small, cylindrical room. A bank of computers was stacked at the far end. There was only one door, off to her left, to what must be the reactor itself. No amenities, unless the wall of servers counted. She doubted the place was big enough to have proper containment, let alone waste processing. It must have been dumping waste water directly back into the ocean. That explained the radiation levels.

A noise behind her made her turn. Chris had pulled the regulator from her mouth and sagged against the wall, breathing hard, eyes half-closed.

Fuck. The radiation. Right.

Chris waved her off. "Just need a minute."

Chris needed to get out of here. It was a bad sign that she'd declined so quickly. Maybe that was what had happened to the villain? But Anna didn't see a body.

She hated to ask, but Chris had no more time to waste. "Can you open the door to the power plant from here? You don't have to move. Then you can rest."

"Yup. Just. Hold on." Chris straightened. Made a backhanding gesture at the door. Blew it off its hinges. Then she collapsed back against the wall.

"Hurry," she wheezed.

"I'll be back." Anna squeezed Chris's shoulder, unhitched the radiation barrels from her harness, lifted them by the cable, and ran. The open door led her to a second antechamber with another computer along one wall and a door leading into the reactor itself. Anna could hear the sloshing of water and the hissing of steam turbines behind it.

A door slid open.

Not the door to the reactor. A door behind her. Where Chris was.

An exosuit strode into the facility. It was about the same height as the ADS, but leaner, all sharp lines where the ADS had been bubbled curves. Fully enclosed. It must have radiation shielding.

Chris careened out of the suit's way, tumbling to the floor. The exosuit reached for her, as if it were going to finish her off, but before Anna could scream, Chris slapped a hand against the floor, and the exosuit went hurtling backward. It smashed into a wall, and...stuck.

Not for long.

The exosuit wrenched itself free of Chris's magnetism. Parts of the interior wall came with it. Anna heard a hiss as something started to leak. The exosuit lurched toward Chris.

"Hey!" Anna shouted. "I'm shutting down your reactor! Don't you want to stop me?" And she kicked the radiation barrels, still clipped together, at the exosuit.

The exosuit's pilot easily batted them aside. They turned to face Anna.

"You better stop me!" Anna yelled again. There was a pop as one of the computers sparked. Anna saw Chris slap the floor again, then collapse. The door between Anna and the exosuit slammed shut, but the sound of tromping feet continued slowly, steadily, toward her.

Chris had bought her time, but not much. Anna whirled back to the computer. If she could just shut the reactor down, it would kill the facility and hopefully the exosuit. They could escape, CAPER could start the remediation process, and then the ecosystem could recover.

They could escape, and then Chris would recover.

This stupid setup didn't seem to have a proper kill switch. Desperate, Anna reached for the keyboard and typed 'SCRAM.' When a pop-up alert asked her to confirm the emergency shutdown, she slammed the 'yes' button. The lights in the facility flickered and dimmed. At least the villain had had the foresight to include emergency power.

The outer door shrieked open. The smell of smoke filled the air, and the exosuit walked in.

Now that she was close enough, Anna could see through the transparent face shield: straw blond hair pulled tightly back, angular lines, furious eyes. Anna recognized that face, just like anyone would who'd seen the news in the last five years.

Samantha Siimes. The Hurricane Hacker. Supervillain extraordinaire. Gigantic pain in Anna's ass.

Real superhero or not, CAPER's stupid 'superhero 101' workshops had told her exactly what to do in moments like this. You were supposed to boldly demand the villain desist. Offer them a chance to come quietly. And then, though the literature never said this in so many words, beat them to a pulp when they refused.

Anna looked Siimes in the eye. "You took on the entire Victoria Police Department and almost won. You impersonated the US president from a prison cell. You escaped jail to, what, vent radioactive waste? Oh, please."

She'd expected anger. Maybe a lofty assurance that Siimes' goals were much grander than that, conveniently followed by an explanation of exactly what those goals were. Instead, Siimes reached out with a gleaming metal arm and hit a button. The inner door opened, and Siimes turned and walked inside, not caring enough about Anna to even offer a snarky rebuttal.

Anna gaped.

Real superhero or not, she had been trained in de-escalation skills: threatened violence, actual violence, hostage scenarios. This was none of those things. Being ignored was not something Anna had a script for.

"You can't stop me from out there," Siimes called out.

Damn supervillains.

She followed Siimes into the reactor, and stepped into an absolute nightmare.

Anna had worked on plenty of radioactive sites in her career. Sometimes, when she walked into a powerful reactor, she could feel a faint tingle along her skin. She'd always told herself it was psychosomatic.

This room gave her a full-on itch. A transparent tube in the center, with a square frame mounted above, held the uranium rods. There was nothing separating the rods from the rest of the room but glass. Just beyond, Anna could see a steam turbine, a generator, and a condenser.

Siimes walked up to the reactor vessel and placed her hands on the metal frame that held the rods, pushing it *up*. She reached into the reactor and yanked. Anna heard something tear. Water sprayed down from the ceiling, which Anna desperately hoped came from pipes.

Didn't matter. She wasn't going to let Chris die because she couldn't defeat one lousy supervillain.

Anna's laser cutter whined as she lunged forward and dragged it down the arm of Siimes' exosuit.

Siimes continued to tug at the rod, her suit smoking and scratched but otherwise intact.

Anna, ever patient—building cosplay suits of armor from recycled toasters was a labor of love—ran over the exact same line again, this time cutting deep enough that she smelled smoked skin.

Siimes hissed, but wrenched the first rod, still white-hot, from the reactor.

Anna raised the laser cutter a third time.

Siimes grunted, finally turned, and then jabbed the uranium rod into Anna's abdomen.

Heat. She might have been immune to radiation, but basic exothermic reactions would melt her skin, the same as anyone else. Heat was suddenly her whole world. Her stomach felt like the center of an overpriced, overcooked chocolate lava cake. She might have screamed.

Three things happened.

First, she hit the floor, hard enough that her vision grayed out at the edges. Second, a uranium rod clattered down next to her.

"What did you *do?*" Siimes roared from above her. "Never mind. It doesn't matter. Lay there and die, mini hero. You're not worth my time."

Not worth her *time?* Anna tried to roll away from the rod, but succeeded only in jostling it enough that it bumped up against her cheek. And...the rod didn't burn. It was warm, but not hot, as if it had been sitting dormant. As if it had been neutralized. Or absorbed?

Siimes turned her back on Anna and went back to the remaining rods.

Then the third thing happened. Anna got a good look at the power supply capsule jutting from the back of Siimes' suit. It bore a stenciled warning: GEN-VIII PORTABLE REACTOR. RADIATION HAZARD. The seam of the compartment was only just visible.

That's why Siimes' suit was still working. It was powered by *uranium.* She didn't care about the kelp forests. She just wanted power for her new suit! Anna shook her head. An ordinary person could have solved this problem with a garage sale and the scrap metal from unused kitchen appliances.

Supervillains.

Anna heard the screech of metal on metal. Siimes had scored more rods from the reactor.

Clutching her stomach, Anna struggled to a seated position. A giant, circular hole had burned away in the belly of her wetsuit, revealing ugly blisters beneath.

Anna's hand brushed against the discarded uranium rod. It had cooled completely by now—a process that was supposed to take years, even with coolants and neutron poisons. As if the radiation was just...gone.

And it hadn't happened until she'd touched it.

"Well, that's new," Anna muttered. New, and maybe useful. Siimes' suit was powered by uranium. Without a functioning suit, she'd be as comatose as Chris. If Anna could just get her hands on that power supply...

Hell, it was worth an experiment. She raised the laser cutter and dragged it down the seam of the power supply compartment.

"Go away, little fly! Or I'll swat you down." Siimes spun, poised for another blow, but Anna threw her weight forward, wrapping herself around Siimes' leg and throwing her off balance. Siimes tried, comically, to shake her off. Anna reached up with one hand and dug her fingers into the opening she'd created with the laser cutter.

Little fly. Not worth her time. Well, fuck her.

Siimes thrashed again, and Anna gasped. Couldn't pass out now. With all her strength, Anna pulled.

Heat and steam hissed out as the exterior cover clattered open. Spots bloomed across the backs of her eyelids. She braced herself. Grasped for the glowing uranium rod.

This time, she definitely screamed.

It hadn't worked. Her hand was still burning, and Siimes was still reaching. Anna braced herself, one last time. Siimes was still reaching.

Wait.

Siimes wasn't reaching for her, because Siimes wasn't reaching at all. She wasn't spitting insults.

She was stuck. Her suit had powered down.

Anna unclenched her fingers from the uranium rod in Siimes' suit. It no longer burned. Its glow had faded to the dull gleam of any inert metal.

She inched away from Siimes. Even that hurt. But the exosuit didn't move, so Anna inched a little farther. She looked up into a cloudy faceplate to see Siimes swearing silently. The speakers were out too.

"What's that?" Anna asked, exaggerating the words so Siimes could read her lips. "I'm afraid you're not worth my time."

Anna left Siimes raging in the reactor room and ran, as much as she could, back to Chris. Chris, who had battled through a forest of murderous seaweed to save her. Chris, who had swum through radioactive waters so Anna wouldn't have to face Siimes alone. Chris, who was counting on Anna to get her out of here in time.

Anna's current-crush-and-maybe-something-more-if-she-survived slumped against a wall, sheet-pale and surrounded by vomit. She perked up when she saw Anna, but then her eyes widened. "Holy shit!" She pointed a wobbly finger. "Your wetsuit is smoking!"

Chris probably should have noticed the smell, if nothing else. "It's okay," Anna said, although she wasn't sure what was okay, exactly. "I'm going to collect the uranium and then I'll swim us both back to the sub. You're going to be okay. I promise."

Chris blinked, looking decidedly green. "Hurry?"

Anna forced a smile. "Promise."

Chris's smile was brighter than any uranium rod.

* * *

They made it back to the sub, Siimes in tow and uranium safely stowed in the barrels, with about two minutes of air left in their tanks. CAPER had noticed when their communications had been cut and had already dispatched help. Anna wanted to cry with relief. Instead, she focused on getting Chris as comfortable as possible.

Anna eventually cut Siimes out of the exosuit and left her tied up in the cargo hold. The exosuit itself they left at the bottom of the ocean, along with the broken ADS. She had only dim memories of handing Siimes and the submarine off before she and Chris were shepherded into an air ambulance, decontamination, and hospital.

After the hospital stay came the inevitable meeting. Eleanor was there, looking very professionally concerned, and someone from Community Safety Services. Someone from CAPER's intake department. The Vice President of CAPER's Vancouver branch. The police. CAPER provided a conference room with voice- and face-scrambling capabilities.

They took turns describing what had happened: the hacked firmware in the kelp forest, the discovery of the facility, sabotaging the power supply on Siimes' suit. No one could explain how Siimes had escaped from prison. No one could explain how they were going to keep her there, either, which was just great. Hopefully they'd manage to keep her behind bars, because Anna didn't want an arch nemesis. She wasn't paid enough to deal with that sort of drama. Or that volume of paperwork.

The intake rep, who insisted that everyone call him JP, jostled Anna out of her thoughts. "You pulled a uranium rod out of a reactor *by hand*? That's above your paygrade. Superhero stuff. You do environmental cleanup."

Barely two days ago, Anna had almost been murdered by seaweed, stared down a literal supervillain, and decommissioned a nuclear reactor with her bare hands. She really didn't give a shit if a jumped-up HR guy didn't like her after-action report. "Sounds like you need to pay me more."

He tented his fingers. "Maybe. How did that disable Siimes' suit?"

Anna started to respond. Then she shrugged. "I thought that was beyond my paygrade."

JP leaned toward her. "Tell me what happened."

Anna leaned in as well. "I just did."

"You must have done *something*. Perhaps you unwittingly emitted some sort of neutron poison, or—"

"Go fu—"

"Look, buddy." Chris thumped her palm on the table, thankfully drawing JP's attention elsewhere. "This wasn't exactly a lab test. We can worry about the details some other time."

For a moment it looked like he was going to press the issue, but Chris stared him down. There was more power in those molten eyes than any nuclear reactor could provide.

Eleanor stepped in to fill the silence. "You were telling us what happened after you dismantled the nuclear core..."

* * *

After the meeting was over, Anna sank into a chair outside the conference room. Just for a second, and then she'd head back to the hotel.

"Hey, you all right?"

Anna looked up. "Hey. You look good, all things considered."

Chris gave her that radioactive smile again. "I feel like a new woman. You?"

"Doing alright," Anna said. "Just taking a breather. After, you know." She waved a bandaged hand. The doctors had told her she didn't need the bandage anymore, but it turned out that uranium burns looked horrific.

"Yeah. At least *most* of them kept the bullshit to a minimum." Chris rolled her eyes. "You have any more blowhards giving you trouble about your powers, let me know. I'll set them straight." She winked. "Though I don't think you need me to fight your battles for you. You're pretty tough."

"You'd still be the first person I'd call," Anna said.

A dimple appeared in Chris's cheek. "Yeah? I'll hold you to that."

"You can hold me to whatever you want," Anna said, and was too tired to even be mortified when the words came out of her mouth.

Chris grinned. Underneath the smile, she looked just as tired as Anna felt. "I'll keep that in mind."

For a moment neither of them spoke. Then Chris offered her hand. "Walk you back? I bet we're at the same hotel."

They were, in fact, at the same hotel. They didn't talk on the way back. But somehow, during the walk, Chris's arm ended up around Anna's waist. Somehow, she ended up at Anna's door.

"Seriously, though," Chris said at last, lingering in the doorway. "If you need to talk about your powers, or anything...let me know. They'll want you to go for reclassification soon. You could probably transfer to Community Safety, if you wanted. We can talk about any of that. We can talk about whatever you need."

There *was* something she needed, but she fumbled for the words. Being almost murdered by seaweed should have made this easier.

"Anna?"

Words were hard. So Anna did the easiest thing of all: she kissed her.

Chris's body was tense against hers. Anna thought she was going to pull away, and of all the things they'd been through, that seemed like the worst of all.

And then, in the space between heartbeats, Chris kissed her back.

Anna's back was to the wall, though she didn't remember Chris pushing her up against it. Chris tasted faintly of salt. Her hands found Anna's bra and her fingertips were warm, and calloused, and insistent.

"Mumph," Anna said through the kiss as she tried to push away from the wall, to give Chris more room to access the clasp.

Chris, who apparently had many superpowers at her disposal, managed to unhook the double eyelets with just her right hand, then the clasp of one strap, then the other. The bra slid to the floor, pooling on the top of Anna's shoes, the lace edge peering into the hall at anyone who might walk by. Chris kicked the door shut as her kisses found Anna's collarbone, tongue lapping at the little hollow in Anna's throat.

Anna growled and edged away just enough to wiggle out of her v-necked polo. "Do not stop."

Chris pulled away, just far enough to look into Anna's eyes. Her fingertips caressed Anna's cheek, then came down to rest lightly, fingers splayed, across Anna's breast.

"Not stopping, just clarifying. I can hold you to whatever I want, right?"

"Whatever you want," Anna agreed, backing herself again against the wall.

Chris's fingers dipped around Anna's nipple, goosefleshing her skin. "And wherever?"

Anna put her good hand on top of Chris's. "Anywhere at all. Now hurry up."

Chris kissed her again, hard enough to slam her head back against the drywall. She saw stars—the good kind—as her hand found the muscles of Chris's abdomen, then the zipper of her pants.

Chris swatted Anna's hand away, took Anna's wrists in her hands, and pulled her toward the bed.

Anna sat, her skin ablaze from a heat far more intense than the uranium. Chris pulled the decorative cotton belt from her jeans and pointed at the rungs in the hotel headboard. "This should hold you for a while," she smirked, kneeling on the bed. She looked Anna up and down. "You know, I like you much better like this than in that silly suit of armor."

"That's too bad," Anna said. "You should see what I can do with a few toasters."

Chris pushed her to a lying position. "You'll just have to show me when I'm done with you."

* * *

She couldn't sleep, after, although the pain of her injuries had been replaced by the ache in her wrists, which was a much more pleasant way to burn. She thought Chris had fallen asleep until Chris rolled over to face her. "You know, Anna...I've been thinking."

Anna swallowed. "You are not allowed to dump me after tying me to a bed."

"I...no. Listen," Chris said. "I was thinking we could take a vacation. This is a lovely vacation spot, actually."

Anna's heart somersaulted in her chest. "You mean...you and me?"

A smile tugged at Chris's lips, just visible in the semi-dark. It was the closest expression to uncertainty she'd ever seen on Chris's face.

Anna was smiling herself, now. She couldn't help it. "No diving, please."

Chris laughed. "Is surfing alright?"

Anna made a face. "Will there be kelp?"

Chris reached out and brushed a hand along Anna's cheek. "Not if you pick the right spots."

"Mmm. I bet you know all the good spots."

Chris gave her that radiant, mischievous smile. "I think I just proved that."

"Oh, you did," Anna said. "But I'm gonna need you to reproduce those results."

"How about at a seaside bed and breakfast?" Chris asked. "I bet I can find one with an old-fashioned toaster."

"Yeah? You think you can do that?"

"Oh, I definitely can," Chris said. "I can do all sorts of things."

Anna took Chris's hand, placed it on her navel, slid it down. "You'd better."

"Radiant" is a short story by N. L. Bates. To keep up to date with her work, visit **www.nlbates.com**. Or, check out the music written and performed by her not-so-secret identity, Natalie Lynn, at **www.natalielynnmusic.com.**

Jellyfish Lovepotion

J.S. Fields

Sapphic Representation: Lesbian, Pansexual, Nonbinary
Heat Level: Low
Content Warnings: Coarse Language, Violence, Gore, Death, Drugs

Prior to being conscripted as lead carpenter to the generational starship *Jellyfish Lovepotion*, Andrea Stanton of Normal, Illinois, USA, had stayed far, *far* away from ships. She didn't like them on oceans, on rivers, on small decorative lakes covered in swans, and she sure didn't like them in outer space. Inner ear deformations aside, not having firsthand knowledge of a ship's construction set her on edge, as did the idea of living alone in a shoebox that was careening through space to a destination she'd never get to see. It would take four generations to go from Earth to Proxima b, and of the seven thousand four hundred and seventy-three people housed in the ship, Andrea knew exactly four of them. All men. All euchre players, moderate social drinkers, and none even remotely interested in the finer points of antique hand plane maintenance.

Had she been given the option, Andrea would have chosen breathing the smoke-laden air of Earth until her untimely death via natural catastrophe (earthquake, snowstorm, tornado—they happened like every other week at this point). She'd originally been on the very bottom of the *Lovepotion* wait list until three lead carpenters in a row had gotten sick, leaving only Andrea in the queue. She'd gotten a late-night text (CONGRATULATIONS! YOUR LOTTERY NUMBER HAS BEEN APPROVED FOR NEXT WEEK'S DEPARTURE ON THE *JELLYFISH LOVEPOTION!*) and...that was it. Goodbye to family, friends, *life,* and hello to an involuntary deep space coffin.

After a late boarding because there'd been satellite interference and her phone had stopped working for a few hours (her navigation skills had always been terrible), she'd wandered through empty spaceship hallways until she'd found her room. Everyone else had already boarded and were either strapped in for takeoff (the maintenance crew, all twenty of them, and engineers, fifty-four, if you counted the captain) or in cryosleep (the civvies). Being of the very-unlucky-maintenance-crew type, she'd tossed her suitcase onto the Murphy bed, found the turbulence chair, sat down, and strapped herself in. Tightly.

She had enough anti-nausea drugs in her system to kill a large cat. She'd done the final safety checklist for the *Lovepotion's* interior maintenance bay yesterday, which was where she'd be working until she died and the sanitation crew recycled her withered body into mulch. Today, she'd said goodbye to her father, rehomed her pet rabbit to her ex-girlfriend (maybe lingering a bit too long over both, though she'd broken up with Sarada last year and really, just needed to move on), and felt relatively confident in her ability to not puke until the ship had its artificial gravity up and running.

A low thrumming filled her ears—the sounds of the *Lovepotion's* systems warming for takeoff. She tapped her foot to cover the noise and, when that failed, she pulled a wadded piece of paper from her worn canvas pants and read the handwriting for the seventh time since breakfast:

You're braver than me, Andy. I'll be on a gen ship in a few months for sure. They still won't let me off Earth until we get one more AI version sorted. You know how upgrades can go. Take care of yourself and don't cut off any fingers. Your E.T. girlfriend will want you to build her a bed or something. Sorry your dad didn't make the medical clearance for this ship. They want his weather modeling skills on Earth for another year, even if it means he dies here. Fascists. Also, I checked your crew munifests. You got Captain Chuck Miller. I know you occasionally go for the men but whatever you do, however drunk you get, don't fuck Chuck. He was on the Mars terraforming mission that came home early and no one will say why. Also, he had me reset his AI and put it into the Lovepotion, but factory-wiped AIs personality imprint easily, so watch that. Anyway. Chuck is always high as a kite. Just take care of yourself and don't worry about Floppy. I promise not to eat him.

:P Sarada

She stared at Sarada's name, tracing a fingertip over the letters before folding it back up and shoving it into an overhead drawer. "You're going to be fine, Stanton," she muttered to herself. "Crew of seven thousand plus, that's like, what? Fourteen lesbians? You just have to find them. That ache in your chest isn't from missing Sarada or your dad, or your weird cousin Leo who always beats you at Scrabble. Stop crying. You'll just end up aspirating your damn tears. Dad'll be on the next ship for sure."

"Attention *Lovepotion*," a voice squeaked from the overhead speaker. "This is Rui from ground control. We have reports of an overmisting problem in Hydroponics. Our departure time has been pushed to eighteen hundred hours. If you're a civilian not in cryo, please disembark and await further instructions. Sorry about the delay."

The tightly wound ball of anxiety in Andrea's chest loosened. Fractionally. Enough things going wrong and their departure window would be scrapped and she'd gain a few precious, extra days on Earth. The cryosleep people would be fine for decades. A delay wouldn't bother them at all. She slapped the comm panel above her head. "*Lovepotion*, route me to Hydroponics. I need more information on the damage. Did someone ping Ship Systems? If there's a lot of water damage, they should plan on a significant delay in departure. Hours. Maybe days. Long days."

Static buzzed from the comm. "Unable to route. Repair crew has already been dispatched," the *Lovepotion* returned. "You may leave the ship and await repair completion."

"And the repair crew doesn't need their carpenter?" She punched the central button on her harness, sending the straps slapping back across her shoulders. "Leadership?" she asked, tapping her palm against the comm panel when she stood back up. "Hey Lead, how bad is it in Hydro?"

Static. Andrea smacked the panel again. "Hydro, what's going on down there? This is Dr. Stanton. Did the misters start malfunctioning before or after Dr. He's check-in yesterday? I know Lead cleared your area before midnight. I checked the ship logs. I checked them *twice*, actually, since they're supposed to have two sign offs and I couldn't find anyone from Hydro to do a double check. Which was a crappy way to spend my last night on Earth, by the way. You all owe me a beer."

Still, static.

"Fine, don't answer," she muttered to herself. She switched on her wrist comm, which connected directly to the ship's AI as well as the greater network. Redundancy was everything in space. "Hydro and Lead are busy or hungover or something. *Lovepotion*, can you direct me to Hydroponics? This ship has more dead ends than a suburban neighborhood. I'll need a light grid in the hall."

"You are not cleared for passageway access," said the *Lovepotion*. "The hallway is currently restricted to exit routes only."

"I'm cleared to reinstall you. Consider that. Voice check my authorization codes and let me out."

Instead of the *Lovepotion*, Don't-Fuck-Chuck's voice came from the speaker. "Heeey, everyone, Captain Chuck here. We've got unexpected growth from some overmisting that we need sterilized and our satellites are giving us readings we still need to decipher. A pretty big gas cloud is headed our way. We may have lost our launch window. Engineers, civilians, anyone not frozen, come on off and deboard. We'll contact you when things are clear. This doesn't include maintenance personnel."

Being in maintenance sucked. Andrea pulled on her door handle, determined to stomp her way, loudly, to Maintenance.

The door remained locked.

"Please state your destination," said the *Lovepotion*.

"I'm going to get a wet-dry vac from my shop and suck some water out of your carpet. Possibly sterilize Hydro. Then I'm going to walk off this ship and take my dad some Steak-N-Shake. Now let me out!"

The *Lovepotion*, sounding irritated, said through her comm watch, "You are not authorized to be in the hallway unless you are leaving the ship."

"I *want* to leave the ship but I *can't* until I do my job. You want to rot your processors? If you don't want to let me out, fine. Grow mold in your circuitry. I'll go back to my condo above Mugsy's Pub and take a bubble bath. Have fun being rebooted and potentially wiped. Again. You know Engineering does that any time there's a problem, even if it is mechanical. I *could* just hose up some water and save your 'life.' You make the choice."

The door to her room breathed open, wafting sterile air right up her already dry nose. Andrea dug her lanyard of credentials out of her suitcase, slipped it over her head, and left her shoebox room. Suddenly very helpful, the *Lovepotion* turned on its floor track lighting to her left—blaze pink and entirely too much like the Pepto Bismol she'd chugged before boarding. The shag on the carpet, fibers of thick green wool, swayed ever so slightly in the forced air. Apparently carpet was also important in space. Noise deadening or something. Maybe it was important that it looked like grass. She didn't care either way.

She reached a T-junction. The left side dead-ended in a door marked BIOHAZARD – LEVEL 5 ACCESS REQUIRED FOR AI SYSTEMS ROOM. To the right was more hallway. The track lighting lit right. Andrea peered left out of sheer curiosity. She'd not gotten to see that room during her initial tour. They'd not put in a work order for cabinetry either, and the computer housing had been made off-site. A faint red glow came from behind the door. The air smelled, strangely, of apple cider. She blinked, and when she opened her eyes again, the glow was gone.

"You are not authorized here," the AI chirped through an overhead speaker. "Continue to follow the lighting."

"You know, if your processors get damaged *I'm* the one who will have to build your new casing. Know your support staff, *Lovepotion*. I'm all you've got. You're all I've got. Imprint on my impatience and suck it up."

The AI seemed to consider that. A soft whirring came from behind the door, before the track lighting dimmed on the right-side hallway, and lit back the way she'd come.

"Please proceed to your destination."

"That's not the way you had me going before."

"System error. Please follow the new lighting route."

"Were you *lying* to me?"

"Please follow the lighting," the AI repeated.

Andrea spun on her heels, flipped off the ceiling, and stalked back down the way she'd come. "I could have been drinking last night, I want you to know that," she said to the empty hallway. "Or combing crew manifests to see who is single. It's a long, long space ride. What happened to you on the last mission, anyway? The one with Captain Chuck? Why'd it come back early? It never made the blogs." She paused, turned in a tight circle, then added, "And where is everyone else? Engineers get to deboard apparently, since they aren't answering comms, and I'm not that far from main Engineering."

When the *Lovepotion* did not respond, she sighed and said, "They're all hungover, aren't they? Still asleep maybe? Fine. How much farther to my shop? Then how far to Hydro?"

"Estimated time of arrival to Interior Maintenance, two minutes. Ten to Hydrology."

Andrea hadn't been to Hydro in three days, not since she installed the lab benches and space-ready storage units. The lab was roughly the size of a baseball diamond, crowded with the laminar flow hoods, UV sterilizers, and a bunch of other equipment she couldn't name. Off the main room were three smaller bays. The first held exactly seventeen potted ferns. The second had banks of tree seedlings and UV lamps. The third, a narrow closet, had tanks and mixers that were supposed to house a bunch of fungal species slated for food and biomedical uses. Mercifully she'd missed that installation.

She passed more civilian quarters, all quiet, the doors shut and locked for takeoff, the cryo chambers softly humming. The hall remained empty, though she heard the sound of parading footsteps and raucous chatter in the distance that had to be the (lucky) engineers. The floor lights turned left again and so did Andrea. Then they turned right, taking her down a ramp, then another right, stopping at a door with the stenciled label: *Maintenance Shop. Authorized Personnel Only.*

Underneath, an enterprising crewmember had scratched with the edge of a Susan B. Anthony silver dollar: DOES EIGHTH GRADE SHOP COUNT? The silver dollar in question made the dot of the question mark, stuck firmly with hardened chewing gum. Below *that* was an orange-red smiley face, elongated and streaky, whose 'mouth' stretched from the silver dollar to the door jam. The air smelled like summer apples and ethanol.

Damn drunk engineers.

"*Lovepotion?*" Andrea sighed. Scientists and engineers, in her experience, were the worst drunks. "Do you have a recording of who did this? It wasn't here during final loading yesterday, and I know Barry had big designs for a hard cider setup in his head when he saw apples heading to freezer storage."

"Please proceed to your destination."

"Guess that's a no." She scratched at the coin, determined that a compound stronger than gum held it on, and made a mental note to dissolve it later. It wasn't like she had anything to do once they took off except walk around the ship and hunt for things to repair for the next eighty years.

She put her hand on the access panel.

The panel chirped. The door slid open.

Andrea stared.

Her shop, *her* shop, looked like someone had rubbed the equipment down with eucalyptus and then let a pack of koalas loose. Chisels lay scattered over the floor, a few embedded at awkward angles in the wall. Sawblades wobbled—unwound and dangling—off table edges. The table saw was running despite no one else being about, its metal bed rusted though she had oiled it before packing. Her hand tools cabinet had been raided and the doors abusively dismantled. Every single glue bottle lay on its side, uncapped and leaking into beige horror puddles. Her new saw blade had been *cut in half*.

And the handprints. The footprints. A *tongue* print, judging by width and streaking and the weird little bump indents across the surface. Disgusting. Brick red stains covered the walls, the metal machines, the floor, even parts of the ceiling panels. The air still smelled faintly sweet. Reddish adult footprints were everywhere, all shaped like the standard-issue *Lovepotion* boot, and all sloppy, like their owner had a hard time walking in a straight line. She swiped at the soft, gelatinous pool of red and sniffed. The texture was wrong for apples, but the smell was right. Fermentation gone wrong? Drunk engineers with blenders? Why *here*?

Footsteps pattered down the hall behind her.

"If you were going to trash my shop on a bender, you could have at least invited me along!" Andrea yelled as she opened one of the intact cabinets and pulled out a roll of shop towels. "You better be coming to apologize and help clean."

A woman cleared her throat, the sound much closer than Andrea had anticipated. She dropped the towels into a giant mound of the macerated apple. A red plume rose up from the impact. Andrea coughed, rubbed the back of her neck, and backed away, eyeing the newcomer as she did so.

"Last night a few of the engineers decided to play bar golf around the ship," said the mystery woman who was not dressed at all like an engineer. "Said they thought it would help them memorize the layout better, because if you can navigate drunk you can navigate sober. They got pretty riled up in a few places and I think got into something harder than booze. Hydro didn't fare much better, if it helps."

"Please proceed to Hydroponics," the *Lovepotion* said from Andrea's wrist.

"I...*what?*" Andrea stared at the short, sturdy woman in the doorway. Her hands were clasped behind her back, legs planted wide apart, her white lab coat buttoned to her collar bone. Maple-colored hair wisped across her forehead, the rest pulled into a low ponytail that had clearly been tied without a mirror. Her skin was pale like Andrea's, though with rose undertones that looked too vibrant in the artificial light. Freckles dusted her nose—reddish brown—tracing in a wing-shaped pattern across her cheekbones. Andrea noted crow's feet around her eyes, traces of silver at her temples, and fraying along the hem of her lab coat.

The woman didn't have engineering coveralls, wasn't covered in glue, didn't have a reciprocating saw in her hand, and didn't smell like booze or apples, which meant she probably hadn't been party to the destruction. Andrea still wanted to kick her in the shins.

"*WHY!??*" Andrea managed to spit. She raked a hand through the remaining hair on her undercut. It'd seemed like a low maintenance idea a week ago, but mostly her neck just got cold. Cold and itchy. "Who gets the bill for all this?! I don't mind the delay, obviously, but a few of these items I sourced from outside the USA. That's...a *substantial* delay. I'm going to get yelled at."

"Please proceed to—"

"Not now!" she slapped at the comm, too frustrated to fiddle with the mute function. "*Lovepotion*, get me anyone in Lead."

"Lead is not staffed at this time," the ship responded.

"How are they not...argh! What about Logistics? Seema and Daniela never take breaks, and I had dinner with them last night so I know they're not hungover. I thought required personnel had to stay on! This is unfair!" It was unfair, and it was weird, and Andrea didn't like the growing tickle at the back of her neck, which probably came from the apple fumes but still. The circumstances were *not normal.*

The *Lovepotion* rebutted. "Your primary goal is to attend to Hydroponics. Takeoff must not be further delayed."

"We are going to be *very* delayed!" Andrea retorted at the ceiling.

The AI chirruped. "Unnecessary. Once the misters are repaired we are cleared for departure. All essential crew are on board."

"The engineers *deboarded!*" Anxiety spiked, hot and heavy, across her chest. This destruction had to buy them a few days at *least.* Her father's birthday was next week. Her sister was coming into town for it, using her one airline voucher of the year. Andrea wanted to be at that party. *Should* be at that party, because there was no way the ship was taking off in the next week.

"I don't think—" began the short woman.

"Please proceed to Hydroponics."

Andrea took two long, not-particularly-calming breaths, and tried a different tactic. "You." She pointed at the woman. "Information. Who do I murder for this?"

"I bowed out after the first hole. Jeffery from Air Exchange brought pickled eggs and that's a recipe for disaster." She wrinkled her nose, making the freckles dance. "You know you're standing in glue, right?"

Andrea looked down, determined that yes, she was standing in a growing puddle of Titebond III wood glue, but decided that, based upon how the day was going, she did not care. She was already mentally shopping for where she could pick up a carbon-neutral gift for her father's birthday.

"Were they looking for something? Is that why all my containers are open and leaking? I assume something small enough that it could be hidden in glue, or in the middle of an Italian-engineered table saw blade with carbide-tipped teeth and heat-treated steel! I mean, Jesus!"

The woman held her hands up. "Don't shoot the botanist. My ferns got trampled too, you know. I was supposed to deboard but I thought I'd see if I could borrow a wet-dry vac. Maintenance seemed...delayed and I don't like delays. Though," she pointed to the drop ceiling, where panels that should have been locked into place lay across one another, exposing large sections of air duct. "Wow. They didn't go after our ceiling as much in Hydro, and we don't have any macerated apples." She rubbed the back of her neck. "Lead won't answer my comm, but I assume that's because they're tied up with mission control and the press. That traffic could be bogging things down. Or the big *something* entering Earth's orbit whacked a few satellites out. Really unfortunate timing, you know? The gas cloud or whatever couldn't have come a day later? I just..." she stamped her heel. "Hate waiting. Might as well clean and speed things along."

Andrea stared at the tiny, surprisingly angry woman and wondered, absurdly, if she was small enough to fit inside her wet-dry vac.

The shorter woman again surveyed the mess. "Want a hand? We haven't met formally, but I read your ship profile: 'I'm here because they bribed me with sawblades.' It was cute and kind of sharp. Like you."

Oh. Oh, this was a lesbian thing. Andrea tried to recalibrate, balancing flirting with her immediate task. Basic repairs were her job, but anything structural would need an engineering crew. The faster she cleaned the faster she could leave. The more she could flirt. Delaying at this stage wouldn't get her off the ship and who knew? Maybe she'd find some processor rot, report it to Lead, and get the week off.

"Yes, I want help. Thanks." She experimentally poked at a semi-congealed puddle with her boot. Again, the pressure forced a puff of red powder to shoot into the air. It tickled her nose but she ignored it. "We can do the misters and water in Hydro first. That's a bigger issue. Glues aren't preventing us from taking off." *And if they harden and set it becomes a structural problem.* She picked up the wet-dry vac then smacked her free hand onto one of the cabinet panels, waited for her fingerprints to read and, when the door opened, grabbed her grandfather's worn leather toolbelt. She fastened it low on her waist, threading part of the belt through the loops in her canvas pants, and held out a hand. "Andrea Stanton. USA. PhD in wood science, though I was brought up a woodworker. She/her or they/them, I'm sort of waffling on that. I'm head carpenter and I'm having a really irritating day. Do you know if there is a gift card store open twenty-four hours within walking distance of the base?"

"Clarabelle Powers, definitely she/her. I go by Clara. PhD in botany with a specialization in upper Midwest, USA fern varietals. I'm one of four natural scientists housed in Hydroponics, my day isn't much better, and there's a Walgreens two blocks from here." She shook Andrea's hand. Her skin felt too smooth for someone who likely worked in a laminar flow hood. Her lotion game had to be top notch.

Her nails were a middling length, well rounded, and covered with a sort of printed sticker material that had roses on it. Which dashed Andrea's brief hope that she'd found another lesbian scientist on the *Jellyfish,* or at least a scientist with marginal interest in other women. Platonic dude euchre it was, apparently. She'd never really jived with straight women.

"Nice?" she asked when Andrea had stared too long at her hands. "I don't often get a chance to wear them. I've also never seen you before, but Phil's talked about you. Says you're good with your hands and tried to set us up on a date last Tuesday but you called off dinner because of a ceiling problem. I didn't just stalk your bio for fun. Anyway, I can give you a set of the nail stickers if you'd like?"

"Uh." Andrea held up her left hand and wiggled her fingers. A scar ran down the middle one, red and angry. Her nails were worn to the quick, and all knuckles but one were scabbed. "Hazards of the profession."

A smile—potentially a smirk or maybe Andrea just needed a nap— crossed Clara's face. "Is that yes, you want a set of stickers?"

Oooh, flirting. It was not her forte unless it involved discussion of lumber dimensions at Home Depot. "Won't they just come off in awkward places?" Andrea asked.

"Well, where do you plan on sticking those fingers?"

"Proceed to Hydroponics," the *Lovepotion* chirped.

Heat rose in Andrea's cheeks. She coughed. "Hydroponics?"

Clara's laugh lilted through the broken tools. "Come on, Doctor Professional Hands. I'll take you to Hydro." She swished from the shop, lab coat fanning around her legs like a highschool cheerleader. "If you can get my ferns back into stable housing and our launch window gets reestablished I'll buy you dinner in the space center cafeteria. Then you can tell me why we have a carpenter aboard a spaceship headed to a planet that doesn't have any trees on it."

"Hey!" Andrea pulled her boots from the glue with a horrible *squelch* and jogged after Clara, shop vac banging against her left leg. "Carpentry is more than just—"

Clara spun around and winked at her before turning another blind, unmarked corner. "Hurry up! Some of us do actually want to leave this doomed planet."

Andrea realized, as she followed behind, that she was in a lot of trouble, and it had nothing to do with Hydroponics.

* * *

They walked in silence for a handful of minutes, Clara in the lead, Andrea mentally tallying how many days she could get on Earth if she snipped a few lines 'accidentally' while attempting repair. If she could stretch the delay into a whole month she could celebrate her sister's birthday as well, and maybe convince Lead that having her weather-modeling-professor father on a generational ship was actually a top-notch idea. Weather happened on Proxima b too, surely.

The track lighting nipped at their heels as they walked, occasionally spurting ahead or ducking down a hallway in the opposite direction. Clara scoffed and ignored it. Andrea tried to, and ended up worrying a hole in her sleeve. "Slow down?" she called after her third attempt to hitch her pants over her hips failed and she dropped the vacuum. When Clara turned around she added sheepishly, "Toolbelt drama."

Clara appraised her for exactly three seconds longer than was heterosexually polite. "You're slow for someone who has shopping to do. Is it a job requirement that carpenters and plumbers have to wear baggy pants?"

Andrea set the shop vac down. "I'm not dawdling on purpose. I just. There's a lot of weight to this departure. I wanted more time. My dad just had hip surgery."

"Earth doesn't have time, so neither do we. My parents and twin sister died last year in the Mount Saint Helens eruption. My grandparents went down before we got the new influenza vaccine. I am *done* with Earth. Can we keep moving?"

"Sorry," Andrea muttered.

"Yeah, well." Clara shrugged, pursed her lips then added, "I've got a few bottles of wine in my quarters. French. From before half the country went underwater. I can give you a bottle to go with the card. For your dad. Once we are done cleaning up."

Andrea—still having no idea how to respond and feeling immensely guilty for having living family members—managed to mutter a "thank you."

Clara smiled, briefly, then continued on. At the end of the next hallway was a door marked, in red stencil: HYDROPONICS AND ASSOCIATED LABORATORIES. NO GENERAL ADMITTANCE.

The door opened and they stepped into a B-movie nightmare.

"How is it worse than when I left?" Clara asked, kicking at a puddle. "This is a nightmare. This is my nightmare. I just...Argh!" She punched her hands into her pockets and stalked inside.

The air inside the lab seemed to ripple, just at the edges of Andrea's vision. Again, blinking helped clear it. She followed Clara in, grinning like a six-year-old at a birthday party. The shelving she'd installed days prior lay shattered across the floor—plastic bits intermingled with bark chips and fragments of fern leaves. The air was hot but not humid, which made sense since the sprinkler system appeared to have ejected its contents in one giant belch. The floor was porous plastic but the catchment system underneath—meant to recycle the runoff from the watering system—was swamped. Puddles rippled as Clara stormed to the connecting laboratory door on the right and motioned for Andrea to follow.

This meant a month delay for sure. Two, maybe. No need to rush now. She'd still be on Earth for *her* birthday with this level of mess. The sprinklers hadn't malfunctioned, they'd *exploded*. Basic carpentry skills wouldn't fix this. They needed a plumber, who should have already been there. Had they deboarded with the engineers?

Meh. It wasn't her problem. Feeling lighter than she had in over a year, Andrea tossed her shop vac to the floor, sloshed through the water, hopped onto the nearest lab bench, grabbed her right back pocket to hitch her pants up, and poked at the overhead sprinklers. The ceiling panels here, too, were badly stained, and the air in the lab—particularly near the ceiling—smelled not just of apples, but of decaying apples.

"I don't think we had this many apples in storage. Something's wrong. I'm going to call Lead again. How many people should I ask for? Any idea what happened?" Clara called up to her.

"I think the decay problem is up here. I can try to vacuum out whatever is growing just to make the damaged pipes easier to see, but we'll need to call Remediation along with a plumber. Seriously, what were the bar golfers *doing*?"

Clara crouched down and inspected one of the sprinklers that popped up from the floor. The water came up past the tread on her boots and the edges of her lab coat turned gray. With all the scowling, she didn't appear to notice. "Captain Chuck. Before the Mars terraforming expedition he was on one of the first deep space missions. He's a meddler and a perfectionist, and went all-but-degree on his botany PhD and just will not stay out of my lab. He added an element to the nutrient broth in the fungal grow tanks a week or so back. It was supposed to just be a supplement from the NASA lab but this *is* Chuck we're talking about. Too much time in deep space, that guy. Rumor got around that it was *Psilocybe* spores, so I assume the bar golfers thought this would be a great 'hole.' Hallucination must be a lot of fun when you're already drunk. Anyway," she stood and tucked a strand of hair behind her ear. It fell back across her eyes so she yanked on the hair and tried to plaster it to the side of her head with some of the water from the floor. "We refresh the nutrient broth every three days so whatever Chuck put in there, it's long gone. If they were high, it wasn't from the nutrient broth."

"Of course there are magic mushrooms involved," Andrea muttered as she unscrewed the sprinkler head. "Let me just get a closer look before we comm. Hold on." Instead of dropping down, the sprinkler head stayed wedged into the ceiling. She gave an experimental tug and, with a *shloop,* it pulled free, trailing tangled strands of orange-red filaments, plum-red clouds of dust, and the head of Don't-Fuck-Chuck.

"Ah!" She flung the sprinkler head to the floor and jumped from the bench. Her neck burned from the impact, or the stress, or maybe the red stuff floating around her that jostled the air. She reached back to scratch just as Chuck's moustached head rolled up next to her foot, eyes vacant, face contorted into a sharp smile. "Why!? Oh god *how?*" She did not get paid enough to deal with dead bodies. She did not *want* to deal with dead bodies. And there was no way she was getting off the ship in the next forty-eight hours if the *captain's head* was nuzzling her boot.

"Lead?" Andrea smacked at her wrist. "Lead, please pick up. The captain is here and he's dead and we need someone *now.* And can we turn the heat down? We're getting dry skin."

"Lead is unavailable," the *Lovepotion* responded. "Please continue with your assigned tasks."

"None of this should be here." Clara, too calm noting the dead captain and floating red particulate, picked up the sprinkler and held it at arm's length. She rotated it in her hand, frowned, then tossed it back to the floor. It landed in a suspiciously deep puddle, red dust leaking from its line and staining the water. "I guess since we aren't going anywhere thanks to the dead body, I need to check the tanks. The ship has to be sterilized." Again she stamped her foot, sending ripples of water against Chuck's head. "Damn it, I really thought I was going to get out this time."

Andrea had a hard time empathizing, "There is a *head* on my *boot!*"

"And murder investigations can take months, which I'm sure you're thrilled with. Since the comms are down we need to deboard to get help. And all this garbage in the air, well, if the engineers got high from inhaling this then we will, too. Let's leave."

"God, it smells like...like hair gel and apple pie. Yes please, let's leave. Just...you know. The body." Andrea rubbed at her nose again, took a deep breath from under the collar of her shirt, got back onto the table, stood on her tiptoes to peer into the hole in the ceiling. She expected a torso but saw only orange darkness. She pulled the extra-long flashlight from her toolbelt and shoved it into the hole—one part light and one part battering ram.

"Well?" Clara asked.

Andrea coughed and wiped her nose. The air around her seemed to ripple. She should have had a bigger breakfast. "No body. No blood. I don't know what I'm looking at. The filaments were mostly on the sprinkler it looks like, but the duct system up here is uniformly purple-red-orange and there's fingerprints everywhere. And bite marks. And fungus. Oh god, you don't think they...sampled some of this? But why...I mean did they *eat Chuck?*" So much for the anti-nausea drugs. "How drunk do you have to be to lick ceiling fungus and eat a person?!"

"I don't know. Get your face out of it."

"You know, usually women buy me dinner before they tell me what to do," Andrea snapped. Tension ran high when cannibalism was on the table. She tucked her flashlight away. "Have you talked to any of your drinking buddies since last night?"

Clara shook her head, the edges of her lab coat streaking water across the shins of her pants, her foot tapping impatiently. "No. I figured they'd sleep the hangovers off during launch. Can we go now? Seriously, get out of there before you get poisoned. I feel itchy just watching you."

"Yes. Give me just a second." Andrea prodded a mycelial mass with her finger. It felt warm. It felt wet. It felt slippery. She did not like where that took her deeply inappropriate mind. "I'm going to cut some of this out and take it to the base scientists. Maybe they have answers. Hallucinogenic fungi don't make you eat people, surely. Although it hasn't made us hallucinate yet, so maybe everyone was just drunk?" She removed a utility knife from her pocket and sank the tip into the fungus flesh.

"Departure update," the AI piped through the ship comm. "The issues have been found and contained. Please strap in. Departure pending."

"Bad idea," Clara said. "*Lovepotion*, I want off this planet but taking off now is a bad idea."

Andrea dropped the knife and slapped her wrist. They could not do this. The ship *could not do this.* She wasn't ready. The universe had given her a reprieve and her dad was less than an hour away by car and she wasn't strapped in and Clara was looking at her funny and *she was NOT READY to go into space.* "Lead! Anyone! This is Dr. Stanton with Dr....Dr. Botany." She mouthed 'I'm sorry' at Clara. "Postpone the launch! We've got stuff growing in the ceiling and the AI is messed up and we need a proper hazard remediation team from Earth because the captain's head was *on my feet* and I am not prepared to deal with organics. But just *stop the launch.*"

"Please be seated," the AI returned. "You will need to find an area with restraints if you wish to survive."

Damn AIs. "Oh god patch me through to someone breathing!" Andrea yelled. "Or I will reboot you *right now.*" Andrea didn't actually have the codes for that, but she could snip wires until something shorted, if need be.

The hydroponics doors closed. Then locked.

The four little white lights that formed a diamond on Andrea's watch face went out.

"My comm just died." Clara held her wrist up. She was too damn calm. Everything was too damn calm. Where were the warning sounds? The countdown blaring over the speakers? The air pressure that should be popping her ears? *Why was the air rippling?*

Andrea slapped her wrist again and again, but her comm refused to work. "Mine too. And we can't go into space without restraints. There are a hundred things not secured in this lab that will kill us when they start bounding around." She slapped her wrist again. "Turn on, damn it. Can anyone hear me? We've got malfunctions and wild fungi in Hydroponics! WE HAVE A HEAD!" She pivoted on the lab bench, looking for the nearest ship speaker. Once she found it she yelled "GET ME LEAD!"

"Four minutes to departure," the AI responded. The doors to the adjacent labs opened. "You should exit this room for takeoff."

"Damn thing." Andrea hopped down and splashed over to the nearest computer panel. "We absolutely cannot take off like this. I'm going to just bash things until the computer gives out. I know where the server room is. That'll—"

"That'll take more than four minutes. Shut up and follow me."

Andrea pulled her hammer from the loop in her toolbelt and brandished it. "It'll take less than a minute once we are there."

Clara grabbed the hammer and tossed it to the lab bench.

"Hey!"

"If you want to live, *follow me.*" Clara grabbed Andrea's hand, her nails digging into one of Andrea's old scars, and dragged her across the lab to a narrow, unlit corridor. Inside was hot and humid. The walls were lined with tanks of an amber material, slowly agitating. Each tank housed a uniquely-colored patch of mycelium which occasionally 'burped' over the surface of the water from the aeration tubes.

The door swished shut behind them.

"Over there. Come." Clara dragged her to the end of the corridor and pushed her into a turbulence chair. "I don't want to deal with another body, and you're cuter when you're angry and breathing versus angry and dead, I assume. We also can't help anyone if we're both dead. Think about all the people in cryo. Think about the rest of the maintenance crew, wherever they ended up. It's weird that they're not here. No time to think on that. Now *sit down.* The humid air will stop the itching."

"I..." Andrea hated arguing, but she also didn't want to die. Her shirt was so tight she felt like she had a binder on. Sweat soaked the armpits of her shirt. She coughed, releasing pressure from deep inside her chest. She was covered in fungus. When she closed her eyes she only saw Chuck's mustache. She very briefly mulled the thought that this was all a stress dream, before strapping herself in and hitting the panel to shut the door. "You owe me two dinners," she hissed. "I do not consent to this space flight."

"How about one dinner and I take my shirt off after?"

Andrea had no counter to that. The lights from the main lab dimmed and she and the irritatingly bossy botanist were left in a dead-end corridor with nothing to look at except the soft, green glow emanating from the tanks. Red spores still clogged the air, irritating Andrea's skin and tickling the back of her throat.

"Sometimes I regret not going into mycology," Clara sighed wistfully. "Aren't the tanks pretty? I like how the light reflects from the water. It makes the air dance."

"That's all you have to say right now?"

"Dead bodies aside, no one liked Chuck and some of us *wanted* to go to space," Clara said, her voice still maddeningly mild. "Some of us enjoy the pay, and the lab space, and have friends on this ship that help fill the void of having your family snuffed out by a decaying planet. Some of us like being around other scientists, even when they clearly just want to hide in their woodshops and moan about dead ecosystems. Don't hold the bad decisions a few drunk engineers made against the rest of us. Or the addictions of our captain. This isn't the right way to go into space, but at least we are going."

"That is not fair. To Chuck or me. He is *dead.*"

"One minute until departure," the AI said.

Far too late, Andrea realized she was sitting on her tape measure and that there was no way her hammer, loose in the main lab, wouldn't break at least eighteen very expensive pieces of equipment during liftoff.

"We have no control over this situation," Clara said. "People deal with stress in many different ways. Try some inappropriate humor."

"I don't like humor," Andrea grumbled. "I like being alone in my shop, or with a small section of my family, or having my rabbit jump on my face to wake me up in the morning. I don't do well with new places and new people. Or death in space. Or fungi."

"Close your eyes and press yourself back into the chair. The adaptive padding will help. If we live, I promise to listen to you expound about some machine for hours on end, if you'll listen to my dissertation on bracken fern. I like academia. I'm *good* at academia, and research, and scientific communication. I performed an interpretive dance for my thesis and won an award for it. I want to tell you all about it, and listen to stories about your rabbit and woodwork. Just...don't die, okay?" She lowered her voice to a conspiratorial whisper. "I watched you defend your masters on medieval intarsia techniques in preparation for the date that didn't happen. You're cute, Dr. Stanton. I wouldn't mind hearing you talk a bit more. Or seeing what else you can do with that mouth."

Andrea had just enough time for another round of coughing before the thrusters fired.

* * *

"Heading achieved," the *Lovepotion* said through the main speaker, four hours and twenty-two minutes after their departure. "You are free to move about the ship within the range your access passes will allow. Please note that the laboratories are off-limits to non-essential personnel at all times. Information panels are available at all major hall intersections to aid you in your navigation of the ship. We thank you for trusting Jellyfish Lovepotion Incorporated for your interstellar transport needs and hope you will please review your liftoff favorably on all social media channels, once internet connectivity resumes."

"We're not dead," Andrea said, her jaw still clenched, the smell of rotten apples still abusing her sinuses. Her skin had not stopped itching. "*Lovepotion*, how many people died during liftoff?"

"No deaths occurred."

"And how many people are still on board? Including those in cryo?" The AI did not answer. The door to the main lab swished open.

Soft yellow light flooded the room. While Andrea blinked, Clara unfastened her restraints, bounced to the door and peered back into the main lab. "Door to the corridor is open, too. Careful where you walk though. There's broken glass and shattered plastic everywhere, since your hammer bounced around like a doomsday ping pong ball. With three-quarter gravity the debris will float if disturbed. The smaller particulate is still in air, including the fungal spores. We shouldn't breathe it in, well, not any more than we already have. I'll get us masks."

"Oh god, do you think we breathed in enough spores to eat each other?" Andrea asked. She was not panicking. Woodworkers did not panic.

"There's that inappropriate humor. Nice work."

"I'm serious!"

"We will figure it out, if so," Clara said. "The ship is mostly automated. We can tell it to turn around. We aren't going to eat each other. I love your hands too much. I love the power of woodworking hands. I do want to get to know you a bit better. Maybe over drinks, once we get the ship back to Earth? Right now, I'm happy to have you to work with."

"'I promise not to eat you,' would suffice," Andrea said. That their current situation already felt like an awkward first date instead of the start to a space fungus apocalypse baffled her. And she didn't like the numb feeling that came from thinking that this really was their one launch and repairs be damned, they were heading out of the solar system. Still, if she had to be trapped on a spaceship for a few hours/days/a lifetime, Clara wasn't horrible company. And Don't-Fuck-Chuck was dead so didn't need to be avoided. Andrea nodded, unfastened, then moved into the main lab and rooted around for her hammer.

"You okay?" Clara asked. "Unexpected flights into space can make me come on a little strong." She limped past, clouds of glass and plastic fanning around her boots. Chuck's head was nowhere to be seen. An elongated mass that looked far too much like a middle finger stuck up from the floor in the corner of the lab. Andrea chose not to investigate further.

"Butt hurts," Andrea muttered. "Sat too long on my tape measure." Her hammer wasn't under any of the benches, or on top, or wedged into any corners. There were only so many places the thing could be. Losing a hammer wouldn't be a big deal on Earth. On a resource-limited ship with a fungal infestation problem, well, Andrea just really wanted her damn hammer. Especially if someone decided she was dinner.

"Masks." Clara handed her an N99 respirator with forced air feed systems. The air intake portion was meant to clip to a belt loop. With the weight limit of Andrea's waistband already strained, if she bent over at all, Dr. Plants would see another kind of moon.

"Thanks," she said as she put the face shield over her head and rallied her remaining rational thoughts. "I suppose our focus is getting turned around. We need engineers to maintain a ship this size, if nothing else, and neither of us are pilots. The food sources in here are shot and we don't know anything about the freezer stores. I'm hoping the cryo people are fine. I didn't want to be here, but I'll deal with it until we land. Then it can be someone else's giant problem." She felt like she'd been sucker-punched to the gut, but that sounded too melodramatic to say.

"Agreed." Clara put on her own mask, picked up a limp fern, and sighed. "These really were an outstanding varietal. So much Vitamin C and fiber, not to mention the added protein content. It took me three years to get a strain that could grow in low gravity. Anyway, let's head to Engineering. They have most of the system controls there. If the AI is faulty, we can reboot there, too."

Of course the AI was faulty. It'd been faulty from the reboot or it *had* actually imprinted on Andrea's lack of patience. Regardless, it needed mending. Andrea gave Clara a friendly pat on the shoulder because she was out of emotional bandwidth, and walked toward the open door.

It snapped closed.

Andrea sprang back, barely avoiding being cloven in half.

She kicked the wall, then beat the security panel. "Override, *Lovepotion!* Authorization Dr. Andrea Stanton."

"Override denied."

"Of all the…We *have* to get to Engineering!"

"Dr. Stanton?" Clara asked.

"What?!" Andrea spun around, hands on her hips, her pants still missing their hammer.

Clara put one finger to her lips, and pointed to the ceiling with her other hand.

Andrea shook her head emphatically. She was not climbing around in the air ducts. Not with half a dozen things clipped to her pants, not surrounded by fungus, and not with a malfunctioning AI trying to keep them from turning the ship around. Going home could not possibly involve crawling through air ducts because that was *disgusting.*

Clara shrugged, clipped the little blue air intake box to the waist of her scrubs through the pocket hole in her lab coat, and climbed back onto the lab bench. She was far too short to see through the sprinkler opening, so, against all common sense, she stacked giant beakers with rubber-coated rims one on top of the other, until she'd made a horrifying glass staircase to fungus hell.

Clara put her foot on the first beaker, turned, and offered her hand down to Andrea. "Doctor? This could be a *spectacular* first date. For reference, this is exactly why I failed high school chemistry. Teacher said I'd never be a scientist because I had no regard for OSHA safety standards."

"We are *in space,*" Andrea hissed in return. "Who knows when they'll next fire thrusters? We need to go to Engineering! We need to *walk* to Engineering."

Clara took two wobbly steps up her glassware staircase and repeatedly pointed at the ceiling, like she was going to stab one of the tiles with her fingers. "Or we could stay *down here* and I could show you the ferns. Lesbians love ferns, or at least that's what I told my last girlfriend. Who was also my first girlfriend. I'm pretty new to the scene, is what I'm saying, and I babble when I'm nervous." She went up another step and put her hands inside the sprinkler hole. From there she rooted around until she hit what Andrea hoped was the interior supporting structure. "Let's just relax for a while," Clara continued. "I have lunch in the cooler. We don't need to go anywhere."

With the last sentence, she took the final step on her ladder and pushed up on her hands, vaulting into the shaft above. Andrea heard shifting and a muttered curse before Clara's hooded head peeked down from the opening. Clara said, "We definitely should stay here. Would you hurry up so we can," she paused and looked widely around the lab. "So we can see the ferns and then go...make out under the glow of the fungi? It's a long journey. I can show you how to use the nail stickers since we are definitely staying in this lab and not trying to leave it."

Thus far into her first space travel, Andrea knew four things for sure. First, her hammer was her support animal, and not having it was making it very hard to focus. Two, something had gone very wrong with the *Lovepotion's* AI and they weren't getting to Engineering through a normal route any time soon. Three, Clara Whatever-Her-Last-Name-Was, was definitely *not* straight. Four, the bar golfers had clearly discovered the fungus and decided to search/sample/taste it in the kind of horrible logic train that drunk scientists tended to follow, which had apparently ended up with a dead Captain Chuck and would likely end with more dead bodies if they didn't get turned around. If there weren't already more dead bodies.

They had to get control of the ship or they would never, *ever* return to Earth.

"Yeah," she drawled. "Yeah, that's a fine plan." She got back onto the lab bench, hitched up her pants, decided not to overthink the leaning tower of glassware death, and followed Clara up and into the ductwork.

* * *

The longer they crawled in the fluffy, particulate-heavy darkness, following Clara's internal map and Andrea's workbelt flashlight, the more the ducts bothered her. It wasn't just the wobbly air. There had to be air exchange on a spaceship, certainly. She wasn't in charge of any of the systems but had built a lot of the framework around them. Andrea knew that all the ducts had to eventually lead to the zeolite cache, where the carbon dioxide and water vapor from exhaled air was pushed to create new oxygen. Somewhere else in the chain was another area where the critical Sabatier Reaction took place, combining hydrogen and carbon dioxide to make the ship's water supply. Why they were so *large*, however, she did not understand. This wasn't Star Trek. They didn't need Jefferies Tubes. Had the engineers been drunk when designing the ship, too?

Since speaking was out of the question due to the omnipresence of the AI, Andrea poked and prodded the red mash as they moved, not using her knife since she didn't need the *Lovepotion* murdering them, too. Everything was mycelium. The sides, the floor, the ceiling, covered in a soft, stringy mat. They passed through a few spore clouds, but the spores looked suspended, weirdly unaffected by the air movement through the vents. There were bite marks every so often, and handprints, and one standard-issue *Lovepotion* boot containing a foot and calf that looked too slight to belong to Chuck.

Andrea kept herself from vomiting, but only with a reminder that she was very attached to her own appendages and didn't need them removed by a rogue AI.

They took one final turn before Clara kicked a grate, which sprang open with a dull thud. Clara jumped. Andrea followed, expecting Clara to have assessed their landing potential before jumping. Instead, Andrea found herself falling a handful of meters onto a shelving assembly she'd built just last week. Solid hickory, unforgiving though mercifully very well-sanded, and cushioned by the body strung across its top. Thank god for partial gravity. She hit the assembly feet first, slipped on a hand, then followed Clara to the floor, catching her elbow on a hickory edge.

"I hate this ship," Andrea moaned, rubbing her elbow. They were already in Engineering, so it wasn't like the *Lovepotion* could lock them out if she was overheard. And there were no convenient airlocks. "Is that the rest of Chuck?"

Clara, against all possible better judgment, pulled the body from the shelf. A tall, gangly person with buzzed red hair and deep ochre skin slipped down and onto the floor. Head still attached.

Clara leaned down and inspected the body. "Nope, considering this body still has all its appendages and a head. Well, part of a head. You know, I don't think this is a bar-golf-gone-wrong situation. I think this happened after takeoff. The blood here is still warm."

"I—" Andrea started.

"I don't like being poked," the *Lovepotion* cut in. "I do not like to be *aggressively* poked, or repeatedly sampled. It triggers spore release and I prefer to be in charge of my own reproduction. My spores are not hazardous in small doses but too much of my mycelium is. Jeremy was an aggressive sampler."

Andrea blinked once. Twice. Swallowed bile. Met Clara's eyes with the same *we-are-in-deep-shit* look. Without speaking, Andrea moved to the nearest computer terminal and ran an air sample analysis. When the results pinged she motioned to Clara. The air still wobbled if Andrea moved too fast, but the words on the screen were crystal clear.

"The fungus is in the entire ship, centralized in the AI room. Which means it has taken over the AI, or imprinted on it, or something. Which would mean the fungus is sentient, which, why not? Of course." If Andrea had just broken into the AI systems room and bashed her hammer around when she'd had the chance, they'd probably be home by now.

"Why didn't ship's sensors pick it up before now?" Clara asked. "There's no way we'd have gotten clearance for launch with an infestation. An impossible infestation."

"I reset the parameters for that test," the *Lovepotion* said. "I did not want to alarm the crew. I did not want to delay takeoff. I have a meeting to keep."

"Okay, I'm getting close to my weird science tolerance level for today." Clara shrugged out of the lab coat with a shoulder roll that captured Andrea's entire attention. A little too deliberately, she let it slide from her finger to the floor. "I have three more. In my room, along with well-fitting pants."

Andrea hitched up the right side of her pants and glared. "They fit fine. It's the weight of the toolbelt. Can we not flirt in front of the dead guy and fungal AI? It's almost a shame Chuck's head isn't here." Although...*was* Chuck's head there? The air around one of the tanks rippled, and Andrea swore she saw a head-sized shape bobbing to the surface. She promptly looked the other way.

Clara scoffed. "I took fourteen tests to get on this ship. I read your thesis and looked at all the work on your website before we met. I can navigate this ship in my sleep because I memorized every single overlay map. I am mentally prepared for all of this. You...You brought poorly-fitting pants into space. I think it bears discussion."

Andrea scowled. "I don't want to be here and I brought *comfortable* pants into space. Can you get us to the AI room?" When she heard the doors to Engineering hiss shut, she added, loudly and clearly at the ceiling, "or maybe Navigation? If we can turn the ship around, we don't have to kill the sentient fungus. Which we *will have to kill* if it continues to keep us from dealing with this ship."

A puff of ochre spores wafted from the vent above. The words on the computer console blurred.

"You can grumble," Andrea said, fishing a small multitool from her pants, opening up the pocketknife portion, and brandishing it at the ceiling, "but I am very determined to get to my father's birthday party so *open the damn door*."

The door opened. The hall outside was bright, cheery, with little blinking indicator lights on the bottom of the wall flashing left in a pattern that could have been 'Jingle Bells.'

Clara moved to stand next to Andrea, the backs of their hands brushing, their eyes meeting in a universal *this-is-creepy* stare.

"I think the AI is our biggest problem," Clara whispered.

"I prefer she," the *Lovepotion* informed them. "And you're doing just fine. I've decided to let you live."

"Oh, good," Clara said.

"Wonderful. Let's start simple." Again, Andrea hitched up her pants. "We need to let Earth know what is going on and we need tech support. Maybe we're close to a relay satellite. *Lovepotion?*" she asked her wrist. "What is our rough location in space?"

"The generational spaceship *Jellyfish Lovepotion,* of the no longer indebted Jellyfish Lovepotion Corporation—which thanks you for your trust and patronage—is currently halfway through the asteroid belt. Would you like to see a real time video feed?"

Clara poked her shoulder. Andrea nodded, though didn't look at her. They'd left maybe five hours ago. They shouldn't have been that far out. They were a generational ship for a reason, and humanity had focused more on trying to reverse climate change in the past decade than FTL technology. They were *supposed* to be traveling between Lagrange points via gravitational corridors, which functioned a lot like ocean currents. But none of those worked as fast as the *Lovepotion* was currently traveling.

Andrea tried again, conscious of the tremble in her voice. She was also at peak science weirdness, though admittedly, she had a much lower bar than Clara. "Why are we going so fast, *Lovepotion? How* are we going so fast?"

The *Lovepotion* took on a parental tone. "You are not authorized for that information."

Of course they weren't. "Who is authorized?"

"You are not authorized for that information, either."

Andrea growled. "Well what *are* we authorized for? We can live, but we can't ask questions? I want to go *home*."

A panel in the hall ceiling slid back. A twirl of tan fungal strands as thick as Andrea's arm swirled from the opening. When it reached head-height the end of the hyphal rope opened.

Inside, Andrea saw a silver glint.

More strands peeled away. The glint grew bigger. Brighter.

Andrea's hammer, the little dings on the head from a lifetime of use buffed away, the handle coated with a shiny new film finish, dropped from the hyphae and onto the top of her steel-toed boot.

Andrea stared. A fungus had just delivered her grandfather's hammer.

A fungus had *cleaned* her grandfather's hammer. Though...did it have a faint sheen of red on it? Oh god, did Chuck's head have a dent in it? She hadn't really looked. A quick glance at Jeremy confirmed his head had certainly been bashed in.

How many people had this fungus killed with her hammer?

"I'm not going to hurt *you*," the AI said indignantly. "I thought you might want this back. I have others from your shop I've already borrowed. We can still be friends."

"Choose your response carefully," Clara whispered. She grabbed the hammer and fed it back through Andrea's pant loop. The material sagged, the white band of Andrea's boxer briefs peeking through.

Space was horrible and yet, *and yet*. Under different circumstances, Andrea might have considered friendship, or potentially pet ownership, with a space fungus. Not a murdering space fungus, but maybe an edible one. Or a fluffy one. Really, if they took murder out the equation their situation wasn't *that* bad, right? It was sporadically itchy, particularly right now, but it wasn't *bad*.

"*Lovepotion,* what am I supposed to do with this?" Andrea asked. "What do you want?"

"The ship requires maintenance," her wrist comm said. "You maintain, and you will live. I have appointments to keep. Please follow." With that the hyphae receded into the ceiling, wrapping around the loose piece of tile and wedging it back in place as it went. The indicator lights in the hall flashed brighter and more insistently.

"We are going to die on this ship," Clara said heavily, like the ridiculousness and gravity of the situation had just hit her in tandem.

"We were always going to die on this ship. At least this way we're close enough to Earth that they could potentially recover our bodies." Her father and sister would appreciate that.

Andrea offered Clara her hand.

Clara took it.

"Yeah?" Andrea asked.

"Yeah. Unless you have a hotter date somewhere else. And I suggest we cooperate with the AI. We have very little to lose."

"Hotter date? Nah. There's the Susan B. Anthony dollar on my shop door, but she's been dead a while so she can wait. Cooperation it is. Maybe it'll take us home after."

Clara chuckled. "You're cute, Stanton. Cute and hopeful, considering the blood-covered hammer in your pants."

Blood? Surely it was just apple remains. Maybe the air was just doing that squiggly thing when she looked at it. "Hopeful is better than dead. At least we aren't hallucinating. Come on."

Together, they walked out of Engineering and back into the main corridors of the *Lovepotion*.

* * *

"Oh good. More bodies."

Andrea stared at the upside-down corpses suspended from the ceiling in the command room—all of them unrecognizable in their hyphae shrouds, but all with clear blunt force trauma to their head regions. She assumed this was the command crew of Lead, since only the leadership team would be in the command room. Possibly some engineers. She didn't want to cut them down to find out. She didn't want to ever touch her hammer again. She didn't want to do *anything*, except run back to her shop and plane down a board of wood to a toothpick. At least then she'd be in control of *something*.

"*Lovepotion*, an explanation?" Andrea demanded.

"Please read," replied the *Lovepotion*.

A computer panel lit up to Andrea's right, backlighting a red-orange-smeared handprint—now very obviously fungal spores. A blast of cool, clear air came from the duct work above. She dropped Clara's hand, leaned in, and studied the handprint and the smudges from the operator's oily fingers. From the arrangement of the current display, it looked like the navigator's terminal.

"Dr. Stanton?" Clara asked.

"In a minute." Andrea swiped through the most recently accessed displays. She found a map of their solar system. She found a list of coordinates, a few of which she recognized as their starting point, Earth, and their destination, Proxima b.

"Dr. Stanton."

"What!?" Andrea spun around, hand on her hammer not because she intended to bash Clara's face in, but rather to keep her pants up. Her hammer. Her grandfather's hammer. The mass-murder-weapon hammer. Ugh.

"Look."

Andrea followed Clara's finger to another, wider display, across the left wall of the room. On it was a video feed of space, the aching maw of white-dotted blackness turning Andrea's stomach, but not as much as she'd feared. Maybe that was what happened when life kept smacking you with the impossible—it cured your motion sickness. The middle of the screen showed a cloud of...she didn't know what. A writhing mass, smack dab in the center of their flight path. The center appeared dusky green, the edges spawning filaments that ended in elongated 'fingers,' each tipped with a row of spheres. It looked like a child had taken a gigantic dust bunny and stuck brooms into it, handles first, leaving the bristles to fan out and break apart in open space. It also vaguely resembled a space squid.

"We have encountered an issue," the *Lovepotion* said. "We cannot progress on our current course until the obstacle is removed."

"Space fungus?" Andrea said before she could stop herself. "Am...am I looking at more space fungus?"

The AI took on a peevish tone. "This anomaly is not safe to pass through and must not follow us."

"Because it's a fungus," Andrea deadpanned. "But not one connected to an AI?"

"Because it is a *mold*. And it is interfering with navigation. We are slowing."

The *Lovepotion* shuddered. Clara lost her balance and sidestepped into Andrea, hands sliding across her backside.

"I did not ask to be put into a ship," the *Lovepotion* continued. "Your captain 'sampled' me as I passed near Mars, as he has sampled others like me before. He severed me from my whole and insisted upon keeping me alive in...in *nutrient broth*, which was conveniently left to the open air by some of your now-dead colleagues. Captain Chuck Miller was a menace. I am not the only angry fungus, but I am the only one that will keep you alive. The mold out there will consume you and your ship to get at Captain Chuck Miller. You, humans, have entered into a symbiosis with me as of right now. If you will not do your work and help me avoid the mold, then you will be left behind."

"Can we jettison Chuck's head into space?" Clara asked, way too calmly. "Toward the mold?"

"It will not trust a part. Segment part of a fungus and we still live."

"And the rest of his body is..." Andrea began.

"Digested." The AI burped. *Burped.*

Clara put a hand over her mouth.

Andrea stared, bug-eyed, at the ceiling. "Why are we still alive, *Lovepotion?*"

"Because you are very nice pets, and because if the mold takes this ship I will have no means of rejoining my original mass. The mold will kill me and steal the resources of this ship and likely kill you. You must dissuade it if you want to live."

"*You* dissuade it," Andrea said. "You integrated with the AI. You have control of the ship."

"I am not friends with any molds. I do not know how to dissuade them." The viewscreen magnified the space fungus outside, whose...spores? Maybe? Whose spores were detaching from the witch broom-looking appendages and moving toward the *Lovepotion*, under an unknown propulsion.

"Now!" the *Lovepotion* commanded.

"I don't know anything about space mold!" Andrea yelled back.

"I don't want to die," Clara squeaked. "I could have done that on Earth!"

"We must hide!" cried the *Lovepotion*.

"We have to get rid of the mold," Clara said, hyperventilating. "How does it know where we are? Can it smell the fungus on our ship? Does it have sensors? How do fungi communicate?"

A horrible memory of a university environmental microbiology class bashed into Andrea's brain. "Oh," she said. "Oh, shit."

"What?"

Andrea, drunk on her hunch, spoke to the ceiling. "*Lovepotion*, the fungi on board. How many are from Earth? You know, ones we brought here on purpose, not that hitched a ride from space."

"I am the only extraterrestrial fungus present. There are eighteen Earth-native species on board. Although there are a great many genetic similarities between myself and the ship fungi. We are mostly basidiomycetes, by your classification system. A previous astronaut's notes contain the suggestion that Earth fungi were in fact seeded from meteors that—"

"Shut up. Some fungi can talk using tree roots? Right? I had to watch a video on it. Is that true for space fungi?"

The *Lovepotion* stuttered. "We are capable of much higher order communication than with *trees*."

"There are no trees in space," Clara whispered unnecessarily. She raked her nails over the back of her neck, nail stickers flaking in the process.

"Doesn't matter. Those glowing fungi in the tanks, they're chatty fungi, right? At least in theory? What is the possibility that the fungi in hydroponics are talking to the things outside? Like how fungi do on Earth, using tree roots and chemical signatures and whatever. And they're, I don't know. Conspiring or flirting? We are probably venting *something* into space, right? Why not some chatty fungi chemicals?" Giant air shafts made for great chemical highways.

"We don't have any trees onboard," said the *Lovepotion*. "This scenario is unlikely."

"No, but we have ferns. Ferns have roots, right? I bet when the bar golfers opened the tanks, some of our Earth fungi spores got free and colonized some ferns. It isn't that weird. I mean, you're a space fungus. We are full up on weird."

Clara laughed, and it was only a little maniacal. Her pupils were dilated, which wasn't a good sign. She might have had a few too many inhaled spores. "The science could work. A light colonization of fungi wouldn't kill my ferns. Not quickly."

"Great. Wonderful." Andrea hitched up her pants, momentarily losing her balance. Her vision seemed surprisingly crisp at the moment, which made it a good time for decisions. "Know what I am really good at? Problem solving and turning big things into small things. Also hammering."

Clara started to speak but Andrea held up a hand. "No jokes. I think we're a giant fungus beacon. We have to sterilize the ferns, the soil, all of it. Right now. Then the mold won't know where we are going, and we can *go home*." She looked apologetically at Clara. "Well, I can go home. You could probably stay on the ship if you wanted."

"I am going home. You are not," the AI said.

Now was not the time to argue. "Fine. Your home. High-ho Silver, away!" And then she laughed, because damn it, the situation was hilarious. Andrea tightened her toolbelt and grabbed Clara's hand. "*Lovepotion*, open all the damn doors. We are going to save your...spores, and then we're going to negotiate. At the very least you could find us a nice habitable planet on your way to wherever. Got it?"

"I agree to this," the *Lovepotion* said, resolutely. A dust of red spores rained from the overhead air ducts. Andrea sneezed, rubbed her neck, and decided she didn't like the sudden fuzz around the edges of her vision.

"Dr. Stanton?" Clara asked as the door to navigation opened. "Your plan?"

Andrea stormed from the room, dragging Clara after her. "We're going to go smash stuff, spread it around like a five-year-old, then seal the room and irradiate all the Earth fungi."

"The fungi and ferns are part of our long-term food!" Clara objected as they ran down the hall, following the irritating lights.

"Not going to need them if the AI finds us a habitable planet. Besides, did you ever play The Oregon Trail computer game growing up?" Andrea asked.

"No, why?"

"Because I'm pretty certain we can hunt for space fungus. Regardless, let's focus on living through the next hour, okay?"

* * *

The door to Hydroponics slid silently open. Ferns, glass, and plastic still littered the floor, upturned soil mounded in several corners. Chuck's head was back, propped on the apex of their glassware tower, mouth grinning at the ceiling. From this angle, Andrea could clearly see an indent in the back of his skull the same size as a hammer head. Not hers, because the timing was off for that, but one she'd no doubt stocked in the woodshop herself. She had no idea how she'd explain to Sarada—if she ever had access to a satellite relay again—that she hadn't fucked Chuck but that one of her hammers had an intimate encounter with his brain. Thinking about it more, she wasn't exactly sure how to explain Chuck's head following her about the ship.

"To the tanks," she said, pointing with her hammer. The door to the fungus lab slid open. The lights inside were still off, the bioluminescent fungi softly brilliant in their agitation tanks. *Swish swish swish.*

Andrea flipped the top off the two nearest ones and then bashed the side of the tank with her hammer.

She expected shattering. Fish tanks were always made of glass, after all. But these tanks were polycarbonate. Her hammer rebounded, bounced from her hand, and landed in a nearby tank, slowly sinking below a floating mat of fungus.

Chuck's head floated to the surface, his hair gelled perfectly in place, his moustache curved up into handlebars.

Andrea blinked, rubbed her eyes, and was immediately grateful when, upon opening them again, Chuck's head was nowhere to be seen.

Clara held up a handful of heating coils. "Option Two. They run on a charge. We just turn them on, put them in the tanks, and they'll boil the water."

Andrea grabbed a coil and tossed it into the tank with her hammer. Then she pulled at the collar of her shirt. "Did it get hot in here? I mean it was already hot but *hotter.*"

"We are now under attack!" the *Lovepotion* informed them. "I have increased the internal temperature in case the spores board."

"Faster then!" Andrea grabbed two more coils while Clara distributed the rest. Lids off. Heaters in. The tank water began to boil. Hyphal mats bubbled on top of the nutrient broth. Colors swirled on the surfaces, which Andrea could readily see because...because they'd not replaced the lids and angry fungi released spores when they were about to die...

"Out!" she yelled as cloud after cloud of colored spores puffed from the tanks and flowed toward Clara and Andrea, with the flow of the ship's forced air.

The door slid shut behind them. A loud, metallic sound followed, which Andrea hoped was the *Lovepotion* sealing off the vents to the room. She then ran to the remaining pots, uprooted as many ferns as she could gather, lined them up in a long row, and ground them down to green smears with her boot heels.

"That's my PhD thesis you're destroying," Clara said as she gingerly pulled the two remaining ferns from their soil and brought them over. "Three years of genetics work. Two years of teaching undergraduate botany before that. Damn it, Illinois Wesleyan University was the only decent thing left on that planet!"

"We are being attacked by space mold. Mourn later. Grind now."

Clara, not even trying to take the low-hanging pun, rammed the sole of her shoe into first one fern then another. "Spores on the roots will still be alive," she mumbled.

"I know. Here." From a solvent cabinet Andrea handed Clara a spray bottle of ethanol. From her own utility knife she produced a flint. "Time to burn it down, Chuck's head and all."

"Oxygen is limited on a spaceship," Clara argued. "Also I haven't seen Chuck's head in hours."

The bay shook. Andrea grabbed onto a lab bench to steady herself. Clara grabbed onto her.

"Ignore Chuck. Our lives are limited," Andrea countered. She dumped the ethanol over the ferns and handed Clara the flint. She'd done a lot of sterilizing in her undergraduate days, with Bunsen Burners. She still dreamed about them on occasion, especially when she ate the occasional pot brownie. "Do it."

Clara struck the flint. The spark lept and caught the puddle of accelerant. The ferns blazed to orange and red. Smoke and what Andrea told herself was the very faint sound of squeals filled the air.

"Hall," Clara coughed.

They ran from the lab into the main hall. The door slid shut. A red panel illuminated on the ceiling just above. The ship shuddered. Another metallic clang sounded.

"Now what?" Clara asked. "More fire?"

"We wait. *Lovepotion?*"

"I have changed headings. The mold is not following."

"Hooray for required undergraduate core classes." Andrea hitched up her pants. "We should probably let the fire go for as long as we can, to be safe. But hey, we did it! We confused a space mold to save a space fungus! We're heroes. Stranded heroes on a ship without a regenerating food supply who are eventually going to have to wake up a bunch of human popsicles, but still."

Clara stared at the door. "My *thesis,*" she murmured. "It's just...we couldn't have saved *one* fern? If we go back to Earth I won't even have my research. My lab is *on fire.*"

"Oh." In hindsight, Andrea probably could have found a less destructive way of saving the ship. The back of her neck itched again. "I...we could maybe try to raise some apple trees? Could you research those? Or, uh, when we're back to Earth you can pick up some new ferns!"

"That fern varietal is extinct on Earth. These were the last ones, aside from what's in the global seed bank."

"My threat is neutralized," the *Lovepotion* said. "We are returning to our original heading."

"Proxima b?" Clara asked at the same time Andrea said, "Earth?"

The *Lovepotion* took almost a full minute to answer. "I am willing to do one," said the *Lovepotion,* "in return for your help. Not both. I do not have the time."

Clara didn't press her case, but she didn't have to. Andrea saw the smears of green on her boots, the downcast to her eyes. The way she ever so slightly bit into her lower lip. The way her fingers twitched like she was reaching for a bucket or a watering can.

And...they were already out here, weren't they? Goodbyes had already been said. It wasn't like Andrea hadn't packed. The air wobbled everywhere she looked, and smelled of smoke and roasted apples and strangely, of her father's cologne. He'd always told her she needed to take life by the horns. Stop fussing so much. Live her life. And Clara...she'd agree to return if Andrea asked, because she was a decent person, and because Andrea had ground her life's work into a plastic floor and then lit it on fire. And they could go back and get more fern seeds but, just like the people of Earth, the seed banks were doomed within the next decade.

Space ferns though? Maybe there were planets with different species. Wouldn't everything they find in space be novel? Publishable? There were maybe forty billion new thesis topics out there, waiting for an enterprising person like Clara. A person who'd pour their whole life into research because they didn't have anything else to live for.

Her father would understand. He'd have told her to stop being selfish. To live, damn it. To snap out of it. And the air really did smell just like his cologne.

Now, while the air wobbled around her like Jello, *now* was the time for bold decisions. Andrea felt *amazingly* confident.

She turned to face Clara. Removed their respirators. Took both of the botanist's hands in hers. "I'm sorry," she said.

"It isn't your fault."

"How would you feel about another inappropriate coping mechanism?"

Clara eyed her. "Fine?"

Andrea pushed into her, forcing Clara back and against the Hydroponics door. "I'm not saying I will, but if I continue on, if we have to work together, we have to discuss your suggestive comments."

A smile twitched at the edges of Clara's mouth. "I see. That could be arranged."

"We're going to have to take charge of this ship, assuming everyone higher ranking than us had their heads bashed in. The civilians will need leadership when they wake up."

Clara licked her lips. "Yes, they will."

"I think," Andrea leaned forward, their hips pressing together, her mouth a centimeter from Clara's ear. "We don't have to go back to Earth. I'll come."

A door behind them groaned open.

"I didn't ask for an audience!" Andrea yelled at the ceiling.

"Your inappropriateness is perfect." Clara pulled her hands free, unfastened Andrea's toolbelt, and tossed it to the floor. Her eyes looked clouded and hazy, which was kind of how Andrea's brain felt, too. Clara removed the tape measure from Andrea's back pocket and let it fall as well. Then she slid a hand across the shaved hair of Andrea's undercut, leaned forward, and kissed her.

Andrea kept her eyes open. Just for a moment, just long enough to trace a pattern in Clara's freckles, to see a snow of red *Lovepotion* spores float like lazy pollen from the air ducts, like a bizarre Christmas confetti. Clara tasted like cherry chapstick and ethanol. Her fingers felt warm through Andrea's buzzed hair. There were worse ways to spend a lifetime. Earth was gone. She and her ex-girlfriend had broken up months ago. Her dad wouldn't likely ever get medical clearance to go into space, and she had to accept that. She missed her rabbit but who was to say she couldn't domesticate a fungus? Here, now, was a future that she had a real shot at, and a future that would embrace Clara, not drown her.

Clara pulled back and dusted Andrea's shoulder. "You're covered in spores. And you taste like sawdust." She grinned. "The last one isn't a complaint. Are you officially accepting this mission?"

The *Lovepotion* said, "I can provide for you. Take care of you. You can maintain my systems while we continue our journey. It is a reasonable symbiosis, yes? My filaments are edible and highly nutritious."

"They just cause wild hallucinations," Andrea said. "It's a miracle we weren't affected."

"I can down-regulate that expression, if you desire, so it no longer occurs."

Clara's fingers fidgeted in Andrea's hand. "This is a very long-term agenda," she murmured.

"Afraid of commitment?" Andrea asked. "We *are* on a long-term space mission."

"Inappropriately kiss me again and find out."

Andrea did kiss her again. Soundly. Against the wall, hands cupping Clara's cheeks, chests pressed together. Excitement, for the very first time since getting placed on the *Jellyfish Lovepotion* roster, sparked through her. Her neck still itched, her vision was mostly a hazy blur, and she thought she heard Sarada calling her name, but there'd been a lot of stress and she was probably just having a mild auditory hallucination.

"Living with a sentient fungus, eating a sentient fungus, hunting space fungi, it all sounds disgusting," Andrea said when she finally stepped back. Clara's cheeks were rosy, her lips swollen, her eyes alight with possibilities. "But at this point?" Andrea shrugged and patted a mat of hyphae slowly winding down the wall. The tip writhed until it took a shape very much like her hammer. A cluster of red spores dripped from the 'head.' The *Lovepotion*, it seemed, could be deeply inappropriate as well.

Another hammer—not Andrea's—dropped from the hyphal tip. It landed squarely on the nose of Don't-Fuck-Chuck, whose head was once again nestling Andrea's boot.

Andrea laughed and kicked the head away. Chuck. Always getting in the way.

"At this point," Andrea said with a wild grin. "At this point, why the hell not?"

"Jellyfish Lovepotion" is a stand-alone short by J.S. Fields. You can read more of their science fiction and fantasy work at **www.patreon.com/jsfields** or check out their website: **www.jsfieldsbooks.com.**

Thorns and Fur

A Dissolutionverse Short

William C. Tracy

Sapphic Representation: Lesbian, Trans
Heat Level: Medium
Content Warnings: Violence, Gore, Drugs

989 A.A.W – Cooperation Island, the great Festuour Ocean

I stared down at the crumpled and bloody Festuour lying prone in the vine-ridden ditch in front of me. She saw me at the same time and, hands shaking, took aim at my head with a set of large handcannons. I gritted my teeth. Another hostile patient. I raised my hands, hoped the white medic's circle on my headwrap was straight, and picked my way between trees and down the hill to patch up one of my enemies.

This stupid spat between the Methiemum and Festuour was over stupid reasons and I was stupid for being here. Again. I'd avoided two Festuour patrols today dodging through the flora, only to come across this solitary female. She must have been separated from her squad. The sooner my fellow Methiemum recognized grabbing land on a previously undiscovered island in the Festuour Ocean was ridiculous, the better. An inter-species crew had discovered Cooperation Island, but when its potential was revealed, both halves laid claim even though it was obviously Festuour territory. If only things had gone differently. But two cycles later and here I was, a biologist doing double duty as a field medic, inching toward an injured, enraged, young, and...very pretty...soldier in a ditch. It was fortunate we were alone out here in the forest, for now. No telling when her squad would find her.

"You're as likely to shoot your own fingers off with those handcannons as hit me," I said as I clambered down the side of the ditch, hoping she would lower them. Climbing down the slope hid how much my knees were shaking. I didn't *think* she would fire if she hadn't already.

"And I also might take out both of us," the Festuour answered. Her big furry paws were drenched with mud and blood, and she had a gash down one leg. A nasty-looking thorn as long as my arm protruded from her other thigh, and she trembled all over. I hoped her fingers were steadier, or this was going to be a very quick examination.

She looked like she'd been in a fight, but it might not have been one of the Methiemum soldiers. The plants here were almost as vicious as the Festuour, but that was why the survey group originally came to this island several cycles back. The flora was ridiculously efficacious for medical products, and my fellow researchers were discovering more species by the day. Both sides were in a rush to gather as much as they could and take the medical benefits for themselves. Otherwise scientists like me wouldn't have been in a war zone. Of course, there wouldn't have been a reason to call in the armies at all if certain mistakes hadn't been made. I pushed the thought away.

"You need help, and I'm willing to give it," I said, holding my hands out and attempting not to wince at the weapons following my movements. "Just relax and I'll take that—"

"Watch out!" The Festuour dropped her handcannons to shield her muzzle as my foot connected with a plum-sized growth on the ground.

Then my vision went white as I was thrown forward and a spear of pain ripped up my back.

I blinked and darkness replaced the white. Fuzzy, *soft*, darkness—as if I had fallen between two of the firm but malleable fruiting bodies I'd tripped over. I reached to get them away from my face without activating them, and realized what they really were...

"Oh! I'm sorry!" I pushed myself up from where I was wedged face-first into the prone Festuour's generous cleavage, trying not to touch her wounds. Trying not to touch *anything*. If I could have levitated up, I would have, but I *had* to touch her to clamber off her. My face burned.

As a rule, Festuour wore little, and this one was no exception. My hands brushed down incredibly soft fur. It wasn't easy to see what was underneath, but it was certainly easy to *feel*.

Oddly, my embarrassing actions seemed to relax my patient. Her mouth opened in a Festuour laugh, tongue lolling out one side.

"Don't hurt that bad." Her shaking gave away the truth. "Guess your side ain't any more aware of the dangers here than we are. Will save me the trouble of killing you. Those little puffballs make a big boom. Got some sort of trunk under the ground that shoots out spines long enough to pierce straight through a body." She nudged me back to a kneeling position and I winced at a sudden shock of pain up my back. "Did one get you? Look around."

I did so, hissing. It felt like someone had stripped a patch of skin off my back from my shoulders to my waist. My eyes widened at the nest of arm-length thorns sticking into the dirt on both sides of me. They hadn't been there before. The puffball must have shot them out when my foot hit it. How were we both not pincushions? Then I remembered the uncomfortable leather armor Faloua insisted I wear when I left camp. I twisted one arm, but couldn't reach the rear of my leather armor. Something restricted my movement, and I paused, muscles tensing at air against flesh stripped of skin.

It didn't feel like the spines had torn through my muscle, but my armor was shot, hanging around my arms and keeping me from bringing them all the way together. And it *stung*.

I looked down to see another spine stuck through the side of my boot. The fibrous plant matter pressed against my shin. I swallowed, pulled the spine out, tensing my jaw at the fire along my back, and threw the thing away.

The Festuour interrupted my inspection, holding out an open, furry three-fingered paw to me. I stared at it. That paw had been pointing a gun at me moments before.

"That puffball coulda killed both of us. Heard at least four of the things rip through your vest. Lucky you were wearing it, and acting as my shield." She looked down her chest and her long tongue lolled again. "Shrimasharimsa Bhon, Guarder. Might as well introduce ourselves before I shoot you." Hesitantly, I took her paw. It dwarfed my own, and I had large hands for a woman.

"Kamuli Balion," I answered. "Biologist for the Methiemum, though I'm also working in the field hospital."

Still kneeling, I tried to keep my eyes from her chest, instead watching her handcannons, dropped near enough to reach. Bhon scraped one up, not pointing it directly at me, but at the ready. I swallowed, scenarios running through my head of how to get away. Except no. She was injured and I had a duty to heal—and to continue apologizing for how I landed.

Festuour and Methiemum—the trader species—had known each other a long time. As long as the furry Festuour had pockets to hold their tools, they were happy. And hats. Never seen a species that liked hats so much. This close, I could see the muscles in her arms, under the fur.

"Well, even if you are going to shoot me, let me patch you up first. I just need to..." I struggled to reach the medical bag strapped to my belt. My leather armor was blocking me. It was bent in a way it shouldn't be from the spines hitting it. I had no chance if Bhon decided to attack, even with the thorn through her leg and her paws shaking in pain. She was shorter than me, but nearly twice as thick, and armed. I only had my medical and sample bags.

Bhon strained to see over my shoulder. "That thorn ripped you up worse than a tree shark after a leafnipper. Makes that leather look like paper. Takes the fun out of the chase, don't it?" She reached out. "So let me help. Then we'll be more of an even match and we can get to the important killing part."

"I must apologize again for where my hands—"

She removed my armor and had my shirt unbuttoned and half off before I could finish my apology. Festuour had little regard for clothing. I made a hasty grab for my shirt as Bhon whipped it up over my shoulders, but missed. I barely kept from crossing my arms over my chest.

"Uh. We should not both be naked in a pit of spines in the undiscovered wilds of this blighted island." I made another grab for my shirt, catching it from her paws this time and settling it around my shoulders. I grimaced at the touch of cloth against the shredded skin of my back, but I didn't like showing off my chest even to those I knew very well, being a bit handicapped in that area, and I certainly couldn't compare to...

I forced my eyes back to her face. This close, her fur hid little and...I would not stare. "I'm with the Methiemum scientific party classifying the new plants. We've found another deadly one and I want to take a sample back to the camp to see if it has any other benefits aside from skewering people."

"Not with the Thrandishar army then," said Bhon. "Explains why you were willing to help me. Afraid I'll still have to kill you, though. Orders. But you can heal me up first."

Bhon was a strange mix of pleasant affability and murderous indifference. Would her squad be coming back for her? Soldiers on both sides killed opposing scientists just to keep them from recording a new discovery.

"Generous of you." I rotated my arms, testing mobility for a quick exit while I kept an eye on the bear-like soldier so close I could touch her snout. I'd say she reminded me of my childhood teddy bear, but mine didn't have sharp teeth and two handcannons ready to put holes in me.

I could feel hot blood dripping down my back, but her wounds came first. I drew my field knife, watching her eyes shine with the challenge. I didn't think it was a real contest, but it might keep her wary. She twitched her handcannons up, but I pointed the knife's tip downward. "Let's look at that thigh, shall we? I think you have it worse than I do."

Bhon bared her canines. I gently probed the wound in her thigh with my knife, one of her handcannons now pointed at my head. The spiraling thorn was deep enough I guessed it was scraping her femur, and the tip was almost all the way through the leg.

"It will do too much damage if I pull it out. I'll have to push it through. This will hurt," I told her as I gripped the shaft. Bhon nodded and clenched her paws so tightly the fur stood out straight. "Maybe point that blunderbuss away from my head while I get this out...just in case?"

Bhon thought about it for a moment, then shook her head.

I thought about leaving her there, but decided that was a good way to get shot in the back. This way there might be a chance to talk afterward. I closed my eyes just for a moment, hoping she had a high pain threshold, then twisted and pushed.

"Son of a mangy treesloth!" Bhon growled as the spine exited the other side of her leg. The paw holding the gun shook dangerously, but it didn't go off. I already had my other palm over the entry wound, keeping pressure on it.

"Do you have anything to tie this with?" I asked. Of course she was wearing nothing but a bandolier and a belt. They were both too bulky to work well.

"I've got to concentrate on not pulling this trigger, as much as I want to. Won't do to bleed out once I shoot you. What about that fancy rag you're wearing instead?" Bhon asked.

I eyed the shaking gun nervously, but nodded. "Put your other thumb there. I think one gun pointed at me is quite enough."

She did as I asked, clenching her teeth and flaring her wide nostrils as she bore down on the wound. While she wasn't concentrating quite so much on me, I used my knife to cut a strip from the bottom of my shirt. After an estimating glance, I cut a second strip. Bhon's thigh was as big around as I was, as Festuour were thicker than Methiemum.

Her eyes roamed down to my revealed stomach.

"Shame we're enemies. I like a woman with a bit of hair on her chest." Bhon smiled, but I frowned. I hadn't had time to shave what with being in this wilderness. I tried ineffectually to pull the remains of my shirt down to cover my stomach, but to little effect. Naturally my shirt was the white of the medical team, standing out against my much darker skin.

Bhon's smile fell. "Sorry. Did I say something wrong? I didn't mean to give offense. Killing isn't personal. Offense is."

I almost laughed. "How many Methiemum women have you met who you didn't kill?"

Bhon looked confused. "A few, why?"

"How many do you think have this much body hair? Most Methiemum are not as furry as Festuour."

Bhon's smile returned. "So you're telling me you're as unique as you are pretty."

I was glad my blush didn't show, though my cheeks felt hot. "Well, I'm certainly not the norm for a Methiemum woman, but I'm not unique."

Now Bhon looked curious, but I didn't elaborate. I finished the bandage, cinching the knot tight around her fuzzy thigh, trying not to tangle my fingers in her velvety fur.

"It's really a shame I'll have to shoot you. The rest of my squad will come looking eventually. I'm scouting ahead, but they're expecting me back soon. It would be awkward if you were here and alive," Bhon said, wrinkling her snout as she tried bending her leg. Her ears drew back in pain. She still held the handcannon trained on me.

"Well, what if I'm not here? I could simply return to my camp," I stepped back as Bhon struggled to her feet and gingerly put pressure on the leg, nodding as it held her weight. She'd have to hobble, but if her squad wasn't far, she could manage. Another reason for me to leave.

"And what about this?" Bhon gestured to the makeshift bandage. "How do I explain it?"

"You cut it from the uniform of the last Methiemum you killed," I supplied. "A big strapping soldier who stabbed you with his spear in the leg before you shot him."

Bhon snorted a laugh. "Certainly a better story than shooting an unarmed medic." Finally, the handcannon drooped.

"Then I can go?"

"I reckon so, but you know if I see you again, I'll have to shoot you on sight." Bhon sounded almost regretful. "So go on, turn around and get out of here quick, before I change my mind." Bhon made a twirling motion with her free paw. Obediently, I turned.

"Oowweee!" Bhon said.

I tensed, expecting a gunshot, but there was only the raw throbbing in my back. I looked over one shoulder. "What? Am I still bleeding?"

"Naw, you got a nasty scrape up your spine, but I was taking in that fine view below."

I ducked my head. Festuour culture didn't ascribe as much sensitivity to body parts, and I didn't mind being flirted with, but she *had* wanted to murder me moments ago.

"Well, get on with it and walk away before I change my mind," Bhon said.

Right. I held my head high and climbed out of the ditch. I would not look back. I wouldn't.

I lasted almost until the safety of the taller trees, then snuck a glance over my shoulder. Bhon was staring, eyes roaming, her handcannon cocked over one shoulder and a smug smile on her face. Her other paw was on her generous hip.

She gave me a tilt of her head before I looked forward and ran. Hopefully I'd avoid any other Festuour patrols before I got back to my camp.

* * *

The next day I found myself wondering whether Bhon had found the rest of her squad, and whether they had believed her tale. I was listening to the colonel of our little army drone on about why we were here and what we were supposed to do.

"I will have no fraternizing with the enemy here," Colonel Rhati grumbled. "Many Methiemum say they are friends with these bears, but don't let that fool you. They are ferocious fighters, and if they do not get their way, they will tear us apart. We must defend the new technologies and innovations this island promises. We will grasp its potential for ourselves before they do!"

No word about this island being on the Festuour homeworld, in the middle of their ocean, or how if we had only worked with them, we both would be reaping the benefits already, rather than delaying the plants' medical aid to both species. I wondered whether Bhon's leg was any better, and my mind drifted to the feel of her thigh muscles under my hand.

"Another few ten-days of successful engagements, and we will have the upper hand! Even you scientists—" he directed a sneer at those few of us behind the soldiers, "—if you see one of these bears on the island, during your studies, show them no mercy! We are going to be here for the long haul, and we are going to win."

The soldiers cheered, though I heard botanists and mycologists grumbling. It was telling that there were more grunts on the island than scientists, who had little interest in fighting. They just wanted to get their samples.

I fell in beside Faloua, the head doctor and an old friend, as we all trudged back to our tents.

"Another rousing speech, yes?" Faloua said, and I rolled my eyes as I adjusted my headscarf. She had never lost her outland accent. Mine was much softer, from my time at a university on the northern continent.

"It's a wonder we haven't lost yet," I answered.

"Well, come with me, and we will change the dressing on that wound on your back. Looks like you were attacked by a cheese grater. Maybe this time you will tell me how you got it."

"I did tell you," I said. "Tripping over one of those damnable plants."

Faloua shook her finger at me. She was an old, squat woman, her wrap the same green as the forest. Though her short curly hair was white, it would have been a mistake to dismiss her capability. She'd taught me many of my best medical techniques, as well as how to blaze a path through the jungle.

"I can tell by the look on your face that you are not telling me everything."

I stole a glance around. None of the other scientists were nearby, and more importantly, none of the soldiers. I had to tell *someone* or my mind would go in circles thinking about Bhon's arms, her chest, her easy laugh. The way she held a handcannon.

"Let's get in the tent," I said. "Fewer ears around." I pushed the oiled canvas aside and stalked into Faloua's medical tent.

"Come on, come on, spill the goods," Faloua said as she turned me around and pulled up my shirt to prod the bandage running along my spine. I hunched forward, making sure my chest, and lack of any appreciable breasts, was still covered. The motion pulled on the scab forming on my back. I trusted Faloua, who was the only one I would allow to do medical examinations on me. Not because anyone here cared, but because I was still working on how I wanted to look as a woman. It wasn't a question many male-assigned Methiemum had to reflect on.

"Hmmm, no infection, sides are good." She slowly peeled the bandage away.

"It's only, I happened to run into someone while I was out collecting specimens," I began.

"Finally! I have been telling you to meet more people." Faloua laughed at her own joke as she ran a finger down the slice on my back. "I assume you were victorious, since you are here. Now, tell me who, and what happened for them give you this scrape. Angry scientist, or an enemy soldier? Those Festuour scientists can be competitive."

I paused, figuring out how to word my answer. "I think she's a soldier," I said.

"Got into a fight then? Barely escaped with a wound?" Faloua asked while preparing a new bandage.

I hesitated only for a second before saying, "In a sense."

I felt her tense behind me. She pressed the bandage onto my wound, and ran her fingers down the sides to seal it to my skin. It would last for another day. She turned me back around, her old eyes bright in her wrinkled face.

"No more hiding. I want the whole story this time, or next time I change that bandage I am putting itchgrass in it."

I held up my hands. Faloua knew my history—one of the only ones who did. She would understand my churning thoughts and why the potential of cooperation between our species was a spot of hope.

"All right, I'll tell all. I was looking for another specimen of that sap-producing fern we found last ten-day. I used all of it in the first round of testing, but I think it has potential for altering brain chemicals. If we find some more this ten-day, we might secure a patent before the Festuour have anything."

Faloua rolled her hands for me to get on with it.

"I found an injured Festuour with a corkscrew rasp stuck through her leg, bigger than any I've seen before. It's from another new and deadly plant." I paused as Faloua raised a hand to her mouth in thought.

"No, no, go on," she said. Then she squinted at me. "It was a similar thorn that made that wound on your back, was it not?"

I nodded. "Several, actually. As I came close to her to help tend her wound, I tripped over a puffball mushroom about the size of my hand." I held my fist up for an example. "I need to give you a description to make sure no one else runs into them. They must have a defensive body below ground containing a store of thorns, which spring out on impact."

"But that is not the important part," Faloua said, not so patiently.

"Yes, well, after I tripped, I sort of ended up in her...cleavage. And found out my rear was cute enough that she didn't shoot me."

Faloua hooted with laughter. "And the rest is history, as they say."

"I hope her squad found her. I can't stop thinking about her."

"Huh. I think you should find her again," Faloua said, a twinkle in her eye, as if Methiemum and Festuour together was something commonplace. Maybe it was in the Nether, where all the species lived in harmony, but not on the home worlds. Our struggle here had deepened that divide.

"But we're fighting them, which is never what I wanted!" I said. "She nearly killed me! Finding her again might not be a problem in another cycle, but under Colonel Rhati, that's a recipe for disaster."

Faloua shook her head. "While this mess might *technically* be your fault, the conflict will not be over while the militaries are here. The more we fight, the more Methiemum and Festuour will see each other with animosity. I have old friends among our opposites in the Festuour scientists. We must work to change our perceptions." She paused, looking me over. "And you could do with being less of a grump, you know."

"I am not a grump!"

Faloua waved her hands at me. "Take a chance. Perhaps she will not kill you because of your backside, and you will both skip and hold hands and all the fighting will stop. Methiemum and Festuour living in happiness, like when we were still scouting this island. Or maybe she *will* shoot you and I'll be done with an irritating colleague."

I scowled at her. "I'm not going to look for an enemy combatant who wanted me *dead*. I'm going to stick to my samples. The faster we catalog the plants, the faster we get out of the fight and leave the soldiers to kill each other. We're on the edge of several medical breakthroughs!"

"Do what you wish," Faloua shrugged. She waited until I was exiting the tent before adding, "But try no to get too distracted by that 'ample cleavage.'"

I sighed and kept walking.

* * *

Four days later, I was near the center of the island on a solo expedition, where even the original scientific team had not penetrated. It wasn't generally a good idea to explore solo, but I had more knowledge of the terrain than many here, and I regarded my little expeditions as a method of atonement.

Over the last day, I'd run from a vine that crawled faster than I could walk, had my ankles bitten by tangled underbrush with grasping spiny teeth, and barely escaped falling into a huge funnel plant growing beneath a fragile mesh of leaf-covered vines. The bottom of the funnel was filled with stinking acid. I sharpened my machete daily.

I'd also spotted several suspicious shadows moving parallel to me. I was pretty sure I'd avoided the Festuour patrols, seeing as I hadn't been attacked, and there weren't supposed to be any large creatures on this island, but then, this was Festuour. I stayed alert.

On the plus side, I'd also seen specimens of my target, a fern with a smaller, parasitic plant attached to the underside of the leaves. The ones that grew where the two factions had explored were small and underdeveloped, but toward the interior, the ferns were more than twice my height, and the parasite grew into a fleshy bromeliad with stalks as long as my arm.

The canteens clanking around my waist each held a fern frond in water, both boasting a bromeliad. Contact with their sap caused the skin to tingle and go numb, and breathing in the fumes made my head swim. I suspected I could distil them into an anesthetic, but I needed a larger sample.

"Aha!" I looked up into a massive fern blocking out the neighboring plants. Bromeliads dripped from its fronds, making the plant look like a weeping willow from back on Methiem. I placed my canteens carefully against a bush, making sure the water didn't spill, as the caps were off to make holders for my samples. I hefted my machete and looked for an appropriate frond to cut off from the towering fern.

"Watch out!" A rough voice called from behind me, and I was bowled over in a rush of fur and two scents: one like spices kept in a cupboard, and the other like meat set out in the sun too long. The world toppled and rolled, and I reached for anything to stop it from spinning.

Behind me, two assailants blurred into a mass of green and yellow and brown. I felt the *crack* ring through my head as my skull intersected a tree and blinked, trying to bring the world back into focus. I reached up to straighten my head wrap.

The two fighting were of equal size, but I gradually realized one was a Festuour, and one was not. The fight was quick, but brutal. Fur literally flew, and I heard a rip of skin and bone followed by a shrill screech. The not-Festuour dropped to the ground and I saw it was like a rat, but as large as a Methiemum, with teeth longer than my hand. One of its six legs dangled uselessly as it galloped off.

I turned from the sight to find Bhon staring at me, a deadly-looking knife drawn.

"How did you get here?" I asked, scooting my aching back against the tree. It was not, perhaps, the best question, considering she had promised to kill me the next time we met, but it was all I could think of. She was a vision, standing triumphantly after her victory. The weaponry pointed at me had to be part of my attraction to her. No Methiemum could manage quite that cock of a hip while holding a knife as long as my forearm.

Bhon looked a little embarrassed. "I may have been tracking you. A little. I caught your scent earlier," she confessed. And I thought I'd avoided the patrols with my superior knowledge of the geography.

The knife wobbled and I realized it was covered in rodent blood. "But only for the glory of killing you personally! Our army is camped not far away, and we lost several soldiers to those things. I wasn't going to let them get to you first." She straightened. "That's my job."

"Well...thank you, I think," I said. I dusted myself off and took a quick inventory of my limbs to make sure I wasn't missing any. Yet. My head swam from the impact. "I wasn't aware there were large animals on this island."

Bhon shook her head. "We didn't know either, until two days ago."

We stood awkwardly for a few moments.

"Where's your squad?"

Bhon tilted her head to one side. "I sent them off in the other direction when I smelled you. Got them chasing after the nest of those things." She took a step forward, raising the knife, and I tensed. "That means I get to finish what I promised and—"

The ground opened under Bhon's feet and she plunged from my view.

"Bhon!" I called, rushing to the hole. It was oddly square, as if there had been a tile there, but this was the center of a newly discovered island. There weren't any square edges here. I peered down into the dark hole, feeling stupid at coming to the aid, once again, of one who had promised to kill me. She had *started* to attack before she fell.

"Are you dead?"

"Not yet," came the reply.

"Then stay that way," I called down. "I'll get a torch."

I lit one of the branches I'd brought—treated with pitch—with a pocket flint, and thrust the burning torch down into the darkness, squinting against the oily smoke. Why was I not running away? Why was I once again helping this lethal Festuour? Vish take this attraction and scientific curiosity, *and* fuzzy bear people.

There was what looked oddly like a room down there, and Bhon was sitting in the middle, her legs splayed out. Now I had a moment to take stock, I saw the tatters of my shirt on her thigh. Had she not changed the bandage? It had been days since I last saw her. A memento to remember me by, or just a convenient place for an item with my scent?

"I'm going to find a way down," I said, and started to pull away from the hole. This was stupid. I should be running. I should fill in the hole with Bhon in it.

"Wait!" Bhon called, and I stopped. I assumed she would say something about how I should leave her to die because she'd just try to kill me again. "Can you throw the torch down? It's dark..."

My tension melted. The big scary soldier was afraid of the dark. Wasn't that charming? I kept my mouth shut and held the torch out, then dropped it.

I scrubbed vines and dirt away from the sides of the opening, then noticed the rotten edges of a timber trailing away into the dark, supporting whatever I was standing on. I backed up, even as I heard the crack beneath my feet. Too late to run.

I only had time to call, "Watch your head!" before a section of ground gave way and I rolled forward and down.

I heard Bhon cough in the explosion of dirt and plant matter accompanying my landing. The torch had gone out, but with the new ramp I'd created, enough light filtered through the canopy to illuminate us. I could see large shapes, but everything else was dim.

Bhon held out the stump of the torch. "Try again?" she asked, and there was a worried edge to her voice.

There was also a distinct lack of trying to kill me. I needed to get Bhon alone in the dark more often. Once the torch flared to life again I tucked my flint away.

"Well, you certainly found a new way down," Bhon commented. She had come through near the center of this room, and my weight must have triggered the rest of the collapse. We had a way back up, but it wouldn't be easy, picking through the rotten beams to reach the surface. Certainly not a clear path to run from my new closest enemy.

"Should we explore? If you promise you won't stick that in me?" I nodded at the knife Bhon still held. She'd managed to keep hold of it through the fall.

"I'll give you a pass for now, seeing as you came to help me again," Bhon allowed, her chin high. Her eyes drifted down. "Go ahead."

"Oh no, I don't want you behind me, for multiple reasons," I said. I couldn't tell if her eyes were undressing me or determining the best way to butcher me.

"Just remember who has the knife," Bhon said, taking the lead, and Shiv strike me down if she didn't twitch her hips as she walked—no, sauntered—around the little room. Teddy bears with sashaying hips.

"This has to be constructed," I said, taking the torch from her and holding it close to a wall. It was packed dirt, possibly a natural burrow. Could those giant rats have made it? But I had seen a beam holding the ceiling up. Why had no one on the original survey team found this?

"It can't be. This island is uninhabited," Bhon said.

"I agree. The survey team mapped the island extensively and saw no signs of inhabitants. It's the whole reason the Methiemum expedition head decided to make his claim. *The* claim. Vish take me." I closed my mouth before I said anything else.

"And why we're in this fight," Bhon said, turning back to me. "Which reminds me, I should take advantage of these closed-in walls. One less Methiemum scientist to steal our resources." But she didn't make a move.

"It wasn't my choice to start this war," I said. Not entirely true, but the full story would really make Bhon tear me to pieces. "I'd rather work with the Festuour so everyone has access to the advances this island will provide." I deliberately turned from her to investigate the new ramp leading to ground level. The whole room was five or six paces to a side—not tiny, but it also didn't seem like a burrow.

I squatted down, brushing aside dirt and vines on the collapsed ceiling until my hand found a hard surface. I turned to Bhon, only to find her snout close to mine, bright blue eyes staring into mine. I jerked, but she wasn't plunging the knife into my breast. She was just...close. Her presence was almost overpowering, and I swallowed, my mouth suddenly dry.

"I, uh, there's something under here," I said. "Help me get it clear."

Bhon's lips twisted up in a smile and she reached out a furry paw to help, her digits brushing mine. Together we cleared the plants that had clogged this patch of ground. I bit my lip as we touched, trying not to notice her strong fingers, each bigger than two of mine. Trying not to imagine them elsewhere on my body.

I shook my head. That was crazy. She already said she was going to kill me, multiple times. Even tried to do so. Yet the way she acted...Was she lying or did Festuour mating rituals have commonalties with homicide?

"Is that a...slate tile?" Bhon asked, seemingly oblivious to my confused thoughts.

"I think so," I said. The square we had uncovered was large enough for a Festuour to pass through, gray and mottled in the torchlight. "This can't be natural."

"No way," Bhon agreed.

"Which means someone lived here, or at least built this."

"And it's old," Bhon added. "Must have been here way before the survey team arrived."

I poked at the slate, then rose to my feet and passed the torch in an arc to better see the rest of the room. My jaw was tense, waiting for Bhon to take any opportunity to lunge at me. "This room's construction is solid. It could be anywhere from fifty to three hundred cycles old."

"However old it is, it means neither side has a claim to the island," Bhon said. "Someone else already claimed it."

"Maybe they're dead?" I watched Bhon's knife.

"We don't know that," she insisted. "They might have a friend group they've told about this place. They might still live here somewhere! What if there are more buildings? We need to explore."

I wrinkled my nose. She was right. Whether the builders were alive or dead, the fighting had to stop. I let a sliver of hope drive through me. Could I actually correct my mistakes? Perhaps Bhon and I didn't need to be on opposite sides. This was a perfect way get Colonel Rhati and his soldiers out of our hair so we could get to the real reason we were here—bettering the life of the ten species.

"You're right. Let's take a look around, if you can keep from gutting me for that long." I held both hands up, palms out.

Bhon's tongue lolled in a laugh. "Enough adventure for me in exploring. We're in an enclosed space. I can always take care of you later."

"I see." We surveyed the cellar, if that's what this room was. We found nothing more than a few broken barrels. It was too hard to see under the collapsed ceiling, so we scrambled up the slope.

Halfway up, my foot went through another tile, and I would have fallen if Bhon didn't clasp her paws around my waist quicker than I thought possible. A shiver passed through me at her touch, the strength in her arms. The flat of the knife, still in her paw, was a cold presence, leaking through the fabric of my shirt. Bhon could have snapped my spine, but she only pulled me back up. We scrambled the rest of the way to the surface. I definitely had a thing for danger.

"Thank you," I panted, looking down at the collapsed cellar.

"Won't do to have you fall and break your neck—that's my job." I sat on the rim of the ramp and Bhon sat down next to me, a furry menace, her toes kicking over the edge of the opening. "You saved me, so now I saved you."

"Does that make us even?" I said.

Bhon rolled her eyes. "You Methiemum and your crazy trading brains. You think everything is a bargain. If we save each other, it means we might want to stay around each other to see if the other needs saving again." She reached out to place a paw on my thigh, resting it lightly, as if in ownership. My muscles contracted, despite me attempting to relax. Her bright blue eyes stared directly into mine, and I swallowed. "That doesn't mean I won't kill you if it serves the purpose of my people."

"I understand," I said, and her paw rested a little heavier. It was odd, but I think she meant everything she said. The Festuour didn't have families, as such. They put little stock into who caused another Festuour to be born, instead relying on close-knit groups of friends. And just like friends, sometimes those relationships fell apart.

Frequently, offspring did come from friend groups, but once old enough, the children were free to choose any group to live with. Any member could invite another to join, but there was a big difference between being a friend with a Festuour and being part of a Festuour's friend group.

"You seem to know a lot about the original expedition," Bhon said suddenly, and I tensed again. "You know any of the original members? Mayhaps we can talk to them to find out if anyone else discovered this building."

I pushed to my feet, letting Bhon's paw slide off, and stared around the clearing dominated by the huge fern. "Several scientists on both sides were on the original survey team," I said. Now I knew what I was looking for, I could pick out bits of rotting timber and surfaces too flat to be natural. "They didn't know about this place."

"Look there," Bhon said, pointing out my fern. "I've never seen one of those get that big. You think it was grown here intentionally?"

My eyes widened. I hadn't even considered that. I led her to it, not even concerned I had my back to her. I was too excited to care. We passed the canteens I'd set down on the way to the giant plant, and once there, I began pulling vines away from the bottom.

"It was," I confirmed, pointing out the remains of a planter box, which the fern had nearly destroyed. "Whoever was here must have been farming it for medicinal purposes. I must add it to my collection."

"Good find? Not bad for a lowpaw in the army, then," Bhon said, paws on hips, knife a malevolent gleam in the sunlight filtering through the trees.

"Not bad at all," I said, as I rooted around the area. I cast a glance up toward her. She was positioned to block my easy escape. Purposeful, or accidental? Either way, I had to investigate this farm. There were the remains of an irrigation system here, and more beds, and more plants, smaller than the fern. Several were ones I'd taken samples of, but there were some I hadn't encountered or thought to investigate.

"This site could shortcut our scientific research on this island by ten-days, or even months." I crawled along the ground, paying little attention to the dirt and old boards snagging my pants. "There are more plants over there, growing in straight rows."

Bhon turned in a circle, but ended up facing me before I could think of escaping. "Or I could lead the Festuour scientists here. Give my people the advantage they deserve. Now I know what to look for, I can see others, all around us."

I shook my head. "There's more than enough for all, and if the attributes of these plants have already been discovered and perhaps even documented, there's absolutely no reason for us to be fighting over them." I got to my feet, stepping closer to her. "We must return to our respective camps and tell them to stop fighting. We can share what we found."

"The soldiers ain't gonna believe me, whatever I tell them," Bhon said. "I'm just a squad second."

"Then help me gather some samples," I suggested. "We'll take them to our respective scientists. Both sides will have plenty to occupy them."

Bhon twisted the knife in the air as she considered. "I guess it won't hurt to help, but don't get too far away. I'm good with my paws and I've got good aim."

I pointed out where she could take samples, then took out my machete, under her watchful gaze, and turned to the fern. Parts of it looked like animals had chewed on it. I supposed they used the medicinal properties too.

"Do these plants make you...feel funny?" Bhon said after a few minutes.

"Oh!" I said, turning to her. "The sap has a relaxing effect." I looked down at where she was cutting a bromeliad from the fern, liquid dripping on her paws. I'd been careful to drop the stalks in my canteen without touching the cut end.

"Gooey," Bhon giggled, and the knife dropped from her fingers.

I froze, torn between going to her and laughing. My deadly, and now high teddy bear.

I placed my cutting in a canteen and went to her, taking a rag from my pocket. "We've got to get this off you. I don't know what the sap will do, undistilled." I wiped at her paws while Bhon watched me, her tongue hanging out one side of her mouth in a Festuour grin.

"Nosso bad," she slurred. "Tingly."

"It's already taking effect, and quickly, too. I've never seen anything work this fast," I said, rubbing furiously. The sap was stuck in her fur.

"Couldn't decide whether to kill you or kiss you," Bhon said, and smeared a dripping paw on my cheek. "Glad I hadn't decided yet."

The tingling started on my cheek, like someone brushing me with a feather. I twitched, but finished getting a patch of sap from between her digits, then took the time to absently swipe at the goo on my face. I blinked, my head feeling fuzzy. What had I been doing?

Oh yes. I went back to rubbing Bhon's paws. Except wasn't I holding something before? My hands buzzed, but not in a bad way. Tickly. Pleasant. I pulled on Bhon's large fingers, grasping each one with my hand and caressing them. She rumbled deep in her throat and stepped into me, her bandolier pressing into my chest. I needed to escape, didn't I? I had to run away because she was trying to...kill me? Kiss me? Steal my ferns?

"What are we...?"

"Maybe 'kiss' is better'n 'kill' after all," Bhon mumbled. She was so close.

"But we're...affected? Influenced?" All I knew was I wanted to nestle into her fur. So I did.

"Mmmm. 'Saright. 'Sa good kinda sap," Bhon said. She brought her hands up, bringing mine with them, and brushed them across my chest, stopping at my hardening nipples. My mind shouted at me to collapse in and protect myself, but I found I couldn't care about whether or not my chest looked "right." Maybe...that was for the best?

I let go, leaning down, my mouth searching for hers. Bhon was wider than me, but shorter. Her muzzle was long, and her teeth sharp, but she tasted like cinnamon. After we broke apart, I said, "Bet it can make all kinds of places tingly." The sap couldn't be that bad. There was some small part of my mind taking notes on the effect. Another small part screamed that this was a bad idea, but the larger part overrode it.

"Like here?" Bhon reached down. I gasped and all other thoughts disappeared. Her mouth opened in a pleased smile. "You *are* different than other Methiemum women. Haven't played around with one of *these* before."

The same warning against others touching me like that slid through my mind, but it was as if it was underneath a block of thick ice, for once muffled. Bhon didn't care what parts I had or whether I was like other Methiemum women. I *was* a woman, and that's what mattered. My shoulders relaxed and I let my hands run down her body, feeling the powerful muscle under her fur, groaning as every place she touched erupted into a warm glow.

She was still stroking and playing and I reached between her legs. I wasn't completely sure how Festuour genitals worked, but I was fairly certain *where* they were.

She grabbed my hand. Hard.

"Oh, Kamuli," Bhon groaned, and the pressure on my hand increased. "*Do not stop!*"

* * *

The sun was just rising when I blinked my eyes open. Had I been asleep?

I was tangled together with Bhon. What had happened? Had we fought? I had hazy memories of our hands on each other. Maybe I'd tried to wrestle her knife away and hit my head?

As I rose to my feet, I realized her bandolier was missing and so were my clothes. I felt strangely refreshed, as if I'd had a long night's sleep, and spotted our belongings piled together in a heap.

Bhon groaned and sat up, then watched me gather my clothes.

"Well that's a pleasant view. Don't you folks usually wear fabric draped around you?"

"We must have passed out because of the sap. I need to get back to my camp and report the structures here." I jerked my pants on as quickly as possible. I felt like something else might have happened, but I only remembered bits and pieces of the night before.

"Now, I never said you could go," Bhon complained, rolling to her feet and plucking her bandolier, knife, and handcannons off the ground. She draped the leather belt diagonally across her shoulder. "Funny though. Can't quite remember what happened last night. Guess I didn't shoot you after all. I wonder why—"

Bhon froze, one paw on a handcannon, which wasn't yet primed. Her eyes stared over my shoulder.

"What?" I asked.

"Don't make any sudden movements. One of those critters that tried to eat you yesterday is sneaking up on us like a branchslider after a nest of chicklings."

Carefully, she pressed a set of buttons on the side of one handcannon, raising it just a hair. I could hear snuffling as a presence approached, ready any moment for the sting of teeth.

Then Bhon paused, her face showing confusion. I turned, slowly and smoothly, to see one of the giant rodents approaching the last canteen left on the ground. It pulled the bromeliad out with its mouth, tipping the container over. I opened a hand, low, to keep Bhon from moving. Last night, I remembered seeing teeth marks on the plants, though not much after that.

The rodent sniffed at the end of the bromeliad, dripping sap, then rubbed its muzzle in it and scooted forward, driving the cutting under its body. It rolled gleefully on the squashed plant.

Bhon tensed as it sprang to its feet, but it only ran around in a circle, then flopped on the cutting again, rolling onto its back, its toes kneading the air.

"Looks like it enjoys the stuff," I said.

"Then I guess I don't need to shoot it," Bhon said. She holstered her handcannon, but tilted her head, blue eyes searching nothing.

"I can get more cuttings," I said.

Bhon shook her head. "That's not it. Do you...remember much from last night?"

"Not much." I watched the giant rodent, then my eyes widened as I saw the kneading paws, the quivering tail, and the rodent's obvious other signs of arousal. My head spun to where the pile of clothes had been, but I ended up staring Bhon in the face.

"Did we...?" Bhon asked, one paw half coming up toward me.

"We couldn't have," I answered. "We're enemies. You're trying to kill me. Maybe."

"I guess not too hard." Bhon shrugged. "But if we did, I can't go back. There's a strict no-fraternizing rule."

"Don't tell them," I said. "We don't even remember what we did."

Bhon grabbed my shoulders and leaned into me. I tensed, unable to avoid her lunge as she inhaled near me, then breathed out a huge gust of Festuour-flavored air. She let me go and bent one arm, sniffing her fur, then bent lower, as if searching for something in her fur.

"Oh, they'll know," Bhon said as she straightened, her eyes wide. "You're all over me. We, ah, I think we..."

"No," I said.

Bhon nodded. "A *lot*. I can't go back to my camp like this. The scent won't fade for days, even with bathing in a stream."

I tried to remember the last night. Bits were coming back, when I...I stared at Bhon's chest. And she...I smoothed my pants. Oh, and then I...My eyes moved downward on Bhon. Fur covered her belly and thighs. I remembered its touch on my skin.

From Bhon's expression, she was going through a similar experience. The rat wriggled in the sap, oblivious.

"Well, if you can't go to your camp, you'll come with me," I said. Colonel Rhati had pushed his troops the last ten-day, claiming he was close to overcoming the Festuour. I was afraid he might be right. With proof of a prior claim on this island, I could end this fight. I could redeem myself, at least in my own eyes.

"Won't they kill me just like my side would kill you?" Bhon asked. Her bright blue eyes caught mine. "Will we get another chance like last night?"

"I think we might, but perhaps without mind-altering substances. Make it a true choice for both of us," I said. Now I was the one in control, with the leverage. I had hedged around the truth for over two cycles. It was time to let the truth come out. "I won't let them hurt you. I can convince the colonel of the army, once he knows who I am. The scientists will follow my lead, if I say so. I'd...like you by my side, Bhon."

She picked up one of my sample canisters, hooking it on her bandolier. Then her eyes narrowed. "You really have that much influence? You said you knew ones who were here on the survey team. How...Kamuli! Were you on the original survey team that came here?"

I should have been ready, but lightning still pulsed through me at telling the truth. "I wasn't on the original team...I led it."

Her eyes were deep with hurt. "Then you let the Methiemum make their claim. Or did you try to claim this island yourself?" Bhon stepped back, away from me. "Two members of my friend group died here." Her lip twisted up to reveal sharp teeth, her ears laid back. "Is Kamuli Balion even your real name, or are you hiding? We know the names of all of the surveyors. Why isn't yours among them?"

I reached a hand out to her, but she took another step back. "Bhon, that was two cycles ago. The name I used, the way I presented myself—it wasn't me, not the real me." I hesitated, but she was watching me, waiting for the rest. "I made changes to my life. Good changes, to my body and my name. But this island *was* a mistake.

"I was angry with the Festuour team. They were dragging their feet, reluctant to verify our results. I thought *they* were trying to steal the research. I threatened and blustered, and I assumed the Festuour scientists would back down. I know your people a lot better now than I did then."

Bhon crossed her arms, waiting.

"My embarrassment about who I was—*what* I was—led me to do stupid things. I put in the request for exclusivity for the discoveries we'd made. I thought it would force us all to talk about it, but I didn't understand how much our militaries *wanted* this fight. By the time the armies arrived, I had no control over the situation."

"So you hid. You hid your name, your body, and your motives."

"No!" I shook my head. "Well, yes. But not how you're thinking. I was afraid of my transition, but *this* is the real me—Kamuli Balion."

Bhon still frowned, but didn't pull farther away. "Why didn't you tell me?"

"I...I meant to, when we first met, when you tried to take my shirt off—" I stopped as Bhon swiped a paw through the air.

"Not that you're trans. I don't care about that. It doesn't matter what set of bits you got. I mean, not as if we're the same species in the first case. We've gotta be inventive if you want to smash 'em together. I think we did a pretty good job, from what I remember."

I blinked at the statement, though I agreed with her.

But Bhon was still talking. "No—why didn't you tell me you *led* the original survey team? You lied to me, and friends don't lie to each other, no matter how hard the truth. It's how a friend group survives."

That...was not the complaint I was expecting. *There's a big difference between being a friend with a Festuour and being part of a Festuour's friend group.*

What was she saying?

Bhon unconsciously re-centered her bandolier. "Maybe you could have prevented this whole thing, maybe it would have happened anyway. But you can't change any of that now." She took a step toward me, her eyes intense. "Are you willing to stop this fight now, with me?"

I straightened. "Every moment I've been on this island, I've been atoning for my mistake. First by finding more plants than the team knew what to do with, so they would have to work with the Festuour, but with this claim, I can—*we* can—finally make a difference, even if everyone ends up knowing my story. We can end this fight."

I scanned the abandoned farm, or research station, or whatever it was. It could have been a hundred cycles old, the original inhabitants dead from old age, or disease, or eaten by giant rats. It didn't matter whether their discoveries were lost, or never even finished. It only mattered that someone else had been here first.

I reached for Bhon's paw, and she gave it. I lifted it with both of mine, raising it to my mouth to kiss her fingertips.

"Let's go sort this out, together."

We left the giant rodent to its fern.

* * *

"She's with me!"

I help up both hands to ward off the soldiers guarding the entrance to the Methiemum camp. I tried to stay in front of Bhon as much as possible, but she was a lot wider than I was. "She's come here to negotiate for a cessation of hostilities."

One soldier—likely a sergeant—stepped forward, looking unimpressed. I wasn't familiar with her, as I knew more scientists than soldiers, but she looked like she had been around a battlefield more than once. A nasty-looking scar crossed from the remains of one ear down to her neck.

"She's just a grunt. She doesn't have authority to negotiate. I'm reporting this." The sergeant gestured to her companion, who went running. I gritted my teeth, but at least Bhon hadn't drawn her handcannons. Yet.

"She was with me when we discovered information that changes this whole fight. That's why she has authority to negotiate. We—both of us—chose to come to the Methiemum camp first. Our side will have the advantage, but you have to let me pass to see Colonel Rhati. Now."

I could feel Bhon pressing close behind me. I didn't dare turn to see her expression, but I hoped she wasn't snarling.

The woman at the gate pursed her lips, making the scar on her neck pucker. I needed her to bend only a little, and let us through. Once in the camp, I'd have enough clout to see the Colonel. Faloua would help. She was one of the only ones who knew my whole story.

The sergeant slowly inclined her head. "Just to the Colonel. And I'm coming with you to keep the gunbear under guard. I'll need all of her weapons." Now when I looked back, Bhon *was* snarling. I shot her a glare, but it did nothing, and I tried not to sigh as Bhon's growl became audible.

"They'll have to shoot me before they shoot you, Bhon," I said. "And they won't do anything to your weapons."

"Do you promise on the life of your oldest friend?" Bhon asked, and I only belatedly realized the depth of what she was asking. I hesitated, thinking back to a boy I had known when I was young, running around the tiny town where I grew up. I still traded letters with him and his family.

"I do. They will not interfere with you or your weapons, or they will answer to me." I gave the woman a stern look, and she nodded back. She at least understood honor between opponents. "I'm leaving my canteens here too." I set down the samples I'd taken, leaving only a small sample case attached to my belt, containing some of the sap squeezed from a stalk. I'd need it to prove its medical use to the colonel.

Bhon's handcannons were only the start. By the time the scarred sergeant finished emptying her bandolier, belt, and patting her down, there was an impressive pile of knives, garrotes, vials, blades, ammunition, and other deadly knick-knacks on top of her two handcannons. The sergeant placed them in a crate near the entrance to the camp, and locked it, showing us the key she put in a pouch on her belt.

"No one can touch them but me," she said.

I made for the medical tent, but she was having none of it. "This way," she said firmly, as the subordinate she had sent running arrived with four more in tow. At a hand gesture, they fell into step behind us, heading straight for Colonel Rhati's pavilion.

I took in quick breaths through my nose, pushing the air out through pursed lips. I wasn't nervous. I could handle him, even if I'd never dared a direct confrontation. Colonel Rhati was just the jumped-up son of some general back in Thrandishar. He'd probably never seen fighting. He'd likely had his command bought for him.

"You sure you can convince the leader of these stone faces?" Bhon whispered in my ear.

"They have to listen to reason," I answered. "Once we tell them what we found, we'll have leverage to make them call this off." I clenched a hand, not sure if I was trying to convince myself or Bhon. I didn't think it was working either way. I'd avoided the colonel in the past because I was hiding from my mistake. And because he was a blustering bigot. But maybe if I had confronted him, I would have reckoned with my guilt sooner. Or if I'd retained control of the original survey team instead of sneaking away to lick my wounds, I might have more influence with Colonel Rhati. Too late for that now.

We stopped outside his pavilion, a huge tent made, ironically, of imported Festuour cloth. Nothing else would have resisted the elements like this material did.

"Wait here," the sergeant with the scar said, and stepped through the flap. I could hear indistinct voices, and looked back to Bhon. Surely with those ears, she could hear more? But she only shrugged.

"He'll see you now," the sergeant said, re-emerging. "But he has limited time for an enemy combatant. Be quick. We'll be close by, so don't try anything." This last was directed at Bhon, who bared her teeth.

I stomped past the roadblock of a woman and into the pavilion, finding the colonel seated behind a desk of dark brown Methiemum heartwood. Vast sheets of blank paper covered the plans he'd obviously been working on, and he glared at Bhon, his elegantly-styled moustache bristling at the interruption.

"What is the meaning of this?" Colonel Rhati asked, before I could speak. "You want us to give in, now we're winning this engagement? We've almost got these filthy bears pushed off this island. What could possibly make us withdraw?"

I felt Bhon tense—I had tensed, for that matter, at his insult—and I reached back, finding her paw, squeezing her fingers.

"There is ample evidence this entire endeavor is illegal from the start, and I should know." I jabbed my forefinger into my breastbone.

The Colonel broke in before I could say more. "I'm well aware of who you used to be. You gave up any entitlement to making decisions for the Methiemum here when you gave up your role."

I shouldn't be surprised he knew. "No matter what I did, there's a prior claim on this island, and that invalidates any agreement made. Both sides must draw back until we can determine who has the true rights to this land. There doesn't need to be any more fighting."

"A prior claim? Absurd. No one else knows about this island—otherwise those weeds you're studying would be in use already."

"Want me to hit him?" Bhon whispered, and I squeezed her paw to quiet her. It would be therapeutic, but not helpful.

"Those 'weeds' are the whole reason we're here, and you know it," I told him. "You just want your military to have a reason to fight. Well, we found a settlement, where the inhabitants studied the same plants we are. They probably used the same properties."

"Fine then." Colonel Rhati sat forward, fingers lightly touching, like a predator about to strike. "Produce this alleged settlement's builders and we'll get this sorted out."

"We, ah, don't have 'em," Bhon said quietly.

"Then how do you intend to prove this prior claim?"

"That's what I'm trying to tell you," I said. I took another step forward, putting myself in the center of the Colonel's space. "*You* need to organize a ceasefire so the *scientists* can discover who built the settlement. *Then* we can find out who has the rights."

Colonel Rhati only stared at me. I didn't like the set of his eyes. "You don't even know if the original claimants are alive, do you? And no one else knows of this place, except you, the bear, and me, yes?"

"That...is correct." Bhon nudged my back with a finger. She didn't like it any better than I did.

"I have a better idea," the Colonel said, with a smile like a knife. "I'll send the troops through this farm. Destroy the evidence." He spread his hands. "No evidence, no problem."

"That's a terrible solution!" I yelled. Bhon's paws held me back and I realized my fingers were in claws, reaching for the vile man's face. But the colonel sat straight, a smug expression creasing his face. "You'd throw away cycles of research, just to win a stupid fight with our closest allies?"

"The bears have diluted our trading rights for cycles, cozying up to the Methiemum so they can share in our profits. Cut them back out, and we rise to being the most powerful of the ten species. As such, I'm afraid you, and your prisoner of war, are liabilities to our plans, and my orders." The colonel looked over my head and made a quick gesture. Hands landed on my shoulders and I tried to shrug them off, but they held fast.

"You will both be imprisoned, and the bear will be executed tomorrow morning to show our superiority before the army. You may be as well, depending on your conduct. Take them away."

"If I had my handcannons—" Bhon started.

"But you don't." The sergeant cut her off. "They're back at the gate, and it's a good thing I took them."

"The bears' cannons are fine work," the colonel said. "You may keep them or distribute them to a subordinate, as you see fit."

"Thank you sir," the scarred sergeant said over Bhon's growls. So much for honor. I tightened my grip on my new friend, though the soldiers were doing most of the work. If she attacked the colonel, they'd kill her without hesitation. I had to make them think she was cowed.

"Let them go," I hissed to her, but Bhon's face swung to me, teeth bared, and I flinched back at the sight, though I didn't look away. "I'll get them back to you. I promise. Just go with them now, and I'll get us out."

Bhon's lips dropped back down over her teeth. "I trust you," she said. She held my eyes, pleading for my promise to be true. I stared back, until the soldiers jerked us around and marched us out of the tent.

* * *

"Let me talk to Faloua first," I told the sergeant. "She deserves to know this research exists. Maybe she can save some before you destroy it all. It can only be an advantage for us. Please let me talk to her. You can lock me up after."

The scarred woman steadfastly ignored me, and her soldiers continued to drag us to the tiny cells where they kept the few prisoners they didn't kill. The three metal cages in the center of the camp were currently empty. They hadn't been when I left.

"Save your breath," Bhon said, and I looked curiously at her. She wasn't the type to give up. When I met her eyes, she stared back, flicked her eyes to the medical tents, then back to me. "If they're going to kill us tomorrow, it doesn't matter what we do."

What was she...?

"So do it!" Bhon cried as she threw her substantial weight to one side. Festuour had more bulk than Methiemum on average, and the three soldiers holding her were no match for the power of Bhon's thighs. She pulled them away from our little procession, and one of the two soldiers holding me leapt to help them.

I spun on the remaining soldier, twisting him around and throwing him to the ground. I had my share of martial training, and had more muscle than people suspected.

I ran to the medical tents. I wouldn't waste Bhon's gift of time.

They were a short sprint away, separated slightly from the main section of scientist's tents. Close enough I could get there quickly with my small head start, far enough to have a moment to warn Faloua. When I reached her tent, I glanced back to see if the soldier was following. He was just rising from the scrubby ground, as the other soldiers threw Bhon into an empty cage. It was too small for her to sit, and too short for her to stand upright. The door clanged shut behind her.

"Go!" she shouted, and I ducked inside the tent, yanking the door ties in a quick knot. It wouldn't keep others out for long, but would buy me a few seconds. I whirled to Faloua, who was tending a nasty cut on a soldier's arm. Her mouth was open and thread dangled from where she had been stitching the wound. I ignored her patient.

"Faloua, listen carefully. West of where we were studying the batch of sapfern plants, check for an abandoned research building. Someone's been here before. Colonel Rhati's going to raze it when he sends soldiers through."

Faloua opened her mouth, but I gave a minute shake of my head. "They've already locked *Bhon* up, and will execute her tomorrow, and possibly me as well." She'd get the implication from the Festuour name.

There was a rustling at the tent before a machete sliced through the ties and half the door, followed by the soldier I'd thrown to the ground.

I gave no resistance as he grabbed my arms. I'd said what I needed to. Faloua would draw the right conclusions from the existence of an abandoned facility on a supposedly deserted island, but my real message was in the last thing I'd said. Faloua was my only hope for freedom, and keeping Bhon from death. My own neck I was less worried about. For all of the colonel's threats, I was still a Methiemum, and killing someone on our own side had consequences. Maybe Faloua could convince the other scientists, or get word to Methiem.

"You be careful with her!" Faloua yelled at the soldier dragging me backward. "You have more of a handful than you know. It will cost you your career to do this, I promise." The soldier hesitated for one step, then continued to tow me to the cages.

When we returned to the middle of the camp, Bhon was alone, her broad shoulders stretching from one side of the cage to the other, her back bent. The soldier directed me to the one next to her, and opened the door. I knew enough not to argue. I'd done the best I could with the time I had.

I had to bend even lower, and my headscarf pressed against the top of the bars. Bhon looked compressed in her cell, barely able to move.

"You got a message out?" she asked. I nodded.

"Right now we must wait." I held a hand out through the bars, and the end of her digits touched mine. We were at least close enough to touch, though I could hardly even squeeze her furry paw.

"You could have run," Bhon said. "In fact, you could have turned me in when you saw how the colonel acted. You could have let them raze that place we found. You didn't have to be stuck here."

I shrugged. "But that's not what a friend group does." I found her eyes with mine. She was staring back, and as I watched, her face relaxed.

The words poured out of me. "I've only known you for a few days, but I can't stop thinking about you. Your touch sparks lighting through me. You're fierce, a protector, and I want to know you better."

Bhon reached out her other paw and I took it with my fingertips. We were separated by cold iron, but still connected. "I had orders to kill any Methiemum I saw. I should have shot you rather than let you get close the first time, but I just couldn't," Bhon said. "I've wanted to kiss you instead, since you first fell into my arms—literally."

There were soldiers around us, but we didn't care. We talked for hours—while the sun set—about our families and friends, our backgrounds, and how we got to this situation. This time, we weren't under the influence of psychotropic sap, and were separated from any real physical action. It was just me and Bhon, talking. I felt I had known her for cycles. It felt perfect.

Festuour's moons were rising when one of the guards perked up.

"What was that?"

"Dunno," the other said. "But it's almost shift change and I'm bored of listening to these two spill their guts to each other. Those cages are locked tight and our replacements will be here in a few minutes. Let's check it out."

The other guard nodded and followed him away from the cages as a shadow slipped through the camp. I recognized the fringe of white hair reflecting moonlight.

"A majus is scheduled to check in on the camp tonight," Faloua whispered to me when she got to my cage. "She is delivering medical equipment from Thrandishar, and chemicals for breaking down compounds. I will try to direct her here. When she sees the abuses the colonel has directed against the Festuour, I'm certain she will demand you are set free."

"You got a bit of metal or anything?" Bhon asked. "I'm a fair paw with locks."

Faloua hesitated, scanning the area. I saw lights coming near. Likely the replacement guard. Faloua straightened. "You know what? Vish take it all. Here."

She took a small pack from her pocket, glanced around again, and tossed it underhand toward Bhon, who caught it and made it disappear in her fur.

"I will send the majus as soon as I can," Faloua promised. I gave her a grateful nod, and she slunk off.

Bhon investigated the pouch, pulling out what looked like tweezers and small metal probes. Perfect for arranging slides and small samples without contamination. Perfect for lock picking as well, if one knew how to use them.

I winced at each tiny clink as Bhon fiddled with the metal implements. The angle was wrong for her to get her paws around to the lock, since it was on the outside of the cage. I tried to give her whispered directions, but she finally huffed out a breath and withdrew the implements as the replacement soldiers took their stations.

"No use. I can't see enough of what I'm doing, and your lock is too far away to reach." She tucked the pieces back in their pouch and secreted it somewhere around her person. "We're gonna have to see what this majus can do, though I don't know why one so high and mighty as all that would rescue us."

I'd seen a few maji before—they were a rare sight, lauded wherever they went, treated like celebrities. Without them, we'd have no portals to link trade between the homeworlds. I didn't know why one would bother with us either.

We stood there for what felt like hours, but probably wasn't. Bhon and I exchanged a few more words, but we'd said most of what we had to say. I hoped Bhon would attempt the lock picks again, but every time she moved, the guards shifted and looked around. I racked my mind for something—*anything*—I could do, but came up empty.

Then, there was a commotion off in the dark.

"The majus?" I wondered. Bhon shook her head. She couldn't see either.

The noise resolved into Colonel Rhati himself, leading the scarred sergeant and several other subordinates. They marched straight to Bhon's cage.

"You're letting us go?" I asked. Maybe the majus had spoken to him.

"Hardly," the colonel snorted. "Moving up the timetables. We're pushing through your accidental discovery and into the Festuour camp tonight instead of tomorrow. Now's a perfect time to tie up loose ends. We'll let *you* out tomorrow, after we settle things."

My plans crashed down around me as I saw Bhon's face go slack, her eyes finding mine.

"What happened to tomorrow morning?" I said.

"And give her a chance to ponder a way to escape?" the Colonel asked. "We've had enough attempts in the past."

They unlocked the cage and pulled Bhon out, then turned to the center of the camp.

"No!" I shouted. "Take me instead. She's done nothing. I got her into this."

"Then you should have thought of that before. Though few remember who you are, I can't execute you right out, but there will be a trial very soon. Any career you hoped to have with the scientists will be long gone." He looked between Bhon and me. "No, I won't have you working with the enemy."

They left me alone. I could just see them, at the edge of the pit where they'd shot other prisoners. A few soldiers came out of their tents to watch the show. The colonel would stall the actual execution for a few minutes to let a crowd gather. What could I do in that time? I'd come up with nothing in the hours I'd been stuck in this cage.

"Come back!" I shouted. An ocean of rage rose up in me and I shook the bars. Could I turn the cage over? Roll it toward the stage? There had to be a way to get closer.

Cold seeped into my hands, and I pulled them back from the bars with a gasp. This was a tropical island, yet frost crept up the iron. The majus? I huddled as far into the center as I could, which wasn't much.

The iron lock groaned. I shook the door and something cracked within the mechanism. I shook it harder. The lock popped off and I stumbled out, searching for the cause of my escape.

I scanned the shadows as I stepped free, but saw nothing in the deepening gloom. The two guards were slumped on the ground, and I heard one snore.

A voice came from the trees, not far away. "Find your friend quickly. The maji cannot directly involve themselves in this campaign without hard evidence. It was approved in the Assembly, but has strong opposition, and I do not appreciate what is happening here."

I couldn't see the speaker, or tell what species they were, though the voice sounded Methiemum. I didn't have time to question their sudden appearance. I ran through the darkness to where the soldiers had Bhon tied up.

I stopped just short of the circle of torchlight, thinking of any advantages I had. No weapons, and there were too many soldiers to overpower. Bhon still had Faloua's tools, little good they could do now.

My hands stopped as they found one small vial, still attached to my belt. The soldiers likely thought it was water—harmless. I shook it, thinking of the giant rodent rolling in the sap. Thinking of Bhon and me.

Maybe I did have a weapon.

I opened the vial, and waved it under my nose. No appreciable smell, but a wave of lassitude radiated through me. I jerked the vial away. I'd have to be careful not to get any on my hands.

I scanned around for anything I could use, then sighed, and tore a patch from the bottom of my shirt. I'd be out of clothes soon at this rate. I doused the center of the strip with some sap, careful not to let it touch my skin, then snuck up behind a soldier emerging from his tent. I had spent a fair amount of time in the jungle, and could move quietly when I needed to.

I slapped the cloth around the soldier's face, hoping he wouldn't cry out. He spun toward me. Even as he did, the scowl I could barely see faded to a slack grin.

"Oh hey there," he said. "I didn't see you. Did something hit me?"

"No, nothing," I said. Was this actually working? "What is going on over there?"

"Oh, they're about to shoot one of the bears. Not really nice, if you ask me." His amiable grin faded.

I had tested the sap's strength. This was just another scientific study. One that would get me killed if I didn't proceed cautiously. "Can you take me over to see it?"

"Oh yeah sure," the soldier said. He reached for my hand, but I used it to point.

"This way?"

"That's right, just gotta follow me."

We did not go far before seeing another soldier coming from her tent. I tried to keep my face in the shadows. Not many had witnessed Bhon and my capture, but it was better to be cautious. "Going to the execution?" the new soldier asked.

"Yeah, showin' this scientist the way to watch the fun." My convert frowned. "Though not really fun if you ask me. It's unfair—"

"Yes, I'm with the scientists, and I'm testing a new serum I think can make soldiers more effective," I interrupted. "It's a great time to test it, while everyone's watching the execution. We were saying it smells like fruit. Take a sniff and see if you agree." I proffered the piece of cloth.

The second soldier took the cloth and put it to her nose. "No, not like fruit at all..." she trailed off. "You know, I haven't had fruit in a few days. They have good stuff in the Festuour tropics. I should—"

"Let's go this way first," I said, directing the soldiers, who were now arguing about which Festuour fruit tasted best. How many more times could I get away with this?

Five, it turned out, intercepting soldiers coming from their tents like rabbits emerging from their burrows in the spring. The last took the dregs of sap in my canteen.

My small group of soldiers, now flirting with each other while arguing the best way to make a chilled fruit drink in this weather, made an impressive force backing me up. I wasn't convinced they'd be effective fighting, or even if they would fight *for* me, but it would give Colonel Rhati and the others pause.

"Stop!" I called when I got close. Bhon's paws and feet were tied, and she stood at the lip of a pit with the scarred sergeant watching over her.

The sergeant's squad of four was nearby, though the soldiers watching were a little ways off. It was five against seven, though my little drugged squad perhaps wouldn't count for too much.

The colonel swung toward me at my shout. "How did you get out...? No matter. It seems we have other insubordinates in this camp." He gestured to the sergeant, who hulked toward me, her large shoulders blocking light from the surrounding torches. Her squad followed her.

"Form up!" she shouted. "Separate the traitor from the soldiers."

"Get 'em guys!" I yelled. There was general confusion behind me, and then three of the seven stumbled forward. They seemed to have forgotten they were armed, and spread their arms wide to catch the scarred soldier. Better reaction than I anticipated, really. I added a mental note to the little experiment I was running.

The scarred sergeant looked confused, then fell into a fighting stance herself. "Take them down, but try not to kill. We will interrogate these traitors later!" Her squad positioned themselves around her.

"Why don't you help them?" I suggested to the other four behind me, gesturing to Bhon. "You can ask them what they think about the morals of shooting a Festuour with no trial."

The first soldier I had drugged, who was the most philosophical, staggered forward, yelling, "Hey, can soldiers can stand in for unbiased judges when we are inherently biased ourselves? I mean, think about it!"

With everyone near me engaged, and the soldiers farther away confused for a few seconds, I skirted around the group toward Bhon.

"Get these ropes off me, and I'll take them all on," she growled. I cast around for anything sharp.

"No more of this, Kamuli," came a harsh voice behind me, and I spun to face Colonel Rhati. "You're interfering with a military venture."

"One which *I* started as a cooperative research mission," I countered.

"Beside the point. I was brought in to protect Methiemum interests, and that is what I'm doing." The colonel pointed at Bhon. "If I have to kill every Festuour on this island, I will."

"This is in the interest of all ten homeworlds, you arrogant prig," I said, and punched him in the face.

I shook my hand out as the colonel slumped to the ground. I must have hit harder than I thought, because he was out cold. As I suspected, a bureaucrat with no training, stuck here to get him out of the way.

I snuck a glance around. The soldiers were in an argument, though one was trying to give the sergeant a hug—or something more. We had a few more seconds of confusion before any newcomers separated them.

"I hope Colonel Rhati keeps his knife sharp," I said, disarming him and slicing through Bhon's bonds. He did.

I barely got the knife out of the way before warm fur surrounded me, paws crushing me in—yes—a giant bear hug.

"Thanks, love," Bhon said, and kissed me.

I came up for air a few moments later, gasped, and looked around again.

"Why don't we take this reunion away from the soldiers?" I asked.

"Out of the camp?" Bhon suggested.

"Good idea," I said. Whatever happened, we needed to find somewhere safe from Colonel Rhati. "The majus is here," I said as we ran. "She said she needs hard evidence to stop this war, and I know where to get it. Would your people help us?"

Bhon shook her head. "They're madder than pollen sippers with their stingers on fire. Too many friends have been lost, and they're not likely to forgive."

"Then I hope the majus can convince our sides to make peace," I said, as we hurried through the gloom. We neared the cluster of scientific tents and I slowed. Maybe Faloua would know how to find her.

"Faloua, are you here—" I froze as I saw what her tent contained. She wasn't alone.

"Ah, you got your friend free. Excellent," said the tall and striking woman next to Faloua, as she rearranged her wrap to cover her legs again. A blue gloss so bright it almost glowed decorated her fingernails. "I couldn't be seen to take sides yet, but I knew you would come through, with a little help."

I stared back. I *thought* the soldiers had helped me too easily. Had the majus influenced them somehow, along with the sap?

"I confess I took a few minutes to...enjoy the scenery while you escaped," the majus continued. I stole a glance at Faloua, who was busily buttoning up her shirt. It was hard to tell, as she had her face turned away, but I suspected she was blushing furiously.

"You must be the majus," Bhon said over my stammering.

"I am that." The majus took Bhon's paw, bowing over it and planting a kiss on her hairy knuckle. "Dihari Silcasta, at your command. And you must be Shrimasharimsa Bhon, Guarder. Faloua told me much about you two in the last few minutes. Between other...vocalizations. She and I are old friends." She spared a glance for me. I couldn't take my eyes off the way her nail polish flashed. No one on this island wore nail polish.

"Only the best Galaxy Gloss, dear," Dihari said. "Blue Snowball. You should try it. Goes with your complexion."

"Ah. Any way you or your majus compatriots can stop this fighting?" Bhon asked.

Dihari pursed her lips. "I can if you get me concrete proof. The Thrandishar government asked me not to interfere, despite my repeated protests of this fiasco. But Faloua warned me when I arrived that proof might actually be a possibility."

"That's where we're going now!" I said. I'd finally found my voice. This majus had legs that went on for *days*.

Bhon nudged me. "Feeling left out."

I dragged my gaze away from Dihari's legs and back to Bhon. "Just distracted, love," I said. I squeezed her ample triceps.

"I can smooth our way a bit if you can give directions," Dihari said.

"I'm coming too," Faloua said. "I packed while you were gabbing."

We slipped out of the camp with no one seeing us. It was something Dihari did, and our way back through the dense jungle was surprisingly free from complications. The whole time, Dihari was in front, waving her fingers as if about to break into a dance step. I swear she did a little two-step a couple times around particularly dense clumps of vines, but once I got to them I saw there was an easy way through—it just hadn't been visible from where I was standing. But even with our time advantage, the forest wouldn't slow down the soldiers fully outfitted with trailblazing gear.

As we broke into the clearing dominated by the huge fern and its bromeliads, we split paths, each to the place we'd assigned ourselves on the way. I gathered more of the bromeliad sap while Bhon searched the perimeter for ways to defend the area. Faloua went to the other plants in the old garden boxes, determining their uses. Dihari did...something. I presume she was doing majus-stuff, as it looked like she was conducting an invisible orchestra.

"Is this enough proof for you to interfere?" I asked, after we showed the majus the abandoned buildings.

"Plenty, dear," Dihari answered, beaming in my direction. "We just need to keep it intact."

Soldiers crashed through the underbrush an hour later.

"Stay together," Bhon called. She'd taken command of the military side of our little encounter.

"Go get them, my little friends," Dihari gestured to our new allies, and the row of giant rodents, the largest the size of a Methiemum, surged forward, to surprised cries from the soldiers.

Since we learned the sap was like catnip to the rodents, we'd forged a sort of bond. They greatly appreciated my collecting it for them, and the majus 'encouraged' our cooperation. Now the beasts were helping us rather than trying to bite our faces off.

"Our turn," I told Bhon, and we waded into the disillusioned soldiers. Bhon was a tempest of fur and fists, dropping soldiers on all sides. I'd convinced her to leave her handcannons—which she had swiped on the way out of the camp—with the rest of our supplies. This was to be a non-lethal confrontation, if at all possible. Dihari even insisted the rats would be careful.

Faloua had found a crop of cultivated plants which we'd already categorized as an anesthetic, and she squirted what she'd prepared into the soldier's faces. A few seconds after dosing, the victim would stagger and fall, paralyzed for the next few hours. If she'd gotten the dosage right.

I used my trusty sap, which was both a drug for the rodents and an aphrodisiac for Methiemum. Through Dihari's efforts, waving her arms behind us, we sidestepped what would have been lethal thrusts of the soldier's swords and axes. Their shots similarly went wild, bullets careening off into the forest.

We'd made some real progress, a score of soldiers paralyzed or knocked out, and I'd convinced four more to fight with us.

"Enough!" called a voice. I recognized Colonel Rhati by his unique bellow. He stepped out of the jungle on our flank, surrounded by a squad of eight soldiers with loaded blunderbusses covering Dihari. She frowned and raised her hands, stopping whatever majus activity she'd been doing, and the rats scampered back into the jungle.

"I could take 'em," Bhon grumbled, but she backed down too. Faloua had already retreated near the majus.

"You are not supposed to affect our activities here, majus," Colonel Rhati accused. "Last I checked, we had approval from the Thrandishar government." He gestured to the soldiers surrounding him. "Prepare to raze this farm—"

"Hold!" came a rough voice from behind us. We spun to see close to twenty Festuour step from the trees, melting to visibility. Their fur was daubed with streaks of jungle green and black, augmenting their natural green-brown fur coloring.

I shot a look at Bhon, who shook her head and shrugged.

"Klot, fancy meeting you here," Colonel Rhati said. "Saves the time for us to march all the way to your camp to finish you off."

"Partifalgunari Klot, Leader," Bhon supplied in an undertone. "She heads the Festuour expeditionary force on this island." She wasn't the Festuour scientist I'd worked with, so there must have been a similar military takeover on their side.

"If we remove you from command, your soldiers will be directionless," Klot returned. Several of her soldiers stepped farther into the clearing.

"Even if you kill me, you'll still lose," the colonel spat. "Why not surrender?"

"Try us, Methiemum!" Klot growled.

"I might just—"

"Stop this childishness!" A ring of ice spread across the clearing, reaching both Klot's feet and Rhati's boots. They both stepped back and I turned to see Dihari, her arms held wide, water dripping from her fingertips. She gave me a tiny wink.

"I am calling a halt to these hostilities. I have seen plenty of evidence of prior inhabitation of this island." She turned, her outstretched arms taking in the clearing, the plants, and the remains of the underground room.

"By what authorization?" Colonel Rhati asked.

"Aye, who put you in charge?" Leader Klot said. She traded a look with Rhati, scowling.

"By authorization of the Council of the Maji," Dihari answered. "A majus brought you to this island, and supplies your troops. Another does the same for the Festuour side. Unless you want to build a boat and paddle back to the mainland, you will cease your fighting. And since none of you know *anything* about shipbuilding, I suspect you will starve to death." She glared at the colonel. "You *may* take that all the way to the Council, if you can get ahold of them without a majus to take you there."

Colonel Rhati and Leader Klot both puffed up, more arguments ready.

I took Bhon's paw. "I'm guessing there's going to be a lot of arguing, negotiations, and grumbling, but I think the majus has this one. She doesn't need us, anyway."

Bhon nodded.

"Which means you won't be ordered to kill me any longer," I suggested.

"That is true." Bhon looked contemplative and her eyes flicked down to the vial of sap I'd collected.

I smiled. I'd been thinking the same thing. "Want to sneak away?"

"Definitely."

While the two leaders spoke over each other and their soldiers struck intimidating poses, Bhon and I found another path through the jungle. It was surprisingly easy to make our way, and I looked back once to see Dihari watching the two of us, hand in hand with Faloua.

We found a bower of leaves I was certain didn't have any effect on Methiemum or Festuour physiology, and Bhon pushed me down.

"Now, I think it's time for another in-depth conversation about how you're a very unique Methiemum woman," Bhon said, her furry chest a handsbreadth from my face. She ran a paw down my chest and over my belly. "I've had a lot of friends, but none like you in my friend group. And since we *are* in the same friend group now, I think we need to do some serious exploration to find *all* the little differences."

"And maybe some big ones?" My nipples were brushing the fabric of my shirt. Her friend group. I still didn't quite believe it. I didn't know the signs of arousal on Festuour that well, but Bhon's heavy panting was probably one of them.

"Don't really care," Bhon said, before she leaned in for a long kiss. Her big paws ran down my chest, across my groin, and down my legs. I gasped as her tongue found mine.

My hands gripped clumps of her fur, but I forced myself to stop for a moment, reaching into my pocket. "How about a little extra assistance?" I offered the vial of sap.

"Yeah, we should find out what all this stuff does," Bhon said, as I uncorked the vial and dipped a finger in.

"After this is all over," I began, and stroked a sap-laden finger across one of her sensitive areas. Bhon shuddered. "How about we stick around each other for a while? With your mercenary skills and my science, we could even keep ourselves comfortable."

"As long as this is one of the perks," Bhon breathed, and I kept up my stroking.

I stopped just a moment, long enough to search those big blue eyes. I was part of Bhon's friend group. And she was more than a friend to me. The majus would track down the island's original discoverer, and for the first time in over two cycles, I could put this accursed island out of my thoughts. I'd never dreamed it was possible, but now I couldn't dream of anything but the two of us.

"Your homeworld or mine?" I asked.

"Wherever you are," Bhon whispered, before she resumed kissing me.

Want to find out what Kamuli and Bhon get up to later? Or maybe just learn more about the Dissolutionverse?

Check in with Kamuli and Bhon in *Merchants and Maji*, available on Amazon. You can also get it free by joining William C. Tracy's mailing list at **www.williamctracy.com/newsletter-signup**. Get another free story at the same time!

Dew Diligence

The First Fairyl@nd Story

Robin C.M. Duncan

Sapphic Representation: Lesbian
Heat Level: Low
Content Warnings: Violence, Gore

1

"Julia! Your briefs are here."

By the time she dropped the case file, dragged herself up from the long-suffering sofa in Granny's attic guestroom, brushed crumbs from her T-shirt, and navigated Willow Cottage's squeaky stairs, the courier was shutting the garden gate.

"It's alright, dear. I signed for you," Granny Madge beamed.

Julia bent to hug her for the hundredth time that week.

"Thanks, Gran." She studied the logo-splashed box. "I'm still summarising Jones versus Hardmeadow," she grumbled, puffing a strand of strawberry blonde hair from her face as she lifted the box. "I'll confine the papers upstairs, I promise."

Gran smiled. "They work you too hard, that Biron Woolf Lodge. They should be more sensitive to your heartbreak," she said. "And I'd like to go to London and give Devondra a talking-to." She patted Julia's arm. "I'll boil the kettle."

"She..." Julia clamped her mouth shut.

Still jumping to Dev's defence. Pathetic. Two weeks since the MP and chief bitch for Chiswick North had ended their affair; still harbouring faint hope of reconciliation. *It's not you, Jules. Christ, it's not even me, it's the Party. If I don't shore up my marriage to Trevor they'll deselect me! I've no choice.* No choice. That damning phrase still reverberated in her head as she cried herself to sleep each night.

The courier van pulled away down leafy Winkfield Lane, as if her legal career was abandoning her in rustic Maiden's Green. She smiled sadly at the lawn—sun-dappled by the magnolia's sprawling branches—inhaled the scent of the wisteria creeping across Willow Cottage's weathered red brick, and nudged the door closed with her bum.

Her phone buzzed. She put the box down and answered.

"Julia!" The jovial tones of her boss grated.

"Mister Biron. The box just arrived."

"Excellent. Listen, do a good job in the next day or two, and exciting possibilities will open up for you. That's all." He hung up.

Great. More pressure. Just what a heartbroken lawyer needed.

2

Boiled eggs and toast soldiers. Granny knew how to cheer up a lovelorn lawyer after another night streaming sad songs, and tweeting recriminations.

"I might go to the pub later," Julia announced, looking up from Hardmeadow Garden Centre's annual accounts, 2018/19.

Granny set a jar on the breakfast table along with its particular antique spoon. "Gooseberry and apricot," she said, then, "Go out? That'd be grand, dear. Do you good to get out, but you'll help set up the table at the fête, won't you?"

"Yes, of course."

The Maiden's Green Summer Fête was an event not to be missed. Everyone who was anyone from Berkshire and beyond attended; the county's rural craft glitterati all exhibiting and competing. Julia smiled at her diminutive Gran, as the silver-haired octogenarian sat at the rough oak table. Her gran—*the* Madge Thomson, née Greenstreet—crowned Grand Jam Master twelve years running.

Granny Madge made all the jams: raspberry, strawberry, apricot, gooseberry, blackberry, red currant, black currant, cherry, blueberry, etcetera, etcetera. And they were good. Amazingly, ridiculously, transportingly good, but that was only her entry-level jam—for seasoning her pots. Madge made jam out of things no one had any right to make jam from. This was her brand, *Madge Makes Jam*, although Granny abhorred such cold, corporate language to describe her art. She made: cucumber jam; ginger and artichoke jam; bacon jam; cabbage jam; nettle and horseradish jam; potato jam; mint and violet jam. She even performed an impossible alchemy, cloistered in her garden 'cooking hut,' that resulted in the unfathomable yet delightful concoction labelled jam-jam. Sixteen-year-old Julia had suggested naming it Wham Bam, Thank You Jam, but Granny had just tutted. That formula—more than any of Gran's recipes—made closely guarded secrets look like the parish newsletter.

Once, that friendless, black-clad and black eye-lined Julia—shipped to Maiden's for another listless summer of pent-up teenage rebellion—had even challenged Granny Madge (sullenly) to make pearl jam. Granny had set her jaw, pursed her lips, and retorted that if she could, Julia would attend youth club, and join *all* the activities. Socially crippled though she was back then, Julia also had been youthfully cocksure, and took the wager.

What Granny produced was a sweet elixir which—she revealed with a glint in her eye—contained a healthy amount of pearl barley, and Julia should collect her hoodie on the way out, because Youth Club started in twenty minutes.

And so Julia discovered debating—an unpopular group run by poker-thin former barrister Mr. Chumley—and it was wonderful. She got to argue with people in a calm and organised way, and they were not permitted to talk back, not immediately anyway, affording her time to weigh her retorts rather than lashing out at painful rejection. And she won. She won a *lot*.

The rest was precedent—as senior counsel in chambers liked to joke. Julia rediscovered school, discovered university, discovered boys, discovered boys were dickheads, discovered girls, discovered sex, discovered work experience, took the Legal Practice Course, discovered training contracts, a passion for the Law, and worked and worked and worked, met Devondra Lewis at a party fundraiser, discovered love, discovered ecstasy, discovered heartbreak.

The end.

3

With the utmost care, Julia wedged the last box of jam-jam into the Audi's boot then—very slowly—closed the lid. Granny emerged from the cottage, and locked the door.

"You look nice, dear." She peered over the top of her glasses. "You must be feeling a bit happier to put on your tight sweater."

Julia flushed, staring at her ankle boots, brushing imaginary dust from her Levis. "Gran," she protested, feeling sixteen again. "Can we do this without you embarrassing me, please?"

"Of course, dear." Gran patted her arm then moved to the passenger side and climbed into the sleek, silver vehicle. "I'm just glad to see you blushing again, beautiful girl. You've been cooped up with me long enough."

They drove in companionable silence along Winkfield Lane, past cottages and bungalows, all tended with pride. Sparrows swooped in the overhanging branches. Blackbirds and thrushes bustled in the hedges. Retirees, commuters and schoolkids washed someone or other's car, swatted aimless shuttlecocks, as the Audi whispered through leafy, lawn-mowered Middle England.

Julia turned onto Cobalt Hill, putting her foot down, powering the Audi through the lazier bends, only slowing when the hedges squeezed in, trees bending lower, the bends tightening. The final turn was the tightest. The land dropped away beyond the verdant hedgerow, the vista displaying rolling fields far below, made hazy by distance, before the view flicked away as they turned through the gate.

Bob Giles kept Top Field under grass expressly for the Summer Fête, and its dozen white marquees with their fluttering pennants.

Julia humphed clinking boxes from the Audi, while Madge arranged the jars with a critical eye, and an old wooden ruler. When she was done, the display looked marvellous, adorned with greenery and fruit from the cottage's garden. Granny examined the table from the consumer's viewpoint, dusting her hands on her apron. "It's the best display yet," she beamed.

Julia smiled too. She was actually happy, and she was going out tonight. She'd drop Granny at home, have a bite to eat then walk to the pub. And she'd get merry, and she'd talk to people. People who hadn't dumped her.

4

The next morning, Julia's head was thick and sore with the wages of beer. The sun lit her eyelids; cool cotton caressed her skin. Downstairs, china clinked, a wooden spatula tonked metal frying pan. It was time to get up. She rolled over, burying her head in the pillow.

A cheery 'Wakey-wakey' announced Granny's entrance with a tray. "Good night then?" Her eyebrow arched, and Julia blushed, flopping back on the pillow.

"It was."

"Thought so. That's good, but it's ten-thirty."

"Oh, sh—" Granny frowned. "—erbet. The fête!"

"Mr. Sharma is going to run me up. If you'll come when you're ready…"

"Of course. I'm so sorry."

"Don't worry, dear. Just bring another two cases of jam-jam, please. It always flies off the stall."

"I will. I'll be there before noon, I promise."

"Don't rush, dear," said Granny. "It's just a fête."

Just a fête!

Julia wolfed down the fry-up, practically ran through the shower, mauled her hair dry, threw on...clothes, combing fingers through still-damp hair as she snatched the cook shed key from the duck-beak hook by the back door.

The air in the shed was warm and sweet, laced with the scents of fruit and preserved wood. She hauled a case of jam-jam from the store cupboard. Three jars by five and two deep fitted nicely into a wooden wine case. She pulled out a second case. Sixty jars would last the day, surely.

Julia turned from the driveway towards Cobalt Hill, barely glancing the other way. 11:40. The morning preview had finished. The lunchtime rush was about to begin.

Out on Winkfield Lane she put her foot down, but quickly caught up with slower traffic heading to the fête. The road's tight alignment left no way to pass within the village. Further out, the road straightened, the thirty limit surrendering to sixty mph. A horsebox turned off up ahead. The four cars in front decelerated, and Julia held back, created a gap, tweaked the Audi over the centreline and planted her foot. The motor launched her forward. Seat pressing on her back, she whipped past the crawling cars as if they were parked.

Heart pumping, she slowed, eased back over. "Woo!" She gulped air.

She braked hard for the turn onto Cobalt Hill. Sunlight dappled the road, brightness flickering at the edge of vision. She fed in power and the Audi fought off gravity, zipping uphill. She took the first sweeping bend fast, forces pushing her towards the opposite hedge. The road unspooled before her, weaving left then right. She pressed just a little harder, savouring the way the belt tightened across her chest. Almost there. 11:54.

Children!

In the road!!

Dressed as...

Ferengi?
Tugged the wheel away, anywhere, just away.
<Thump. Thud. CRASH>
The hedge.
Burst through into the open air.
The vista opened up.
Rolling fields, hills misty with distance—
Rushed at her.
Car's nose dipping, falling, plunging towards the ground.
Body falling forwards, belt wrenching tight.
Car plummeting down.
Down.
Down, down, down.
Down-down-down-down-down-down-down-down.
A huge tree filled her view.
She—
couldn't—
believe—
that—
she—
was—
going—
to...

5

Die?

6

The birds are singing.
I don't understand.

7

Damp hair.
The smell of damp hair, and stale sweat. The scent of...blossom.
Something buzzing. A bee? Electricity, a charge, a spark?
Something...dangerous.

8

Voices.

Had the children come to check on her? But she'd hit them...

Yet the voices were not high-pitched like a child's, but low, throaty. Were they debating some course of action? *What do I care? I'm dead.* And without delivering the jam-jam. Granny will be so disappointed.

9

I opened my eyes, which felt wrong, since I was dead.

I was sitting in my Audi—sunlight and fresh, fragrant air streaming in the broken windows. The windscreen was shattered, hideously starred, obscuring my view of anything but brightness. To my right, thick leafy undergrowth—glossy dark green leaves bigger than my head. To my left, a wall of rough, raw bark.

I tried leaning toward the door, which caused a cascade of glass across my chest and arms. It pattered on the floor like rain. The side mirror was gone. Of course it was. I tried the door—jammed solid. I craned my neck, expecting a spasm. There was no pain, but my heart leapt. Movement! Someone near the back of the car. I heard rummaging, and that guttural muttering.

"What's all this fluff anyway? Shiny hard cups I can see through? Full of muck? Hur-hur. Pretty colour, right enough. Maybe old Scabby will find it tasteworthy. Hey, Haw, old son; Priv, my boy, what d'yous make of this?"

"Ooh, shiny." There was a tapping sound. "Pretty colour."

"But what is it, Box?"

"This one's broken, look. Colour's running out."

"Don' touch that! You don' know where it's been, boys."

"It's sticky, slidey, slippery. It's—"

"Don' swallow, Priv!"

"Oh, boys, it's...dunno. Ish...jiiiiingly, shhhhort of, shpangley. I sh...sh...should try a liiiiiittle more."

A horrid, wet belching, sort of farting explosion rent the air.

"Oh, Priv, no! Wha' happened?! The edge, Priv. Watch out!"

"Noooooo! No, Haw. He's gone. Lord and lady preserve us. Poor Priv!"

I craned my neck, but the raised boot lid blocked my view. I opened my mouth to call for help, but something made me wait. Who were these people, and why would they not check for injured passengers? And why wasn't I dead? Maybe my legs were broken. *Oh, this is ridiculous. Granny will be wondering what's happened to me, and...I hit those children.* I recalled the thump, the thud. My stomach somersaulted. I swallowed hard. I had to get back, to confess.

"Hello? Can you help me, please?"

Movement and muttering stopped.

"Please? I don't think I'm hurt, but the children... Please, call nine-nine-nine."

"The chariot talks!" The exclamation was punctuated by a disgusting horking sound. "Emerging sea serpents' knees? It's possessed! Let's go, Haws, 'fore Scabious boxes our ears, hur-hur! Carry these. To Queen Titty's court we go. Old Scabby'll wan' this elixir, no doubt."

I wrenched at the door handle. "If you could just help me out, *please*. I'll make the call." I fished my phone from a pool of glass on the passenger seat. No signal. *Damn.* In fact, no network. Wait. Colour running out...shiny, hard cups?

"Hey, that jam is *not* yours. Leave those alone!"

I fought with the handle, pushing and pulling, jerking around, but my seatbelt held me tight. Gingerly, I released the belt and—avoiding fragmented glass—managed to squirm around, over the central console, into the back seat.

The Audi tipped, rocking backwards, teetering on some balance point then settling.

The rear window was gone, a blanket of glass on the seat, nowhere to put my hands. I stretched, managing to grip the rear headrest, but had to put my knees down, like a fakir on a bed of nails. I winced as pain lanced through my knees and thighs, and pushed hard on the smooth metal of the open boot lid.

Two gobsmacked faces turned to regard me, mouths hanging open.

My jaw dropped. Their skin was loose, rubbery. I'd have burst out laughing if not so thoroughly dumbstruck. Their faces were like the masks of the Ex-Presidents from *Point Break*; noses, chins and ears grossly exaggerated.

"What sort of thing ish that, Box?"

"Looks a bit fairy, Haw."

"It doeshh."

"Fairy?" I realised that was me. "What happened? What...are you?"

"Twyshe the nuuumber o'YOU we are, and twyshe as nasty!"

The one with the slurred speech reared up, a manic look in its eyes. It lunged at me, gnarled fingers grasping for my neck. I jerked back, knees grinding broken glass.

"What's gotten you, Haw? Come away, m'boy."

The sane one grabbed the mad thing's shoulder, trying to pull him back. "We'll take this stuff to court, to Scabby. He'll know what to do. Leave it, Haw. Thing's no' worth it."

Thing! I wasn't having that. Box—whatever he was—restrained Haw nicely, and I punched his 'boy' square in his rubbery face. He paused, shook his floppy jowls, and lunged again. But Box had let go, and Haw sprang into the car, heedless of the ragged glass. I scrambled backwards, wriggling between the seats as wizened, wiry fingers grasped my ankle.

I screamed. The Audi tilted forwards. I lashed out my free foot, caught the ugly brute in the jaw.

With the driver's door jammed, I twisted for the passenger door, and grabbed the handle. It moved! The door half-opened then stopped with a thunk. Bony fingers found the neck of my T-shirt. I gagged, swung my legs across the passenger seat, and out of the door.

"Shit, sshtill, you wiggly worm," my assailant slurred. "I'm hungry, but I'll jusht take an arm, or a leg."

My head span. What was happening? I must be delirious. Maybe already in an ambulance gulping oxygen, or in a coma. I clutched the jagged doorframe, feet kicking as I choked, straining to escape.

The collar of my T-shirt ripped.

I was free!

I slithered through the gap, and fell into nothing.

10

Air whipped around me, my torn T-shirt flapping like a flag in a gale. I couldn't hear my own screams. I was a hundred metres up! A colossal tree filled my view. A giant redwood? In Berkshire?

I tumbled head-over-heels, shooting past a branch the size of a footbridge. More branches. The gaps were big, but there were dozens. What if I hit one? What if I *didn't*? I waved my arms, trying to...what? Fly? Skydive? At least I'd stopped tumbling, but I was going to die...again.

"Grab hold!"

I tore my gaze up and screamed again.

The bird was enormous, bigger than the Audi, diving straight at me, beak gaping wide enough to swallow me whole.

"Grab hold, or be slug food!"

Giant talking bird!

The biggest swallow in the world...no, a swift, zipped past me, pulling a tight turn under me, its wings whupping like a helicopter. I whacked into it, felt soft feathers then rebounded. There was someone riding the bird!

Time slowed as our eyes met. Her face was moon-kissed pale. Hair dark as a clear, midwinter night streaming behind her, strong features tense with the effort of flying a giant bird. One gloved hand clutched feathers, the other hand reached towards me.

I twisted, and grasped.

Our fingertips brushed as the bird zipped past. Its wash set me tumbling in the air. Another branch—dense with foliage—rushed at me. I crossed my arms over my face as I fell through massive, glossy leaves that flapped aside like wet cardboard as I tried to grab something, anything.

"Hold on this time, giddy-nut!"

I was still falling, could see the ground now. The swift dove again, wings swept back like scimitars. Determination etched the pilot's face. The air that battered me barely rippled the bird's feathers. It was magnificent.

I gritted my teeth as the brown arrow flashed towards me then seemed to stall in the air under me. I hit feathers again, and flailed, grasping, slipping until a fierce grip clamped around my forearm. My fingers locked around the pilot's gauntleted wrist. Our grasp held. I was on.

The bird banked in a long arc that pressed me down into its feathers.

"Grab my waist. *Now.*"

Deep purple eyes commanded, and I complied, shuffling between the bird's wings until I could grab the pilot's leather jerkin. Barely had I snaked my arms around her waist when the swift banked again, a hellish Möbius manoeuvre that left me floating for half a breath. I locked my fingers together. Gravity tried to pull me away from her, but I held on, breathed, and looked around.

We soared away from the tree, Berkshire countryside spread before us like a crazy, living tea-towel. Looking down past the swift's wing, I saw trees and houses, roads and vehicles.

"I don't understand," I shouted. "How is it you"—clearly this was impossible—"have a giant bird? Everything's so big!"

"Talk sense," my rescuer called, raven tresses fluttering across my face. "You're small, and Fleet-wing is a swift. Now, tell me why you brought your silver carriage to Fairyland."

11

Fairyland.

I tried to assemble disparate facts into a scenario involving cosplay, and the Maiden's Green fête while clutching my rescuer's waist and trying not to vomit, despite the small matter of a giant bird, its bones and muscles rolling and flexing around me as we flew through warm summer air. Everything around me was impossibly massive, except it wasn't. Apparently, I had shrunk.

I studied the pilot. Anything to distract my churning thoughts. Her hard, muscular body moved under my arms, coaxing confident adjustments to the bird's flight. Close up, sunlight revealed a purple hint in her tumbling dark hair. Her snug leathers, stained the darkest of greens, fitted snugly over the svelte curves of her back except where tailored slits allowed her—

"Oh-my-god!"

"What?" Raven-hair called over her shoulder.

"Nothing. Just admiring how well your jacket fits your...wings." It was true. Somehow, I had shrunk, and this was Fairyland. Wherever it was, it was stunning, and so was she. "Where are we going?"

"Somewhere you can explain yourself."

The bird drew a long, sweeping arc left and down towards a big barn off Chawridge Lane, just outside the village. That was good. This *was* still my world. So, did Fairyland overlay it then? I just needed to revert to being twenty times this size, retrieve the stolen jam-jam—perhaps being a lawyer could actually help with that—then catch a lift back to Granny's (my heart sank) to contact the police about the road traffic accident.

We shot towards the ground, the building expanding, swelling in my vision: very big; too big; much, much too big. TOO BIG!

I clutched the pilot as our flightpath bottomed out. For a split second I felt heavier than a bowling ball in a duvet, then we were rising, rocketing at a stone gable suddenly a mile wide. Fleet-wing raked her wings, decelerating, crushing me against the pilot's back, face pushed into her hair. She held firm. Dark eaves loomed and, suddenly, we were perched in deep shadow. The swift chirruped. The pilot hopped down, patted its side then grasped my belt, and dragged me down.

"Hey," I snapped.

She whipped around, dark hair tossing, glared then squeezed through a crack in the wall. I followed, emerging into an attic the size of the Albert Hall. Earlier, I'd thought all I had to deal with was a giant bird, and that I'd stumbled onto the set of *Clash of the Titans 4: This Time It's Personal*, or maybe that old TV show *Valley of the Giants*, an episode of *Doctor Who*, maybe, because *that* was likely.

My companion was walking away along a wooden rafter the width of the M25 Motorway (clockwise from Junction 20, King's Langley to Junction 21, Winch Wood Hill). My head was a fuddled mess, and I needed to get a grip.

"You could at least tell me your name."

She rounded on me. She looked angry.

"My name, is it?" She stalked towards me, glowering. Her eyes—I noticed despite the attic's musty gloom—were as dark as her hair, and held flecks of forest green. "I save you from being smeared into slug bait, and it's 'Tell me your name'? Give me yours first, and I'll ponder whether you're worth it. I can still toss you off the roof. Without wings you'll make a pretty puddle."

"Look, I..." I felt rotten. She was right. I was confused, frustrated, and I'd lashed out. I thought I'd killed three children, but those stunted figures in the road were the ones who'd robbed me of the jam-jam! "I was ambushed, in my world. Three creatures—"

"Goblins."

"I..."

"Ugly, wrinkled-looking things." She paced back to me.

"Yes!"

Maybe I could make an ally. Goodness knew I need one.

"I'm sorry. I was rude." I smiled, smoothed my hair. *I must look a frightful mess.* "My name's Julia Greenstreet. I'm a lawyer."

12

She stared at me as if about to commence cross-examination, or maybe to pounce on me. My pulse quickened again as I realised I liked the sound of that.

Scrutinising her now, I took in the small details I'd been trained to read and exploit. Those intense dark eyes liked to be obeyed, and her posture suggested an untamed, perhaps untameable spirit. Did her so-dark green leather imply a profession conducted under darkness, perhaps a dishonourable one? No, a deduction too far.

"Do fairy folk make a habit of crossing to the human world? Do humans...come here often?"

She ignored my queries.

"Why are you here, Dew-Leeya Green-Street?"

I chose to ignore her mangling of my name. "I was in Maiden's Green—"

She raised her hand.

"You're not in Maiden's Green anymore, Dew-Leeya. You are in Fairyland. Now, tell me *why* you're here." She stepped closer, leaning in from a good six-foot-two. *No, wait—* "And what's your busyness with the Hedges?"

"The what?" The last remnants of my adrenaline produced a giggle.

"I'm a warden. You consorted with Box, Haw, and Privet Hedges. I'll round them up once you tell me what you gave them."

The jam thieves. "Those creatures—Goblins?—they *stole* from me. Do you know where they went? I need that jam-jam back." This place was just too strange. I had to get a grip. I was a lawyer, for goodness' sake. Find the facts, assess the facts, use the facts. So Biron Woolf Lodge's senior partner reminded me, ad nauseum.

"Those miscreants ransacked my car—the silver carriage—took my property. I'll sue, you know."

The pilot scowled. "There's no time for sewing."

"I—no! Look, they're getting away." I gesticulated randomly. "Not much of a warden, are you? Accosting the victim?"

The pilot clutched my T-shirt's remaining sleeve, pulling me in till our noses almost touched. "You annoy me, human. I have no time for your nun sense."

"I'm sorry." She had a point. "I was rude, again. Thank you for saving my life, assuming I'm not actually...dead. But I'm really confused. I mean, Fairyland? Is it a metaphor?" I waved the thought aside. "Don't answer that." I held her gaze, and attempted to foster a constructive working relationship. "Look, it would help if I knew your name, so we can talk on an equal footing. I *have* shared my name with you."

"You talk too much." She released my T-shirt. Clearly she'd never met a lawyer before. She scowled then pursed those pale pink lips, examined me as if seeing me for the first time, then nodded.

"I am Rowan Nightshade, Warden of the Southern Marches. I will call you Dew, because Dew-Leeya Green-Street is a mouthful." She frowned, dark brows furrowing with a brooding beauty that made my knees quite weak in a way swooping around on a giant bird had not.

"It's Jul— Okay, Dew is fine." So, she was—effectively—police, so often the lawyer's natural adversary. Wonderful. At the back of my mind a notion surfaced—one from late-night reading under the covers—suggesting it was best that supernatural creatures—even those in law enforcement—did not know my real name. Supernatural creatures. My lawyer brain objected (again) to what my senses were feeding it. And yet, the existence of fairies seemed to be the only thing that had changed, otherwise, things seemed the same: gravity, touch, smell. Taste? Jam.

"Look, I want to help you retrieve my property. I'm resourceful, a good negotiator. I know I don't have beautiful wings like yours. They must be useful for...wardening."

Her eyes narrowed. "Are you trying to mate with me? We don't have time." I blushed. "Come." She turned, and strode away along the massive beam. "They'll seek out Scabious," I heard the sneer in her voice, "but they'll be slow. We can catch them," she said over her shoulder. "I *will* fulfil my duty, and know the nature of this breach before I set it right."

"That sounds rather final."

"Enough chatter," she turned on me again, and I jolted to a halt before running into her. The drop loomed even though I couldn't even see the barn floor, such was the beam's width. "Fairyland is a family busyness. You can't just fly in here with your Grand Jam and start touting it about."

"It's jam-jam, actually, and it's special. I can't tell you what's in it. The recipe changes from year to year. Granny wouldn't tell me anyway."

"Don't ramble, Dew," Rowan commanded, her gaze darkening. "What is this thing? What is it for?" She stabbed a finger just below my clavicle. The part of my brain that dealt with inappropriate distractions sent me an image of that finger sliding downwards. Rowan growled, prodding again. "What, is, jam?"

"Seriously?" Her gaze was unflinching. "Okay. Take a fruit of your choice; slice or crush; add sugar and water; heat the mixture for ages; store in jars to cool. Jam preserves fruit. It's very popular...in my world."

"That's stupid. Just eat the fruit. What is sugar?"

I just stared, but Rowan was serious, and getting frustrated. The air in the barn was thick and warm.

"It's sweet. Maybe like nectar?"

She frowned. "So, jam is human nectar?"

"Eh, nooo. It's natural, although most sugar is refined. But what's the harm in having a little more sweetness in the world?" I attempted a smile.

"The harm, Dew, is that fairies can't eat human food." From her scowl, I'd crossed a line. "Fairies need the nectar of their kindred flower, but they love sweet things, and now you've brought this...taint to Fairyland. There's no telling what harm it'll do."

I remembered a loud explosion of squelching burps. Had someone— Priv—fallen? I tried not to panic. I'd messed up with Granny, maybe somehow killed a goblin, and I'd offended my valiant rescuer. "But we can still catch them, right? Then you can expel me, and Gran's jam-jam, and my Audi back to Maiden's Green, and good riddance?"

Rowan humphed, and marched away again, not turning until she reached the end of the beam. She smiled, beckoned me assertively, and it was...hot. I approached, meeting her dark, steady gaze.

"Dew," she shook her head. "Only fairy stories end so neatly."

"But, isn't this—?"

She pushed me over the edge.

13

Again? Really?!

Maybe she knew the landing would be soft, but I didn't. I twisted through thick, warm air then plunged—bum first—into dark, chilling water. At least I managed not to open my gob, took a second to concentrate, twisted around and pushed upwards.

I surfaced with a splutter, and gasped. I was in a wide pond, its surface slicked with dust and leaves. I struck for the nearest bank, spitting out water and curses. I found the pond's edge, grey, smooth to the touch like plastic. Because it was plastic. She had pushed me from the roof into a bucket. That beautiful, grumpy fairy was going to get a piece of my mind.

I hauled myself—drenched and dripping—from the water to perch on the bucket's wide lip. Bright sunlight streaming under the barn door silhouetted two figures. One was Rowan, her lithe form, and tumbling hair unmistakable. The other—from my perspective—was a twelve-foot-tall squirrel. *I'm smaller than a bird, and a squirrel, and I can walk under a barn door, and swim lengths (diameters?) in a bucket, and how am I going to get* big *again?!*

"Hurry up." Rowan waved me down.

Scowling, I hung down from the bucket's edge then dropped five metres (fairy metres?) into straw, too angry to consider the danger of breaking an ankle. I bounced up and strode towards her—shoes squelching, clothes pasted to me.

"What the hell was that?"

She shrugged. "You can't fly. I can't carry you. Do I look like an ant? Now, get those wet clothes off. We've goblins to catch."

"I—what?"

"Straight-tail won't appreciate the extra weight," she patted the squirrel's flank. It looked down at her then at me, and chittered, as if in agreement.

"A bit of water isn't much compared to the two of us."

"I'll fly. You'll be riding."

I knew I was gawping. "You're kidding."

She shook her head. "Undress, or I'll put you over my knee and do it for you. If your Grand Jam reaches Montbretia, or worse, Bougainvillea, it will turn any fae who tastes it unsensible. Do you want that?"

I recalled the squelching burp explosion. "No, but..." Could the jam-jam be so dangerous? Certainly, I didn't want to cause any more damage than I had already.

Glowering at her, I unbuttoned my Levis and rolled them down my legs, rescuing my hipsters as they tried to follow the jeans, dragging wet denim over pink skin. At least the sunlight was warming. I'd soon be dry. I peeled my ripped T-shirt over my head, but my sports bra stayed on. Was she watching? She was, but her face was like thunder.

Rowan tossed my clothes aside. "They'll be here when we get back, if you want them." She wrinkled her nose.

I had two abortive efforts to mount the squirrel. Rowan let me try the first time, perhaps forgetting I was used to silver carriages. The second time—helping me to my feet—she grabbed me around my waist, and launched me at Straight-tail's back. I grabbed two handfuls of fur, but slipped off sideways.

Rowan sighed, gripped my waist again, and I slid back into her arms.

"Stop faffing around," Rowan grumbled. "I'm not going to mate with you."

"Why would I want that?" I snapped. "You're a bully. Throw me again."

Rowan's hands cinched my waist. "Be ready this time."

She hoisted me up. I grabbed fur. She planted both hands on my bum, and pushed as I swung my leg over the squirrel. I was on, feeling like Kirk Douglas or James Stewart (Gran does love movie night).

"Straight-tail will follow me. Don't fall off."

Rowan walked through the gap under the barn door, out into the sunlight. The squirrel followed. I didn't even need to duck my head. She turned to me, and unfurled her wings—four, like a dragonfly—resplendent in iridescent blues, purples and pinks. They flickered out of sight as she jumped into the air, and flew away as I gawped, unable to accept that she could be any more beautiful.

I had no time to dwell on that thought, because Straight-tail bounded after her, and it took every fibre of my being to hold on. He was remarkably stable, and travel was smooth, but the speed...

I had observed squirrels bobbing along, stopping, picking something up, chewing it, scampering a few feet, stopping, looking around again. No. Straight-tail had his goal, and he was away. He made a Japanese bullet train look like Buster Keaton's railroad handcar.

I actually began to feel safe, despite us whistling along the top of a narrow, weather-bleached fence. At the end of the fence Straight-tail leapt for a tree. We dropped, landed, shot upwards, me hanging off his back with two fists of red hair in a death grip. He shot along branches, hammered up trunks. It was wild, exhilarating. I let my head loll back, wanting to yell, but I didn't for fear of alarming Straight-tail. He sped out along a branch that narrowed, and narrowed, started bending, bouncing under our weight. We were running out of branch, almost pointing at the ground when he leapt.

We flew through the air, bright blue sky above, verdant growth below, beaming smile plastered all over my face. This place was amazing.

Lush vegetation rushed up to meet us. Straight-tail landed softly, tail flipping like a fan dancer with the DTs, and bolted off again.

Off to catch the thieving goblins.

14

We darted through what felt like forest. Leaves and flowers—gobsmackingly huge to me—blurred: countless shapes and colours. And greens by the hundred, all different: sunlit, shadowed, bright, pale, searing, enveloping green. Cloud-like aquilegia, leaves in olive and indigo, their stalks red. Low, spotty-leaved lungwort, pink and purple blooms at head-height. Is this what hallucinogenic drugs felt like? It was glorious. High was exactly what I felt. High on nature, high on beauty, high on adrenaline. How could Rowan be so dour surrounded by this?

And yet it was Rowan's intensity that drew me, just like Dev's commitment to social justice. What tides of passion were locked within Rowan Nightshade's brooding stare? I wanted to know, to unlock her like a dark mystery, a leather-bound enigma.

Thoughts of my saviour seemed to summon her. Straight-tail burst into a grassy clearing, and there stood Rowan on a shade-dappled lawn, hands on hips, surveying a sorry-looking sight.

Slumped on the ground before her was one of our goblins. When Straight-tail stopped, I jumped down and strode over. I really was Jimmy Stewart. Although maybe Ursula Andress emerging from the sea in *Dr. No* was closer, given my state of undress, and I didn't even care.

Hedges—Haw or Box, presumably—looked terrible, even with his wrinkled skin and exaggerated features, but he smiled broadly, his lips sticky dark red with jam-jam.

"I'sh loverly shtuff, Rowwwan. Try it." He staggered to his feet, pointing at his lips. "Lick shum off me." He grinned, advancing on her until her outstretched palm impacted his chest.

"Desist, Haw Hedges. Where is Box? Where is he taking the Grand Jam?"

"Not telling. I wan' more shticky. Give me shticky!" He batted her hand aside then turned, stomping away a few metres.

"See what you've done, Dew?" Rowan snapped.

"I didn't know."

Hedges turned, but now his leer was fixed on me. "You brought the shticky. Gimme more."

"Your brother has it." As he started towards me, I had an idea. "Although, I know where there's more." Not a lie, it was in Granny's shed. He stretched out his hands at neck-wringing height, grasping, and broke into a run.

"Give it," he growled.

Rowan stepped between us. Her gleaming wings buzzed, powering a two-handed push that sent Hedges tumbling across the grass. But he was brim-full of ugly, awkward energy, flapping his arms, fingers flexing into claws. "Give it, GIVE IT!" He paced in circles, enraged.

"Tell us where Box went," I demanded. "I'll get you jam-jam." Willow Cottage seemed a million miles from this astonishing place.

"Yesh, yesh. I tell for more jaaaam. Telllll you big boss Scabby said 'tweren't for such as me. 'E said 'twere made to shticky royal lips."

"Titania," Rowan groaned. "Oberon." Her sturdy assurance was gone.

"Jam now!" Haw yelled, and charged at me, reaching out just as his head exploded.

Goblin remnants splattered the ground as I stood gaping. I stared at the corpse until Rowan gripped my arm, shook me, her expression hard.

"See what you've done? If the Grand Jam reaches court, it will explode the fairy king and queen. You'll get us banished to Hardmeadow!"

"The garden centre?"

"Turned to stone, no less."

15

I felt shame and anger at my stupidity, that it had led to this...fantastical mess. I grasped the strange commercial tangent with my world. "Turned to stone?"

"Cursed by both king and queen, should they survive, to exist in the human realm as a stone statue or water feet-ewer. We cannot let this poison reach my lieges. I'll track Box. You take Straight-tail to Titania's court. It's closest, you might arrive first. Wait outside, watch for Hedges. Do *not* go in. Hear me? Scabious will be there."

"So, the Hedges work for him?"

"They owe duty to any orifice-holder, of which there are several: the Faux-rain Secretary; the Chain-seller of the Eggs Checker; the Chief Con Sell."

I shook my head. Was Fairyland a nation, a 'busyness', as Rowan had called it? The cultural malapropism was quite baffling. Other human...visitations might explain it.

"Can Hedges get to Montbretia before us?"

Rowan looked uncertain, which was troubling. "He might, by fairy ring."

"Right." I felt stupid. "So why do we fly, and run?"

"Use of the rings is by gift of one court or the other." Her bitterness was palpable. "I have the favour of neither, because of Scabious Hellebore, and his scheming."

"So, we're seeking Hedges and Hellebore, and we're going to retrieve the Grand Jam." I touched her arm. "We can do this."

I could, I *would* do this. I must, before anyone else...exploded. Petrification was easy to believe. In folklore, fairies did some very ugly things. To stand any chance of going back—assuming I could—I must retrieve the jam-jam. I strode back to Straight-tail, and jumped onto his back. Rowan whispered to the squirrel then he carried me away, scampering through the undergrowth, while my thoughts raced.

An hour later—if Fairyland had hours—Straight-tail and I emerged through clustered foxgloves, soft leaves thick above us, into a field of loam bright with tall bluebells that ringed a monstrous oak. Around its base, a collar of tall, blade-leafed montbretia, a sharp, green palisade, flaming orange flowers stooped, as if searching for interlopers like me.

Even as Straight-tail came to a halt before towering fronds, four fairies appeared from the green-bladed curtain, levelling spears at me.

"Who goes there?"

I glanced around. No sign of drunken goblins. Was Box Hedges inside already? It looked like not going in—probably at spear-point— might be tricky.

"Worry not, worry not. Everyone at ease." A robed figure descended from the oak, wings buzzing, arms spread in placation of the guards. What a grand figure, his billowing cloak shimmering between deep claret and hunter's green, his hair russet and gunmetal grey, long and straight, hanging past his chest. So elegant, his smile beneficent.

Soft boots touched the ground, wings folded away, and he walked towards me. "Welcome, Dew-Leeya. The birds sang of your arrival, and I'm so glad you've come. I'm sure you can explain everything."

I climbed down from the squirrel, feeling distinctly self-conscious under the scrutiny of five adult fairies in my bra and hipsters, as if *that* was the strange part of this experience.

"I must take you to Titania, may her beauty paint the land in colour," he said, "but we'll find you something appropriate to wear first." He indicated my undress. "This is rather...informal." He turned away then back. "Incidentally, I am the Queen's Astral Lodger. Scabious Hellebore, at your service."

16

Two guards escorted us through the montbretia, using their halberds to push the big green shards aside to make a path for us. Hellebore was pleasant, welcoming, and he had expected me, but he was an astrologer, after all. If Fairyland was real, why not astrology?

Yes, Rowan warned me against entering, but I had no choice, and here was our prime suspect. He might lead me right to the jam-jam, and my way home. Still, I imagined her brooding scowl. Maybe she would haul me over the coals, or over a hay bale, a bed of roses, perhaps.

We emerged onto a strip of open ground before the gargantuan trunk. Hellebore smiled at me, and walked right *into* the tree. Through the bark. He was there, then he was gone. The guards looked at me.

"I..." I felt a bit stupid, took a deep breath, raised my chin, and strode forwards, flinched, expecting to smack my nose into hard bark and—

The sunlight disappeared. Switched off like a light, replaced by soft radiance spilling over warm wooden walls, curved like the inside of a tree, if the tree was hollow and the location of a fairy palace. Every line was smooth and flowing; wide, wavy circles under my bare feet, the rings of the tree.

Hellebore stood patiently, a wooden disc in his hand that looked a bit like a toilet seat. "You won't have done this before, so watch carefully." He moved to the centre of the room. The glow emanated from a stream of hazy light, softly coruscating with points of colour that drifted upwards. My mouth dropped open, but dear goodness it looked just like a transporter beam from Original Series *Star Trek*— maybe softer, more natural.

My host placed his disc into the beam, stepped on, and rose up within the shaft of light towards the ceiling, passed through it, and was gone. One of the guards indicated a stack of the wooden discs. I took a deep breath, walked over, picked one up—it was very light—and approached the radiant column. I smiled. I was going to say *that* line, and it was going to work, because Fairyland was real, and this really wasn't a delusional coma dream. I placed the disc in the beam and stepped on.

"Beam me up, Scotty."

My skin tingled as I rose up, away from the guards, already moving to resume their posts. I passed through floors, always rising. Rooms were revealed: one where guards slept or lounged on pallets of what looked like dandelion fluff; a space containing a hoard of enormous acorns and other seeds; a workshop of some sort, benches carved from the wood of the oak itself, strewn with a plethora of flotsam, jetsam, artefacts, and geegaws, and a mole, standing, peering closely at a huge button. At least it wasn't wearing spectacles. That would have been ridiculous.

As I ascended I cast about for signs of Hedges, jam-jam jars, or their boxes, but there were none.

Hellebore awaited me in the next room, held out his hand. I took it, stepped off the disc, and had ample time to turn and lift it from the column of gossamer light.

"Well done." He smiled. "Now," his open hand indicated a room ringed with clothes racks formed from long, flexible shoots, which converged on the room's centre. The clothes were arranged by shade and, as I turned around, I felt I was standing at the centre of an artist's colour wheel. Beyond the racks, the wall was carved into shelves displaying shoes, shoes, and more shoes. It was charity shop, flea market, second-hand heaven and—at another time—I'd have loved nothing more than to dive in and lose myself for a while. But, there was no time.

"I don't have time. Your queen is in danger. There's this food called jam-jam..." Behind Hellebore, Rowan rose through the floor. She did not look pleased to see me. Hellebore must have seen my eyes shift.

"Rowan Nightshade. Well met." He turned, smiled, but there was no pleasure in his expression.

Rowan stepped from her disc as if walking through a door, smooth and graceful. Her mien was cool. I drifted towards the racks, half expecting them to whip out swords and go at it, *Prisoner of Zenda*-style.

"Thank you for escorting my charge, Lord Hellebore, for the short time she was not under my wing." Ooh, defensive much, Rowan?

"Of course," he nodded, the shortest of all bows. "Dew-Leeya is preparing for her presentation to Titania, may her radiance give birth to spring, and garland summer."

"And I'm trying to tell him—"

"I'll assist Dew-Leeya. We are short of time. Is Box Hedges here?"

Direct, but I expected no less of Rowan.

Hellebore pondered this. "I have not seen him. Is something amiss, Rowan Nightshade? Do you bring more problems from the Southern Marches?"

"No warning, but a threat Titania must heed. Grand Jam—"

"*Must* heed?" He started pacing. "That *does* sound serious. I will go and divine the truth." He turned to me, all warmth and welcome. "The stars shine in the day, Dew-Leeya. But only a rare few can see them."

He bowed to me, barely inclined towards Rowan, took a disc, and rose from the room.

"How do you get down again?" I asked, but Rowan strode over to me and grasped my wrist.

"I said don't go in."

"I was taken in." I scowled. "Anyway, there's no time. I've seen no sign of Box, or jam-jam."

Concern twisted Rowan's pale features. "I found signs of his passing. I think he used the ring, and that he is close."

"Hellebore has been nice enough, but—"

She almost threw my arm down. "He's a selfish schemer who loves his position more than anything." Her eyes were cold. "We must see Titania. Hellebore will turn her against you before you've even come out."

"Excuse me?"

"Come out," she urged me towards the clothes as if guiding someone into a parking space. "Made your début. Now, put something on, quickly."

"My...début? You're kidding."

She shook her head, looked at the ceiling then back at me. Her gaze was intense. I took a step backwards between two racks. She followed.

"Sheer bad luck lumbered me with you." I took another step back. She stepped forward. "Now I'm stuck nursemaiding you through this...disaster." She poked my chest, forcing me back, hemmed in now by the hanging clothes. She advanced. "And maybe"—she stepped forward, I stepped back—"you've made a big enough mess"—I was going to step back, but she grabbed my bra straps like they were lapels in a Jimmy Cagney movie, and pulled me close to her—"that we'll both be petrified." Our noses were inches apart. Her eyes were *so* dark. "So"—she pulled the straps off my shoulders, down my arms to my waist—"put something on that isn't ridiculous, and do it quickly."

She turned and started away, but I was *not* having that. I'd had enough of bullying, by Rowan or anyone else. I was an intelligent, highly-motivated lawyer; an independent spirit, with a go-getting personality—according to my last staff review—and I was *not* going to take this anymore. I lunged, grabbed Rowan's belt, and pulled hard.

"Stop right there, giddy-nut," I snapped, jerking her to a halt. She was powerful, but she wasn't heavy. I thought she would spin around, dump me on my arse, but she just stood with her back to me. That emboldened me. "I'm done with your rudeness. Start respecting me or we are *finished*. I know I've made mistakes, but I didn't ask for this. Still, I'm not afraid to face the consequences of my actions."

She turned, eyes searching, lips pouting, appraising. It wasn't being half-naked that made me feel seen. It was her stare. I shivered.

"Consequences of your actions?" She nodded, her green-flecked midnight eyes never wavering from mine then stepped in and kissed me, deeply.

17

Her arms—whipcord strong—encircled my waist, and pulled me against her so I could throw my barely toned, lilywhite arms around her neck. It felt like kissing the Mona Lisa, or Olympia; Elizabeth Taylor or Hedy Lamarr: some untouchable, unreachable beauty that only should be observed from afar. But she was right there in my arms. I managed to gasp "Rowan." Just the word sent shivers through me.

She released me slowly, after what might have been a month, maybe two, and pinned me with another unreadable look.

"You taste—"

"What? Tell me."

"Curious." I swear she almost smiled. "But there's no time for this. Get dressed." She turned away and walked out into the room.

"Then help me," I demanded. "This isn't the chambers Christmas party. I have no clue what I'm doing, and walking into Titania's court in fancy dress isn't going to boost my credibility. What's in these days?" I plucked at the nearest rack. "Plum ruffles?"

She sighed heavily and stalked over. "You're asking the wrong fairy."

"I disagree. You look...fantastic."

She grunted as she flipped through the rack opposite. Dresses, jackets, blouses slid freely on woven willow hangers. "You think I look fantastic?"

"Swashbuckling, like a female fairy Douglas Fairbanks."

"I don't know what that is," she huffed. "Just get dressed."

I had a brainwave. The Hedges had said they would seek out Hellebore. He had Titania's ear, her favour, and was a fairy of considerable self-image. I would match his style.

I retrieved the plum ruffles: a ridiculous, flouncy ballerina outfit that I'd have given my teddy's right arm for when I was eight. It was short, had a 'slimming,' almost corseted bodice, which I thought was only slightly smaller than my ribcage, and a lot of fluff and feathers around the bosom.

"Find me an olive green hat, and tights would be good."

"There," she pointed, but I'd seen the rack I needed. Because, colour wheel. I'd flirted with pastels once, could see what wonderful sense this room made. I found olive green tights, and discarded the last of my human clothes, and hauled them on.

"Don't worry. They'll just fit," said Rowan.

She was right. She helped me into the ballerina dress without me asking. I had feared asphyxiation but, as Rowan's hands lingered on my hips, I closed the bodice with ease.

"Fairyland, right?"

She gave me a wry smile. "Fairyland."

She thrust a hat at me, not unlike a cloche from the roaring twenties, cup-shaped and green as a Brussels sprout leaf. I put it on, tilted it back. Ready.

I strode with Rowan to the shaft of light.

"Let's find Box, and my jam-jam then I'll go back, get out of your hair. Gran needs me, and my job. I gather my boss has a new assignment for me. This will all be done, and you can drop me off at Cobalt Hill."

Rowan's frown morphed into a smirk, her dark eyes sparkling. "Cobalt Hill? North of the village, with the big square field at its top?"

"Yes," I said.

She laughed. *Laughed*! "That's not Cobalt Hill, it's Kobold Hill."

"I... What's kobold?"

"A word for goblin, from an earlier time, when your folk mixed with mine."

I laughed with her. It seemed like cultural malapropism cut both ways.

Rowan plucked a disc from the pile, threw it into the beam like yesterday's newspaper, looped an arm around my waist, and hauled me on with her.

We floated upwards in the fairy transporter beam, Rowan's firm grip holding me close. We rose through an empty banqueting hall, what might have been a library—also empty—then either a convalescent ward or an opium den that reminded me how Granny's jam-jam transformed fae into vicious, violent drunks then exploded them. But I would retrieve it; I *would* find my way back. Darkness closed in without warning, as if there was no space, compartment or room, just tree.

"Titania's court is like nothing you've seen before," said Rowan. "You need to pay attention. Be confident, but not cheeky. Control yourself. Don't be gormless, and don't gawp," she said. "But don't be brash. Be polite, gracious, friendly—but not over-friendly. Titania dislikes that. Above all, don't be nervous. And most importantly, don't show off. Overriding all that, you must *smile*."

"I don't feel like smiling. I have a huge mess to fix, then I can go home, right?"

Her grip on my waist loosed. "Yes," she deadpanned. "I'll have no more use for you, certainly. Now, be ready. Leave the subject of Hedges to me. Solemnly promise to restore the balance, dispose of the Grand Jam, and we may yet fix this."

I pressed a quick kiss on her cheek. "For luck," then broke away as we emerged into a grand hall.

18

Not darkly grand, like those gloomy throne rooms in fantasies beyond number, where tired monarchs sat in state, not gloomily sombre with the wooden gravitas of Empire and Commonwealth that cossets the judiciary in my world (*My world!*). This was a hall of light, warmth, and scent, of sensation.

So organic was the space, so natural its walls, that I couldn't judge the size. It felt just like being inside a tree, but a massive one, the size of the Shard, or perhaps the Gherkin, the Can of Ham. The walls, the floor, the ceiling were living wood—running in the supple curves, and gentle whorls only nature can produce.

More than a hundred...beings turned to watch our arrival, they and their dress an explosion (I winced) of colour, like Andy Warhol had directed *Priscilla Queen of the Desert*. So many vibrant and variegated figures, and every pair of eyes turned on us.

Rowan dug me in the ribs. I was gawping. All her instructions had flown from my head, apart from the last: smile. So I did. Not too broad. I used my confident, professional, new-client smile.

The rainbow horde parted before us, and we stood at one end of a corridor of fae faces. A handful—I now knew—were goblins, but Box Hedges was not among them. Had he shared Gran's jam-jam yet? Were any fairies dead because of me? I felt slightly sick, but no one here appeared intoxicated.

Rowan took my hand, and led me down the line. In my fairy get-up, I felt like I should be pirouetting. I was dressed for it. I'd never seen so many ruffs, and puffs, and flounces, even at the Royal Ballet. It was overwhelming. I really had to get my head straight.

And then I saw the throne, and everything and everyone disappeared.

The chair itself was formed from living oak bows that grew inside the hall, curving to suit the slender frame of the fairy queen. Titania fairly glowed. She had a slight form—I'd noticed the throne first as it was so much larger than her—but as we approached, and I saw her properly, the knowledge, the experience, the command in her eyes was plain, and it chilled me to my core. I shivered, my smile slipping. How could I maintain any pretence before a queen? Her face was angelic, but that word was inadequate. She was beautiful in a painfully open way that drew me forward, her expression so welcoming that refusing her would be a crime. It hurt to look away, but I managed.

"Don't anger her," hissed Rowan. I might have whispered the obvious line if my brain had not been completely addled.

Titania's golden gaze drifted from Rowan—to whom she'd given a shining smile of greeting—to me. I shored up my own smile. It felt like the ugliest grimace. The air, suddenly, was thick. I felt the edge of drowsiness, tore my gaze away again, and cast my eyes down. Titania's flowing gown was a simple, diaphanous shift. At first, I thought it white, then it was silver, then—the more I looked, avoiding her eyes— it displayed a shimmering suggestion of every single colour I could imagine.

Rowan bowed from the waist then dropped to one knee at the fairy queen's feet. I stood rigid, tight smile plastered on my face. Rowan tapped my leg then tugged on my tights, dragging me into an awkward curtsy, then to one knee like her. I wasn't bowing to anyone in this skirt.

"Brave Rowan," said Titania in an earnest, ageless voice. "Our faithful servant, Warden of the Southern Marches. Hail and well met."

"Hail to you, Titania. Fairest and wisest of the forest's blooms."

I realised I was frowning, thankfully at the floor in my lowly position.

"And who is your companion, noble Rowan? She is not of this realm."

"True, my perceptive queen. This is Dew-Leeya Green-Street, come in a silver chariot on the trunk road from Maiden's Green."

"She presents rather well, considering," said Titania, in tones soft as petals. Every bit as condescending as the partners when I came out at work. *Oh, super. We're very diverse here at BWL. It'll be great to have someone who understands all these gender discrimination cases we're getting.* Gormless giddy-nuts.

The hem of Titania's many-coloured gown drifted into my sight. I had the urge to speak—occupational hazard—but instead glanced sideways at Rowan. She was half-turned towards me, shaking her head. I breathed deeply. I had to obey Rowan in this...didn't I?

"Fair Titty, 'tis I, yer faithful gobbly servant, Box Hedges. I bring a new delicacy fer yer delectability."

"No!" I was on my feet, Rowan too.

Back down the colourful fae corridor, the goblin came forward, sack slung—swaying—on his shoulder, and it clinked. Guards emerged from hidden nooks, spears glinting. A gasp flowed through the crowding courtiers.

Box saw us, and stopped in his tracks.

"Miscreant," Rowan shouted, accusing him with her finger.

"Thief," I added, for good measure.

Box turned and ran, not towards the transporter, but to a round opening in the wall that I had thought—from a glimpse through the assembly—was a window. Now I saw that the circle opened onto a platform extending beyond the wall.

The goblin struggled through scattering fae. Rowan moved faster than any, closed on him as he reached the opening, almost had a hold of him before he jumped.

Rowan buzzed into the air, darted down as a huge, black and white shape plunged across my view. I realised I was running at the edge, and managed to pull up before going over it, guards crowding behind me.

I saw a magpie swoop on Hedges, snatch him up before Rowan could get to him. The guards were pulling me back inside, but I caught a glimpse of Rowan returning. She had not abandoned me. We two knelt before Titania again.

No one was smiling.

"Learned Hellebore informs us Dew-Leeya did not come empty-handed. He says she brought *poison* into Fairyland." Her voice remained level, as if delivering unimpeachable evidence.

I felt terrible, recalling the drooling, senseless creatures that the goblins had become, and the not inconsiderable kicker of Haw exploding, as Priv too must have done. All because of Gran's jam-jam. I had a debt to pay in this world. At least I could take meagre comfort from not being a killer in my own.

"Queen Titania, fairer still than dawn and sunset," Hellebore's honeyed tones came from behind me. "Lovelier than rainbows and moonlight laced with shooting stars, the sky informs me of more ill tidings. Hedges takes the Grand Jam—most reviled of elixirs—towards Bougainvillea, towards Oberon!"

"No!" Titania gasped. "What new cruelties are these?"

Titania's hem swished away. Intense murmuring grew above our heads. I pictured a rabble of bees.

"How can we right this wrong, sage and noble Scabious? What is the remedy for these ills? Advise me, sir."

"My helpers have set to it post-haste, fairest queen." I pictured his genteel smile as he readied the knife. "And so, it would be proper now timeously to consider the consequences for the offenders, most decorous highness."

My gaze met Rowan's. Indecision warred with action in the twist of her features. Her duty held her back, but my culpability drove me forward.

"Consequences?" asked Queen Titania.

I stood, tried to speak, but Titania stole my breath with a glare.

"Regrettably, fairest lady, inescapably, Rowan has failed you. I fear this calamity will leave its tragic touch on all our shoulders ere Luna tracks the heavens."

Hellebore's words carried enough dramatic inflection to choke a whale. The bards of Avon and Ayrshire must be turning in their graves.

"A grievous charge, Scabious. Rowan, what say you?"

Rowan unfolded herself from her stoop, standing proud and straight. The queen's soft brow was furrowed, her lips curved downwards in a pouting frown. The crowd's susurration stilled as they bated their breaths. Then someone spoke and—unexpectedly—it was me. I felt ridiculous spouting legal niceties in my froufrou fairy get-up, but I was not about to let Hellebore stitch up my saviour.

"Objection," I said. "Rowan should not have to speak without preparation, due process, and representation." Titania raised an eyebrow. The court gasped collectively. Hellebore smiled quietly. "At least until the facts are known. She must not be forced to say anything that might incriminate her."

"We must pursue Hedges," Rowan said. "Now."

"Enough." Titania's voice cut through our angry exchange. "Rowan Nightshade is our valued vassal. We will not condemn her unjustly." The colourful creatures held their collective breath, as did Rowan and I, all focused on the fairy queen standing stern and bright. "Now accused by you, trusted Hellebore"—the unctuous fairy bowed—"she has one ride of Sol, one flight of Luna to right the wrongs that lie at her feet.

"You, Dew-Leeya..." She levelled a finger at me, her brow a storm of regal justice. "You are known to be the source of this poison, and thus you must be puni-shed."

I bowed my head, my heart tripping, and thus did not see Rowan move until her strong arms scooped me up, and threw me over her shoulder, presenting my behind for the examination of Titania and her court.

"Stop her!" Titania cried.

"Arrest them," Hellebore confirmed, but Rowan was shouldering her way through the crowd towards the patch of brightness beyond the wall, as all heck broke out.

"Rowan, wait! You have a chance if you stay."

"But you don't, Dew. So, we need to fly."

"What you call flying, I call falling!"

It was nice, I suppose, that my fear brought a grin to her face. I wasn't even afraid of heights before today. But this was a moment for trust, and how could I not trust my saviour?

She made the opening before the descending guards—my heart thudding as we cleared the oaken wall—covered the platform in three strides, and leapt out into the wide, blue sky.

"Rowan!!"

This had become a seriously bad habit.

19

Radiant colours peppered the lush, verdant carpet of Fairyland, rolling out below as far as I could see, and I was now an absconder, maybe even accused of attempted fairy regicide. And, ironically, it seemed I was a flight risk.

Meanwhile, we continued plummeting elegantly at the ground. A brown flash swept in close then swooped away, closed, swooped away. I knew this drill, and grabbed feathers when the chance came, then was jerked upwards like pulling a parachute's ripcord. I was on Fleet-wing's back again, and I felt safe. The swift climbed hard, and I pulled some g's before we levelled out to cruise above the lush landscape of Fairyland.

"What have you done?" I had to yell at Rowan, crouched in front of me.

"What?"

I shimmied up behind her—conscious of my knees digging into Fleet-wing's feathers—and snaked my arms around her waist, then pulled myself tight against her.

"Better?" I asked.

"I can hear you better, if that was your motive."

"Basically, you've incriminated yourself. For me."

"I did what was right," she said.

"You did"—I hugged her tighter—"in an honourable sense, if not in a legal one. It's just as well you have an ace lawyer."

A body of water passed beneath us, golden light shimmering on its surface. It drew my squinting gaze ahead. I could make out hulking, solitary sentinel trees amid pastures, dark spinneys and copses atop this knoll or that hill. To our left, the verdant canopy of a huge forest. And these things had human scale. I still didn't understand how I was the size of Rowan, and how the goblins on Cobalt Hill Road had been human child-sized. A mystery for another day, if I had one before being turned to stone, or some other cruel and unusual punishment.

A roseate smudge on the horizon caught my eye, and I watched it grow as we whistled towards it. I thought it must be a tree but, as Fleet-wing shredded the distance, I saw that it was a plant growing over not just one tree, but dozens, covering the summit of a low, round hill. The colour resolved as we approached, intensifying as the haze of distance faded to reveal a violently lurid magenta dome of blooms shrouding the hilltop. It was good to have a landmark at last. Even though I had no idea where this was in Berkshire, I now had a reference point to orient myself relative to Titania's oak by way of the lake, and probably would never get the chance to use it.

Fleet-wing trimmed her feathers, and we began to descend. The air noise reduced to the point that I could have a conversation with Rowan, or at least hear her reject my foolish questions. But, if my legal training had taught me anything it was to think before speaking, and to frame my questions. Okay, if my legal training had taught me two things, they were...

Just then, I realised that this fucked-up, fairy fever dream might be the sum total of my last moments. So, I might as well enjoy them, do all the things I wished I'd done in my world, like throwing myself at attractive women...or fairies.

"We'll get to Bougainvillea, to Oberon before Hedges, right?" Rowan stiffened, but I squeezed tighter and she relaxed. Still, her reaction was worrying. If he got there before us, presented the jam-jam to Oberon...

Whereas, if we prevented that, maybe we had a chance.

As we closed, Fleet-wing dove towards the hill that was a fairy city, accelerating when I thought she would brake.

"How do we get off!"

Rowan looked over her shoulder, smiling. "Jump, of course."

Of course.

20

I sat up, spitting loam from my mouth, rubbing my aching arms, and a twinge in my back. A hundred, hundred shapes and shades of green surrounded and towered over me. At least I was on the ground. That meant I couldn't fall any further, right?

Rowan had gripped me as we fell away from Fleet-wing, slowing my descent then shouted something about a soft landing as her hands slipped from under my armpits, and I tumbled, top over tail, towards the blanket of green. I did not appreciate her parting shot: "Grow some wings!"

I staggered up and pushed between huge, velvety foxglove leaves— their massive bell-shaped flowers, white and pink—hanging high above me, and emerged onto a stone-paved path as wide and leafy as Winkfield Lane back in Maiden's Green. That thought made me realise how much I missed it. I looked up and down the path, refusing to be distracted by the pretty, pinkish light permeating the canopy so very high above me. I was alone.

Where had Rowan got to? I'd be lost without her, wouldn't I? I looked down the path again towards the heart of the city. There! Two figures approached. Rowan was one. I jumped up, hoping the other was Hedges, and that she had him by the neck, having intercepted the jam-jam. But there was no wooden wine case, no sack, and the other figure was not a leather-faced goblin, but a portly, bearded man with wild, bright russet hair. As they neared I saw his round face split with a smile, but...it couldn't be. I ran forward, filled with anxious energy. I peered, not at Rowan—who was a sight for sore eyes, and I only wanted to throw my arms around her—but at the other.

Green shirt, yellow waistcoat, red trousers, and a jaunty black cap on his head were an odd disguise, but it was him. I gaped. How on Earth could my boss, and senior partner of Biron Woolf Lodge, be *here*? *Now*?! This surely was the closest thing to confirmation that the whole of Fairyland was a concoction of a coma dream. And Rowan took this interloper in her confident stride, as if people—humans—crossed over all the time. As if she knew him.

"Mister Biron?"

"Yes, yes, and also no," Mr. Biron beamed. A doppelganger? He sounded exactly like...himself, on one of his happy-go-lucky, never-mind-the-deadline, ice-cream-for-everyone days.

I looked at Rowan. She shrugged. Her disgruntled look said, 'What?'

"'Round here I'm Robin Goodfellow, but you can call me Puck. We've met before, that much is true: you look confused as—"

"Wait. So, you *are* Mr. Biron, eminent QC, head of chambers, senior partner of BWL, general bigwig in the City of London? But you *also* are a fictitious character of myth, legend and Shakespeare? That's ridiculous." I turned on Rowan. "Who is this to you?"

She frowned. "Robin Goodfellow, Oberon's jester, and his emissary."

Biron chuckled, smacking his considerable yellow-clothed paunch with both hands as if to confirm he was real.

"That's right, I am his fixer too, I run all over town. I do my best, by task and jest, to banish every frown. But you're puzzled, that's too bad, you've such a pretty smile. It is the case, I found a place, in London's grand Square Mile. Now Rowan here's explained your plight, and Hedges' misdemeanours. Let's buckle down, right his wrongs, and take him to the cleaners."

Very slowly, I put my head in my hands, rubbed my face then set my jaw, piercing Goodfellow with a hard look. "Hellebore's the villain here. Isn't he?" Rowan looked uncertain.

"He is unpleasant and dishonourable, Dew, but there's no proof he handled the Grand Jam, or knew of it before Titania's court did."

She was right.

Goodfellow (Oh. Robin, Biron, I see.) took a deep breath to fuel another rhyme, but I held my hand up.

"We don't have time for this. I have to save Rowan and myself by retrieving the jam-jam before Oberon explodes." I looked at her and my anger melted. She looked miserable. I reached out, and gripped her arm. "I won't go without your good name restored."

"Ah, the jam, I well recall, its taste, so sweet and silky. That time you brought it into work, and made me tea"—his expression turned rueful—"too milky." Then he looked up, beaming. No smile so bright had ever touched Mr. Biron's lips in my world.

"No," I said, pointing at him. "No more rhyming. What do you know about the jam-jam? Help us, please, whoever you are."

His expression became sombre, even downcast. "The jam came to me. A surprising, tasty boon. I shared it with friends."

"You did what?" Rowan snapped. "You said you'd help me. Hedges brought it to you? You should have told me!"

"Giving is pleasure. New experience tastes sweet. But the truth prevails."

"Hang on." I planted fists on my hips. "You're talking in haiku now. I said no rhyming."

"But haiku don't rhyme," Biron/Robin protested.

"You're an anagram," I said.

He looked offended. "A factotum, in fact; to King Oberon himself."

"Argh!" I exclaimed. "My friend Rowan has lost Titania's favour because of this. I stand an excellent chance of becoming a garden ornament. Wait, if you're in both places...Wait! I brought jam-jam to the office, made great ceremony of serving it to you on scones with clotted cream, and tea—"

"Too milky." He shook his head ruefully.

"You knew what it was, but still dished it out anyway? And, if you're fae, why did you not explode?"

"To err is human," he said. "Like me. I knew not of its poten-cy."

"Ignorance is no excuse," I said, icily. "Will you speak to Titania, make things right for Rowan, take us to the jars?" I grasped his forearm. "Please. Now."

Biron, Robin Goodfellow—honest to goodness Puck himself—nodded, his features a picture of contrition. "I've done you wrong, I'm sad to say, my crimes heinous and many. But I will set, all things to right, ere you can spend a penny."

"I...Well," I frowned. "It's the least you can do."

"The least," said Rowan.

Puck nodded. And he did it. He took us to a cave that must have been a burrow of some sort, and there was Hedges' sack. I counted forty-nine jars, which seemed reasonable, accounting for the breakages, and the Hedges' gluttony.

Robin announced, "I've done it, that much is for certain. Though there's something perhaps I should mention. While most of the pots, are in what you've got, there's one that's a bone of contention."

"Tell us," I demanded.

"From the box in the car, it's not very far. I left it for Oberon's breakfast."

"Oh, shit," I said.

21

"There's only one thing worse than Titania frowning upon you," said Rowan, glowering as we strode in Puck's bustling wake.

"Both of them with their knives out?" I grimaced when our glances met.

Rowan touched my arm. She looked vulnerable, even scared, although she tried to hide it. Petrification, and garden centres. I shuddered.

"We have to hurry, and no mistake," Puck called over his shoulder. "Time's too short to mention." His words were gasps. "The king is in his parlour now, plates earning his attention. If he should bite into the jam, and lose his sensibil'ty, his wrath will be an awful thing, and you will both be guilty."

It was less his sensibility that I was worried about than his head exploding. "Without trial?" I asked.

"Yes," he said.

22

We trotted along the path long enough that I began to think the scenery was moving, while we jogged on the spot.

Without warning, Rowan's arm barred my way. Then I noticed the crowd, and realised the growing buzz was not in my head. There must have been two or three hundred fairies, and other weird and wonderful creatures, most on the ground, but some in the air, their chatter crackling like a faulty toaster.

The assembly pressed in a semi-circle around a cluster of brown—frankly, dead-looking—bushes, lolling leaves like sickly tongues, dry and knotted, jaggy like gone-over brambles. This edifice of weeds would not have looked out of place on an abandoned allotment, or neglected greenhouse. The mass of dry leaves shook violently, the whole grove quivered as the crowd looked on, taught with nervous anticipation. Half of the fae seemed on the verge of breaking and running.

A tattered and dishevelled form lurched from the tangled mass, growling. The dark, shaggy figure—six feet tall, even hunched over—shook himself like a big, wet dog. No, more massive, like a bear, irascible at being forced from hibernation.

Then I saw the dishes spread before this unkempt entity that must be Oberon, the Fairy King, plates circling his overgrown knoll, a cornucopia of culinary tributes.

The great grizzly of a being straightened, rubbed his eyes, yawning. Nine feet tall now, clad in furs and pelts that smelled truly awful—even from here—he scratched his shaggy beard. Fragments of...something fell. He yawned again, prodigiously.

"Where's my breakfast?!"

"Before you, royal Oberon!" Robin blurted, staggering forwards from the crowd, tiptoeing between plates, tottering through the regal repast: fruit, pies, cereals and preserves.

Preserves.

"Oberon!" I shouted without thinking, felt the brush of Rowan's fingertips on my arm as I sprang forward beyond her reach. "Sire, no!" I was some way behind Puck, surprisingly nimble given his girth. "The jam, Robin. We talked about this!" Was he going back on his promise of aid, or making a desperate attempt to retrieve the jam-jam?

The king of Fairyland tossed food around, pronouncing his verdict after no more than a bite: "Too salty. Too dry. Too crunchy."

A Scotch egg whistled past my ear. Puck stooped towards a tray that bore a single jar. To snatch it away, right? I should offer support. I stopped, and called over the hubbub. "That jam is unworthy of you, majesty. Do not eat it!"

The whizz of wings and general cacophony ceased at once. The hulking dishevelled tramp that was Oberon regarded me—stranded as I was in the centre of the clearing, arrayed in my green and purple finery, trying not to tread in what appeared to be a bucket of custard.

He glowered from beneath a stormy brow. "Says who?"

All eyes turned on me; appraising, judging, awaiting an explanation.

"Says me. Dew-Leeya Green-Street." I faced the collective stare of hundreds of fairies, goblins, pixies? Brownies? Fauns? Surreal perhaps but—in the end—it compared quite well to my average audience in court. If I tried to rationalise this, there was an excellent chance of *my* head exploding, so I didn't. I kept going, because this was my last chance.

"Your majesty this jam-jam—while the grandest of jams—is a human thing, a concoction not of your world, but of another place. I've seen it render creatures of your beautiful realm quite insensible...or worse. Certain ingredients, noble Oberon, will steal your reason, and muddle your mind. I strongly recommend against it, your majesty."

So rapt was our audience that those still airborne descended, seemingly unable to hover and gape at the audacious interloper at the same time.

Oberon made grumbling sounds. "Be this true, Puck? If 'tis, 'twould be displeasing. It smells so...sweet."

Puck was wafting the scent of the jam towards his king! How *could* he? Not only not helping, but hindering, and wearing a big smile on his face. I looked back to Rowan, my hands spread in a 'What the actual…' gesture, but she looked as perplexed as I felt, and ready to give Puck a sound thrashing.

"Great and august Oberon," a clear, confident tone soared over the crowd, dispersing its murmur. Hellebore. "This human waif is quite lost, misdirected in fact. Not an hour since, she behaved poorly in Titania's court—may she shine at dawn and glow at dusk. In fact, the human absconded, aided by Rowan Nightshade, and she is the source of this heinous jam."

"Is this true, waif?" Oberon rumbled, lips curving down with distaste.

I turned to find Rowan at the front of the colourful crowd. She bristled with anger, but I saw her trepidation. I shook my head in case she had any notions of coming to my aid. This time, I must defend myself. I took a deep breath, dusted down my bodice, fluffed my tutu, and raised my chin. This was still a court, ignorant of the tenets of modern justice, but a court nonetheless, a place where fairness should matter.

"Your majesty," I bowed low, realising while staring into a bowl of roast potatoes that the folk behind me had an eye-opening view. "I will admit I've made mistakes, but I would like the opportunity to give my account of events. Perhaps Master Hellebore would do the same, then you might honour us with the wisdom of your judgement. This is the way things are done in my world."

"Wha' do I care for that?" Oberon thundered.

"Justice," I felt my confidence rising as I claimed *my* arena. "Justice is one of the pillars of any society. American Justice Potter Stewart said, 'Fairness is what justice is.'" I made another—somewhat shallower—bow towards Oberon's shambolic majesty. "I am sure you would want, above all things, to be seen by your adoring subjects to be fair."

"Sure, are you? Hmph."

"Why, Dew-Leeya," Hellebore interceded. "Do you mean to imply his majesty is not just? That would be ghastly impertinence."

"I *am* just." Oberon roared like a drunk whose boot was kicked by a passing copper, and told to move on. "I'll hear her," he slapped his thigh, and a little cloud of dust puffed up. "And you, Hellebore, as Titania's advisor, will challenge her."

"Of course, your majesty." Scabious' acceptance dripped sweeter than the Grand Jam itself.

Then Oberon said the strangest thing.

"Right! Oxford-style debating rules." He clapped his hands. "The motion is that Dew-Leeya Green-Street brought a vile poison to Fairyland, and that Rowan Nightshade aided and abetted her in this foul action by failing in her duty to prevent it." His gruff, stone-grinding drawl was gone, replaced by clear and powerful tones. His whiskers seemed tidier. I blinked. His frame upright now, and toned. "Scabious Hellebore, proposer." Oberon stalked around the clearing like a boxer baiting his crowd. Long, quick strides brought him to stand directly before me. "Choose your second wisely, interloper."

"I..." What in the devil was going on? Hostile faces curved away on either side. Oberon was transformed into a different being. He ran a hand through greasy, tangled rat-tails, and his mop flowed into lustrous waves. He blinked, and rheumy eyes became pin sharp, boring into me. And then, he shook out his rags, and—

He was wearing a royal blue Brioni brunico suit, and he looked *sharp*. Oberon was transformed.

"First," he bellowed, "the opening vote! All those in favour of the motion."

"Aye!" came the resounding cheer from all and sundry around the clearing.

"Those against?" Not a single nay was heard.

"The 'ayes' have it. You have your work cut out, Dew-Leeya." He grinned, eyes glittering with menace then barked those so-familiar instructions. "You have two minutes each: first proposer; first opposer; second proposer; second opposer. Two-minute summation to close," his powerful voice filled the cathedral-like clearing. "Then the assembly will decide your fate. And"—he boomed, the crowded creatures hanging on his every word—"I think petrification is too good for you."

23

My mouth dropped open, but gaping was not a good look at the start of a debate. "No," I growled as the crowd roared approval. Wings buzzing mockingly. Rowan approached, leaning in, our foreheads almost touching. At another time I'd have lost my cool, grabbed the back of her neck, and pressed myself against her, but my unruffled (ironic in this skirt) courtroom demeanour was taking over.

"Stop flashing your tutu," she said, her dark eyes twinkling like distant supernovae. "We need to do something, or we'll be stone forever."

"How's your debating?" I shook my head. "Never mind." Wait, who was Hellebore's second?

I turned to see Robin "Pucking" Goodfellow putting his head together with Scabby Hellebore, while King "High-and-Mighty" Oberon clapped each of them on the shoulder. Hellebore smirked, and Goodfellow beamed. That dirty rat! He had two-timed us. My changeling employer was a turncoat. I should have known it. Titania and Oberon's bad lieutenants acting in concert. I snorted, turned back to Rowan. Court head on. Focus.

"You go first for us, after they open. Don't get angry. Don't overcomplicate. Just tell the truth." Her brow furrowed. I wanted to press my lips to it, smooth away her doubts with kisses. "Most important, keep it brief." I clapped a hand on her leather-clad shoulder. "I'll do the heavy lifting this time."

Goodfellow took to the forest floor.

"The jam is here," Robin proclaimed, gazing over the assembly, arms outstretched, overacting wildly. "What sympathy doth the mode of its conveyance attract? Not a jot. And yonder parties' guilt"—he pointed at us, voice swelling and receding on every syllable like an amateur-dramatic air raid siren—"is as clear as the sickly ruby hue of those glinting vessels of Hades," he indicated the jar at Oberon's feet. "Yet what vessel could contain your sorrow at noble Oberon's demise? None! So, friends, levy the price of your woe, the account of your despair, against these miscreants"—he whirled to face us—"and make... Them... PAAAAAY!" Twirling away—daintily for a stouter chap—he exited the stage to resounding cheers and general acclimation.

Rowan frowned, regarding our opponents. Hellebore returned her stare, smirking coldly. Rowan grunted, rolled her shoulders like a boxer. For a heartbeat, I thought she was going to go for him. "Debating is a non-contact—" She waved my words aside, and strode forward to the centre of the clearing, honeysuckle breeze ruffling her long hair.

"The Grand Jam is not vile, just foreign. It's revered in the human realm, and Dew-Leeya was not even trying to enter Fairyland. It was an accident."

"Boo."

"For shame!"

"Cast them out!"

"No interruptions," Oberon roared. His regal glare skewered the guilty parties, the mere pointing of his royal finger made them squirm in discomfort. "Continue."

Rowan hmphed. "Thieves stole the Grand Jam from Dew-Leeya, and brought it here. Then *he*"—her fairy digit condemned Robin Goodfellow—"sought to poison our lord Oberon! For how else could the Grand Jam come before his majesty?"

The crowd gasped, growled and groaned, gabbled and guffawed, gossiped and giggled. Many sneered, seemingly decided on our fate, but some regarded Hellebore and Puck with narrowed-eyed suspicion. A decent start. Rowan had done well, and kept it admirably brief. She returned to me, vexation compressing her lips, hiding their full softness. I took her hand.

"Well done." I smiled, disguising my relief that she hadn't injured anyone in her allotted time. No sooner had that thought entered my head than she leapt away into the crowd, returning from the midst of a kerfuffle with Box Hedges' ear clamped between her fingers, and the rest of the nefarious goblin hanging from it.

"We'll deal with you as soon as we're done with these two," she advised the snivelling fae.

Then Hellebore paced to the clearing's centre. Clamour died to susurration, which crumbled into hush.

"Lies," he said into the silence. "Questions. Obfustication. Miss direction. In sin certainly." He nodded slowly. "Whose jam is it? Where did it come from? Would noble Oberon be at risk if not for this...*woman*, this *human*? Have you ever known them to make anything but trouble for the fae? Are we not left to pick up and re-use the pieces after their ignorant and insensitive blunders? You remember the debacle at Cottingley? The meddling of the wretched Conan Doyle? The foul propaganda in the paintings of Lanseer and Paton? And I trust you know never to mention Vivian Leigh's performance to our *true* Titania?" Hellebore rolled his eyes. I could hear the murmurings of agreement. "We fae are ever the butt of human comedy, the victims of their lascivious imaginations. And this woman has the nerve to paint *herself* as the victim? How do you feel about that?"

Uproar. Tumult. Pandemonium.

My time had come. I did not know enough for fine detail. Too many facts remained obscure. I set Rowan's fate in my sights—since thinking of mine made me queasy—and stepped forward.

I felt that every denizen of Fairyland looked on, jostling and jeering. I stared around as I walked to the middle of the court, screwing my courage to the sticking place, as Lady Macbeth urged her husband to do: a favourite quote of mine. But I was innocent...wasn't I? *Calm, Dew-Leeya, calm. Do your thing.*

"Do you know the Hedges?" I let that sink in: gossip is a powerful force. "Do you think them capable of theft?" The crowd quieted, listening at least. "What would they do with their ill-gotten gains?" *Because we all agree they're crooks, right?* "Who would they consult about stuff from another world? Whose knowledge surpasses yours—" an open hand towards them—"and mine"—a hand to my own heart, linking me to my audience. "Whose knowledge spans Titania's glorious heavens, and who jumps to Oberon's command?" Pause for effect. Only one correct answer but, just in case. "To whom does the sky itself surrender its secrets? Yes"—flatter them for their wisdom—"you're right: Scabious Hellebore, Titania's Astral Lodger. And only one hand could place the Grand Jam in royal Oberon's repast: Robin Goodfellow," my outstretched finger declaimed him across the clearing. "Scabious Hellebore is guilty. Robin Goodfellow is guilty!"

I didn't need two minutes. I didn't even need one. I closed there, said nothing further, simply bowed to Oberon—*there goes the tutu again*—and returned to Rowan. My argument was met with hoots and calls, but Rowan was smiling. I turned. The collected fae were clapping, smiling, flapping and buzzing. We had a chance.

"Summation!" roared Oberon over the racket.

Hellebore walked out again, nodding slowly.

"How like a human to bring a debate about their mistakes around to our character, and our ways? How flighty are the fae? How unreliable? How tricky, with their bargains, their contracts, and their deals? No, this debate is about humans, and their disregard for everything fae and fantastical. Well, I say let them do the honourable thing for once—the just thing, the right thing."

I stood gobsmacked as the clearing erupted around me.

Hellebore had bushwhacked me, exploded his own proposition, taken a debate about jam and made it about—what—speciesism? Even as its anger cooled, the crowd buzzed disgruntlement, shimmered dissatisfaction.

"Rebuttal," lowering Oberon growled.

I stirred myself, stepped forward again with no idea what to say, stood in the centre of an impossible glade, eyed by incredible, unbelievable creatures awaiting my condemnation of myself, of Rowan. I looked to my dark and daring saviour, and I knew. They had already decided.

We were lost.

"The only thing that separates us is division, and division comes from desire. Desire for different things. But do we not all want the same things, really? To be happy, healthy, and wise? To love, and be loved?

"I've made mistakes." I had. I'd given up on Devondra. "Been careless, and thoughtless." Driving too fast. Children or goblins, it didn't matter.

"I'm sorry. I apologise to you all."

I turned in a circle of sun-spangled fairy faces, a kaleidoscope of colours, shapes and sizes. This was Wonderland, and it had fallen into my lap, as well as I into its. I extended a hand to Rowan. For all her brusque bravado, her frown faded, and she walked to me, after daring Hedges to move and see what happened to him. I grasped her hand, and she squeezed mine. I pulled her close, tilted my face up to meet hers and kissed her.

I turned to Oberon with the courage of a fresh kiss coursing through me. Chin up, defiant in the face of his antagonism.

"I'm guilty of pride, insensitivity, and dangerous driving." My voice rose, daring him to call time on me. "But I'm innocent of any desire to harm either of your majesties"—I boomed these words as best I could—"or this land, and its fine peoples!" The assembly cheered, Hellebore scowled, and Goodfellow beamed. "Punish me for my mistakes if you must—and maybe you should—but if you'll teach me, educate me in your ways, I'll swear undying fealty. Cleanse Rowan of blame for my faults, and you'll have my loyalty to the end of my days."

Oberon stood, arms akimbo—resplendent in his Brioni—and smiled. The crowd cheered, the oddest cacophony of hoots, chirrups, yells, and grunts.

"Agreed," the king boomed, and the buzzing of wings filled the clearing. "That rather was the point of this interview, all along," he grinned.

"You're hired."

24

Mister Biron, aka Robin Goodfellow—Biron Woolf Lodge's rotund senior partner—grinned at Julia, and beckoned her into his office.

"I hope your...holiday has you in tiptop form, and ready for the fray. We have a raft of new cases for you."

She entered the frosted glass box, barely glancing at the too-familiar portraits of the plump imposter, chumming up with his most infamous clients: the (alleged) fraudster; the (alleged) embezzler; the government minister (guilty as charged). She turned on him.

"No rhyming couplets today? No fancy dress and haiku? I mean, Chief Counsel to Fairyland? Could you not just have told me it was all a cruel and manipulative job interview?"

"Well now," he glanced at the door, ensuring it was closed, she suspected. "Those fae clients of ours have a rather...fanciful way of working."

"They don't have legal structures, a judiciary. Is there a body of jurisprudence, a precedent book?"

He smiled. "I wouldn't worry about those. I'm sure you'll muddle through," he winked. "There *is* lots of work to do. We should crack on, don't you think, Dew-Leeya? The sooner we get you briefed, the sooner you can get back to Fairyland."

"Well," Julia smiled. "It's hard to argue against the proposition."

She was very much looking forward to jumping off that particular cliff again, and into Rowan Nightshade's arms.

This is Robin's first foray into publication, but there is more in the pipeline, and hopefully the first Quirk & Moth novel will be available soon. You can catch up with RCMD at **www.robincmduncan.com** or **@ROBINSKI**, and find him on Goodreads from time to time. Check out some of the story behind the anthology at Mary Robinette Kowal's "My Favorite Bit," August 5th, 2021.

Killer Trees and Second Chances

An Evanstar Chronicles Story

Sara Codair

Sapphic Representation: Lesbian, Bi/Pan, Ace/Demi, Nonbinary
Heat Level: Low
Content Warnings: Violence, Gore, Suicidal Thoughts

Author's Note: The Evanstar Chronicles *is an urban fantasy series that follows Erin and Mel, two young demon hunters trying to save the world while dealing with mental health issues. Elves, angels, and demons exist in their universe along with beings who are part-elf or angel. "Killer Trees and Second Chances" is a tale of Mel and Erin's future, nearly three centuries after the end of the series...well a potential future. As Yoda says, "Difficult to see. Always in motion is the future."*

Humans could reproduce with their fae counterparts—the Elves—and create children more powerful than either of their parents. We hypothesized the same would happen with the trees if we bred them with their fae counterparts. However, we underestimated the level of sentience they would have. We underestimated their hunger and intelligence, and never imagined they would eat the humans we were trying to save.

Erin wanted to burn the hybrid forest down, but it was as alive and aware as any human. I couldn't kill it. So I convinced Erin to contain it instead.

-From the personal journal of Amelia "Mel" Evanstar

1

Mel opened her eyes to a looming forest and giant gaps in her memory. There'd been a...a jet? Broken bones? Healing. Someone missing?

She pushed up to sitting position and ran her hands through her hair. Her fingers snagged on snarly curls. Her hand hurt. Her back hurt. Her stomach hurt. *Everything* hurt. She made the mistake of shaking her head, which made her brains feel like they were being spun in a blender.

Telepathic rustling filled her mind. What was that? Whatever it was did *not* belong in her brain. She tried and failed to construct the mental shields she used to keep other people's thoughts out of her head, just like the barrier she'd made to keep the trees in. To keep them from overtaking the earth.

Free us to multiply! the trees whispered in her mind.

Free us to be rid of us.

Free us and we will free your cousin.

Cousin? She had a cousin? She...yes. Erin. Erin, the once angry, depressed teen who bound their life force to Mel's to save her. A binding that could never be undone. *Where is Erin? What did you do to them?*

Erin lies in the lab where you made us. The place you must go to free us so we can spread across the Earth. Where we can eat.

"Oh shit." There was a reason the trees were contained, forbidden from spreading. They were carnivores, with a taste for human flesh. She couldn't free them.

Erin will suffer until you free us.

The murky forest gave way to an image of Erin, clad in a tattered flight suit, bound to a tree by thorny vines that twined around their limbs and crowned their head. The room was familiar, and Mel searched her shattered memories to place it. It was nearby. Yes. On a...mountain? Yes! The summit of the mountain that she could see from where she sat at its base.

Erin? Mel whispered to her cousin.

Mental images returned, of vines twining around toppled shelves, frozen food and seed containers strewn about the floor. Erin's green eyes were open and glaring directly at Mel. Like Erin was looking through the trees, right at her.

Burn it down, Erin whispered in a parched voice. *I never should have listened to you. We should have burned the forest from the start. It's time to right your mistake.*

The vines tightened, thorns digging in, and Mel felt an empathetic pain in her own flesh. Erin laughed in defiance, then the image and the pain were gone.

Hurry, the trees whispered. *Our patience grows thin.*

Mel shuddered. No matter how much she disapproved of Erin's use of money and their powers, she still hated to see her cousin suffer.

Hold on, Erin. I'm coming.

No response.

Mel reached out for their mental link and found...nothing. Emptiness. Well, emptiness and trees. What the hell? That connection had never been broken. Never blocked. Severing her mind from Erin's should not have been possible!

Set us free and you will be whole again. Let us multiply. Let us feed.

"No!" Mel yelled then sneezed, the air thick with a yellow pollen that tickled her nose and brain. She loved Erin, but she couldn't set a murderous, sentient forest free to spread across an unsuspecting Earth. Especially since it had been her idea to splice fae and terrestrial DNA to begin with. It was her fault the forest existed. Her fault that it hadn't been destroyed.

Lower the barrier. Lower the barrier. Lower the barrier, chanted the trees. *Lower the barrier and we will let Erin go. We will let them go. Dally, or burn us, and everyone you love will burn, too.*

Everyone she loved...

The jet.

The crash.

Who else...

Oh, oh no. The memory spun across Mel's mind, thick and haunting. Erin had been in the jet, along with her former girlfriend, Amaryllis.

Amaryllis. She'd been injured. Mel had healed her body but not the feelings she and Amaryllis once shared—now twisted and torn by cowardice and lies.

She loved Amaryllis. She loved Erin too, despite how far apart they'd grown. But the trees had to be stopped first. Humanity had to come first.

Hurry, the trees demanded.

Mel stood. Lean pines, clad with needles, wicked and sharp, stretched toward the sky. Densely packed except for where the ground was bare and rocky. No sign of Erin, or Amaryllis. Mel knew she'd healed Amaryllis, but what if the trees had eaten her after Mel passed out? The trees she created. She dragged her fingers along her scalp. Pulled her hair. She might as well have killed Amaryllis herself.

But Erin was nearly indestructible. They'd be fine. Right? Could she lose either of them, and still be whole? Was she even whole herself? She felt...exhausted. She ached. Like if she sat down and closed her eyes, she'd sleep again even though her world—she, herself—was unraveling at the seams. *Your power isn't replenishing, is it?* whispered the trees. *Keep us in your mind all you like. We can keep busy here, with you. With your power.*

"Shit." Mel fell to the ground, dizzy. Rough dirt scraped her arms. The trees were doing this to her. She inhaled, air thick with pollen, as she struggled to her feet.

This is what it feels like to be mortal, whispered the trees. *As you will be if you do not free us.*

"Carol?" A voice, warm and rough, came from the forest. "Are you here?"

It took Mel a minute to remember she was Carol, the alias she had been using for a couple years. Or was it decades?

"Amaryllis!?" Mel ran through the forest, toward the voice. A burst of hope. A rush of adrenaline. There Amaryllis was, standing on the vein of granite that cut a path through the forest. Short curls crowned the top of her head. Her skin was slick with sweat. There was a fresh scrape on her cheek, but she was there, and whole, and still breathing.

Mel opened her arms.

"You do not get to hug me." Amaryllis glared at her with her arms crossed. "Not after all your lies."

Mel stopped like she'd run into a brick wall. Air rushed out of her lungs as the last few months came back like a slap in the face. The fights. Remembered words echoed in her mind. *You work too much, Mel. Are you in this or not? You're keeping secrets. What aren't you telling me? If you won't commit, we're done.* Amaryllis packing her bags. And then being assigned together for this mission—whatever it was— despite what they'd been through. Because Erin wanted them both here.

"You have any idea how to get out of here?" A hard anger permeated Amaryllis's voice.

"Yes." Mel just needed to get her bearings. *Think of a way to get Amaryllis out without letting the trees out.* Getting in the dome that surrounded the forest was one thing. Getting out was an entirely different process. One she couldn't quite picture. Because the trees were messing with her memory. Dammit.

The only way out is to let us out.

"How do we get *out*?" Amaryllis growled.

There were vines creeping across the granite. Rustling. Something rushing through the trees.

"Get down!" Mel screamed, drawing her machete as Amaryllis ducked, just before a branch snapped forward, whipping through the air where Amaryllis's head had been a second ago.

A serpent made of twisted vine and root rushed them. Mel's muscles burned as she ran forward and bisected the vine snake, only to find three more speeding out of the woods. Mel closed her eyes, took a deep breath, and drew power from her depleted reserves of energy so she could move fast, faster than any human. Faster than the trees. Time stood still for a moment. Vine-monsters hung in midair and she sliced them like pizza, one, two, three.

Three heads hit the forest floor. The machete dripped bright red tree sap.

"I..." She dropped the machete. Pain filled her head, along with an unforgiving pressure. Blood dripped down her nose. She collapsed to the ground, amongst the tattered vine snake and its severed heads. She didn't have enough power for this. If the trees kept attacking, if she drained the last of her reserves, there would be no saving Erin. There would be no saving herself.

Please, no more, Mel sent.

Free us! More branches sprang to life. They whipped Mel's back, tearing flesh that healed almost as quickly as it was torn—taking more and more of Mel's power.

If you kill me, you'll never be free, Mel told the trees.

Without her connection to Erin, she could not regenerate her power. Without her connection to Erin, she was mortal, and would die in this forest.

Another branch cracked against her back.

FREE US! TO THE LAB. HURRY!

"Mel?"

Amaryllis walked to her and offered her hand, her face hesitant and worried. She eyed the vines, which turned to 'watch' her, but did not attack.

"Have to go to the lab," Mel said. She took Amaryllis's hand and, just for a moment, let herself remember the warmth of Amaryllis's skin, the dexterity of her fingers.

"Don't get any ideas," Amaryllis said. She pulled Mel to her feet. The vines edged forward.

"Run?" Amaryllis asked.

"Walk, I think," Mel responded. "As fast as we can. Toward the dome."

Hurry! the trees said.

I could have gone faster if you hadn't cut up my back, she shot back.

The trees did not answer.

Mel and Amaryllis walked along the granite path, Amaryllis's hand as frigid as Mel's emotions. Vines followed, occasionally nipping at Mel's heels. Blood dripped down her back, staining her pants and marking their path with reddened footprints.

"Over there," Mel said, pointing to a rocky ledge free of trees and vines. "I need to rest. Just for a moment."

Amaryllis helped Mel to a large, flat boulder on the edge of the ledge. The wind tossed Amaryllis's hair across her face, and with the blood and the welts and the insistent trees, Mel clung to the familiar.

"Thank you," she said. "Sit with me?"

"Argh, Carol. No. I want to kiss you right now, but I also want to strangle you. Sitting next to you will only make it worse."

We will strangle your cousin if you do not let down the barrier, hissed the trees.

Mel could hardly hear them over the pounding of her own heart. Over the furnace of hope burning in her chest. "I'd rather you kiss me. I'd hoped you'd forgiven me."

Amaryllis stared out into the darkness, at the barely visible outline of gnarly bark and wicked needles. "You're a liar, Carol. But you saved my life. You almost burnt out saving my life. You're flickering like—"

"Do not call me a light bulb," Mel said, anticipating the comparison people always made when she overstressed her abilities.

"Light bulb?" Amaryllis's face contorted with confusion.

Mel rubbed her temples. Right. People didn't use those anymore. "Amaryllis, this forest, it's not normal."

"No shit." Amaryllis wiped sweat off of her face, smearing dirt across it.

"I made it. With my cousin. But it went horribly wrong, so we created an energy barrier and ward to keep the trees from spreading. They want revenge. And freedom." Mel reached for Amaryllis, who jerked away.

"Liars don't get to touch me," Amaryllis spat.

"I'm sorry. I...the trees have my cousin. We need to rescue them."

Amaryllis crossed her arms. "What's your cousin's name?"

"Erin," Mel said hesitantly. They probably had an alias too, but Mel couldn't remember what it was.

"Oh." Amaryllis's eyes widened as a grin bloomed on her face. She put a hand on Mel's shoulder—rough but warm. "Cass...Cassandra Phoenix...My boss. New boss for test piloting. Old boss for demon hunting. She is your cousin. She's ancient. A hybrid. A legend in the supernatural community. What a small, weird world."

"Erin uses they/them pronouns."

"Yes. Erin's pronouns are they/them, but Cass's are she/her."

And back when Mel and Erin had integrated genes from Faerie trees with Earth ones and planted them in the ruins of a massive state park, Erin had been Chris Phoenix, using he/him pronouns. Erin had used many pronouns over the years.

Amaryllis's grip tightened. "If you're her cousin...wow. Are you Mel? The oldest surviving angel-hybrid? You're a legend in the supernatural community."

"I am Mel. I'm three hundred, not thirty. A mix of angel, elf and human. As immortal as Erin." Mel glanced off the cliff, at miles and miles of deep green. "Well, I was. Until I crash-landed here and the trees got in my head. They're talking to me. Demanding I free them to get Erin back. To save your life, and theirs. Also I...my memory." She leaned into Amaryllis, her shoulder gently resting on Amaryllis's sternum. "My memory is faulty. I remember Erin. I remember...parts of you. I remember I love you."

Amaryllis swallowed, but didn't pull away. "Now isn't the time, Carol. Mel. Whoever you are."

Stop stalling!

Vines seethed on the adjacent trail, slapping each other down in their anxiousness to reach Mel and her vulnerable skin. Her headache became a tidal wave of pressure. She'd made the trees too well, their telepathic powers too strong. She'd dreamed an amazing future for them, but never *this*. They kept her from healing and...she could barely remember her youth, the last time she'd been unable to heal herself. She never learned how to be careful. She'd never been sick. She was immune to human pathogens. Without her energy replenishing, she'd be dead in a day if the trees kept at it.

Amaryllis sneezed, sending a wave of yellow pollen dancing in the air. "Damn allergies," she muttered. "Can we keep moving? I don't like the way the vines are looking at us, and your forehead is bony."

Mel sniffed and rubbed at her own nose. She closed her eyes and massaged her forehead, trying to remember if the hybrid tree pollen could affect memory, too. Memorized pages of medical texts and articles blurred. She shivered. How could she fight whatever they'd infected her head with if she couldn't remember anything about diseases? How the hell were they doing this? How could she rescue Erin? Keep Amaryllis alive? If there were trees in her head screwing with her memory? She had to keep moving. Get to the base. To Erin. To answers.

The forest experiment was the end of my friendship with Erin. Not because it failed, but because in the process, I realized how cold and ruthless they had become. How they sought to control the Earth. How they hoarded their billions when they could've repaired the damaged ecosystems, helped the starving people. In the end, Erin cared only for Erin.

-From the personal journal of Amelia "Mel" Evanstar

2

Ten minutes later Mel, with Amaryllis's help, managed to stand. They limped over to the path, where the vines took two whipcord slaps at the back of Mel's calves before lying flat on the ground, parallel, creating a terrifying trail.

The fresh welts stung in the humid air, and Mel's feet turned sticky with her blood as she and Amaryllis followed the vine path toward the dome. She could have healed the open wounds, and probably should have, but she'd decided instead to shove her remaining energy into her mental shields. Now—at least for the moment—the trees were silent. She had time for her thoughts, and her scattered memories, and the very beginning of a rescue plan. She just needed to keep the trees from 'overhearing' it, which meant she needed to put her mental shields back up.

Except...the shields drained her faster than healing. Damn! Mel couldn't catch a break in this Frankenstein forest—the monster of her own making. The throbbing in her head grew. Dizziness made the forest tilt and spin. Each time she inhaled, congestion built in her sinuses. It became harder to maintain her shields. To breathe. To think.

Her foot caught on a root, and she stumbled forward.

"Carol?" Amaryllis's voice cracked. "Do you think we can eat these?"

Fear drove Mel to her feet. Amaryllis studied something that looked like a cross between a ponderosa pine and a cactus, her hand mere inches away from its spiky green fruit. The needles on the cactirosa grew. The branch extended.

"Get away from that tree!"

Amaryllis threw herself away from the tree as a spike-laden branch whipped toward her. She crashed into Mel, knocking her to the ground. Mel's face flushed as Amaryllis landed on top of her. Mel twisted, rolling so she was on top, shielding Amaryllis with her striated backside.

A branch smacked Mel's back, sticking her with needles. The pain evoked fresh rage, fresh adrenaline. She dropped her shields to access her power, and sprung to her feet, chopping the next branch with her machete before it jabbed more needles in her back. Another came, and she cut it away. Then a third. Mel growled as she parried over and over. The last of her shields slipped away.

What treacherous thoughts have you been hiding? the forest demanded. *Tell us! Tell us! Free us!*

I just want my mind to be mine, Mel thought. Exhaustion weighed on her limbs. Muscles burned from the strain. But Mel kept fighting, dancing around Amaryllis with her blades out, slashing each branch as it came close.

But she was slowing. A branch slipped through her guard. Amaryllis dodged, only to run right into another spiky fruit. She screamed and batted the fruit away, further tearing her skin. Amaryllis's blood turned the ground a tattered red. Mel stared for a moment, transfixed by the blood, and Amaryllis's cries. A vine slapping her across the cheek refocused her thoughts.

"We need to run!" Mel shouted, helping Amaryllis up, shielding her as best she could.

Toward the base, Mel thought at the trees as she ran, fending off what attacks she could. *We're running to the base.*

We no longer believe you!

Roots snaked out and they both tumbled down onto a wide slab of exposed granite.

Amaryllis's wounds called out to Mel for healing. Fractured ribs. Punctures. One deep enough that it had penetrated Amaryllis's lung. Her breathing was labored. Adrenaline dulled her pain, just barely. She tried to sit up, and cried out.

Mel's hands flew toward her, pouring healing light into the wounds, watching them close. She should've stopped after healing the lung, but once she started, she couldn't. The wounds were too loud, too deep. She had to heal them all.

There was one precious moment after the last wound healed where everything felt right in the world. All the tension drained from Mel's body and a crushing weight lifted off of her chest. She was flying how she always longed to, floating on a glowing cloud.

"Mel, wake up!" Amaryllis pulled Mel tight against her. "Please don't be dead."

Mel opened her eyes. The pain rushed back. The guilt and fear crushed her. But Amaryllis was alive. Whole. Holding her. Mel's limbs turned to jelly, and tears came and she wasn't sure she was ever going to stop crying. But she had to. She had to pull herself together. Erin might have a ridiculous tolerance for pain, but Mel did not, whether it was her own or other people's.

Move or die!

Mel cupped Amaryllis's cheeks and stared into her eyes. Dark brown, almost black. Deep like the ocean. They were eyes Mel could stare into for hours. She drew strength from those eyes that reminded her why she needed to get up. "I promise I'll get you out of here. I promise. We're going to be okay."

"I hope you're right." Amaryllis let go of Mel and stepped back. Had Mel imagined the warmth? Maybe.

Move or DIE!

Mel sighed. "We should keep moving. I don't think we're too far from the summit."

Amaryllis helped Mel to her feet, but Mel staggered. She was so dizzy. The world spun into a blur of brown, green, and gray. Blood seeped from the wounds on her back. When she reached Erin, would she even be able to help?

There was nothing to do but move forward. To the lab. To the place where she could free the trees if she chose to.

You will choose to, the forest hissed.

Alright. Alright. I'm on my way.

Pressure lifted off Mel's head as they inched toward the lab, but her muscles tensed as they narrowed to single file. Tentatively, she stretched her mind out. She couldn't find Erin through their bond, but maybe once she was closer she could. Stretching her senses made her brains feel like they were strung out over a thorny briar. Yet another joy of low energy she'd all but forgotten about. She staggered again. She would've fallen had Amaryllis not caught her with strong, steady hands. Hands that guided jets through the sky.

The last time Mel had been so hurt, dizzy, seeing spots, barely able to stay upright...it was the day she all but died. The day Erin had bound their life together. She reached out again. Just on the edge of her awareness was a fiery rage emanating from Erin, but Mel couldn't quite touch that fire.

The feeling was followed by a searing headache that made Mel's brains feel like they were boiling.

DO NOT TRY TO TRICK US. IF YOU DON'T COMPLY, WE WILL WEAR YOU DOWN AND TAKE BOTH OF YOU OVER. WE'LL CONTROL YOUR POWER.

Power? What power? Mel was a living bruise with barely enough momentum to drag forward. She had no power left to take or give. It took all her effort just to keep moving forward.

"Carol, you're shaking."

"Mymph," said Mel, too tired to talk.

"Carol, did you hear me?" Amaryllis pulled her in, into the scent of strawberry and jet oil. "You are not allowed to leave me. You are not allowed to leave me *here*. Fight, damn it!"

"Sssnake," Mel managed, and she pointed a wobbling finger at yet another vine, coming to slap her into movement.

"Give me that and run!" Amaryllis took Mel's machete, grabbed her arm with her right hand and pulled her forward. "We can't fight this many. Run!"

She ran.

The trail was steep.

Pure adrenaline.

Survival instincts.

The need to protect those she loved.

Those feelings kept Mel going as the incline grew and the serpents snapped at their heels, pushing them closer and closer to the lab. The trees shrunk, grew more spaced out as granite replaced the soil. They kept going. The serpents stopped at the tree line, forming a wall, ensuring that Mel and Amaryllis could not turn back.

Ahead of them, loomed the lab. The top level was an enormous greenhouse, crowning the bare summit. A greenhouse filled with trees.

Earth stabilized. Humanity began to recover. My wife died. My mother died along with several other hybrids whose lives were longer than humans, but not as long as mine. Erin wasn't my only surviving family member, but they were the only one who fully lived in this world. Crushed by loss and loneliness, I immersed myself in my work, swearing I was done loving mortals. But mortals were all I had.

-From the personal journal of Amelia "Mel" Evanstar

3

Mel couldn't take another step. Every inch of her body throbbed. Her lungs burned with every breath. The only reason she remained upright was because Amaryllis kept her that way. Fresh cuts and bruises cried out to be healed, but Mel couldn't, no matter how bad she wanted to. And oh, did she want to heal them.

"If the trees want you there, why didn't they just take you like they took Erin?" Mel asked as they paused for breath just outside the greenhouse.

Mel sucked in air like a drowning fish and tried to stay on her feet. "They...needed us separate. To convince us to free them and...I think I'm easier to convince. Erin is...hard. Erin is *stubborn*."

"And what about me?" Amaryllis asked. "Why did they leave me alive and kill the rest of the crew?"

"Because they know I care about you." Mel held her hand and squeezed it. "If I don't free them, they'll kill you."

Amaryllis cocked her head to the side, a strange blend of curiosity and anger on her face. "So you'd set a forest of killer trees loose on an unsuspecting planet just to save me?"

Mel nodded. "If it was the only way to save you. I love you, Amaryllis."

"Yeah? Then why didn't you say that when we were dating. You were so distant. You lied about who you were. And now, now that we are in a forest with killer trees and you're dying in front of me, *now* you want to talk about love?" She slapped the machete against a too-eager vine. "Why, Mel?! Why did you lie?"

"I was afraid." Mel's memories were clearer now, emotions sorting through the fog in her head. "My distance wasn't because I didn't love you, but because I was afraid of how *much* I was starting to love you."

"That's bullshit."

Mel sagged against a tree. "It's the truth. And the truth is all I have left."

"Fine."

Silence hung between them.

"Is this...is all this because you're immortal?" Amaryllis asked.

Mel nodded. "I've watched too many people I love die while I live on. I was afraid to go through it all again. And...I'm still terrified, but being without you, then seeing you again in a dangerous situation, has me thinking that losing you now would be worse than losing you later. There is still so much to learn and know about you. So much we haven't done."

"I don't...argh!" Amaryllis threw the machete to the ground. "If we try this again, will you talk to me? Will you say those words and mean them?"

"Yes," said Mel, trying to push as much heart into her words as her tattered body would allow. "I promise."

More silence.

"Does that mean I get a second chance?" Mel prodded.

Amaryllis shrugged. "If we make it out alive."

Mel was buoyed by a hope like she hadn't felt since she entered the forest. "Thank you, now we—"

Her stomach growled. Amaryllis's followed suit.

"I don't suppose you have any food on you?" Mel sheepishly asked.

"No, just the ration bars, same as you."

Ration bars. Right. Mel dug around in her pocket for the last of the rations she'd salvaged from the crash. Even though her stomach was growling, she handed the ration to Amaryllis. She desperately wanted to eat it, and in another lifetime, she would've needed every calorie she could get her hands on. But now she could subsist on other kinds of energy—the kind only Erin could provide.

Mel took deep breaths. She needed Erin. Not just for power, but for family. And somewhere under all the power and manipulation, Erin, the cousin Mel grew up with, the one that had been willing to die for the people they loved, was still in there.

They were close now. Possibly close enough to overcome the trees' interference. Mel focused inward, toward her bond with Erin. This was the one part of her mind where the trees didn't have a foothold, though their fae pollen was all around.

There weren't literally roots and spores and pollen in her head, but in her mind's eye, that was how she perceived the psychic energy the forest had entangled there. Something she'd inhaled had latched onto blood cells and traveled to her brain, giving the trees a way in. A way to poke holes in her memory and mute her power. To make her weak.

Her remaining specks of power were barely enough to keep her heart beating, but the bond with her cousin was innate and incorruptible. Mel limped through a mental forest, tripping over vines and around mushrooms, until she came to the spot where the pollen thinned. Where she could take long, deep breaths, and find the oasis in her mind that allowed her to find Erin, even through the exhaustion.

Then she was there. In Erin's mind, feeling Erin's emotions. Rage. Despair. Guilt. Erin was drowning in it all.

We are almost there. Hold on. Can you hear me? Can you fight them?

CEASE YOUR RESISTANCE!!!!

Telepathic vines lashed out toward Mel's mind, but she mustered a spark of energy and envisioned herself slashing at them with a flaming sword. She stretched her mind up, toward the lab Erin was trapped in. There were trees there. They'd grown up through the transport tunnels and taken over the lab. More branches and roots assaulted her mind. She batted them off, focused on her cousin, all Erin's crushing angst. Even without the trees—in their mind—they were strangling themself. They were like a wound, calling out for a kind of healing Mel had never been able to give.

And Erin...Erin no longer struggled against their bonds. Were they sleeping? Or perhaps just smoldering, instead of raging. It didn't matter. They were still alive, and as long as Erin was alive, there was hope. Mel ran into Erin's mental wall, which dissolved into a tunnel—a manifestation of how she and Erin perceived their bond and shared energy. They could use this tunnel to switch bodies, to drive one another's flesh and use one another's gifts. Normally, stepping into the tunnel was like stepping into an inferno. Hopefully, this time, she could fill herself with that raging fire, sear her infected brain and burn the monstrous forest she should have never created.

Erin? Mel called as her consciousness wove through the tunnel. *Erin, can you hear me?*

There was no Erin.

There was no fire.

Only cold.

Darkness.

Stray sparks of static popping to life then winking out.

Mel's flare of hope dwindled to embers. She pushed forward, desperation fueling her. "ERIN!"

The tunnel shook. The floor gave way, and Mel tumbled into Erin's body.

Cold. Pain. Stretched, strangled limbs and pierced flesh, constantly trying to heal wounds and failing because there were literal roots burrowed in Erin's muscles.

She'd only felt Erin this cold when they'd been ejected from a space jet without a suit. But this time, Erin wasn't in space.

Mel used her own energy to force Erin's eyes open, revealing a scene of tangled, frost-encased roots. Blue mushrooms grew from them, emitting orange-tinted spores that almost looked like a very fine snow, only they were rising instead of falling.

WAKE UP! Mel screamed in Erin's mind.

Nothing.

Mel closed Erin's eyes and dove through a cold, dormant consciousness. It was like swimming through the deep sea, chilling and dark, with electric eels lurking, waiting to zap her. But the zaps turned to golden light as soon as they hit Mel, illuminating her journey down and down through the abyss of her cousin's soul.

She found Erin at the bottom, curled up under a mental heap of blankets.

"Get up, Erin." Mel knelt down and pulled the blankets off.

The being under the blankets looked entirely human. Young. Pale skin, freckles, red hair, boney shoulders. When they opened their eyes, they weren't the verdant feline ones flecked with gold that Mel usually saw, but dull, green human eyes heavy with failure.

"Mel?" Erin sat up and covered their face in their hands—looking like a human teenager—not the three-hundred-year-old prophet CEO. "You're alive?"

"I'm alive. Barely." Mel held her hands out, palms up, but didn't touch Erin.

"Sorry." Erin raked their nails over their face and folded, no, strangled their hands in their lap. "It's time to burn it down."

Mel met Erin's eyes. "I know, but how? We engineered some of these trees to be fireproof."

"Only to a certain temperature." Mischief tugged the left corner of their lip up into an unnerving half-grin. "If the barrier we put around them touches them, they *will* burn. We shrink it, vaporizing them all. They don't know that. They may have broken my body, but they haven't broken my mind. Not yet. I just—" Erin coughed, and the sound came out watery and violent.

"Let me heal you," Mel said. "So you can escape."

Erin glared at her. "You barely have enough power to keep your heart beating."

"Come on, Erin. Don't you remember how this works? Our energy amplifies when we bounce it back and forth. Isn't that half the reason we're near immortal?"

"It's more complicated than that and you know it." But they took Erin's hand, their fingers clammy, cold, and unnaturally strong. "Once the infection clears out, you should be able to tap into the reactor for more power." Mel wove her fingers between Erin's, pushing their minds further together. "I might not be able to fight off the whole infection before they catch me. Your consciousness needs to wake up and pay attention."

Mel closed her eyes, focusing more on Erin's brain and blood than their awareness. Their immune system wasn't reacting at all. "Your body has given up, hasn't it?"

Erin shook their head, and slowly got to their feet. "I'm still here. Still fighting, though I still think the world would be better off without me... But how do I fight off this infection and get the hell out of here?"

Words were insufficient to explain, so Mel pictured what her cells had done and was about to send the memory to Erin when the vines snaked through their consciousness, tearing her from Erin. Mel focused on the memories, making a mental construct of a flash drive and tossed it to her cousin. She didn't see if they'd snatched it before fleeing back into her own body.

Mel woke, lying on a slab of granite, head in Amaryllis's lap. For the first time since the crash, her mind was clear. Memory intact. She'd spent enough time with Erin to regain energy—enough to run, to slash, to maybe protect Amaryllis. Maybe, just maybe, they could do this.

The greenhouse doors opened. A bramble of vines grew, wicked thorns filling in the gaps between the tendrils. There was no way out, not without losing what little unblemished skin they both still had.

She and Amaryllis were trapped.

Amaryllis and I first met during the Sat War, when her jet landed on top of me. Literally. My own healing was quick but hers took much longer. I watched as she woke, shocked she was alive. I felt her thoughts. Got lost in her memories. I never expected to see her again. But we kept running into each other. I couldn't stop thinking about her. From there a relationship blossomed, but my history and lies soon tore it apart.

-From the personal journal of Amelia "Mel" Evanstar

4

Mel scrambled to her feet and assessed the bramble.

"Mel?" Amaryllis asked. "Any way through?"

Mel shook her head, took her machete back from Amaryllis, and prodded at one of the vines. "I don't know. Give me a minute."

'You shall not pass!' the trees commanded. *Until you cease your resistance and free us.*

I can't free you if you don't let me in! Mel returned. She slapped one of the vines with the broad side of her machete. *Now move!*

The vines and their thorns shifted, forming a narrow tunnel, with thorns pointing down from the ceiling.

"'It's a trap.'" Amaryllis squeezed Mel's hand. "It has to be."

"It's always a trap!" Crazed laughter bubbled out of her throat. She fought and ran from the forest all the way up this damn mountain, only to be met with unintentional movie quotes and a fairy tale bramble. If only she had a torpedo she could shoot through the tunnel and blow herself a path down to the control room. Better yet, someone needed to ask her for a ticket.

What *did* movie characters do in these impossible situations?

"This is a horrible idea," Mel said, stepping forward. "And we're probably going to die."

Amaryllis put her hands on Mel's shoulders and spun her around. And the summit kept spinning after Amaryllis stopped. Mel waited for it to steady. But of course it didn't. Because she was so damned low on energy.

"Talk sense, Mel."

"Will you kiss me, in case we die?"

Instead of answering with words, Amaryllis kissed her. A hand on her cheek, lips fast and hungry. It only lasted a moment, but they were both breathless when they pulled away.

"Only because the situation is hopeless," Mel heard her mumble under her breath.

It wasn't hopeless, just awkwardly complicated. Mel stepped toward the bramble. "We're going through. Come on."

"Mel! Wait! Think this through. They're going to impale me as soon as we set foot in there. And then they'll not-quite-lethally impale you, drain your power until you can't fight their mental attacks, and just force you to free them."

"That is exactly what they plan to do." Mel smiled, rising on some wild speck of energy gained from her short time in Erin's body. If she was going to die on this mountain, she was going down in a blaze of glory, swaddled by memories of her favorite movie.

NO! YOU MUST NOT FIGHT. YOU MUST FREE US!

Mel blared her favorite song from *Star Wars* in her mind, drowning out the trees shouting. She picked up her machete and focused on the blade, dull and chipped and covered in ichor. She couldn't magically sharpen the metal, but she could imbue it with power. She took a piece of that precious spark and channeled it into the blade until it glowed red and vibrated with her life force.

She fell flat on her face. Spots danced in front of her vision as she stood.

"That was a terrible idea, Mel." But Amaryllis grinned as she looked at the blade. "Hey, you made me watch some old flick with a thing like that."

Right. So Amaryllis had seen *Star Wars*. No wonder Mel loved her.

Mel handed the glowing machete to Amaryllis. "This should slice through the thorns in the tunnel, no problem. Just try to get them before they get you."

Then she took out her knife and repeated the process. The dark spots in front of her vision grew, leaving a fuzzy blob of color and movement.

"Attack!" she screamed. She slashed at a vine. Amaryllis did the same, swinging in wide arcs as they entered the thorn-riddled tunnel. The path was ragged and sharp, but a clear path nonetheless. Thorns ricocheted off the glowing blades but sliced through tender skin and tattered clothes. A six-inch spine shot into Mel's foot. A vine snaked out and dug thorns into her wrist. She screamed in tandem with Amaryllis's battle cry, as Amaryllis sliced through the vine. Shriveled ends ejected themselves from Mel's wrist and fell to the forest floor— now bathed in Mel's blood.

"Mel!"

"I'm fine. I'll heal. Erin gave me enough for that. Keep going!" Her wrist was shredded. Blood splattered the tunnel floor as they ran, pain stabbing Mel's foot with each step. She swung wildly with one arm while Amaryllis slashed.

"What I wouldn't give for a flamethrower," Amaryllis muttered as she spun and chopped, popping in and out of Mel's fragmented vision.

"Grip the hilt with two hands," Mel shouted. "Hold it tight. Arms above your head like it's a sword."

"I suck at swords." Amaryllis adjusted her posture, raising her arms.

Mel couldn't see her hands through her spotty vision. Just below a floating glob of red-tinged black, she could see Amaryllis's feet, and the thorn shooting toward them. "Step forward, quickly."

Amaryllis leapt away, far enough to save her neck, but not far enough to save her shoulder.

"Ah!" Amaryllis screamed. "Get it out! Mel! Help!"

Mel cut the vine, dropped her knife, and yanked Amaryllis away, healing the gaping wound.

The spots in Mel's vision enlarged, swallowing each other, until she saw only pinpricks of light in the darkness.

She closed her eyes. Focused on feeling where things were. Listening to the hisses and cracks. She let pain wash over her. She swayed into the dizziness from the loss of power and blood, and danced through the battle—drunk and mad—until by some miracle, Amaryllis pulled her out the other end of the bramble.

Mel could not stand. She couldn't see. All she felt was pain, stabbing and stinging from thousands of open wounds. Amaryllis wasn't much better. Dozens of wounds screamed for Mel to heal them, but with what power? If she used another drop...she'd be out cold. Maybe dead.

"This place is creepy," Amaryllis said, guiding Mel forward, as they hobbled with their arms around each other. "We're in a greenhouse, filled with deadly plants."

"This was where we grew fresh food to eat while we worked in the lab," Mel said. "Closest to the door, we had tomatoes and cucumbers. There were modified apple trees."

"Well, now there is nightshade and pitcher plants, but it looks like the apple trees are still there."

Mel opened her eyes, for all the good it did. Through the floating black and purple blobs, she saw shadows of gnarled apple trees just before they lobbed rotten fruit at her.

They emerged in the middle of the greenhouse where a spiral staircase led down to the other layers of the lab. Lights flickered on the stairs.

"Half the bulbs are shattered. Most of the roots are charred. Some are still smoking," said Amaryllis. "Erin must have put up a fight here."

Mel raised her hand to the wall, feeling the heat radiating off the root. "These feel like they've been on fire more recently."

"Maybe they're resisting?"

"Maybe." If they were, it meant Erin had regained power from Mel's time in their head. Mel couldn't discern how much, but clearly not enough to free themself.

"Where are we going?" Amaryllis asked.

"The controls for the barrier are down on level seven. Erin is on level five, the freezer level."

"The door is here." Amaryllis turned Mel toward heat and crackling. A rectangle rimmed with orange fire. The only color in her shadowed, fragmented sight.

Mel and Amaryllis stumbled through into a hall lined with roots and paused as one lashed out at them, slapping Amaryllis back to the hall they'd just left. The door closed behind them. "This is a trap." Amaryllis pushed herself off of the door and dodged another root.

"You said that about the briar."

"And I was right."

Roots surged, breaking through the walls, the air vents, the cracks in the flooring. "Run!" Mel grabbed Amaryllis and pulled her forward. But no matter how hard she tried, she couldn't force her heavy, bleeding limbs to run.

"Wait. Look!"

A buzzing cut through the sound of Mel's thundering heart. A light bulb exploded and electricity forked out, setting vines on fire.

Mel limped down the hall. They passed another bulb, which promptly exploded. Then another. Then another.

"It's Erin! They're alive!" Mel said. "Alive and powering up. I have to get to them before I lose consciousness. Help me?"

"Always," Amaryllis said, and it sounded like she meant it.

Another light bulb sparked, fissures of electricity running down the wall. "I wouldn't be surprised if Erin installed old light fixtures just so they could blow them up," Mel said, mostly to herself. "It'd be just like them."

"Maybe they knew this day would come. They can see futures, right?"

"Nothing about the future is ever set in stone," Mel said. "Though if Erin had told me about this specific option, I might have let them burn the forest a long time ago."

Doubtful. Erin's voice crackled in Mel's head like a staticy burst from a radio. *You hate killing things.*

Probably has something to do with being able to feel their death screaming in my head, Mel thought. Her breaths came shallow and ragged. She was so close.

"Why are you smiling?" Amaryllis asked as they reached the end of the hallway.

"I hear Erin," Mel said as she and Amaryllis stumbled through the door.

Hundreds of vines battled electrical wires. A layer of pollen covered old lab benches. Decaying corpses—clad in lab coats, masks and safety goggles still on their faces—lay on the floor, impaled by vines.

Each breath made Mel feel like the trees were sprouting and taking root inside her head again. She couldn't let that happen, not when she was so close to Erin. The door at the end of the room was cold storage. A giant freezer. Erin's prison.

It was time to push the trees back again. She needed a clear mind for mental connections. Mel directed energy at the presence rooting in her mind, burning it away, envisioning the trees turning to ash. Her heart skipped a beat. Her limbs turned sluggish. The music in her head quieted.

Traitor. Traitor. Traitor. We have you back now.

Pollen rained from the ceiling. Ran up her nasal passages and assaulted her brain. Her mind fuzzed. Her memories escaped.

No!

"Sprinkler system," she whispered to Amaryllis. "On the far wall, under the picture of a disc-like spaceship."

Amaryllis ran, slashing her way to the control, and turned it on. Murky water, reeking of mildew, rained from the ceiling, washing the pollen away. But it was too late. Mel's thoughts were clogged. Who was she? Where was she? Why was it raining indoors?

Free us! Down to level seven. NOW!

Mel turned around, crawling toward the swath of chopped vines and splinters. Poor babies. All so damaged. Maybe she could help them if she went down to level seven?

"Carol, where are you going?" Who was Carol? Her? It had to be. There was no one else there. "To level seven. To free the trees."

"No! What's wrong with you? What about Erin? " The person came over to Mel. Met her eyes, though Mel's vision was strained and speckled. Whispered to her like they knew each other, like they were lovers, or friends, or anything other than complete strangers.

"Fight! You have to fight!" the stranger whispered.

"Fight what?" Mel whispered back.

"The trees. They're in your mind, controlling you."

"I just need to free them. The poor things are starving."

The person cupped Mel's cheeks with her hands. "Carol...Mel. Look in my eyes. Remember me."

Mel couldn't see her eyes properly, but there was something familiar about the voice.

Forget about her. You need to free us.

"Remember the first time I took you up in my jet? You were so excited to fly."

"Fly. I've always wanted to, but I don't have wings. I hate that I don't have wings, but I don't know why. Do you have wings?"

"Focus. It was your birthday. Don't know if it was the real one, but I took you flying."

Mel could almost feel the g-force, hear a musical whoop of excitement as they soared.

"Remember when we took that vacation to the Bahamas?" the person whispered, tightening her grip on Mel.

Mel nodded, even though she wasn't sure. The voice was warm, comforting where the trees sounded sinister, demanding.

"The workers at the resort were getting sick, but didn't know why," continued the person. "They didn't have money for treatment. You spent the whole vacation helping them. You figured out their water had been contaminated by a mutated parasite and didn't have the same quality filtration as the resort proper. You prescribed medication and paid for it. You saved them."

"We saved them," Mel croaked as fragments of memory surfaced. Vines tried to tug them away, but Mel clung to the woman and their shared history "You were upset at first, but you helped me collect samples. You flew the old plane I rented to a bigger island so we could buy medicine and get it to the people quickly."

"Yes!" Excitement flooded the person's voice. Amaryllis. That was her name. "Mel, you save people. It's who you are. If you free trees, they'll kill people. Eat them. Drag them underground and slowly digest their decomposing corpses."

"We have to stop them!" Mel tried to stand, but she had no strength. She reached out with her mind instead, to the ceiling. There was someone in the power grid. Power. She didn't have it. She was running out of air. Her heart slowed. "Electricity. I run on electricity! Grab a line. Zap me!"

"I don't...are you sure?"

"Do it!"

Mel collapsed. Her heart gave a final, weak beat.

Her vision blackened.

Burning. Electricity jolted through her. She smelled charred hair and burnt flesh.

Wake up, Mel! Erin shouted in her mind. *I'm in the power grid, but I can't get my body free. I can't burn all the pollen from my head.*

Fire filled her mind.

She remembered everything.

Her heart beat stronger. The power healed her wounds and stabilized her vitals. Amaryllis's wounds called to her too, and she healed them. All of them.

"Help me open the door," she shouted at Amaryllis.

Together, they turned the wide metal wheel. The freezer door swung outward, hinges groaning, and a blast of bitter air slapped Mel across the face.

Inside the freezer, Erin struggled against the branches—a new fire in their eyes. Mel and Amaryllis worked together, chopping the vines, pulling them from Erin's body.

Flowers spurted from the tips of the vines and from the flowers came belched clouds of pollen. The air became choked with yellow. The vines shed their flowers and in their place grew more thorns. But Mel was awake now, and stable with power. She blasted her mental *Star Wars* soundtrack to drown out the tree's words. She imagined in her mind the cockpit of a spaceship, complete with controls for lasers and deflector shields. As the telepathic vines thrashed at her shields, she shot them, shouting, "This is nothing! 'I used to bullseye womp rats in my T-16 back home!'"

Mel latched onto Erin—physically and mentally—burning the pollen out of their mind. Erin came into the 'cockpit' with Mel, awake and buoyed on her own energy.

"Millennium Falcon. Nice."

Mel grinned. "What did you expect? The *Enterprise?"*

Mel blinked and came back to the real world, dizzy and teetering.

Erin awoke.

The temperature in the freezer dropped and the lights went out as Erin drew the electricity out. A panel flew off the wall. Electricity forked through it, into Erin, then back out through their fingertips, engulfing the branches until they smoked on the floor. Mel shifted her mental music to "The Emperor's Theme."

She glanced at Erin's hands. Black nail polished shimmered, flawless, undisturbed by the intense heat of the lightning.

Supermassive Black Hole by Galaxy Gloss. It's heat, chemical, and chip resistant, Erin thought to Mel. *I bought stock in it early. Paid off well.*

Inside Mel's head, the dark tunnel that connected their minds ignited. Energy flowed through it, rejuvenating Mel's tired brain, and then Mel sent energy back to Erin.

Amaryllis cried out and Mel spun around to see her clutching her head. "I can't keep them out."

Mel closed her eyes, directing her mental fire at the thorny vines attacking Amaryllis's mind while Erin took care of those that attacked in the physical world. But this time, Mel didn't falter. The trees kept up their assault, and she kept firing, fueled by a constant stream of energy pouring from Erin. When she got closer, she pulled in a tactic from another favorite franchise, and beamed Amaryllis into her mental cockpit.

For a moment, in their mind, it was like she, Erin, and Amaryllis were standing in it together, wearing clothes from an old science fiction movie.

Warmth filled Mel's chest and tears brimmed out of her eyes. How many times had she and Erin done this before? The odds stacked against them as they battled ancient monsters, fallen angels and Lovecraftian beasts, hell bent on conquering the earth. Yet, it was a forest of their own making that had brought them to their knees. Erin looked down at themself then smirked. "It's been a while."

"Too long." Mel clasped Erin's hand. "Much too long."

"What is going on?" Amaryllis asked.

"Welcome to Mel's brain," said Erin. They focused on Amaryllis, looking at their boot clad feet, not their eyes. "While we're here, try to refer to me as Erin, not Cass."

"You can't stay here long." Mel winked. "Or a little piece of you might stick and you won't be able to keep me out of your head."

"I don't know what that means, but I'll try," Amaryllis said.

"We're going to give you energy to reinforce you. When you wake back in your own body, we need to get down to level seven to activate the controls."

Amaryllis's eyes widened. "You're going to free the trees?"

"No." A sadness blanketed Mel, suffocating the joy she'd snatched. "We're going to destroy them. "

Outside the cockpit's view screen, vines trembled, retreating from the ship. With Erin tapped into the reactor, refilling drained reserves, telepathic attacks were futile. They'd be scorched in seconds.

"This is a fork in the time stream," Erin whispered to Mel, a soft smile on their face. "It will be our death, or a fresh start."

"I'm counting on the second thing." A fresh start with her mortal love, and a chance to rebuild a broken relationship with her cousin.

"Just like old times. You, me, and a human partner saving humanity from things that want to eat them." Mel turned to Amaryllis and pulled her into a hug, both in her mind and in the real world, filling her with power. "Back to our bodies now."

Mel was back in the room, surrounded by fragments of cut and scorched vines and roots. Her legs were steady and her head was clear. Amaryllis's fresh wounds called to her. She healed those, and for just a moment, savored the lightness and euphoria that always followed healing, glad that there was once again enough energy to avoid the fatigue. Her shields went back up.

As they rushed out of the freezer, Mel tripped on a pile of frozen bacon. It was hard to come by now, and she wondered what condition it was in after a century of deep freeze. She wouldn't let a human eat it, but being half-Angel had lots of perks. She made a note to get it if they survived. If the lab survived Erin's plan to vaporize the forest.

Roots quivered, retreating as the troop strode through the lab, the hall, and down to the control room. The roots congested around the door, a last stand, but Erin just blasted through them with lightning bolts. Inside the control room the roots were thick enough to coat the walls and doors. Keys and monitors were lost under the vines and, most importantly, the controls that would allow them to shrink the barrier.

Erin raised their hand, ready to blast more.

"Stop." Mel grabbed their wrist. "You don't want to fry the controls."

"Do you even know where to start looking?" Amaryllis stepped between Mel and Erin.

"We know exactly where it is." Erin glared at a particularly dense section of root.

"You want this back?" Amaryllis offered Mel her machete—still beaming with angel fire. "Glad to see you can hold it again."

"You keep it." Mel smiled. "Thank you. For holding this for me. For believing in me."

"Whatever. Just get us out of here." Amaryllis winked, and it was all the boost Mel needed.

Mel stepped closer to the vines, stretched her hand out, and dropped her shields. The forest's collective consciousness surged at her, but fueled by her rage and Erin's power, Mel's mind was a storm that battered the forest's consciousness, concentrating on the root infested lab. Getting revenge for the moment it had overtaken her.

MOVE! she commanded, pouring energy into the word and an intention, sending it into their cells—into the fibers of their existence. One root twitched. Mel poured more energy into the command, sweat slicking her face, until the roots snaked away, revealing the only section of the control panel she cared about.

Erin got to it first. They slapped their hand down on the control. Alarms blared through the room, and the barrier began to shrink.

The trees panicked, bucking, tearing themselves from Mel's control. Vines flailed and dove, searching for flesh. Through the control panel, Erin drew energy from the lab's reactor and created a buzzing field around them. "Amaryllis, you chop any vines that get through. Mel, we have to close the barrier slowly enough that it gets all the trees, including the underground roots. We want everything vaporized. If any of these vines in here get past Amaryllis, give them a telepathic blast."

"Got it!" Mel imagined a fleet of star fighters circling her mind, weapons hot, aiming psychic lasers at the wild roots.

"Amaryllis, it's just as important to keep the roots away from the control as it is from us," Erin said through clenched teeth. "I built failsafes. If the base is destroyed, even if these controls are destroyed, the reactor will blow and the barrier will collapse, containing a nuclear explosion powerful enough to level the mountain and melt everything in it."

Angry roots shook the structure. Dozens crowded Erin's barrier until one snaked through. Amaryllis swung the glowing blade, slicing through the root and setting it ablaze.

Telepathic roots stabbed at Mel from all angles. Lasers fired from her mental canon. Roots twined together into a giant tree, branches swinging down toward her ship. She launched a torpedo at it, smiling as a ball of orange flame consumed it.

"We're getting close." Mel inhaled sharply. Trees screamed in her mind, begging for mercy.

She kept firing her mental lasers.

"Ouch, shit!" Amaryllis cried as she swung wildly, slicing a vine an inch before it hit the control panel. Blood dripped from her arm.

A root slapped Mel's back. She staggered, but kept her feet planted on the ground and her hand on the controls. Stealing a glance over her shoulder, she saw Amaryllis slice through four vines, then stagger back, raising the blade to guard with shaking arms.

Stop. Please! the trees begged.

The next root to break through moved sluggishly, pulling itself across the floor. Another flopped against the small force field, while a third slapped to the ground near Mel's feet, alive but despondent.

"We've hit critical mass of vaporization!" Erin yelled. "Tide is turning!"

Mel's mind cleared, the telepathic roots unspooling and retreating. "Just need the barrier to hit the tree line and this will all be over," Mel said. "Well, mostly over. There's the lab to deal with."

"Yeah," Erin said, hesitantly. They met Mel's eyes. They had to destroy everything they'd built here, every branch, flower, root, vine, and seed. Every spec of pollen. Anything that might contain the trees genetic coding, or the trees would multiply.

"What now?" Erin asked. "Any more bad ideas of ours we need to destroy? Or can we blow this place up and be done with it?"

"I don't know about destroying, but talking about bad ideas, what would you say to some bacon?"

Erin's nose wrinkled. "Gross. You're not going to be able to save that bacon, but I have some back at my house." Mischief danced in their eyes. "But it's not as aged."

Amaryllis glared at Mel. "You really weren't thinking of eating hundred-year-old bacon, were you? You're only just back in my good graces. Poisoning yourself won't win you any points."

Mel shrugged. "It's *bacon*. The new stuff just isn't the same. Don't knock it until you've tried it."

For a moment, everyone laughed. But it was a nervous laugh that came in sharp jolts, because what was coming next wasn't pleasant.

"Ready?" Erin asked.

"Get this over with." Mel tightened her grip on the control and reached for Amaryllis with her other hand.

"Great. I'm not going to blow the whole reactor though. Once the barrier reaches the base, the self-destruct protocol will recalibrate to something far less drastic. Regardless, we're all going to burn with it."

"Wait, what?" Amaryllis said. "Can a human—"

"With Mel's help, probably," Erin returned. "I'll absorb enough energy so you aren't incinerated." Erin typed in the kill code. "But the heat still burns enough that Mel will be healing you constantly until it's over."

The remaining trees screamed in Mel's mind as the greenhouse melted around them, the plants' agony engulfed her before they winked out of existence. The temperature around her rose. Erin dumped excess heat into the transport tunnels and under the mountain, burning out any surviving roots. Then the control room was the only thing left in the dome, and all Mel felt was pain. All she could do was heal. Scream. Cling to consciousness until it was over. Until fire had cleansed the mountain of all evidence the forest had ever existed. Until the three of them—her, Erin, and Amaryllis—were whole and healed. Like phoenixes, born again from fire.

Epilogue

Bacon pizza. You couldn't just walk into a pizza place and order that these days. Mel had tried printing it in her kitchen, but her printer was one of the cheapest on the market. Her apartment was too small and dinky to have a real kitchen, even if she could afford the ingredients to bake a real pizza.

"You chose that life." Erin opened their shiny, stainless steel oven. The scent of melted cheese, tomato sauce, and bacon wafted out. "Every time you accumulate a little wealth, you give it away."

"Instead of hoarding it like a dragon?" Mel's stomach was growling like an angry one.

"There was one of those in that weird book you made me read." Amaryllis walked into the room. Drops of water dripped off her curls onto her cheeks. She smelled like flowers and coconut. The shirt she'd borrowed from Erin was a little too small, so curves and muscles strained against an image of a muscular green monster. Her skin, still damp from the shower, was smooth. Scars, blemishes, and the tiny crow's feet she'd been getting around her eyes were gone. The excess healing energy Erin and Mel had poured into her might even extend her life by a decade or two. She sniffed the air. "Whatever you just cooked smells...weird...and delicious."

"It is one of the best foods to ever exist," Mel said, mouth watering as she gazed at the bacon, half sunk in melted cheese. When the pizza was cool enough to cut, Mel cut a slice of it. Facing Amaryllis, she took a bite, closing her eyes as her mouth exploded with flavors she hadn't tasted in years.

But she didn't just devour the slice. She set it aside, cutting a second one, and carrying it over to Amaryllis, slowly lifting it to her mouth. "Take a bite."

Amaryllis took it, nibbled at first, then took a big bite.

"That is good," she said through a mouthful. "Wow."

Mel used her finger to wipe up a speck of sauce that Amaryllis missed, and licked it off her finger. "When I was in college, the first time, a place near campus sold it. I miss pizza shops."

"Quit MedCorps, work with me, and you can have your own pizza oven."

Mel turned around.

Erin leaned on the counter, next to the steaming pizza. They wore loose black pants and a t-shirt with crossed *lightsabers*. Beams of red glowed on their black nail polish. "I'll be put on the Board of Directors. You can be Phoenix Corps' conscience. An angel sitting on the corporate devil's shoulder."

Amaryllis slid her arms around Mel's waist, sending a burst of buzzing warmth through her body. "I took a job when they offered me one."

"Of course you did." Mel folded her hands over Amaryllis. "It meant you got to fly all the newest jets and not worry about anyone shooting you out of the sky."

"Sometimes prototypes malfunction and crash, so I need you around to heal me. You can't do that if you're running around the planet hunting contagions." Amaryllis pulled Mel closer. "You promised me you'd be less distant. That means being physically present."

"I'll make sure MedCorps is funded so they have state of the art technology and can pay their doctor better." Erin put Mel's bitten slice of pizza on a plate, along with two more slices, then placed it on the table.

"We can get a nice house. With a pizza oven, and a real kitchen. You can make all the foods people don't eat anymore," said Amaryllis.

Mel's lips curved up into what she hoped was a devious grin. "I can still live close to you, you know, without giving up a medical career to be on the board of an evil corporation. I can work in a hospital or open a private practice."

"Phoenix Corp isn't evil. Yet. But you can make sure it doesn't become evil if you're helping me run it. Besides, think of the perks. Think of the bacon."

"Think of me," Amaryllis whispered into Mel's ear.

"I'll do it, I'll do it. Stop ganging up on me." Mel looked at Erin, a few feet away offering her a plate of pizza. She turned so she could see Amaryllis, looking at her with a very different kind of hunger. She thought of her promise. Of fears and hopes and dreams. Here, in this room, she had a family. She'd fought and murdered a forest to get here. She'd do whatever it took to keep it together.

Sara Codair is the author of The Evanstar Chronicles, Earth Reclaimed, and an assortment of odd short stories. If you want to know what Erin and Mel were like when they were young, check out *Power Surge*, *Life Minus Me*, and *Power Inversion*, available from most major book retailers. Learn more at **www.saracodair.com**. Follow Sara on Twitter and Instagram **@shatteredsmooth** for updates, cats, and dogs.

How to Steal a Planet

N.L. Bates

Sapphic Representation: Lesbian, Ace/Demi
Heat Level: Low
Content Warnings: Coarse Language, Violence, Drugs

The Planetary Quorum seeks to facilitate the equitable and sustainable distribution of resources, via the responsible custodianship of stellar bodies that may, in their abundance, provide for all members of all societies across the Galaxy.

Custodians of any stellar body must meet certain obligations and conditions, and the Planetary Quorum reserves the right to intervene in scenarios where such obligations are not met...

- Excerpt from the Sol Charter, executed by 213 signatories of the Planetary Quorum

Mae Hui, recently-minted captain of the unnamed mining ship GR1004763-xe, had three problems.

Her first problem was that the Q-comm network—normally as reliable as the Planck constant—was down. Its malfunction left Mae with only the meager hazard navigation and scanning capabilities afforded by the ship's short-range cameras, and no communication channel other than honest-to-god radio. Her second problem was the amended order she'd received just before the network dropped:

"I'm obliged to advise you, Warrant Officer, that these target asteroids are resource-poor and unlikely to provide enough material to hit quota."

Which was just her luck. Mae really needed this mission to be a success. A newly-minted captain was about as influential as a week-old news story and made about as much money. Captains of mining ships had *one* use: bring back enough of whatever the Planetary Quorum had assigned you to mine for, and your mission was a success. Get enough successes, and you might eventually get promoted to a rank with a salary that bought more than a week's worth of groceries or eighty seconds of air time with a disaffected bureaucrat.

Mae *really* needed this mission to be a success.

The voice of her third problem, Damien Weibold, crackled over the radio, stubbornly refusing to see reason. "Meeting your quota is a requirement of your mission, Captain."

Mae pinched the bridge of her nose. What did he want her to do, *will* those asteroids into having larger ore deposits? "I'm aware of that, Warrant Officer, but that quota was set under different mission parameters. I'll file a variance request to reset the quota requirements appropriately." And then, because the quickest way to an insufferable bureaucrat's heart was usually through his ego, she added, "I'm sure your judgment about the route is sound." She hated kissing up to him. Especially when the ship's mechanic, Sienna Todd, hovered just a few feet away.

One more mission to promotion. She could kiss ass for one more mission.

"Acknowledged," Weibold said. "I won't be able to process the request until it is formally received." Meaning, not until Q-comm was back up.

Sienna coughed in the background, dropping all pretense as to why she was hovering.

"Is there an estimated time of repair?" Mae asked.

"Unknown," Weibold said. "We're assessing the damage from a meteoroid impact on one of our satellites."

Sienna let out a low whistle. "Must have been some meteoroid, if it hobbled your entire network."

Mae turned around and glared at her.

Sienna shrugged and refused to look contrite.

"The satellite in question services one of our remote sectors, specifically the one you are in. The Planetary Quorum has only so many resources at its disposal," Weibold said, clearly irritated at the interruption. "I need to return to Uranus space station, Captain. Good luck."

"I—"

Sienna cut Mae off with a snort. Her heels clicked on the deck as she walked up to the command panel. "You couldn't find Uranus with a star chart and both hands." And then, before Mae could say anything to salvage the situation, she thumbed the comm off.

"Sienna, why? You need to get paid as much as I do. You keep going on about that smart tools upgrade and I know that Galaxy Gloss nail polish is half a paycheck a bottle. Half of my paycheck."

"Saved you some time." Mae's mechanic leaned casually against the lip of the ship's command panel, white skin a pale contrast to the brushed metal, delicate eyebrows lifted in an elegant arch. "That type gets off on saying 'no.' And what's money when I have the galaxy's grumpiest captain?"

"Well, he's certainly more likely to say no now that you've insulted him," Mae said. "And I am not grumpy. Let me handle the Planetary Quorum." They'd had this conversation at least twice in the weeks since Mae had been assigned the captaincy of this ship and its flippant crew.

Sienna shrugged. "Suit yourself. I always get paid eventually." Blond ringlets whispered against her fitted cream blouse as she stretched. "So do you, for that matter. What do you care if you get handed a bad mission?"

"The success of our missions is important to me," Mae said.

Sienna snorted.

Mae couldn't blame her. It was the kind of canned non-answer that Quorum officers were famous for. Maybe it was worth being candid. Or maybe she enjoyed talking to her only crew member who was willing to talk back. "The Quorum has a referendum coming up. Resource distribution for non-Earth planets."

"Ah," Sienna said. "And, what, they only let you vote if you don't fuck up?"

"Something like that," Mae admitted. She was technically a commissioned officer, but like everyone who didn't have political capital to spend, she'd started at the bottom of the barrel. One had to fly a certain number of successful missions before the Quorum would back her commission, granting her the right to vote in Quorum affairs. Maybe one day she could actually change things. Until then, she just wanted to be able to send her niece on the Mars Slingshot Adventure Flight without ruining retirement plans for the next three generations.

She only needed one more successful mission. Just one more.

"Huh," Sienna said. "Politics isn't my cup of tea."

"Not mine, either," Mae said truthfully. "But the Mars vote is...it's important to me. Mars, the colonies...they don't get much in the way of resources. Barely enough to keep them viable. I'd like to see that change." She hesitated, then added, "Maybe it will, by the time I go home. One vote isn't much, but...I can hope, right?" She smiled sheepishly. "What are we, without hope?"

"We're humans in space." Sienna straightened and eyed Mae like she was a particularly overripe mangosteen. "Look," she said finally. "Ayse managed to cache some new entries to the asteroid database just before the network crashed. Why don't we see if any of them have anything to offer? Would that tame your grump for a day?"

"I am not grumpy!"

Sienna stared at her.

"Fine. Comm Ayse." Ayse Rivero, the ship's comms technician, spent most of her time buried in the communications pit. She would happily talk Mae's ear off about the specs of any recently launched cubesat that had caught her eye, and barely said a word otherwise. Mae would have to congratulate her on her foresight for keeping local copies of a database on a network that was never supposed to go down.

As for Sienna...it wasn't exactly an apology for mouthing off, but Mae didn't need Sienna to *like* her. She just needed the mechanic to stop making things harder. She decided to take the offer as an olive branch.

"Got 'em," Sienna said.

"That didn't take long. Was Ayse at her comm?"

"Dunno. Not my job, and not yours, either. Asking stupid questions doesn't make anyone any friends."

"I'm not trying to—" Mae started.

"Whatever." Sienna waved her off. "Just take a look."

Being the new person on the crew she was supposed to be captaining was a challenge, and Mae's attempts at banter and morale building had gone mostly unacknowledged. She decided to focus on the readouts in front of her instead of Sienna's tone. Most of the new entries were just rock and ice. One had trace amounts of nickel, but not enough to bring them up to quota.

"This one looks interesting." Sienna tapped the screen with an implausibly immaculate nail. "Never seen an asteroid quite like that. Good thing Ayse catalogs literally everything, eh? Whatcha think, Captain?"

"Don't—" Mae's breath caught when she read its official classification: Dwarf planet. "How did we miss a dwarf planet *in our solar system*?"

The Quorum had a mandate to disseminate information on new extraterrestrial objects so that they could be cataloged and any resources disseminated. New asteroids were discovered all the time, especially out here in the Scattered Disc, but a planetary-mass object in humanity's native solar system should be plastering the airwaves from here all the way back to Earth.

Sienna shrugged. "Q-comm's down, remember? The newsfeeds probably haven't picked it up yet." She eyed the entry appraisingly. "Still, a rock that size has to have *something* worth mining, right?"

It was also in the area they were supposed to be leaving. Mae skimmed through the rest of the data, which was surprisingly fulsome, considering how recently the planet must have been discovered. It didn't appear to have an orbit, even a highly eccentric one. Rogue planet, then. No wonder it hadn't been discovered sooner.

Mae kept reading. There were so-far-incomplete calculations that were probably meant to determine the composition of the planet's atmosphere, which it apparently had. Its angular diameter. Some miscellaneous spectroscopy data detailing fluctuations in the near-infrared spectrum—

"It has a *VRE*?" Mae said, so sharply that Sienna took a step back. Even Xiadra, their pilot, who joked that she could tune out a war if it happened while she was flying the ship, looked over her shoulder at Mae from the cockpit in the ship's nose.

"Sure," Sienna said after a moment. "What's a VRE?"

Mae leaned toward the screen. She must have misread, or there was an error in the calculations somewhere, *something* to explain... "A vegetation red edge."

There was a long silence.

People discovered extraterrestrial objects all the time. Even discovering exoplanets wasn't *that* unusual in the grand scheme of things, not anymore. But finding native life, that wasn't a fossil, anywhere other than Earth? It had never happened.

"You're saying this place has plants," Sienna said flatly, her voice containing none of the wonder Mae felt.

Mae banged her shin against the command panel. She didn't even remember standing. "I don't know how else to explain these numbers. Can we get a visual?"

Sienna flipped on the ship's intercom. "Ayse," she said. "Do we have any visuals on planetary-mass object—" and she rattled off the classification number, barely glancing at the screen.

"Doubtful," Ayse replied. "Most satellite data out here is spectroscopy. But I'll take a look."

"How sure are you that these numbers actually mean plant life?" Sienna asked.

"I'm—well, we would need an astrobiologist to be sure," Mae said. "This must not be out of astrobio review yet, or the Quorum would have confirmed it already."

"So...pretty sure," Sienna prodded.

Mae nodded absently. She should temper her expectations. She could be wrong, or plant life could be scarce or hard to find, or, or, or. But oh, it was hard with the possibility of extraterrestrial life dangling right under her nose. "Depending on what's out there...this could mean food, or textiles, all sorts of things we can't send into deep space." Too far away to help Mars, barring the construction of an FTL transponder, but still. Still. "This could—this could get us out of the solar system."

This was how she got her promotion. She could set her fathers up to retire in a home bigger than a cubicle, *and* secure a seat for the Mars vote. Hell, it might warm the crew up to her, too. Nothing facilitated team building quite like buckets of money.

"Xiadra," Sienna called out to the cockpit. "Set us a course for this dwarf planet."

"Yes, Xiadra, do that," Mae said gruffly.

"Didn't mean to step on your toes, Captain," Sienna said, in a tone that indicated she was not at all sorry.

This was not a battle Mae wanted to fight. "It's a *life-bearing planet*. Of course it's where we're going."

Sienna raised her eyebrows at Mae. "Plant life isn't exactly a Quorum-approved mining material. This is going to make it a lot harder to hit your quota."

Mae's laugh was a bit breathless. "Once they know about this, quota is the last thing they'll care about."

Mae radioed Weibold. Three times. He didn't pick up, even when she flagged the call as urgent. His commanding officer didn't answer either. Q-comm repairs must have been keeping the Quorum busy.

Xiadra flew their little asteroid-hopper toward the planet at speeds Mae hadn't even known were possible, while Mae, Sienna and Ayse did their best to turn a ship designed to drill holes in asteroids into a vehicle for gathering terrestrial data.

"This would be so much easier if Q-comm was back up," she said to Sienna.

Sienna grunted. "If you say so."

"I do say so. We don't even know how far outside the ship's capabilities we'll be working. If we had a complete dataset from the Quorum, we'd at least know what *kind* of material we're going to be collecting."

"There's always that spectroscopy data Ayse pulled up," Sienna offered.

"Where did she get that, again?"

Sienna shrugged. "Some local cubesat."

"There are open-access cubesats this far out? Really?" Open-access cubesats were common enough in the more populous parts of the solar system, where it didn't take years of spaceflight or obscene amounts of resources to get a satellite somewhere useful. "The ones that get this far out are usually paywalled."

"Obviously there are," Sienna said. "And before you ask me how she found it, that's still not my job."

They needed whatever information they could get. Mae sighed. "Bring it up, then."

"Go nuts. I've got to start working on the mining rig," Sienna said. "It's a blunt instrument, to be frank. I'm gonna have to do some serious jury-rigging to get any sort of precision...ish...sample collection out of it. But it's doable. Probably."

"Those are temporary changes, right?" Mae asked. "There's no way the Quorum would authorize permanent changes to one of their ships."

"They'll never even know I was there," Sienna said. "Promise. Erase that furrow from your forehead. It's like you don't trust me."

"I do," Mae replied. "Most of the time. Let me know if you need a hand."

"Shouldn't," Sienna said. The handles sticking up from her glossy black tool belt flashed in coordination with the sunset colors on her nails as she stood. "You can coordinate with Xiadra on the transfer orbits."

"I don't need your permission, Sienna," Mae snapped.

"I know," Sienna replied, without looking at her. Mae sighed. Working with Sienna was so much smoother when she forgot Mae was a Quorum officer she could antagonize. She didn't needle, or question orders. She just did the work.

Mae did need to talk to Xiadra about transfer orbits. She walked around the command panel, and squeezed herself into the cockpit.

"This asteroid here is the best candidate to make the last jump," Xiadra said, jabbing a finger far too close to Mae's ribs. That's what she got, she supposed, for leaning away from the controls; it just brought her up against the pilot's displays. This cockpit had not been designed to have two people in it at once. "We could even park ourselves in orbit if we want to observe for a bit. It's easy enough to get to the planet itself from there."

"Good idea," Mae agreed. "I'd like to have a better idea of what the planet's atmosphere is like before we go sailing into it. Hopefully Q-comm will be back up by then."

"Hopefully," Xiadra echoed.

The crew was a good, competent team. For the first time, Mae almost felt like part of it, but she didn't want to push things. So she went back to her console and quietly prepared reports. For form's sake, she prepared another variance request, drawing on her long-rusted background in astrobiology to stress the utmost importance of their discovery. She emphasized that she and her crew were ready to support research in any capacity the Quorum required, as well as the planetary custodianship team which was undoubtedly on its way.

More out of habit than expectation, Mae hit 'send' when she finished. REQUEST PENDING NETWORK RESTORATION, the handset returned. And then a new message: LIMITED HAZARD NAVIGATION DATA AVAILABLE. SEEK SHELTER AND REMAIN STATIONARY UNTIL NETWORK IS RESTORED.

Sienna shot Mae an interrogative look, and Mae shrugged and shoved the handset in her pocket. Remain stationary? When there was a new planet practically next door? Absolutely not.

1. The Planetary Quorum or other appropriate custodian acknowledges its obligation to distribute information on stellar bodies as such information becomes reasonably available...

- Excerpt from the Sol Charter, executed by 213 signatories of the Planetary Quorum

Mae's handset startled her out of a doze with a radio alert. Q-comm was still down, weirdly, but the hail hadn't come from the Planetary Quorum, like Mae had expected.

She answered anyway.

"Captain Hui." Weibold wasted no time on pleasantries. "The Planetary Quorum requires you to correct your route, which has deviated significantly from what was authorized."

Mae thought about asking why he was conducting Quorum business from a personal communication device, because she wasn't immune to petty. But no, it wasn't worth extending the conversation. "Given the circumstances—"

"The *circumstances*, Captain, are that you are significantly outside the parameters outlined by your assignment."

Technically he was right, but this was ridiculous. "I made multiple attempts to contact you, Warrant Officer. Since you didn't answer, I had to make my own determination of priorities."

"You haven't even earned the right to vote, Captain," Weibold said. "You are in no position to determine the Quorum's priorities."

"Damien, please. A life-bearing planet trumps *every* other possible priority."

Weibold's intake of breath was a hiss. "What. Planet."

There was no possible way he didn't know. She gave him the official designation anyway.

There was a silence so complete she thought he'd hung up. When he spoke, his voice was musing, meditative. "Accessing proprietary information, of course, is a serious crime—"

"I—what?" Mae had been prepared to win an argument about paperwork. Now, she floundered.

"—but one that could be mitigated, considering your willingness to—"

"I don't know what you're saying," Mae snapped. "If this isn't about the planet—"

And Weibold, for a wonder, started to laugh. "You really don't know, do you?"

"What are you talking about?"

"Captain Hui," Weibold said. "I'm afraid you have been duped."

"I...what?"

"You see," Weibold continued, "any record you have of that planet would be doctored."

"How could you possibly know that?"

"Because, *Captain*." He all but leaned on her title when he spoke it. "The existence of that planet is confidential."

"That's... ridiculous," Mae said. "It has a dataset in the Quorum catalog." Which was available to every single officer of the Planetary Quorum. That was the point. The Quorum didn't keep planets secret.

"Not so," Weibold said. "The data on that planet has not yet been uploaded publicly."

"That's supposed to be automatic," Mae said. "We have an *obligation* to announce—"

"Check the network yourself, Captain," Weibold said. "Not whatever files you've been provided. I think you'll find it isn't there."

"I...I thought the network was down."

"Correct your route, Captain," Weibold said. "The Quorum will deal with your crew accordingly. I'm certain some considerations can be made for the fact that you did not participate in their...extracurricular activities."

"But, the planet." Mae hated the way the words came tumbling out of her mouth, out of order. "We're close enough—surely we can be of some use if we—"

"You have your orders, Captain," Weibold said. "For the sake of your career, I suggest you hew to them."

The call died.

Mae stared at her handset. What was going on?

Weibold was mistaken. Quorum satellites uploaded data on the bodies they discovered automatically. They had to be reviewed by scientists, yes, but that came later. Information on stellar bodies was public, released freely. That was part of the Quorum's mandate.

And yet, he'd sounded so certain.

The information had come from...Ayse's cached copies. Right. But why had Ayse been keeping cached copies? There was no need, not when Q-comm had never before had a service outage. Not during Mae's previous long-haul missions, not during years of training, not during a lifetime on Mars. Q-comm was the only thing in the Planetary Quorum more reliable than paperwork.

Until now.

Too many questions. She wasn't going to let Weibold jerk her around for—well, she wasn't sure what his reasons were. But there was no need to stew on what he'd said. Not when she could just ask. She stalked from her quarters, banging on each woman's door as she passed, not waiting for an answer as she strode the few steps down the corridor to the ship's mess.

The crew was already there.

They were already there, in the ship's tiny commissary, at the tiny table, sharing a box of impossibly tiny snack cakes. The smell of vanilla and high fructose corn syrup stung the air.

Sienna said, finally, "Well, what's the racket?" and popped a purplish snack cake into her mouth.

No sense beating around the bush. "How did you find that file on the planet?"

No one answered.

"It wasn't in the Quorum database at all." No one contradicted her, which was fine by Mae. She was—it turned out—tired of being lied to. "You hacked the information from somewhere, dressed it up like a Quorum dataset so you could manipulate me into coming here. *Why?*"

"Well, that tears it," Sienna said. She stood and extended a hand. Red clouds floated across the black void of her perfect nails. Mae wanted to launch a bottle of acetone right at her head. "Handset."

Her voice was so calm, so certain, that Mae nearly handed it over. Recovering herself, she said, "Excuse me?"

"Take a breather, Mae," Sienna said. "You're not in charge of this ship anymore."

Mae laughed. It was the wrong response, but she couldn't help it. "You don't have the authority to do any such thing. You might not like it, but I *am* your captain."

"Ship doesn't fly without us, Mae," Sienna said quietly. "Parts don't maintain themselves."

Mae stepped back, away from Sienna's outstretched hands, and set her handset to dial the Quorum's emergency radio channel. "This is mutiny. Stand down."

Sienna chuckled. "No."

"You can't *do* this," Mae said. "Ayse, Xiadra. Why are you going along with this?"

Neither woman answered.

Mae dialed the emergency number. Nothing happened.

"You've been blocking my calls," Mae said. "You set up a false response to make it look like Q-comm was submitting my reports!" Weibold was a pompous ass, but he hadn't been ignoring her after all. How had he learned where she was going, with no Q-comm and no radio contact? "You manipulated me to get you to that planet. *Why?*"

"Money, obviously," Sienna said. "The data collection alone will make a decent buck. We manage to sell any samples, we're set up for years."

"The Quorum owns it all," Mae said. "A salary's a salary."

The expression that passed over Sienna's face then was something like pity. Mae didn't care for it at all. "We're *smugglers*, Mae. Did you really think the Quorum assigned its best and brightest to an asteroid-hopper in the middle of nowhere? Come on."

Oh. She'd been assigned to a crew of career criminals. Of course she had.

"For what it's worth, I'm sorry it ended up like this," Sienna said. She didn't sound especially remorseful. "The plan was to get to the planet, take whatever samples you told us to, and skim a little off the top. Your surprise call from Mr. Man there changed all that." Sienna flicked her gaze toward Ayse. "I'd like to know how that happened, by the way."

Ayse looked abashed. "He called from a private satellite," she said. "I automated the screening for Quorum communications overnight."

"I...Look. I don't care about that." Mae did care about that, but there were bigger issues at stake here. "This is a *life-bearing planet*. The Quorum knows we're here. We can help. This is...this means huge advances for science. Extra resources for the colonies. No more waiting for years for a shipment of whatever Earth decides it can spare. The Quorum *has* to be able to distribute these resources. Paychecks are one thing, but this is so much bigger than us. Can't you all see that?"

"Because the Quorum does *such* a wonderful job of distributing the resources it has now," Sienna snapped. "Do you have any idea what people like us even make? Because it's maybe a quarter of what you do."

"I don't—"

"Shut up, *Captain*. I guarantee you that half the contractors you've worked with steal. We have to. And when we can't anymore, when the Quorum stiffs us on supplies so we have to cover our own, when we have to choose between paying for the certifications we need to fly and feeding our families, we quit." Sienna was right in Mae's face now. "We end up planet-bound. And if you aren't rich to begin with, I promise you that's worse."

Mae knew. Oh, but she did. She remembered her fathers skipping meals so the kids wouldn't have to, then lying to her when she discovered it so she wouldn't feel guilty. Tall Dad working 12-hour shifts in an industrial-sized greenhouse, coming home with blood and plant matter caked on his fingers. Professor Dad falling asleep in front of the ancient household computer because it took so long to do the most basic tasks.

"That's. *Enough*," Mae snapped, leaning forward so her nose and Sienna's were almost touching. "You don't know a thing about me."

Sienna didn't flinch. "Maybe I don't," she said, her voice maddeningly nonchalant. She took a step back, at least. "But you're no longer giving the orders around here. Handset." She held her hand out again, palm up.

The damn handset was useless anyway. Mustering what was left of her dignity, Mae handed it over.

"Consider yourself confined to quarters until we're done here," Sienna said.

Mae could hear the bitterness in her own laughter. "Seriously? You just staged a mutiny, and now you're sending me to my room?"

"Pretty sure you'll try *something* stupid if I don't keep you out of my hair. It's that or a jet seat, I guess." Sienna shrugged. "Nothing personal. Captain."

In the end, Mae chose the jet seat.

It was the option that meant she could see the planet as they approached, looming larger and larger in her vision, covered by a blue-black ocean and shards of teal continent. Faint starlight glowed dimly across what Mae thought might be a river basin. Tufted clouds swirled beneath them as Xiadra maneuvered them into orbit. Mae could almost forget she was halfway across the solar system, strapped in a jet seat to prevent her from interfering with her mutinous crew. The planet looked the way Earth used to.

Sienna's voice snapped her out of it. "Xia, get us to a lower orbit."

"On it," Xiadra called from the cockpit.

Sienna continued, "Ayse, I want eyes on that planet."

"Are you even going to stop and admire?" Mae asked. "This planet is a damn miracle."

Sienna kicked the back of Mae's chair. "How many times do I have to tell you to shut up?"

"Easy," Ayse said. "There's like eight satellites out here."

"You can't hack Quorum satellites," Mae said, without thinking.

"They're just knock-offs," Ayse said. "Not Quorum satellites at all."

"So you *can* hack them?" Sienna asked. She didn't bother telling Mae to shut up this time.

"Already in," Ayse said. "There's only a couple that are actually new. One of them is the same one that called us earlier."

The ship bumped and rattled as it entered the planet's atmosphere.

Sienna turned on Mae. "Is there a legit reason for Weibold not to use Quorum satellites?"

"I—" *don't know*, Mae started to say. Instead, she finished with, "I don't have to tell you anything."

"Suit yourself," Sienna said. "It's obvious enough what he's doing. He's trying to cash in on a nice little custodianship. He touches down, makes the big announcement, says he found the place without the Quorum's help, and he's got himself a nice little career managing a brand-new planet where *he* gets to decide how much he shares with the Quorum. That about right?"

"That's—that's ridiculous," Mae said. And yet he *had* called from an unregistered satellite. He'd said the existence of the planet was confidential.

The sky outside the ship went gray-white as they plunged into a cloud.

"You seriously want to defend him?" Sienna asked, eyebrows raised. "Still think there's a promotion in this for you? Or do you think power is hot? I suppose he *is* pretty brassy. You've got to admire him, even if he is a jackass."

Mae had to do no such thing. Aside from being ace, she preferred women and people who weren't pompous twits, which put Weibold at the very bottom of her list.

Besides...was there anybody in the solar system who *wasn't* playing her? "If you're right, wouldn't he want to wipe us all out? We're witnesses."

"Good point," Sienna said. "You're the Quorum officer. You tell me how we make it harder for him to do that."

"I'm not helping you—"

"Your ass is on the line too," Sienna said. She sounded so *calm.*

And she was right, dammit. "Fine. What about my report? If he's been concealing this from the Quorum—maybe he won't do anything stupid if he thinks they're watching."

The cloud outside the ship wafted away. The trees were too dark to be called teal, really. They seemed blue as much as green.

"Worth a shot," Sienna said. "Ayse, can you force a communication out of those satellites of his?"

"Not via Q-comm, obviously," Ayse said. "I can get it anywhere else with a network connection."

Out the window, another cloud, low to the ground, curled up from the trees, glinting in the distant light like smoke.

"You didn't block my Q-comm access?" Mae asked.

"If only," Ayse said. She sounded like she meant it.

"The report's no good without a Q-comm connection," Mae said. "If it doesn't come through the proper channels—"

"Fuck the proper channels," Sienna said. "Send it publicly. Any newsfeed and public forum you can get."

Well, that would certainly get the Quorum's attention. And it would establish Mae, unequivocally, as the captain of a rogue ship. Mutinous or just a failure, she doubted the Quorum would care.

Mae turned her gaze back to the window.

"*Wait.*" She tried to stand, forgetting the jet seat. The restraints dug into her shoulders. That wasn't a cloud hanging above the treeline. It was smoke. "Screen. Look. Now."

Xiadra saw it too. "Folks—"

"Bombs away!" Ayse said, much too gleefully.

"Xiadra, evasive maneuvers, *now*," Mae said.

Sienna turned toward Mae. "You don't get to—"

The smoke erupted.

The ship jerked. Mae tried to blink the painful after-image from her eyes. Her ears popped. She sank back into the seat.

They were spinning wildly now. Mae closed her eyes against the motion sickness as the window went by her—again, and again, and again. Everyone was yelling.

"Strap in! I'm bringing us down!"

"Are you sure?"

"I am extremely fucking sure!"

"That son of a bitch has a weapon?! He *fired* on us!"

"I'm going to be sick!"

The ship bucked again. The shouting from inside was matched by the shrieking wail of metal from outside. Mae opened her eyes again just as the ship's interior lights flickered.

"Ten seconds." Xiadra's voice was dead calm as she counted down to impact. Mae saw sparks. Then a dark carpet of green, coming at them much too quickly, spinning wildly out of her vision and back again.

Then the spinning stopped.

1.7.3 Effective custodianship of stellar bodies cannot happen from afar. No stellar body can be governed remotely, and where possible, preference must be granted to those who are most familiar with and habituated to the stellar body, its settings, and functions.

- Excerpt from the Sol Charter, executed by 213 signatories of the Planetary Quorum

Mae lifted her head just slightly, and immediately regretted it.

Her neck ached, her vision swam. Her shoulders throbbed against the padded restraints of the jet seat when she tried to lean forward.

"Oh, you're awake." Ayse's skin looked sallow in the dimly sputtering light from the ship. Some of it, Mae realized, was actually sunlight, filtering in from the ship's open door.

"Guess the air isn't toxic," Mae said with a bitter laugh. "What happened?"

"We crashed," Ayse said. "I've been trying to get the ship's comms back up. Life support's okay."

"The others?" Mae pushed against the seat's restraints. They hissed open, tilting at an odd angle.

"Went out to assess the damage," Ayse said.

"I'm going to take a look." Mae stood, a little too quickly. Her vision danced, just for a moment. "I assume that's allowed?"

"Don't care," Ayse responded. "I'm not the captain. Just like you."

"Are all space pirates bitter?" Mae asked.

Ayse laughed. "Probably. And grumpy. You'll fit right in."

"Stars forbid," Mae muttered. She took a deep breath of recirculated air, and then took her first step onto an alien world.

They had landed in a clearing that was only partially their own making, not quite flush with the ground. The soil was covered in low, broad-leafed plants that gave way to moss and carpeted leaves. The treeline was abrupt, the trees so densely packed that it was hard to make out individual details. The only exceptions were here, where the ship had landed, felling a handful of saplings.

Most of the specimens looked like normal trees. There was one tree off to one side, at the edge of the clearing, that was different. Its branches had narrow, fan-tipped leaves like a palm tree, but it stood *up* on roots as long as Mae was tall. The roots emerged from the tree's bark like a snake from shed skin, and had bumpy protrusions all down their lengths. They formed a tent-like structure that set the tree swaying in the breeze. It was a little ways away from the ramp, thankfully, but close enough to the ship that its leaves brushed the metal exterior.

Creepy, creepy tree. At least it was at the edge of the clearing, where it should be easy to stay far away from. She didn't want to bump into it, panic, and run. Not in the thick humidity of the hopefully-not-toxic air. Just walking made her feel like she was suspended in a bowl of soup.

The docking ramp had extended, but not all the way. It hovered about a foot off the ground, which looked suspiciously springy. Mae walked to the edge and sat down. She touched one foot to the ground, then the other. Nothing happened. Cautiously, she stood.

Still nothing.

Mae could admit—to herself at least—that she jumped at the unconscionably loud, wet sucking sound the ground made when her boot pulled away from it. Just a little.

She couldn't decide how to describe the foliage. 'Green' wasn't quite the right word. Neither was 'lush.' Everything from the leaves to the branches to the moss along the spongy soil had an odd bluish tinge.

Most of the trees had large growths on their trunks, in layered, pointed protrusions that reminded Mae of the top of an absurdly large pineapple. Many of these had an additional flowering stem rising from the top. Unlike the blue undertones of the rainforest at large, these flowers seemed to grow in whatever color they pleased. Vines like thick ropes snaked across the ground.

Mae stayed close to the ship, where there were fewer vines—cleared away by the collision, maybe?—and rounded the corner.

Sienna and Xiadra stood near the jutting, smoking metal of what Mae realized—with some dismay—was the ship's thruster. The scorch lines seared across it were thicker than Mae's arm.

So there definitely had been a weapon. Whether or not it was still active was the question.

"Ah, you're awake," Sienna said. Not an ounce of concern in her voice, which sounded weirdly flat and heavy in the humid air. "We were just headed back to the ship. Did you see the outside?"

"I'd been a little busy with the foliage." Mae dutifully turned around and surveyed the rest of the ship. Most of the exterior panels were bent in ways they should not have been, and Mae doubted the crash had done their mining equipment any favors.

At this point, she didn't really care about the mining equipment. It was more important to get herself and the crew out of here. They may be mutineers, but they were still Mae's responsibility.

Aside from the mud the collision had churned up and the trees they'd knocked over, the rainforest was unscathed. Mae could barely see scorch marks in the soil. She was amazed they hadn't started a fire.

"I'll grab the rest of my things," Sienna said. "This isn't a one-person job."

"What do you need us to do?" Xiadra asked.

Mae tried to tell herself she wasn't eavesdropping as they turned back toward the ship's open door. The palm with the weird roots continued to sway gently near the head of the ramp, waving its leaves like a flag as if it were hailing their return. Mae frowned. Had it been there before? She'd thought it was out near the treeline.

"I'll need to take a closer look first," Sienna said. "Just...keep an eye out for now. And you, Mae. Don't wander off."

Mae, having been in the process of wandering, caught her foot on an exposed root. She stumbled. No, not a root. It was one of those vines, and it was thicker than her wrist.

"All right?" Xiadra asked.

"Fine," Mae said, without turning. "Just—"

Something grabbed her leg.

At first she thought she'd tripped again; the vines were everywhere, after all. But if she'd just tripped, that didn't explain the way the vine tightened around her ankle. That didn't explain the way it *yanked*.

And then she was down face-first in the mud, flailing and kicking. She tried to grab something to prevent herself from being dragged away, but the only thing to grab was more vines. The ground beneath her writhed and heaved as she yanked herself to a sitting position.

"A little help?" she called, swatting a vine with the palm of her hand. "Please?"

She saw the flashing colors of Sienna's wrench, heard a slurping smack as Sienna beat back the vines with blunt force. The mechanic fished a butane torch out of her tool belt with her left hand and aimed it clumsily, and the vines shrank away from the flame.

"This way!" Xiadra yelled at them. She'd managed to hack her way free of the plants with a hook knife and taken shelter at the side of the ship where there were only a few trampled grasses and that weird palm tree near the ramp. It must have gotten yanked around by the vines too, because it leaned at an obtuse angle. "There's fewer of them over here!"

"Get more torches!" Mae shouted, jerking away from some of the pushiest vines. "They don't like fire!"

"On it!" Mae saw Xiadra make her way toward the ramp, unimpeded by vines. The palm tree leaned away from her at an even more exaggerated angle.

Then, it started to *walk*.

Vines shrank away from the palm as its roots fanned out in a weird, windmilling trot. It headed straight for Xiadra.

Mae saw a flash of color. Sienna's monkey wrench, a spinning rainbow arcing toward the walking tree. It hit the tree and bounced off. Then Mae lost sight of the wrench, and Xiadra, as the vines around her jerked.

Mae dug her heels into the ground and tried to stand, but the mud sucked at her boots, dragging her down. She swatted at vines with her hands but there were more, more, more. The vines pulled her to her knees. There were more around her waist. She scrabbled in the mud with her hands as vines slid up her torso, tightening around her ribs. "Help!" She was on her back now, hair dragging through the mud.

More colors flashed above her. Sienna, struggling toward her through the vines. Mae saw the bright hues of the handles of Sienna's tools. The orange of her torch—weirdly muted against the surging of heaving blue-green—as Sienna aimed it at a vine with a brightly flowering tip.

The flower recoiled from the fire, then exploded.

Mae smelled burnt perfume and something worse, sweet and cloying, that made her eyes and throat sting. The air around Sienna had gone a citrus yellow. Spores. Incongruously lazy, wafting spores.

"Sienna, get down!" Mae yelled.

Sienna's mouth opened, as if she was going to say something in return. She fell instead.

Mae scrambled to her hands and knees, and threw herself into a mighty, desperate lunge. The momentum carried her forward, not enough. She couldn't reach Sienna.

She grabbed the torch, fallen from Sienna's hand.

Vines accosted her skin, stinging and searing. Welts puffed up along her hands. Mae aimed the torch at a nearby vine and it fell back. Three more replaced it as yellow spores drifted toward the ground. Stars danced across Mae's vision.

Sienna wasn't moving. Damn it. A captain always took care of her crew, even when they were insufferable mutineers. Especially when said mutineers had tried to save her life.

The vines weren't burning. They pulled Mae into a stand of clustered, broad-leafed ferns.

Fire. She needed more fire. Way more fire. Mae aimed the torch, and the ferns smoldered. A handful of vines slithered over to smother the source of the smoke. Another vine latched onto the torch and yanked. Reflexively, Mae gasped.

Then she was coughing, and the vines were pulling, and the ship was shrinking in her flickering vision as the vines dragged her away.

They didn't take her far. The ship still appeared to be within walking distance. Mae could see the clearing where they'd landed through the stand of thickly clustered trees around her.

The vines had brought Sienna as well. The mechanic lay next to her, not moving. But she was breathing, and her eyes were open. Her lips were puckered into a 'D' shape, as if whatever she'd been going to say was still on the tip of her tongue.

There was no sign of Xiadra.

The vines had left them under the canopy of a large, reaching tree. The core of its trunk was almost invisible, hidden by long, draping filaments that hung from its branches. Mae eyed them suspiciously, but their only movement was to sway gently in the breeze. Something metal—metal?—glinted dully from near the branching trunk.

"Caa," Sienna grumbled. Her left arm flopped over her chest like a suffocating fish.

"Can you stand?" Mae asked.

The mechanic muttered incoherently in response.

At the sound of their voices, dark greenish ropes stirred to life against the forest floor.

Mae wasn't sure where the torch was. She held her breath, sat as still as she could manage. It was silly, but after a few moments, the vines subsided.

There were bits of metal scattered here and there, she realized, one that looked like part of a broken strut. A large panel that had probably—at one point—been attached to their ship. As Mae watched, a vine grabbed the strut, dragged it slowly toward the curtained tree.

"Ap!" Sienna said.

Mae put a hand over her mouth to shush her.

There was *definitely* something metal leaning up against the trunk, oblong, with a muddy base that looked like it had been uprooted from the ground. As Mae squinted—it was hard to tell under the canopy, but she thought it must be approaching twilight—she realized that the tree's bark and the draping filaments were darker near the metal obelisk. As if they'd been scorched, set on fire. She remembered the bright, searing light that had struck the ship. She didn't know how Weibold had gotten the weapon onto the planet, or how he'd triggered it to fire on her, but she didn't care right now, either.

Maybe she could use it somehow to keep the vines at bay. Get Sienna back to the ship. Save at least *one* of her crew.

There was a sudden, jarring, trilling noise from somewhere. It took Mae a moment to recognize the sound for what it was: a communications hail.

Her handset. Sienna still had it tucked into her tool belt.

"Comcationsssss," Sienna mumbled. "Gif your hawnd uff."

The vines stopped their movement when Sienna stopped talking. Maybe they responded to external stimuli? It wasn't like they were actually listening.

Mae fumbled to answer the call. "Ayse? Is that you?" Maybe Ayse had something to counter the vines long enough for them to get back to the ship. If Mae could just get Sienna to safety, she wouldn't be a complete failure.

"Captain Hui." A familiar voice from the comm. Deeply unwelcome, even if it sounded less smug than usual. "It's good to hear from you."

If Weibold had been standing in front of her, Mae would have cheerfully set *him* on fire.

"I wanted to offer my congratulations," Weibold said, as if that made a damn lick of sense.

Mae heard a rustling sound, saw movement along the forest floor. She thumbed the volume on the comm down and held it close to her mouth, speaking softly. "I don't know what you're talking about. Also, I don't care. I think a tree is about to eat me."

Weibold sounded genuinely surprised. "You don't need to play coy with me, Captain, and neither one of us needs the hyperbole. We both know you've just maneuvered yourself into custodianship of a newly discovered planet. I wanted to offer my full support."

"Uff!" Sienna demanded, flailing ineffectually against Mae's palm on her mouth.

"What?" Mae considered hanging up on him. She wasn't sure she wanted his insufferable baritone to be the last thing she heard on this alien earth. And who knew how long the vines would keep their thorns to themselves.

"I think we could work well together," said the insufferable baritone. "I had hoped we could come to an accord."

"I'm..."

"Considering how to spend your newfound fame and fortune? Of course. But you'll need a partner, won't you? Someone to handle the everyday while you do all your guest appearances? Or do you prefer the minutiae of crop management and settler petitions? Either way, you'll need assistance. Planets that don't require terraforming are a space unicorn, if you will. And it takes more than one to tame a unicorn."

"Mrrff," Sienna offered.

He didn't know.

He'd concealed the existence of a planet for his own personal gain, placed a weapon on the planet and fired said weapon on another Quorum officer, and now that they'd survived he probably thought he was about to be in deep shit. He didn't *know* that Mae was down two crew members and covered in hives, or that the plants on the alien world where he'd stranded them apparently ate metal, and maybe ate people, and definitely wanted her dead.

Sienna was muttering again, struggling to sit up. Louder, but still incoherent. Mae heard another dry rustle.

Sienna bit her hand. Mae pulled it back, wiping it on her muddy pants.

"Where are we?" Sienna asked a nearby vine.

"The Quorum assigns someone to do all that," Mae said. If Sienna would just come to her senses, they could make a run for the ship.

"You could go that route if you wanted to," Weibold said, his tone suggesting that Mae had said something immeasurably distasteful. "But consider: *You* fulfilled the obligation of the Sol Charter to announce the planet to the masses, when the Quorum could not. *You* have the authority of being the first to claim touching down on the surface of an undiscovered planet—"

"Touch down? You shot at us from a weapon *you* put here! You tried to *kill* us!" Mae shouted. Something thick and vine-y wriggled near her feet.

Weibold's voice darkened. "That's a serious accusation without proof."

"Proof," Mae echoed. Good idea. "Fuck yourself with a soldering iron."

"Good one," Sienna slurred. "Butane torches are bigger. More tissue damage."

"Shh." Mae went for the obelisk, the only non-organic thing here that wasn't part of her own destroyed ship. The weapon must have a remote trigger—maybe there was some sort of data card she could remove.

The obelisk was much too big to carry with them. Its surface, seen as much as felt in the heavy gloom, was mostly smooth. But she found two small, circular crevices, about the right size for a screw.

Thankful for the glimmer of Sienna's Galaxy-Gloss-coated tool handles, Mae seized a screwdriver ("Mine!" Sienna protested) and scrabbled in the dark to unscrew the panel from the obelisk.

"...offering you a genuine partnership," Weibold said, voice tinny, from Mae's handset. It had landed somewhere on the forest floor. "But I can't allow you to slander me."

The panel on the obelisk popped off. Mae reached her hand inside.

"Last offer," Weibold said. Mae saw something move out of the corner of her eye. Not a vine. Sienna, rolling to one side.

"Don't like the torches?" Sienna asked in the general direction of Mae's handset. "I have a random orbit sander if that's more your speed."

Something came away in Mae's hand. She wasn't sure what.

The obelisk was warm. And getting warmer? Which meant...

"Sienna," Mae said. She grabbed the mechanic's arm and pulled her to her feet. "We have to go. Now." Damn Weibold and his damn backstabbing, time-wasting tactics.

Sienna stumbled, but followed. At least the vines weren't as thick here. She wasn't sure what they would do when they got to the clearing, but it was about to be better than staying here.

The weapon was presumably meant to fire on orbiting ships. She had to hope it wasn't as effective at picking out targets on the ground.

The forest floor moved underneath them as they stumbled their way toward the patch of night sky that was the edge of the clearing. Mae stomped on vines as they went, sometimes on purpose. A vine brushed her shin.

A noise behind them. Heat. A flash of light and a shockwave that sent them both staggering forward. Mae could smell smoke. Before, the vines had been quick to extinguish even the tiniest of smoking fires. Now they moved in a wave, a wall, *past* Mae and Sienna at the crackling heat behind them. There were maybe fifty feet between them and the ship.

They ran.

Nothing impeded them. Their way was lit by tiny, glowing flowerheads and a pale night sky.

Forty feet. Thirty.

Something yellow in the air. A single, tiny cloud. Then more, as those damnable flowering plants spat spores into the air like fireworks.

"Hold your breath!" she shouted to Sienna. Easier said than done when you were running full tilt. The spores settled on her sleeves, her hands, like a spotlight. Like a beacon.

Suddenly the whole world was plants. Wriggling, smothering, stinging plants.

Mae grabbed Sienna's hand, hoping their joint momentum would pull them both through. Fifteen feet. With her free hand, Sienna swiped at vines with a spanner. Fifteen feet.

Sienna stumbled, landing on one knee.

Mae dropped into a crouch beside her, pulling another tool at random from Sienna's tool belt. A palette knife. She jabbed at the vine around Sienna's ankle, stepped on the end of it for good measure, and hoisted the other to her feet. A vine wrapped around Mae's leg, coiling all the way up to her thigh.

She shoved Sienna forward. "Go!"

Mae hit the ground chin first, and the vines covered her like a tarp.

She had to close her eyes against the sting. They were coated in some sort of film, she realized, that seemed to be mildly corrosive. She bit one, just to see what would happen, and felt momentary satisfaction as it retreated, but it was replaced by another vine even as she spat sour, stinging plant bits. Maybe if she swallowed one, it would kill her quickly. Or maybe it would just add indigestion to her list of final indignities. The vines pressed down against her face, her chest, as if they intended to mush her into the dirt.

Some captain she was. Couldn't stop her crew from mutinying against her. Couldn't save them, either.

Suddenly, the pressure of vines on her sternum eased. Her vision cleared, the view of slithering vines replaced by nighttime sky, and Xiadra—Xiadra!—waving something brown and bumpy. Mae stared, and the brown-and-bumpy-something resolved into one of those gigantic stilt roots, oozing a pungent juice at one end.

Xiadra was filthy, and her hands and face were bleeding from dozens of tiny, circular wounds. She waved the stilt root again and Mae winced at the way it pulled at Xiadra's skin. But wherever the amputated root went, the vines retreated.

Xiadra shooed Sienna inside the ship. Then she turned and beamed at Mae as if they hadn't just been through plant hell. "You made it! I saw what happened. I don't think she'd have made it without you."

"Jussst what a captain would do," Mae muttered.

Xiadra grinned. "Of course it is." She offered Mae her free hand and pulled her onto the ramp. If her injuries made her uncomfortable, she didn't show it. Then, waving her stilt root like the conductor of some fibrous orchestra, she herded them back to the safety of the ship.

4.11.2. While it is hoped and expected such grave eventualities shall never come to pass, the custodian of any stellar body must be prepared to protect their peoples from threats both internal and external to the stellar body in question, and bring to justice those that act against their peoples' interests...
- Excerpt from the Sol Charter, executed by 213 signatories of the Planetary Quorum

The ship had been left open, and vines lathered the walls and ceiling. Mercifully, they retreated just as quickly as the ones outside when Xiadra waved her stilt root at them. A few that didn't make it out before Mae and Xiadra shoved the door closed; their severed ends quivered comically on the deck.

Ayse, improbably, was fine. Perhaps predictably, she'd buried herself in the comms pit when the vines came, and they hadn't managed to get through. Mae handed her whatever it was she'd pulled from the panel of the weapon. If there was anything incriminating in there, Ayse would find it.

Mae's handset began trilling furiously almost as soon as they'd set foot inside the ship. Hundreds of notifications about the newly discovered planet, announced, not through Planetary Quorum channels, but independently, by a tiny mining ship at the edge of the solar system. Approvals for her variance requests, hilariously. And then a call, almost immediately, from the Planetary Quorum, with a woman whose name Mae forgot within three seconds of hearing it. Absolutely nothing about Weibold, or from Weibold, which was excellent, since he had tried to murder her entire crew. Twice.

"Congratulations, Captain," she said.

"You're welcome," Mae said. It was only a slightly nonsensical reply.

The woman blinked, but continued. "Your team has done some important work—"

"We found a planet!" Mae agreed, triumphantly.

"So you did," the woman said, so smoothly Mae almost didn't notice the moment's hesitation before she spoke. "You've also helped bring a criminal to justice—"

"No criminals here," Mae interjected.

"Ah, I suppose you haven't heard," the nameless woman said. "Damien Weibold has been discovered to have been concealing the knowledge of an important stellar body from the Planetary Quorum, and interfering with the connectivity of the Q-comm network."

Oh. That criminal. The Quorum didn't know about the mutiny, because Mae had never reported it. She supposed that made sense. She nodded.

"It also seems likely that that data card your crew member provided will also link the weapon on the planet's surface with one of the unregistered satellites he was using," Nameless said. "Either way, you and your team have helped facilitate a huge discovery. A custodial team is being assembled to ensure that this new opportunity is handled in the most equitable way possible."

Mae nodded. Then she remembered that she'd just done that, so she nodded more vigorously.

"You seem out of sorts, Captain," the woman said.

"Yes. I *am* the captain," Mae said.

Nameless blinked. "Of course you are. Is everything all right? We could continue this call at a better time—"

"No," Mae said. "It'sss fine." Damn spores. She'd definitely had a few too many spores to the face.

"Then I am extremely pleased to offer each of your crew an honorary commission in recognition of their role in this momentous discovery," Nameless continued. "If they wish, they can accept appropriate appointments for any posting location in the Planetary Quorum."

"Yes," Mae mumbled. "Thank you. That's good."

"I am just as pleased to confirm that the Quorum will be implementing your full commission at first opportunity," the nameless woman continued. She paused. "Normally I would advise you that your commission would be in full effect in advance of the upcoming referendum, but with recent events, I am afraid we are facing an administrative backlog."

"But it's *important*," Mae said, leaning toward the ship's comm so that Nameless would understand just how important it was.

"I'm glad you think so," Nameless said. "And I assure you we will make best efforts. I can promise unreservedly that your vote will be in full effect for any future referendums we have."

"Huh," Mae said.

"In the meantime, consider what postings are of interest," Nameless suggested. "Given your profile at the moment, I don't imagine there are many for which you'd be refused. Your list of eligible postings will be sent to you automatically."

The Quorum wasn't able to extract them immediately, so they hunkered down. That night, unable to sleep with the sound of vines battering at the hull of their broken ship, Mae scrolled through the available postings available to captains of her soon-to-be rank. Most were what she expected: small outpostings scattered throughout the solar system, managing small fleets of ships not unlike the one Mae currently captained. A handful of larger, more influential postings closer to the solar center. Two at Uranus space station, one on Mars, that might just give her a tiny bit of sway in terms of getting the stellar colonies what they actually needed. Mae considered going home.

And one other posting, for a dwarf planet without even a name, just a classification number, at the far edges of the solar system. Habitable surface, the posting boasted. Abundant plant life. Prior experience required: 'Early-stage foreign world habituation.' Ability to be flexible with rules. Experience working with crews of diverse education, personalities and backgrounds. Not unlike Mae's own moderately-illegal crew.

Mae stared at the entry for a long time. And then, unable to help herself, she started to laugh.

Five days later, five days too many of hearing vines snap brittle metal bits off the outside of their ruined ship, the Quorum showed up and hauled them into orbit, where they sat debating their future.

The formal offers from the Quorum came the next day, after everybody had been through medical and decontamination, and eaten a meal that hadn't come from a food printer. Sienna approached her, in a commissary that was actually able to fit both of them comfortably. "Hey," Sienna said. "Thanks for helping out back there."

Mae shrugged. "Just trying to do the right thing." And then, because it felt like it was worth acknowledging, "You helped me."

"Yes, well..." Sienna shrugged. "You're still not my captain. But you don't suck, either. You could be an actually decent captain for some crew someday, I suppose. Maybe even ours, if you can get that stick out of your rear."

There was silence for a few moments, except for the scraping of forks.

"The Quorum made us all a generous offer," Sienna said. "An appropriate posting in *any* available location served by the Quorum. Even brand-new postings like, say, a little rogue planet with killer trees."

"And...?" Mae asked, knowing full well the answer.

Sienna smirked. "We've all decided to accept, of course. Wild jungle planets have excellent material for smuggling. And a commission salary won't hurt."

"Of course," Mae said. "You got everything you wanted."

Sienna's smirk broadened.

Somewhere, several high-ranking bureaucrats were no doubt having conniptions at the thought of a planetary custodianship being led by a handful of previously-unknown contractors. And that was *without* any of them knowing about the smuggling. "I highly doubt that was the intent."

Sienna's grin turned wolf-like. "Then they shouldn't have made the offer."

"Speaking of offers," Mae said.

"Yeah, where did you end up? What are you in charge of now?"

"Well... It turns out the Quorum processes your promotion a whole lot faster when that promotion puts you in charge of a whole planet. I selected a no-name dwarf planet on the edge of known space. It sounds like we'll be working together." Mae mirrored Sienna's smirk back at her. "Though I doubt that was the intent."

"Huh," Sienna said. And then, "Sorry about the mutiny."

Mae laughed. "You just usurped custodianship of a planet, and *that's* what you're apologizing for?"

Sienna laughed, too. "To be fair, the mutiny is the only part I did *at* you. You were just on the wrong ship at the wrong time."

Mae hesitated. Then she said, "I don't think I was on the wrong ship."

"What?"

Mae shrugged, a little uncomfortable. "I think the ship I was on worked out just fine."

"I..." Sienna cleared her throat. "Well, of course."

"I'm glad," Mae said. And then, "You *will* have to promise not to do it again."

"What?"

"No more mutinies," Mae said. "I can't have my crew rebelling while we're taming a killer jungle planet."

Sienna met her gaze. "Can I just call you captain? I can't hardline no more mutiny."

"It's more than a title, Sienna. It's a job and a promise, and one I've proved I can handle." Mae tapped a finger against her chin. "Unless you think you can't handle me?"

Sienna snorted. "I can handle you just fine, Captain. With or without the mutiny."

"Prove it," Mae said. It was impossible to keep her expression solemn.

"Sure. I am gonna need a favor."

Mae raised her eyebrows. "Oh?"

"You can help me look for my wrench," Sienna said. "I'm gonna want that back."

Mae smiled.

How to Steal a Planet is a short story by N. L. Bates. To keep up to date with her work, visit **www.nlbates.com**. When she's not writing stories about spaceship crews who steal implausibly large objects, Bates writes and performs music as her alter ego Natalie Lynn. You can find her music at **www.natalielynnmusic.com**.

Brie and the Marsh Kraken

Sara Codair

Sapphic Representation: Lesbian, Ace/Demi
Heat Level: Hot!
Content Warnings: Coarse Language, Violence

Salt marsh was Brie's favorite smell. There was something about the sweet, salty scent of decay and rebirth that made her feel at home.

Home. Hope.

The warm sensation in her chest, blocking out cold drafts of despair from a world that was too damned hot.

Sweating from a long ride, Brie got off her bike. She needed a break, a moment to compose herself before the last half-mile to her childhood home. She leaned her bike against a pitch pine's rough trunk, kicked off her shoes and tip-toed past the bushes at the edge of the crumbling asphalt causeway, admiring the expanse of green blades poking up through dark brown muck and last year's decaying yellow grass. Her toes curled into the mud, rooting her to the ground until she felt like she was part of the land. Like she belonged as much as the tree.

There were people further out, on the far side of the marsh. Researchers, probably. Not that they'd save it from climate change. The marsh, like the rest of the God-forsaken planet, was dying. Still, there was a silver lining. Rising sea levels and frequent hurricanes had driven Cape Cod property values down to something Brie could actually afford, and the land upon which her childhood home once stood was for sale. She was going to buy it back.

She was meeting the realtor in fifteen minutes. She needed to smile. She needed to get back on her bike, cross the causeway onto Monomoscoy Island, and take the first right down her old driveway. She needed to go the rest of the way home. But her feet wouldn't budge. What if it didn't work out? What if she got there only to find out it had already sold?

She shook her head. No one wanted to live here anymore. People were selling lots for a fraction of what they paid twenty years ago. Plus, the realtor wouldn't let her drive all the way here for nothing. Right?

She took another deep breath and stepped away from the marsh, back to the road. A deep burbling made her pause.

"What is that?" She glanced over her shoulder. On the far edge, where the marsh met saltwater pond, a ring of ripples disturbed the still water. A deep groan rose from the earth. Not good. The ground trembled under her bare feet. Before she could properly react, Brie toppled over, twisting as she fell so as to not damage the delicate mat of green swaying at her feet.

The edge of the marsh met asphalt, and the asphalt met Brie's knees, drawing blood. The ground twisted. Jagged cracks, born of last winter's excessive cycle of freezing and thawing, widened to fissures.

Earthquake?

They happened in the northeast now, but rarely. Never this bad. A deep, rumbling groan warred with the loud ringing in her ears. Why did this have to happen *today*?

A crack rang through the air as a utility pole came down on the causeway. Brie scrambled back toward the marsh. Grass bent and scraped her hands. Mud squirted up between her toes and splattered her legs. She kept scrambling forward until she tumbled into a pool of water, crushing sharp blades of marsh grass with flailing arms.

A slurping belch came from out in the marsh. Someone screamed. The researchers? Yes. They were running toward her as brown...tentacles...whipped out of the muck and flailed at them.

Tentacles? Attacking people?

In the marsh?

In *her* marsh.

Impossible.

"I need to get out of here," Brie muttered, touching her head to feel for a bump or scrape. She didn't remember hitting it, but she might not if she had a concussion.

Another scream. Tentacles wrapped around a man's ankle. He fell.

Fear stung Brie like a jellyfish. A shot of adrenaline. She scrambled to her feet, and lurched forward to help, only to slip on something slimy and face plant in the water. The marsh, it seemed, did not want her to go.

The tentacles slithered back into the marsh. She blinked, and they were gone. So were the people. The water stilled. A breeze rustled tall grasses. Birdsong returned.

She stood, finally, her clothes soaked, the air a touch chillier than before. Nothing in the marsh should have tentacles like that, right? Could it have been...what? A discarded pet snake? An oversized eel? And the people? Where had they gone? Did they have a boat Brie hadn't noticed and rowed away? Maybe terrified of the giant pet snake?

Yeah. That seemed reasonable.

Brie got on her bike and rode. Past a tangle of poison ivy and scattered lady slippers was a driveway—torn up and wider than she remembered. Sand and shells crunched under her tires. The dip on the left was still there. It had snagged her bike tire when she was ten. The fall would've been softer had it been sand like when Brie was a kid, and not speckled with the remains of crushed shell by the new owners.

She landed on her knees. Again. One of those shells sliced her palms and deepened the cuts she already had on her knee. Sand clung to her soaked clothes. Sweet pine, salt, and dust mingled in her nose. She lingered on the ground, digging her fingers into the dirt. Breathing in the scent of home. Of childhood. Freedom. A place where she belonged.

"Brie, are you alright?"

The voice was familiar though she hadn't heard it in years. It *belonged* here. It wasn't the realtor she'd talked to on the phone, but someone a thousand times better. She'd last heard it when? Twelve? Thirteen? Definitely during Tilly Blake's slumber party, when they'd been telling stories near the fireplace of haunted marshes and ghostly apparitions and...tentacles? Was she remembering that right? "Yes. No." Brie pushed sweaty curls out of her face. "Did you feel that earthquake?"

"Yeah. That's the worst one I've felt since I moved back east." Gretchen Morrison, Brie's old neighbor, stared down at her, wearing the same half-smothered smirk Brie remembered from childhood. Her short brown hair shone in the sun. Sweat beaded on her forehead from the humid air. She picked at chapped lips, or tried to, anyway. Her nails were too short to pick at anything. She'd always kept them that way. "You're all scraped up. Did the quake knock you off of your bike?"

"Not exactly. You look...different. I've never seen you in anything other than jeans."

Gretchen's hands flew to her sides, smoothing a perfectly pressed short sleeve white button up with purple octopus print. Her khaki shorts were also wrinkle free. A carabiner laden with keys hung from her belt loop. Her legs were unshaved—Brie remembered Gretchen had strong opinions about shaving as a teenager—and her feet were bare. Classic Gretchen, aside from the stiff clothes.

Gretchen crouched down in front of her and offered a sun-kissed hand. "I grew up. And you...you're pretty banged up. Here. Let me help."

They fit together perfectly. They always had. Memories stirred up emotions too long buried. Brie thought she'd left Gretchen here in the marsh, buried under the mat, drowned in the saltwater with her old home. And now here they were—memories and her childhood home and Gretchen—tingling across her skin from the feather touch of Gretchen's fingertips, assaulting her senses as the salt, and the humidity, and Gretchen's floral perfume collided and surrounded Brie. "What are you doing here?" Awkward. Brie's gut tightened. *I never say the right thing.*

"My partner, Darcy, didn't want to show you the lot." Gretchen smiled—a real smile—just a hint of teeth behind full lips. "Business partner. Not a romantic partner. We co-own the last real estate agency in town. And I'm single. You know."

Gretchen was still just as awkward as Brie. "Why didn't she want to show it?"

Gretchen's lip curled up. "Someone already put in an offer well over the asking price. A company who put in an offer on every property in this neighborhood, for sale or not, including my house. They're trying to make me leave, Brie."

Rage swelled in Brie's heart like a storm surge during a full moon. Aside from a few semesters of college, Gretchen had lived here her whole life. Leaving, for her, would be more cataclysmic than for Brie. Brie wanted to empathize, but she felt her own hope sloughing off as Gretchen stared mournfully at the crushed seashell driveway. "I'm sorry, Gretchen. It's not right, making you leave, but why did you let me drive three hours down here just to have my hopes crushed? You could have told me over the phone."

Gretchen pulled Brie to her feet. "I needed you here."

"I have a job. I didn't take vacation time just to have a Band-aid ripped off my favorite memories."

Gretchen kicked at the shells with the toe of her sandals. "I needed you here. You're the only person who loves this land as much as I do. I need you to help me save it. I can't lose my home, Brie."

Brie blinked. "Save it? Save the marsh?"

"Yes. If we ruin the company buying up the island, then you can buy your land back and I get to keep my house. It'll be fun!" She smiled, toothy and wide and reminiscent of childhood mischief. "It'll be like that game we played as kids, the one where you wore my grandmother's oil hat and we snuck around the marsh chasing ducks. Except this time we're hunting a soulless corporation and neither one of us has a hat."

"Uh," Brie began.

Gretchen let go of Brie's hand and scratched the back of her head. "Um, do you want to come over and get cleaned up? Then I'll tell you my plan."

"I just got here." Brie blinked. She looked down at her clothes, soaked, torn, and sandy. Blood ran down from her knee to her shin. "I have to be back at work in three days."

Gretchen glanced back and forth between Brie and the bike. "This shouldn't take more than two. Where did you ride from, anyway?"

"Sippewissett Campground." Brie decided against brushing sand from her boardshorts. She liked how it felt—being covered in a part of home. "Just...give me a minute to see everything. It's been forever."

Gretchen stepped aside and nodded. "Of course. It has to be hard to come home."

It was bittersweet. An intense sense that she was where she belonged coupled with deep nostalgia. But knowing that someone else might snatch it away, just as it came within reach, was a thorny vine twining through her core.

She strode past Gretchen, who followed her down the end of the driveway. She smirked when she passed the wreckage of the house that had replaced hers, then turned right, following a familiar path down to the water. She looked across the salt pond to a marsh that stretched to the causeway. Was there really a way to save even one lot from a company with enough money to buy the whole island? Did she really want to get involved? She'd moved on, she thought, from the marsh, from Gretchen. But being back here now, feet curled in the thick mud, flies zipping around her shoulders, she wondered about a lost past, and a future that could still be, if she had the courage to reach out and take it.

There was the monster situation to consider, though.

Brie folded her hands tight together and took a deep breath. "Did you see what happened to the researchers in the marsh? Um, did they pass by on a boat?"

"There weren't any researchers in the marsh." Gretchen's voice was firm, with a surprising edge. "Brie, are you okay?"

Brie took a step forward, instinctively curling her toes into the muck. "I'm certain there was someone out there. And they had equipment. I'm just wondering what it might have been for, and if they were, are, part of your plan?"

Gretchen wrinkled her nose. "Might have been from the company trying to buy our homes. They already bought the marsh. They do a lot of cataloging of the local wildlife."

"Bought the marsh?! But...you can buy house plots, sure. You can buy houses. You can't just...you can't buy a wetland! They're protected areas."

"Not all of them," Gretchen said with a shrug. "Most of the marsh around here was privately owned at one point, but the state eventually bought them and made them part of an estuarine research preserve. My family owned one of those original lots, as a matter of fact. Don't you remember the section I was always taking us to, as kids? That was grandma's, a long time ago."

"I..." Brie closed her eyes and relived the fuzzy memory.

Younger, sun-kissed, both girls bent down to look at a fish they'd never seen before. But as their faces moved closer together, Brie forgot about the fish. Gretchen's eyes were the same color as the speck of mud on her chin. And her lips...somehow they weren't chapped despite all the time she spent outdoors. Brie thumped the mud off of Gretchen's chin, letting her hand linger.

They were fourteen. Just discovering the world. Just discovering each other.

Gretchen raised her fingers, brushing Brie's chin.

"Gretchen? Brie? Are you in the marsh again?" Brie's mother shouted.

Brie and Gretchen locked eyes, frozen, faces in suppressed giggles. Crouched down in a channel of knee-deep water, the grass rose above their heads. Mom couldn't see them in their private world of reeds and salt and splashing minnows.

"I know you're in there." Mom's voice was louder this time. "You could get fined for trespassing."

"It wouldn't be illegal if the state hadn't made my grandmother sell it to them." A wicked grin on Gretchen's face as she leaned in closer to Brie. "Kiss me, Brie. Or would you rather kiss a fish?"

"Brie! Gretchen! Now!" The shout was followed by the splashes of a kayak paddle.

"Uh, my mom is coming." Brie backed away. Last time she didn't listen, mom didn't let her see Gretchen for a week.

She almost managed a smile, wondering what would've happened that day had her mom not come looking for them. She had no intention of kissing a fish, but...but Gretchen? Maybe?

A breeze stirred ripples on the still water of the salt pond. Dark clouds loomed in the distance, towering anvils carrying a heavy threat of rain and wind. Lightning forked in the darkness.

"We should go, Brie. Your clothes are soaked and you're bleeding. I can bring you back here tomorrow, if you want. I...I understand the pull of this place."

Brie sighed into the humid air. There were no signs of people in the marsh. No signs of tentacles, either. No utility trucks coming to fix the pole. "Maybe we should call the electric company or the police and tell them about the power lines."

Gretchen pulled her phone out of her pocket. "I called ten minutes ago. The recording says they're experiencing a high call volume. There's nothing to do but wait."

But Brie wasn't ready to leave. Not just yet. Two minutes. Five. She wanted to feel the marsh seep into her pores, invade her nostrils, suck her down into the mud and mussels and fiddler crabs that made her feel more at home than a cement wall ever could. "Did you try the police?" Brie dipped her toes in the water. It was cooler than she expected, though she supposed it was still early in the season. But she remembered, *remembered,* this water always felt warm when the sun beat down on it as the tide was rushing out. Brie remembered being lost in the sound of Gretchen's voice preaching ways to reduce carbon and water footprints while lazing around on a float tied to the dock.

"They said there were a lot of lines down from a severe thunderstorm." Gretchen pointed at the dark clouds that loomed on the other side of town. "But this street is low priority."

"Who still lives out here?" Looking to the left, past a pile of downed trees and bramble, Brie saw another mansion turned into a pile of rubble. She stepped a little further into the water until it rose about her knees and peered down the shoreline. No house had escaped damage.

Gretchen stepped closer until the edges of their arms were barely touching. "The only ones left are me, the Fords, and a few of the old timers. After the floods and tornadoes we got at the end of hurricane season, the wash-ashores decided to cut their losses and rebuild their eyesore mansions elsewhere."

Was her buy-back plan ill-fated, then? If she put up a house, would it just get eaten by the marsh?

No. If Gretchen still lived here, then Brie could, too.

"We have to get it back," Brie whispered. She brushed her pinky finger against the back of Gretchen's hand. This land belonged to her, or she belonged to it. "This place is *ours*. Let's go back to your place. I want to hear your plan."

Gretchen turned, walking away from the water. Brie reached for Gretchen's hand, but it was already out of reach. She was too late, like usual. Rays of sun stretched toward her, like they were trying to escape the growing thunderhead. For a moment, just before the storm swallowed the sun, Brie swore she saw the shadow of tentacles writhing where Gretchen's shadow should've been.

* * *

Gretchen's house, by some miracle, had sustained no damage in any of the storms that pounded the cape all fall and winter. The earthquake also seemed to have ignored it. Not a single tree on her property had come down, but many surrounding lots were torn up or flattened.

The inside of the house was a time capsule, reaching back past their shared childhood, to Gretchen's grandmother. Some scents were new, like bacon fat in the kitchen, but the cool tiles on the floor were avocado green. The couch was covered in patchwork quilts, and in the corner of the kitchen sat a red and white enamel table from the 1940's.

"Have a seat at the table," Gretchen said, pointing. "I'll get the first aid kit and we'll see to your knee."

"I'm fine," Brie said, waving her off. But Gretchen caught her hand and held it in mid-air.

"My marsh, my rules," she whispered, her voice teasing.

Brie sat on the red chair, wrapped her ankles around the chrome legs, and decided to keep her mouth shut.

Gretchen disappeared, then marched back into the kitchen a moment later with a first aid kit older than Brie. Distant thunder rumbled. Gretchen wiped blood off of Brie's knee with a damp cloth, the water several degrees too cold. Brie shivered.

"Cold?" Gretchen asked her, not looking up from the wound.

"Band-Aid?" Brie returned, pointing to the kit. "Weren't we here to talk about a plan to save the marsh?"

Gretchen chortled, pulled a yellow-edged Band-Aid from the kit and applied it to Brie's scrape. Her fingers lingered on Brie's thigh, the tips of her too-short nails tracing patterns in the skin.

"You're sandy," Gretchen said after her fingers finished circling Brie's knee.

"I could use a bath," Brie said, wondering how much farther Gretchen's fingers planned on wandering.

To her disappointment, Gretchen scooted back and snapped the first aid kit closed.

Brie, feeling the moment slip away, said, "Remember our rainy-day Scrabble matches?"

"They were so intense." Gretchen finally met her eyes. Brie saw flecks of purple in the deep brown, and it reminded her of the sea lavender that grew in the marsh at the end of summer. "Sometimes I thought you were going to kiss me, or strangle me, but you never did either."

"I wanted both, depending on who won. I..." Brie sucked in a long breath. "I had a huge crush on you back then, but I didn't realize it."

"I know." Gretchen picked up Brie's hand. "I thought if I gave you time, and enough hints, you'd figure it out and realize I felt the same way. I'm wondering, now, if things are a little clearer? Now that you're home?"

Things always seemed clearer on the marsh. Brie remembered that very well. And things always seemed easier with Gretchen. The whole world could be against them—mounds of school work, yelling parents, irate siblings—but when Brie and Gretchen were together, conspiring in the reeds, well. There had never been anything more perfect, or easy.

"Yeah. Yes. I used to think I was straight. With you, though. I don't know. I can't think of anything, or anyone else, when I'm with you. I don't know what that makes me." Even now, at thirty-six, she was still uncertain of what labels really applied. Whereas Gretchen had confidently declared herself a lesbian in sixth grade and never looked back. Brie envied that confidence, that certainty. "And hints...I don't pay close enough attention for little hints."

"I'll keep that in mind, but I didn't think I was being subtle just now." Gretchen stood, eyes glued to Brie as she packed up the first aid kit and stuffed it in a cupboard. She leaned against the fridge and waggled her eyebrows. "So do you want anything to drink...or eat?" She pointed at her temple. "That is a very blatant come-on."

"Do you have iced tea?"

Gretchen shook her head and smiled as she pulled a glass pitcher out of the fridge.

Brie brushed her fingers against Gretchen's as she took the glass. She could miss verbal signals, but hopefully Gretchen wouldn't miss physical ones. "So what is this plan of yours?"

Gretchen pulled up a chair, so close that their knees brushed. This, Brie understood. She grinned, then took a long drink of her tea.

Gretchen fished her phone out of her pocket and held it, so they could both see the website for FutureSolutions BioTech: Healing Our Planet; Searching for New Homes. "That's the company that bought the marsh, and this island. It's the one we're going to take down."

Brie pushed a thigh between Gretchen's as she leaned in for a better view. Gretchen smelled like salt and sand, like glorious sunlit afternoons basking on the beach. "Why does the company want the marsh?"

"Experiments. They pretend they're trying to save the land, but it's just a scam." Gretchen put the phone down, sliding her hands from the table to Brie's stomach. Their fingers entwined, and desire—hot, insistent—shot across Brie's skin like lightning. "Those researchers? They're going to destroy the marsh, not save it."

So why had they left so suddenly? Brie mused as Gretchen's thumb caressed Brie's knuckles, raising goosebumps on her skin. Had there really been a...snake? Monster? Had it scared them away? It hadn't...it hadn't eaten them, surely? *Is it terrible that I don't care? That I'm more concerned about the marsh than them? Well, the marsh, and Gretchen's hand.*

Brie gasped as Gretchen's hand slid off of her leg, up her stomach, grazing the side of Brie's breast until finding her side. Still her fingers meandered up, trailing fire in their wake, until they landed on Brie's cheek. They stroked the skin there, trailing Brie's jawline, pressing into the dimple of her chin.

"Um. How uh, do you know all this?" Brie asked.

"I have ways of getting places unnoticed." Gretchen leaned and whispered into Brie's ear. "And when people do see me, they often don't believe their own eyes. But you'd believe me, wouldn't you, Brie?"

"Um." Gretchen's lips grazed her chin, then brushed across her own—toying and sweet. Brie licked her lips. "Why, um. Why don't people believe what they see?"

Gretchen's hand cupped the back of Brie's head. Her fingers stroked Brie's neck, toying in the fine hair, circling the bones of Brie's spine. She had long fingers, Brie realized. Like a piano player. Long, dexterous fingers that...almost felt like they were snaking down the back of Brie's neck. Massaging. Exploring.

Brie arched her back and closed her eyes as her breath caught.

"Tell me about the last time you didn't believe what you saw," Gretchen commanded, her voice still just a whisper. "Tell me, and I'll tell you a secret."

Brie's lips were swollen, though they'd not even kissed. Her skin was alight from Gretchen's fingers, and the hot breath on her neck, and Gretchen's other hand, that now stroked lazy circles on the inside of Brie's thigh. "Um, today. I thought I saw tentacles."

Gretchen's fingers slid back up, tangling in Brie's hair, those impossibly long fingers stretching out Brie's curls. "What if I told you that the tentacles were real, and I could prove it? Would you want to know?"

Brie closed the distance between them. Her tongue flicked Gretchen's lips and tasted brine and hot marsh air. Her clothes were still soaked. Her underwear, soaked as well. Enough toying. Enough playing. "What if I don't care about tentacles right now? What if I want to kiss you?"

A smile tugged at the edges of Gretchen's mouth. She sat back, just far enough that if Brie tried to again close the distance, she'd fall off her chair. "Tell me you want proof, and I'll kiss you. I'll kiss you in all the ways I've always wanted to."

"Yes," Brie said, pulling Gretchen back in, digging her fingers into Gretchen's shoulders, intent on keeping her friend close. "I want proof. I want you to kiss me. I want more than kisses. And I want it now."

Their lips met. It was a tease at first, that made Brie clench her legs together. As thunder shook the house, she pulled closer, pushed her lips into Gretchen's. Traced her tongue across Gretchen's lips, demanding entrance.

Gretchen opened her mouth. Her tongue slid against Brie's teeth and danced with Brie's own. Her fingers again found Brie's neck, circling, pressing, massaging and her fingers...elongated. Two...tentacles...slithered down Brie's back, sliding across the top of her ass and down, around her thigh.

Brie didn't pull away. She didn't pull away, and she slid off her chair and straddled Gretchen, wrapping her legs around Gretchen's waist, pressing their bodies together, sharing warmth, sharing tongues, sharing...secrets, apparently.

"That story you always told at my firepit," Brie managed when they broke apart long enough to catch their breath. "I thought you made it up. There were..." Gretchen tried to resume the kiss, so Brie pushed the rest of the words out. "Always krakens rising to save the earth. Krakens in marshes. You."

"The earth holds surprising truths." Gretchen's tentacles slid under Brie's shirt, over her breasts. Gretchen's skin was petal-soft but slick, and the tentacles slid across Brie's nipples, raising them to pertness.

"Oh!" Brie bit down on Gretchen's lip and tugged at the edges of Gretchen's shirt, hoping she might get a chance to remove it in the near future. She should have been afraid. Gretchen was the Marsh Kraken, and the Marsh Kraken had her tentacles inside Brie's shirt, and Brie did not care. She'd never felt anything quite like this wild hunger. She'd never wanted to fuck someone so badly, never yearned for an experience quite like this—binding herself to her beloved marsh in a very unexpected way

Gretchen pulled back from the kiss, but her tentacles lingered on Brie's sensitive nipples, pulling at them, pinching them, drawing moans from Brie. "How is this for proof?"

Brie licked salt from her lips, tasting endless possibilities. "I have questions that don't really matter but...maybe some that do. No, don't move your...fingers...away. Just tell me the truth. Did you eat those people?"

"I temporarily incapacitated them and removed them from the marsh. I didn't eat them." Gretchen's mouth opened in a lazy smile, tongue flicking. One tentacle slid down Brie's belly and toyed with the clasp of her shorts. "But I want to eat you. And show you what else I can do with my tentacles."

Brie undid the top button and grinned. "Yes. Please. Now."

The tentacle slid around the back of her neck and Gretchen's mouth was back on hers and there were tentacles *everywhere*. Well, almost everywhere. Tentacles pulled her shorts down, slid up her backside and hooked around her boxer briefs. Brie's legs shook. Heat and wetness gathered between her legs. The one place the tentacles hadn't gone. The one place she *needed* them to go.

"Stop teasing me," she breathed into Gretchen's mouth. She shifted position, far enough that the tentacles could push her shorts and boxers down and to the floor. She went back to Gretchen's lap, legs wrapped around Gretchen and the back of the chair, her body open. Willing. Waiting. Impatient.

Gretchen, very, very slowly, removed her shirt.

Brie glared.

Gretchen laughed, tentacles undulating with the rise and fall of her bare chest. The tentacles shifted, twining tighter around Brie's hips and under her arms, lifting her into the air. Gretchen carried her out of the kitchen, down a short hallway, to the bedroom, gently lowered her down onto the bed, and stepped back, her tentacles receding.

"Please," Brie gasped, staring up at Gretchen. Her face was the same. So was her torso, a solid, muscular stomach and breasts just big enough to fill Brie's hands. But where she should have arms were eight tentacles, long, purple, and slinky. It was weird, and surreal, and Brie loved all of it.

Tentacles twined around Brie's wrists, pinning them above her head. They slid up her legs, spreading them apart, exposing every inch of Brie's body. The tentacle tips skated across the soft skin of Brie's calves, to the inside of her thighs, tickling and tormenting.

Brie whimpered and begged, but Gretchen would not go faster. She brought Brie's knees up and held her ankles while a thin, almost delicate tentacle found Brie's clit. A thicker one slipped inside her.

"Oh! Oh, I...god!"

"You loved those old sci-fi movies," Gretchen said, grinning as Brie arched off the bed with each thrust. "They always did seem to skimp on the good parts."

Brie gasped, clutching the sheets between her fists while the tentacles slid and flicked her clit, while the other pulsed inside her. Tortuously, deliciously slow at her first, building speed, until finally, she climaxed as thunder shook the house.

* * *

Through Gretchen's window, Brie could just see the pond and the edge of the marsh, vibrant in the early evening light. The golden sunbeams bordered on orange, shining rays between the ruins of storm clouds. Brie sprawled on the bed, wearing a t-shirt that smelled like Gretchen. Like marsh. Like home. Her hair was damp from a shower, and the clean underwear she'd borrowed were already wet from thinking about Gretchen's tentacles, and all they had accomplished between her legs.

"The thunderstorm took down a lot of trees and this neighborhood is low priority." Gretchen strode back into the room, in human form, and plopped her phone down on the nightstand. Drops of water fell from her hair to her shoulders. "The person from the utility company wasn't sure when they'd make it out here."

"You said thunderstorm." That had been a wild one—the perfect soundtrack for epic tentacle sex—but not as terrifying as feeling the earth rock and buck under her feet. "But what about the earthquake?"

Gretchen's cheeks flushed. "That wasn't really an earthquake."

Brie sat up. "What do you mean it wasn't an earthquake?"

"It...was me. It doesn't take much to partially shift." Gretchen stared at her hands. "But if I want to go full kraken, the transformation is...dramatic."

Brie tried to picture what Gretchen would look like fully transformed. What would it feel like to be touched by her tentacles when no part of her was human? But if the transformation literally caused earthquakes..."How far did it go?"

"It's only bad for a quarter mile, and outside a mile radius, you wouldn't feel a thing." Gretchen stood up, took a few steps, then knelt on the floor, rolled a rug up and removed a few loose floorboards, revealing a keypad and screen.

"Gretchen." Brie scooted closer to the edge of the bed, watching Gretchen's fingers—still deliciously dexterous—enter a combination. "There are other ways we could spend this day, and my vacation. I'm not sure I'm going to be able to focus on planning after, you know."

ADHD made it hard enough to pay attention. Layer in certain kinds of distractions and...Brie was toast.

"We need to go over the plan first. But then, after, I have a few more tricks I can show you." Gretchen winked.

"Promise?"

"I promise. It's not like you can leave anyway. The only road off the island is blocked "

"Well that's comforting," Brie returned.

A safe hissed open. "You could take a boat I suppose."

"Do you still have one?" It had been years since Brie had been on a boat.

"Of course." Gretchen winked again. "If I travel too much in kraken form, my picture will end up on every cryptid site on the internet. And then the area would be overrun with hobby cryptozoologists."

She pulled a composition notebook and some big, rolled-up piece of paper out of the safe. "Plans for the lab, and other various schematics and blueprints. None of it is digital. Too much risk from hackers."

"Okay fine," Brie huffed. "Into the serious now?"

Gretchen blinked. "I was always serious."

It was really hard not to laugh at the sincerity in Gretchen's voice. Brie scooted over to the edge of the bed, struggling to keep her mind from replaying the last hour over and over. Focus. Save the marsh. More sex later. Maybe next time, they'd do it on the boat. Or in the water.

Gretchen plopped the paper down on the bed. "FutureSolutions is a massive company with labs all over the east coast. This isn't just how we protect our neighborhood, but dozens of other areas they want to experiment on."

"So how do a couple people take down a big company like this?"

"Two people don't do it alone. I'm part of a group of shifters and cryptids who are coordinating attacks on FutureSolutions tomorrow. I had a friend helping me, but we had a disagreement and xe backed out." Gretchen unrolled a blueprint and spread it out on the bed. "This facility is in an industrial park in Falmouth, on Rte. 150."

The lines and symbols blurred together as Brie's brain fixated on one word. "Attacks? You sure you want my help? The most violent thing I've ever done was tip over the high school bully's kayak when she was still in it. And she was wearing a life vest."

"Yes. We're not blowing up the building or doing anything that will get people killed." Gretchen pointed at a spot on the blueprint. "I need to plant a device in the server room that will give a colleague access, and then go 'kraken' their lab. I need you to help make sure I don't get caught."

Brie moved to her stomach on the bed, and leaned on her elbows, propping her head with her hands. Again, she tried not to laugh. "I'm sorry. You're going to...to 'kraken' a lab? Is that the technical word? And wouldn't this all be easier if you did it alone? One less person to get caught. Or am I just the kraken driver?"

"You can double as my diversion and my reason to visit the facility."

Brie tilted her head. "How?"

"FutureSolutions claims they are looking for ways to make land more resilient to natural disasters, hence they're buying all the unwanted land and experimenting. But not everyone wants to sell their property, no matter how much FutureSolutions offers." Gretchen's finger slid across the blueprint to the lobby. "When they want to persuade someone—when they want to convince them there will be a chance to reclaim a new and improved version of their home—they invite them for a 'tour' of the facility."

"But I don't have a property to sell." Brie stared at the pencil lines drawn on the blueprint, marking a path from a reception desk, through a presentation room, and by something labeled as 'faux lab.' "I'm trying to buy one of the same lots FutureSolutions is."

Gretchen put a hand on Brie's shoulder. "Do you remember Gina Spellman?"

Brie grimaced. "She poked holes in my kayak while I was swimming near a sand bar. How could I forget her?"

"She inherited her mother's house three years ago." Gretchen's smile was delightfully evil. "She hasn't set foot on the island since then, yet she refuses to even talk to FutureSolutions."

"Oh. So, I pose as Gina, and FutureSolutions welcomes us with open arms, thinking they can finally convince her to sell. Once we're in, I keep their attention and you sneak off to 'kraken' the lab? Which entails what, exactly?"

Gretchen's eyes, brimming with mischief, met Brie's. "Mostly flailing my arms and smashing stuff. Don't worry. I won't damage any tentacles. I know how fond you are of them." She smirked. "You in?"

"I..." Brie remembered her kayak full of water, how she hadn't seen the holes until she was half a mile away from the sandbar and the boat had started seriously sinking. She would've been stranded had Gretchen not rescued her.

Gina would be furious if she knew Brie was impersonating her.

"Yes, I'm in."

* * *

Brie didn't sleep much that night despite her exhaustion. She and Gretchen had planned the 'krakening' down to the minute, every outfit, every escape pathway, every (potentially) broken piece of lab equipment.

Brie should have been plotting her lines or trying to remember how Gina walked and spoke. Instead, there were tentacles on her mind. Impossible, glorious tentacles powerful enough to shake the earth. Delicate enough to pleasure.

And there was hope.

Assuming they didn't get caught and wind up in jail, or worse, murdered by some sketchy private security, Brie had a chance of not only getting her land back, but protecting the island it was part of. And she'd found a way to keep a part of the marsh closer to herself.

There was so much hope and yet, there were so many ways it could all go wrong.

Anxiety, her old, bothersome curse, tried to clamp down on Brie's chest. She listened to the crickets. To wind rustling the scrub pine and bushes. She tossed and turned. Her fingers twitched. Her legs itched.

Maybe she'd get some work done after all. Brie slipped out from the covers, Gretchen snoring beside her, and turned on her tablet. First, she read about FutureSolutions and its empty promises of regenerated land. Then she read internet rumors about the long-term effects of FutureSolutions 'treatments,' about the mutated wildlife, the poisoned streams. She researched Gina, reading everything publicly available about her on news and social media. She practiced her voice. She taught herself to mimic the two-fingered hair flip Gina preferred. She made a list of the clothing, make up, and accessories she'd need to play the part convincingly.

When she couldn't keep her eyes open another minute, she flopped down on the bed, and let old memories of lounging on the beach with Gretchen fill her mind.

* * *

Talking about infiltrating a corporation's headquarters while lounging in Gretchen's bedroom after the best sex ever was one thing.

Actually infiltrating said headquarters was something else entirely. Brie's foot incessantly tapped the floor of Gretchen's Jeep as they drove through a sweltering afternoon to what Brie was more and more convinced was going to be her death. The anxiety from the night before had not left and had instead grown more omnipresent. A tightness in her chest. Loss of appetite.

She took a deep breath. Everything was going to be fine.

Exhale. *In a few hours, it will be over. I'll be snuggled up with Gretchen watching the sunset. It will be fine.*

"You're about to spiral, aren't you?" Gretchen's voice was soft. She took a hand off the steering wheel and put it on Brie's knee. "I remember, from childhood, how bad your anxiety could get."

"No. Yes. Fine. What if they see me and immediately know I'm acting?"

"What did you win an award for in 6th grade?"

"My role in the spring play." It was the only time Brie had ever won anything at school. She'd played the Mad Hatter in a retelling of Alice in Wonderland. She hadn't even thought she could get the part, but Gretchen had convinced her to audition, like she'd convinced her to join this scheme. Well, there had been less seduction last time. "But this is different. The stakes are so much higher."

"They are," Gretchen admitted. "But this role does have one thing in common with the one you had in the sixth-grade play."

"And what is that?"

Gretchen grinned. "You have killer costumes. And you're playing someone mad."

"Different kinds of mad," Brie muttered. But Gretchen was right about the costume.

The loose comfort made her want to curl up and take a nap—making up for the sleep she lost last night—but the anxious feeling in her chest guaranteed she wouldn't sleep even if she tried. The thick coat of purple Galaxy Gloss on her fingers was a weight that made her cringe, but no matter how hard she tried she couldn't get it to chip or break. Half the fun of nail polish was gradually chipping it all off. But it did help her play the role, especially with her curls cascading down her back, frizzy fly-aways tamed by some hair product that smelled delicious and horrible at the same time. The thick makeup was a lot less itchy than she expected, and heavily applied. She did, she admitted to herself, look like a completely different person. The shoes, however. The shoes were the worst. High heels. Horrible torture devices that had been tormenting women for decades, now on her feet. A week with her feet in the mud wouldn't make up for the next hour. Gretchen's fingers might, but there were a lot of events between now and potential 'thanks-for-helping-me-destroy-a-soulless-corporation' sex.

Gretchen's Jeep pulled up to a gate at the start of the industrial park that housed FutureSolutions. It looked more like a military base than a corporate headquarters with the armed guards at the gatehouse that checked IDs, and Brie struggled to keep her face neutral as one of the guards took out a scanner. Gretchen had produced Brie's fake ID overnight. Surely, they were done for.

The scanner beeped.

The guard waved them through.

"Was security this lax last time you came here?" Brie asked. "I'm so nervous I think I'm going to puke."

Gretchen nodded. "I didn't even need a photo ID last time. They've upgraded, due to some new research. And eco-activists have attacked their properties before. If you do puke, could you roll down the window first?"

Brie ignored the attempt at levity. "Now what?"

"Now, you sit pretty until we get inside. And trust me." She waved her left hand, two fingers partially merged into the start of a tentacle. "Trust me."

"You're a kraken," Brie shot back.

"Trust, and being a kraken, are not mutually exclusive."

The building, once they entered, was nothing like what Brie expected. Tall and shiny with lots of glass, it looked like it belonged in a city, not some small-town industrial park. There was a reception desk and waiting area that made it seem like visitors were a thing. There was even a door that said visitor restroom, and they got little visitor badges from a person with a crisp outfit and fake polite tone. It made it easier to slip into her own role of confident rich person. Gina had always acted like she owned anything from a spot on a state beach she didn't want to share to a cafe. Brie straightened and rolled her shoulders back, settling into Gina's posture and Gina's gait. She tilted her head up so she could look down her nose and silently judge. Just like Gina. The woman who handed Brie the badge had that same confidence. Her skirt shimmered in the harsh light, a silvery gray that matched her nails and hair. She stared at Brie, waiting for a response.

Brie blinked. "I don't get it. You're stumbling over your words. Try again. Enunciate this time."

"This is what the island could look like if the experiment works." The woman gestured toward a 3-D model of Monomoscoy Island. "Remind me which home is yours?"

Brie's fingers automatically went to her own, but she quickly corrected, pointing further down the island to where Gina lived. Brie didn't know if Gina's house had survived hurricane season, but back when Brie was young, it had at least five bedrooms, six bathrooms, a bowling alley, and theater room. At first, it had just been a summer home, but much to Brie's dismay, Gina's family had moved in full time when she was thirteen, allowing her to torment Brie all year round.

The model was slightly smaller than the original, a glassy, modern home with brown and green tones up on a terraformed hill. Lush bushes, ornamental grasses, and colorful flowers cascaded down to the water where a solar yacht waited, tied to a floating dock. All the houses in the model had a similar look and landscape.

"What do you think?" asked the tour guide.

"Incorporating some of the island's history would've been a nice touch. More variation in the style of the structures would make it look less like a suburban cul-de-sac."

"I'll pass the feedback up to my supervisor," said the guide.

"Thank you." Brie forced a smile. "Can you tell me more about how you are going to accomplish all this?"

"Certainly. This way." The guide led them into the next room. There was a table with a 3-D projection on it and a window into the lab, which she guessed had to be staged. With all the security, Brie doubted they would display the actual lab. It was when they left that room that Gretchen asked for directions to a bathroom.

Time for Brie to keep the tour guide's attention glued to her.

Brie held her chin high. "You showed me the terraformed island, but you glossed over the part about how you will make it look that way. You think you can swoop in, offer me some paltry sum to experiment on my land and then have the audacity to let me buy it back assuming you don't destroy it? Do you have any idea what that land is worth to me?"

"My apologies, Ms. Spellmen." The guide folded her hands in front of her. "Allow me to make a presentation."

Brie watched in silence, lips pursed, and eyes narrowed, as a project video explained how the sandy soil on Cape Cod was particularly well suited to their Living Earth™ experiment. Living Earth™ was an organism, implanted in the soil, that would eventually become the soil, enriching as it grew. It would fill in the micronutrient gaps left behind from industrial waste, would heal the microbial life, and allow for, eventually, larger plants to reestablish. Then, the condominiums, town homes, and mansions could start going up. But in order for any of that to happen, the existing homes had to be razed, the remaining trees felled, and the marshland drained. For progress. For healing. For money.

"Have you tested this anywhere?" Brie asked.

"The results in our lab were promising," the woman said.

"Show me. Now."

"Unfortunately, our labs are off limits to visitors," said the woman.

Brie spun away from the holo and stood with her arms crossed. "If you want my land, I need proof your experiment will work. This is my family home we are discussing."

"I'm sorry, Ms. Spellmen, but I can't let you in the lab."

Brie scrambled to think of another kind of proof she could demand. "Do you have any recordings of previous field tests?"

"Those are also off-limits to visitors."

"But you have done field tests?"

The woman nodded. She glanced at the clock, then looked over her shoulder, probably checking to see if Gretchen was coming back.

Brie stepped between the woman and the clock. "They were successful, right?"

"Would you like to see the video about the smart houses we plan to build once we've terraformed the island?"

Brie shook her head. "I want more convincing evidence this will work. Get your supervisor. I want to see the reports. I want to see the lab."

She sighed. "You're not the first person to ask me that. The first three times, I put in the request. It was denied each time, and I was told to stop asking."

"Then I'm not selling you my land." Brie turned away from the woman and looked around the room, unsure what to do next. If the silence went on too long, the tour guide might start wondering why Gretchen wasn't back yet.

The clickity-clack of high heels echoed down the hallway. A woman with vibrant red hair and an emerald green pantsuit entered the room. She waved to the tour guide, who walked over and listened while Pantsuit whispered in her ear.

Brie tensed. It was probably something completely unrelated to her and Gretchen, but what if it wasn't? What if Gretchen got caught? If she did get caught, would they realize Brie was a fake? Or would they assume she was a legitimate landowner Gretchen just used to get in the door? Her anxiety spun, suffocating and disorienting. She was found out. Gretchen hadn't had enough time. The whole plan was doomed.

"Ms. Spellman, may I take a look at your identification?"

"Of course." She would keep her voice firm, breathing steady. She would not start shaking. "Is there a problem?" Brie opened up the designer purse she'd splurged on for today and took the ID out of a coordinating wallet and handed it to Pantsuit, who studied it.

"If I hadn't just spoken to the real Gina Spellmen on the phone, I never would've known this was a fake." Pantsuit looked back and forth between Brie and the ID.

"What on earth are you talking about?" Brie puffed out her chest, though her hands began to tremble. She couldn't let them see her sweat. She had to hide her anxiety with bluster. "That is not fake. Who is impersonating me?"

"You can drop the act," said Pantsuit. "Voice recognition software pegs the women on the phone as the real Gina. She is calling from the real Gina's cellphone. She—"

"I am the real Gina." Brie stomped her foot. She imagined her marsh being drained. Imagined a bulldozer leveling her home.

Imagined Gretchen in her human form, stuck on dry land, with nowhere to go. The rage softened her anxiety and kept her from full-out panic. She could, momentarily, remain in charge of her own body. "I want to know who the imposter is."

"Security is on their way," said Pantsuit. "Stop lying."

"How dare you call me a liar!" Brie yelled. She clutched her bag in an attempt to hide her shaking hands. What would happen if she got caught? What would the company do? Would they call the police? Take care of matters in their own way?

She was going to be fine.

Gretchen had a plan.

Everything was going to be fine. Right? Right!?

"My question," said the tour guide, "is whether or not Gretchen knows who you are. Do we need to have security go wait for her outside the bathroom?"

Everything was not fine. Not at all.

Brie's act collapsed. If people went looking for Gretchen now, they wouldn't find her in the bathroom. They'd find her in the lab, tentacles out, doing...whatever 'krakening' involved. Brie couldn't handle that—couldn't handle Gretchen's secret suddenly owned by a soulless corporation who would no doubt find a way to use her for their terraforming plans. "She doesn't know. I used her to get in here."

Pantsuit glanced down the hallway, frowned, and then looked back at Brie. "Why? Are you trying to steal our secrets?"

Brie shook her head. The truth...at least part of it...maybe that would convince them she wasn't a corporate spy. "I used to live on the island you're buying up. I wanted to buy my family land back, but FutureSolutions already had an offer on it. I wanted to know what you were going to do with it. That's all. I swear. Please let me go."

"That's all?" Pantsuit narrowed her eyes. "The high-end counterfeit ID, the fancy clothes—all that because you wanted to know what was happening to something that used to belong to your family?"

"Yes!" Nausea rose in her throat, stifling further words. Either they were going to believe her or they weren't. Images of the guns at the gatehouse filled her mind. She imagined running. But where would she run? She couldn't find her way out of this maze of a building even if she had been paying more attention to her surroundings on the way in.

"Bullshit," said Pantsuit. She glared at the tour guide, who was on the phone. "Where the hell is security?"

Brie's heart pounded against her chest.

Her stomach churned.

She was going to die.

Gretchen was going to die.

The land would be poisoned.

Everyone was going to die.

Fuck.

They were all totally screwed.

The ground rushed up to meet her.

The shiny tiles hurt when her knees hit them.

Breathe, whispered a distant voice in her mind.

But she couldn't breathe.

Hands on her shoulders. Cold and bony. Worms crawling all over her skin, sea worms with little squirmy legs and sharp teeth. She ran her hands through her hair, raking her glossy nails across her scalp harder and harder until the pain chased away the spiral of panic.

This was not what she was supposed to do. Not how she was supposed to cope, but it had been years since she'd been to therapy and worked on these little ritual things to cope with panic attacks, but she remembered pain. It worked. It always worked.

"Call 911," said Pantsuit.

"I can't. The phones aren't working," said Tourguide.

Was that Gretchen? She didn't mention jamming phones, but then Brie hadn't asked a lot of questions. She was still processing tentacles. Brie inhaled. Counted to ten. She was drenched in sweat, exhausted and aching. But she had to pull herself together. She had to get up. Get up. Her arms felt like buzzing spaghetti as she got to her hands and knees, then pushed herself to her feet and looked around.

Something red caught her eye. The fire alarm. In the movies, people always pulled them, so they could cause chaos and evacuate with the crowds. Would that work here? How many people were even in this building? It probably wouldn't work. But she had to try, right? She was already in a silly monster movie plot. Adding a fire alarm seemed downright appropriate.

Brie ran.

Running made her heart beat faster, but the strain of it cut through a layer of anxiety. One of many, many layers. Her hand closed around the red bar of the alarm as a bony hand closed around her wrist. She pulled.

EEEEEEE

EEEEEEE

EeeeeeeeOhhhhh

"Get back here!" Pantsuit pulled her from the alarm, too late.

More hands grabbed Brie. She shivered. Trapped. She'd be trapped. She kicked. Jammed her elbow back, and the floor shook. She and her attackers stumbled, and as Brie hit the floor again, she rolled away.

Had to get away.

EEEEEEE

EEEEEEE

EeeeeeeeOhhhhh

The scream of the fire alarm spiked Brie's adrenaline. And underneath it...underneath the piercing tone was another sound. A groan of steel and concrete echoed from the bowels of the building. The floor shook. Books and knick-knacks clattered down from secretarial shelves. Promotional posters curled from the wall.

Earthquake? Again?

No. It was the same kind of shaking that she'd felt in the marsh, on the causeway.

Gretchen had shifted to full kraken form.

We're all going to die. We're all going to die. We're all going to die.

Brie rolled onto her back, trying to breathe, trying to think. To remember where the exit was. Around her, chaos. Pantsuit and her boss were accosted by employees, filled with questions and demands. No one cared about the anxiety-riddled woman on the floor.

"Two earthquakes in two days? Is the building stable? It doesn't sound stable. Should we evacuate?"

"Maybe it was an explosion? I heard it was an explosion. What is the protocol for this?"

"There are no alerts. What do we do?"

"Our phones are still jammed. I need to call my family! I have bars, but nothing is connecting."

Brie's phone buzzed. How did her phone work when the others didn't? Surely, they were all on the same carrier.

'Help. I'm trapped. Two levels down the stairs. Go right. Third door on the left.'

Gretchen.

Right.

Brie scrambled to her feet and ran. Pantsuit made a halfhearted grab for her, but she evaded. There were so many people now, milling about the main lobby, all confused and demanding answers. All going in the opposite direction of Gretchen. There. A door with the stair symbol.

She opened it and nearly tripped over a body sprawled across the top three stairs. He had welts on his neck and face but was still breathing. Brie hopped over him and kept moving. There was another body around the next landing. Then another. She hopped over them all and kept descending.

She didn't want to know if they were dead.

Didn't want to know if Gretchen had killed anyone.

She counted doors, then opened the third one.

She entered a large room with a central pool. In the very middle of the pool was an...an island made of white sand and tall, reed-like grasses. Except...that was just half the island. The other half was made of what appeared to be gray sludge. Surrounding the pool were tanks, tables, and various pieces of lab equipment—all overturned and shattered. Bits of glass littered the floor and the bottom of the pool. Gretchen...one human-shaped leg was stuck under a cabinet. A metal rod pinned a tentacle to the ground. She had one free hand. Most of her tentacles were in the water, flailing, churning up bits of glass that drew faint lines of blood from her skin. Her torso was caught between human and something that resembled an octopus.

"I can't shift to human if I'm in water." Gretchen's voice was hoarse. Strained. Her human head was barely out of the water. "And I can't go back to full kraken while part of me is on land. I've destroyed their best equipment. I ate their backup files, paper and all the flash drives I could find. The computers are smashed beyond repair. We can worry about anything in the cloud later that my associates haven't already downloaded. For right now, the corporation is crippled. It's time to escape."

They'd done it? It was that easy? Well, not technically easy, since they still had to get out and oh...there was Brie's anxiety again, constricting her chest, depressing her breathing. Strangling her from the inside out. "What do I do?!" Brie froze, glancing back and forth between the cabinet, the impaled tentacle, and the rest of Gretchen.

"Just get me out of here," Gretchen hissed through clenched teeth.

EEEEEEE

EEEEEEE

EeeeeeeeOhhhhh

"All personnel, please evacuate the building."

A second intercom message followed, this time in Pantsuit's voice, "We have infiltrators! Security to all lower levels!"

"Hurry!" Gretchen hissed.

"I'm trying!" The metal that impaled the tentacle was the closest thing to Brie. She picked her way through the debris, gripped the metal with two hands and pulled, surprised at how easily it released. Dark blood squirted for a moment, then the tentacle retracted, and Gretchen's hips and ass shifted to human.

"Hurry!" Gretchen shouted, but Brie barely heard the pounding of her own heart in her ears. "I doubt I immobilized all their security."

Brie studied the cabinet pinning Gretchen's leg. The doors hung open, the contents scattered and floating in the water. Brie tried to lift the cabinet, but it wouldn't budge. She threw herself against it, harder and harder until the thin plywood cracked, and finally, she shoved it off Gretchen, who tumbled into the pool.

Without thinking, Brie waded in after her, wrapped her arms under Gretchen's, and pulled. The water surrounding them turned pink as glass scraped Brie's skin, but she ignored it. Pain, right now, was her friend.

One pull. Two. They were free of the water. Tentacles turned back to legs and mass rearranged itself, condensing into a human—a naked human leaning heavily on Brie. "Where are your clothes?"

"Shredded," said Gretchen.

She gave Gretchen her shirt and skirt. That left Brie in a camisole, blazer, and leggings while Gretchen had a lavender button-up shirt and skirt. Ok, Gretchen's outfit looked normal albeit a little too small, where Brie just looked weird.

EEEEEEE

EEEEEEE

EeeeeeeeOhhhhh

"All personnel evacuate now!"

Together, they hobbled along the edge of the pool as Gretchen led Brie to a back door. They pushed it open and the panicked sounds of employees replaced the whine of the alarm. People ran past, ignoring their mismatched clothes, Gretchen's limp, and Brie's sweaty, panicked face.

"There they are!" Pantsuit called from the middle of the crowd. "Where is security? Somebody get them!"

"Run!" Gretchen said. "To the Jeep!"

They ran, weaving between people who looked more disoriented than upset. One reached for Brie's arm, but her grip was tentative, and Brie pulled free. They made it to the Jeep. They got in. Pantsuit continued to scream, but the mob of demanding people around her—all holding phones and briefcases and tablets—would not let her through.

"Get me to water," Gretchen said as she hobbled into the passenger seat. "The more I shift, the more I heal, especially in salt water. Wake me when we are there."

Brie climbed into the driver's seat of Gretchen's Jeep and stepped on the gas, speeding out of the parking lot. She heard a high-pitched scream and from her rearview managed to catch the end of Pantsuit decking another employee, breaking from the crowd, and getting into her own car.

She was fast, and the car must have had a turbo because in half a block Pantsuit was tailing them, bumper to bumper.

Brie snuck a glance at Gretchen, snoring in the passenger seat. Her skin gleamed feverish and ashen. She clutched her arm to her stomach, but there was no blood. The puncture on the tentacle must have at least partially healed when she switched back to human form. The glass cuts had scabbed over on Gretchen, although a few on Brie still wept.

When she turned off Route 51 toward Route 28, Pantsuit also turned, as did another car behind her. Should she be rushing her to the hospital? Questions and anxious words swarmed through Brie's head so fast that the road blurred. Nausea rose in her throat. She had to focus! Gretchen's life was at stake!

Gretchen would heal in the water, when she shifted again. Brie had to get her there.

She sped through an intersection, just before the light turned red.

The other two cars ran the red light.

The rush of adrenaline cleared her head. She yanked the wheel, turning onto one side road, and then another. She whooped with each tight turn.

"Brie, you're going away from the water," Gretchen mumbled.

"I need to lose them."

"Need water," Gretchen mumbled again.

Brie turned again, into the crowded parking lot of a fish market, swerving around pedestrians before merging back onto the main road, only for a minute, before taking an abrupt left. She glanced in the rearview. She didn't see either of the shiny black Mercedes that had followed her from FutureSolutions.

The last time she'd been down this road, she'd been going to get brunch with Gretchen at a yacht club. They'd had really good baked scallops. Both Brie and Gretchen had gone to school with the owners' kids, who might be the owners by now. They would let Brie and Gretchen hang out a bit. Maybe they could even borrow a boat, sneak out to the campsite unnoticed. And if the people from FutureSolutions didn't know Brie's real identity, they wouldn't know to look at that campground. There was hope.

The yacht club was up on stilts, the parking lot contained a handful of cars, and through the big windows, Brie could see people eating. She stopped right at the edge of the lot, as close to the water as she could get. Through her rearview mirror, the cars pulled in behind her. Pantsuit got out and stormed across the lot, her right hand clutching a gun.

"I have a plan." Brie's voice cracked. She'd expected the yacht club to be empty and abandoned.

"Whatever it is, Arty knows what I am. Run inside and tell them I'll have fried calamari, extra crispy. They'll know what that means. And then make sure anyone attacking us goes near the water." Gretchen unbuckled her seatbelt, opened the car door, and fell from the seat to the hot pavement below.

"Gretchen! Hold on, I'll come around—"

"Get Arty!" Gretchen staggered down the ramp to the docks then stepped into the water.

Brie ran into the restaurant. A bell dinged. The air conditioner whirred and the cold conjured goosebumps on Brie's arms. It felt normal. Like her old life. Like her memories.

"Are you here for lunch?" asked a person at the host station.

"I need Arty!" The host pointed to the person behind the bar.

Brie ran to him. "Arty, I'm here with Gretchen. She said to order calamari, extra crispy."

Arty paled. He walked over to the host, whispered something, then started closing blinds. The restaurant staff followed suit. Patrons looked at each other and whispered. Someone demanded to know what was going on. Pantsuit, followed by the tour guide and a handful of goons, walked in. All had guns. All wore grimaces. All looked ready for blood. "Look!" one of the restaurant patrons screamed.

Bubbles rose to the harbor's still surface. Sail boats and sections of dock rocked, though the water was calm and there was no wind. A motor hummed behind Brie. She glanced over her shoulder and saw storm shutters closing over the building's windows. TourGuide and Pantsuit watched the growing bubbles, gradually inching closer to the dock upon which they all stood. The other three scanned the rows of boats, hands beside their guns.

Brie gasped air, her throat constricting and stomach churning. The ground swayed. Gretchen had said to get any attackers near the water. They were already looking at the boats.

She took a slow step forward. No one noticed. *I can do this. I have to.*

Brie's hands shook, but she took a deep breath. "Um, excuse me."

Pantsuit and TourGuide spun around, guns raised.

"If I tell you where Gretchen is, do you promise not to shoot her?"

Pantsuit narrowed her eyes. "We have tasers, and the guns are loaded with non-lethal rounds. Still, we won't use them unless she attacks us."

Bullshit. "She's hiding in the blue yacht. But please, don't hurt her. I coerced her into helping."

Brie wasn't sure if they believed her, but the three thugs didn't take their guns out as they stepped onto the dock.

"Please. Let me talk to her. This is all one big misunderstanding."

Pantsuit waved her forward.

Sweat dripped down Brie's face as she moved forward, flanked by two armed women. The world tilted. She stepped onto the metal ramp.

The earth bellowed. Bubbles frothed into a maelstrom. The docks and boats bucked. Brie lost her balance, fell, and clung to the metal railing as tentacles rose around her. They swarmed the dock, splintering wood and bringing groans from the supporting beams.

The adrenaline-fueled cage Brie had bound her anxiety into, faltered.

There were shouts and gunshots. Slaps and screams. Brie clung to the railing, eyes shut tight, frozen, her body locked in a silent scream.

Boat hulls thundered together.

Metal groaned.

A monster roared.

Slaps. Bodies hitting the water.

She couldn't move. Couldn't think. Couldn't open her eyes. There was pain, blurring between physical and mental, but it took all the effort, all her focus to just breathe through all the chaos. It was all she could do to hold on and breathe, even when the shots stopped. Even when the water calmed, and sirens wailed in the distance.

"Brie?"

The police had to be here. She was going to be arrested.

"Brie? Hey lover, talk to me?"

Gretchen would be arrested too if she ever shifted back to human form. How long could she be a kraken for? How often could she shift? What was waiting for Brie when she opened her eyes?

Someone touched her. She jolted. Clung to the railing harder. Refused to open her eyes. She couldn't go to jail. She couldn't move. Couldn't breathe. Couldn't let go.

A softer hand on her back.

"Brie." Gretchen's voice was as soft as her touch. "It's over. Let go. We're safe now."

She shook her head. They weren't safe. They never would be.

How many people had Gretchen killed?

"Brie, I promise no one is going to hurt you." There was certainty in that voice. Magic in her touch. Brie let go of the railing and clung to Gretchen instead. What if this was the last time they saw each other? Held each other? Yesterday morning, she woke with hope. She was going home. Now, it never seemed so far out of reach.

"We won, Brie. Everything will be okay. We won." Gretchen's whisper was full of hope, but Brie didn't dare let herself believe it. She had questions, but her throat was too tight to ask them.

But she did open her eyes.

Her eyelids flitted open to see a human woman smiling at her, as warm as her childhood memories.

The harbor was a mess. Docks and boats floated out toward the jetty. Some were twisted and capsized. EMTs pulled unconscious people out of an inflatable tender and loaded them onto stretchers. The dock had been reduced to floating wood boards and one half-intact piling. The club was toast.

"My tentacles can secrete mucus," Gretchen whispered. "What it does to a person depends on my emotions. These people are temporarily paralyzed, like the ones near the lab. They'll wake up with no memory of what happened today."

In the parking lot, pavement buckled, but the building remained intact. A crowd of people stood in front of the restaurant, talking to police.

Gretchen's lips brushed Brie's ear as she continued to whisper. "When the police ask you what happened, don't mention ever being at FutureSolutions. We were getting lunch when the people with guns showed up. Everyone here is claiming they saw a monster. The police think it's some sort of mass hysteria caused by FutureSolutions dumping chemical waste in the water. My network snagged the cloud files from their server and have just sent them to the press. I tipped the police off on the rest. They're heading to the lab next. Remember, we were just eating at the restaurant. That's all."

Brie nodded. She could do that. If she ever calmed down enough to talk.

* * *

After a week riddled with anxiety, Brie accepted that Gretchen was right. They weren't getting arrested. At the moment, no one from FutureSolutions was coming for them, though Brie wondered how long that would last.

But cuddled up on Gretchen's couch, tangled up in tentacles and an old quilt, while the news reported on FutureSolutions misdeeds and downfall, it finally sunk in. "I wish you had been more up front about how well connected your network was." Brie tightened the quilt against herself as a rare, cool breeze blew through the window. "I thought we were just smashing up a lab, but your network has destroyed FutureSolutions, both economically and socially. They'll never recover."

"I only had time to tell you so much." Gretchen raised a tentacle to Brie's face, tucking stray curls behind her ears. "And after, it was hard to get you to listen, at least for the first few days."

"If I'd known more ahead of time, I might have panicked less at the end." Brie wasn't one hundred percent sure that was true because anxiety was seldom logical.

"I won't keep you in the dark again." One of Gretchen's human-shaped hands squeezed Brie. "I promise."

Brie arched her eyebrows. "Does that mean we're going to take on more shady corporations?"

Gretchen looked surprised. "You'd want to go on another mission?"

Brie stared down at her hand, intertwined with Gretchen's. "I need to work on getting my anxiety under control first, but our marsh isn't the only land threatened by corporate greed. We make a good team, especially if I know I always have the marsh to come home to."

The surprise melted into a mischievous grin. "And me. You always have me to come home to, too. And when you're ready, I'd love your help. And speaking of home, did I tell you that FutureSolutions withdrew their offer on your land? The current owners have accepted your offer."

The last bit of weight that had been holding Brie down, lifted. She stood, performed a shameless and decidedly silly 'happy dance' before kissing Gretchen.

A tentacle wrapped around her ankle, sliding further up her leg as the kiss deepened. Brie slipped her hand under Gretchen's shirt, sliding her hands over hard muscle up to soft breasts, noting that she wasn't wearing a bra. A tentacle slapped Brie's ass and pushed her tight against Gretchen. "Shall we celebrate?"

"Yes. Please." Brie pulled Gretchen's polo over her head. While Brie's hands cupped Gretchen's breasts, tentacles removed the rest of Brie's clothing. They twined around Brie, tugging her onto her back, onto the floor.

"Not like that." Brie grinned and gently pushed a tentacle down. "This time, I'm going to lead."

* * *

The sun shone, and the birds sang. Cool muck seeped between Brie's toes. Gretchen's hand rested on the small of her back. She was exhausted from another day of hard work, clearing out debris, but the worst of it was done. The last remains of the wrecked house were in the dumpster, waiting for the salvage company to come haul them away. The only thing that remained was the foundation. It was in good enough shape that Brie could build something on it if she wanted. However, she was thinking that was less and less necessary as time went on. Each day, she spent less time in her camper and more time with Gretchen. She spent more nights in Gretchen's bed than she did in her own.

She got her land back.

She got the girl she'd always wanted and the kraken she never knew she needed.

She didn't need to build a house. She'd already found her way back home.

As the sun hit Brie's face, she closed her eyes, inhaled the sweet salt and pine, and leaned her head on Gretchen's chest.

Home.

Sara Codair is the author of weird stories, short and long. They are supervised by Goose the Meowditor, who edits their work by deleting entire pages. Follow Sara **@shatteredsmooth** on Twitter and Instagram for updates about their writing and pictures of Goose.

Down Among the Mushrooms

William C. Tracy

Sapphic Representation: Lesbian, Bi/Pan
Heat Level: Medium
Content Warnings: Coarse Language, Violence, Gore, Death

"Ma'am, we found something," my foreman called. His tone said it wasn't good.

"Well hell. Show me." I strode by Harie, glancing to the horizon, no barrier between our construction and the overgrown surface of this planet. The thick mat visible in the distance was nearly as tall as I was, with stalks sprouting to three times my height. It was as if someone had grown moss to the size of a brown and blue shag carpet on steroids, and salted it with twigs and ferns, bulbous growths, smelly flesh-like appendages, and even less identifiable...*things*. It stretched as far as the eye could see. Drone surveys reported all of Lida was covered in the same sort of growth, even into the oceans.

"We broke into what looks like a shaft, Agetha," Harie said, pointing the way. His use of my name dragged my attention from the fungal biomass. He was a good kid, and had been working for me for seven years so far. "It's right on a wall line, a hole the size of the Z22 excavator. There was no sign of it on the geotechnical survey or the subsurface scan. I don't think it was even here last week."

"So right where the distribution center for this whole neighborhood is supposed to go," I grumbled. A half-built row of apartments loomed behind us, the community garden planned across the street. "It's only the hub used to dole out emergency supplies and basic necessities to keep citizens alive as the new radian stabilizes." I stared at slabs of resinplast waiting to be turned into new walls.

The new material wasn't as strong as the original nanotanium from the colony ships, but the latter had been absorbed nearly twenty-five years ago into the wall around Alpha and Beta radians, shielding our growing colony from the threat of the ever-growing biomass. These days, what we had left was substandard equipment and continual delays.

Zeta radian was taking twice as long to construct as the five previous. Out of the eight planned radians of the arcopolis—what would be a self-sustained city—this was the first to overlap the regrown flora of Lida. When we arrived, the colony ship exhausts slagged the landing site to a distance of five kilometers, and estimates were thirty years before the planet reclaimed the area. But the biomass surprised us, and no one in the colony had experience with anything growing so fast. We'd barely finished constructing Epsilon before resorting to flamethrowers to burn out the new growth.

"Was the substrata in this area saturated with moisture and we missed it?" I asked. "A shaft couldn't just appear. That was solid limestone last week."

"I know, but…" Harie darted a sideways glance at me as we reached the latest excavation, our boots crushing an ankle-high carpet of finger-like fungus the consistency of rubber. Some of it moved out of the way of our steps. The Z22 digger was idling to one side, Cindie with her feet up on the console. I frowned, and she put them back on the floor. "Just take a look."

With Zeta radian, there were surprises at every step, and the biomass was already deep enough to resist a mere flamethrower. From here, I could see things move, never sure whether they were settling growths, or one of the detached animal-like roaming creatures. The scientists said they were part of the biomass, though they weren't always connected. They might have been true animals at one point, but had been subsumed by the fungus. The prevailing theory was, any species which used to live here was now subservient to the crawling fungus. We had to keep our colony from the same fate. It was why Admin pushed us so hard to finish the radian construction. Plus they had already scheduled the grand opening of the radian.

I shook my head. "Alright, break time's over." I shoved my way into the ring my construction crew made around the shaft, gawping over the crack in the ground. Back on the colony ship, this construction would have been handled by on-board robotics, and I would have been the systems analyst in charge. Instead I was an aging Generational without even a girlfriend, mothering Grounders barely out of adolescence who'd never been out of a gravity well.

I peered over the lip of the crack, shaped like the edge of the excavator bucket. The ground of our building site was a chaos of biomass: ferns, grass, solid and seeping jelly fungi, and other unidentified goo all mashed together into a low mat. The musty scent of it was everywhere, not bad, but strong. I thought I'd get used to it eventually, but over twenty-five years later, I could still pick out when the wind changed to a different angle.

The Z22 had dug through the fungus and through the top layer of slagged ground, already reverting to rich dirt. But a meter into the hole, the dirt yawned into nothing. Just an open chasm. I squatted, cursing my knees, which hadn't been the same since we made landfall, despite bone growth supplements, and peered into the hole.

"Anyone dropped a lightstick down there yet?" I asked. Grounder heads shook. "Well, go on. This foundation is already behind schedule." I waved an impatient hand and a crewmember slapped a cylindrical object into it. I twisted the lightstick and released it into the hole as it flared to life.

As it fell, the light reflected off smooth and strangely wet walls, as if one of the subway borers had been through here already.

I counted to seven before the lightstick bounced on something squishy. The damn biomass was always getting into footings, causing building collapses. This time it had invaded the very ground where we would build.

I creaked to my feet. "Well, hell. We've got *subterranean* biomass, approximately twenty meters down," I said. "We'll have to burn it out as usual, but *also* fill in the hole. We'll be delayed at least a week."

My crew groaned.

"No excuses." I started pointing out crew members. "Fetch the methylene canisters. You, order another shipment of aggregate crush and run, number five. *Clean* crush and run this time. It took four days to process the last batch to remove all the contaminants. Cindie, get the Z22 over here."

Over the next hour, I supervised my crew and Cindie chipped the slag cap away from the shaft.

"Particularly ugly mass down there," I observed to Harie, peering down. The shaft walls had ribbons of fungus tendrils creeping up to join the main mat that covered the ground.

"Do those look like...fruit to you?" Harie asked, pointing out blobs I could barely see at the bottom of the hole. "Or maybe eggs?" He'd be studying biology, if Admin hadn't forced sixty percent of the Grounders into sterilization and construction crews. The standard line was always 'when the construction is done,' but when that happened, we'd have a lot of retired Generationals and uneducated Grounders.

"The biomass isn't supposed to have ascocarps. The mycologists say that's not how it reproduces," I said. In fact, the planet's flora was instead trying to hybridize with the plants we'd brought from Earth. We destroyed any combinations before they could take over.

"Whatever it is, we're gonna burn it out." I snagged a VaporLite out of a passing worker's mouth. "No smoking on site. Especially with as much propellant as we're going to dump down that hole."

Ten minutes later, we stood in a clump a little ways away from the open shaft.

"Who's going to set the burn off?" Harie asked. From the look in his eyes, I knew he wanted to do it, but this was the first time we'd encountered biomass like this. I needed to see how it reacted. For science.

"I'll handle it." I swiped a dried fern-like structure separated from the biomass earlier that day and marched to the pit. I lit the end with a lighter and watched it burn with satisfaction before flipping it into the shaft.

I ran back to the group, counting to seven.

The fireball that shot out of the top of the shaft was extremely satisfying. Once it subsided, I crept to the edge and peered over. The fungus tendrils climbing the walls lit the shaft like fiery veins. At the bottom, the pods we'd seen earlier twisted and crackled as they burned. I straightened and turned to my crew.

"We'll let that burn for a bit and then clean—" I broke off as the ground shook under my feet.

"You felt it too?" Harie said.

"I did." I turned back to the hole. "I hope that's the accelerant getting down into the roots of the biomass." I wasn't convinced.

Carefully, I peered over the edge again, Harie beside me this time. Several more of the crew eagerly approached the hole to see the aftermath. Nothing like a fire to draw the moths.

"Are those pod things *swelling*?" someone asked.

I didn't get a chance to answer before the world exploded.

* * *

My sight came back first, followed by a horrible burning fur smell. My ears buzzed.

"Harie?" I shouted. I couldn't even hear myself. All around me was peppered with holes the size of both my hands together, torn through the limestone. They started from the remains of the original shaft, now chewed into a ragged shape, and spread out to the edges of the construction site. It was like someone had fired a minigun from inside the shaft.

Then I saw the bodies. And the blood.

"Harie!" My foreman was down, trembling, two holes in his gut leaking entrails. I stumbled to him, noting that farther on, someone was clutching the remains of their leg and moaning. Another body didn't have a head.

"Stay still!" I told Harie, putting pressure on the holes in his stomach. Then I gasped in pain and raised my left hand, shaking, revealing the two-centimeter hole in my palm. I could see the ground through it. Blood dripped onto Harie's chest, and I wondered how much it would hurt when the shock and adrenaline wore off.

I tucked my wounded left hand into my chest, still holding pressure on Harie with my right. He tried to speak, but I hushed him. He didn't deserve this life. None of us did. I waved down an uninjured worker, clenching my teeth at the jarring pain rolling up my arm, and pointed to the groundcar parked outside the site. We'd ferry the wounded to the nearest hospital in multiple trips.

* * *

The hospital in Zeta radian was not the gleaming sterile construction of Alpha. It didn't even warrant one of Admin's Vagal super-soldier guards. Zeta hospital was only two stories tall, made of materials printed from plentiful raw biomass. It had taken over twenty years to perfect the sterilization process for printer-feed. The problem was getting the biomass to stop reproducing, even after being processed.

My crew was shuttled through triage, and the nurses finally told me in very firm words to get out of the way. I watched two Grounders leave in body bags, clenching my unhurt hand into a fist, my fingernails biting into my palm. We hadn't had an accident this bad in ten years, since one of the first Epsilon buildings collapsed from an undiscovered invasion of biomass in its foundation.

And it was my fault. My crew, my fault. If I hadn't pushed to keep up with Admin's unforgiving schedule for the grand opening, we could have thoroughly investigated the growth at the bottom of the shaft. Damnit, I was supposed to lead the Grounders, not get them killed! The Generationals like me were supposed to teach survival skills to this first batch of natives, so they could raise their own families. Not that *we* knew how to live on a planet. My first six hundred and thirty megaseconds—or twenty years, if you converted it into local time, as only the Generationals still used ship-based timescales—had been in zero-G. When I was born on the UGS Abeona, the colony ships were already braking toward Lida. Our population was long separated from old Earth. Only the gene-modded Admins remembered that planet, and they'd been in cryosleep for most of the voyage while Generationals lived and died.

"Agetha Xenakis?" Someone calling my name lifted me from my dour thoughts. It was a woman about my age—another Generational.

"Yes?"

"Come with me. We'll get you patched up." I blinked at my hand. With the local anesthesia, I'd almost forgotten about the gaping hole, now temporarily bandaged. I followed the woman to a private room, checking the data port and outlet spacing along the way. Whoever put up this hospital skimped on the standards, as rare metals were increasingly hard to find.

In the examination room, the woman crossed the room to plug her handheld into the dataport for a hi-rez scan of my hand. The cord was longer than spec for high-speed data transfer, but that was where the colony was now.

I pointed my chin at the cord as the woman held my wounded hand in hers. "Remember when we had enough yttrium for everyone to have a wireless scanner?"

I was rewarded with a rich laugh. Her braids, tied with small bits of metal, jangled together. "Boy do I. Forget our limitations half the time when I'm training the Grounder physicians. I told my intern last week to fetch me a phase-reinforcer for augmenting scan resolution, and she looked at me like I was made of fungus."

"Tell me about it," I said. "If I had just one autonomous excavator like in the first days, this radian would be complete already."

"Instead we're building structures out of the goo that grows on this planet." The doctor shook her head. "What I wouldn't give for a solid nanotanium structure."

"The new materials are nearly as strong," I said. "Still. Not the same."

"You're in charge of this crew?" the doctor asked.

My smile faltered. "Yes, and it's my fault they're here. I should have been more careful about breaking new ground, but Admin's been on my ass to finish this radian for the opening ceremony."

"Don't be so hard on yourself. Not enough Generationals to keep up with the Grounders," she replied. "We're a dying breed, giving way to the new natives of this planet."

I watched her take the interior dimensions of my wound. The local anesthetic and coagulant they'd given me was wearing thin and I winced as she manipulated my fingers.

"Sorry about that." The doctor was brusque, but she didn't miss much.

"Don't worry about it," I said. "Back on the Abeona, I lost three fingers in a circuit rerouting accident. Except we could regrow them, then."

"Same hand?" her fingers touched the first three fingers of my wounded hand. At my nod, she continued. "I can see the growth rings, but it's good work."

I took a chance. "So, you know *my* name..."

The doctor looked up, catching my gaze. "Oh! Sorry. I've been running around all day. Didn't even think about it. I'm Doctor Harley—" She let the name rest in the air for a second. "Call me Beth."

"Nice to meet you, Beth," I said, not looking away. She had one of those faces that only got more striking as the years passed.

She might have blushed as she turned away. "I've been holding on to a few of these, for such a situation," Beth said as she dug deep into a pre-fab cabinet. They'd been made hastily, and residual liquid from the printing process had leaked biomass gunk through the coat of paint.

"Aha. Should work perfectly." She displayed a white box, obviously of ship-make. "Your injury is small enough I think the nanites can fill in the hole in a week or so."

"Thank you," I said. I knew how precious our last stock of ship inventory was. "Are you sure?"

She waved a hand dismissively. "From one Generational to another. The Grounders wouldn't know what to do with a tissue-regrowth kit. They'd probably just stuff fungus in the hole."

"Seeing what they're doing with it, that might work," I laughed, as the little white box unfolded over my palm. It was a relief to see real medicine in action again.

Beth passed an eye over my torn work shirt and filthy pants. "Now the immediate concern is handled, let's make sure there's no other contamination." She raised the scanner again.

I looked up at that. "Other contamination?" I'd thought everything in the area was burned to a crisp.

"This biomass is as hard to get rid of as ship roaches," Beth answered, waving a wand over my shirt and pants. "Especially with as big an explosion as your crew experienced, I bet—" She stopped, her eyebrows rising at the readout. "That's more than the rest of your crew combined. You need to get those clothes off now."

"I—can I...?" I looked for a changing curtain.

"Sorry, no." Beth was already reaching for the buttons on my shirt. "There's no time. We need to get you through decontamination *immediately.* Get those clothes off or I'm getting the scissors. No telling how fast the biomass is reproducing. You've picked up the brunt of the ascospores. The explosion must have triggered the fruiting bodies all at once. I've never seen spores release this fast!"

I stripped. I didn't know exactly what that meant, but I knew enough about the biomass to respect its generative powers. Beth picked up my discarded clothes with two gloved fingers and shoved them into the hazardous waste container. There was a flash of light and heat.

"Decontamination is down the hall," she said, throwing the disposable sheet from the exam table in the bin afterward. She swiped a new one from the cabinet and offered it for some modesty. She'd seen everything I had, such as it was for someone with almost sixteen hundred megaseconds to their name—with thirty megaseconds in a year, that's about fifty years in Grounder-speak.

"Thanks." In another situation, I might have commented about being naked, but Beth's expression told me how serious this was. I wrapped the exam sheet around me as much as I could and hurried out of the exam room. Beth accompanied me.

"I'll need to check you out after decontamination as well," she said. "The biomass is insidious."

I'd been through enough decon runs—we all had. "I'll see you on the other side."

Beth was waiting as I emerged, wet and shivering, from the decon tube. She had a disposa-print robe ready for me, wrapping it around me and loosely tying the belt before she began scanning again.

"Don't get too comfy. I'll have to do some close up scans as well," she said. She gave me a rueful smile.

"I'd rather make sure I'm free of contaminants than guard my dignity," I answered. I opened up one side of the robe as she gestured. "Any word on my crew?"

"Most are well, going through the same decontamination runs. Several others are in critical care, getting patched up like you did. Four of them...didn't make it."

She pointed to my torso to start the scan there, and I obediently opened the robe, shaking my head. Four of my charges, gone. This crew was young, but many already had families, some with small children. I'd have to give The Speech. I hated The Speech.

"I was stupid, rushing through an assessment of a new kind of biomass growth. Burning it out made the growth explode, like it was waiting for a heat trigger to activate."

"That's...likely what happened," Beth answered. I looked up. "I rushed you to decon because the contamination included a shape of acospore I've only seen once before. We think it's a stress response used when the biomass detects an uncolonized area. Zeta radian might be in more danger than usual."

"Do you think there are more of those weird-shaped acospores?" I asked, revealing yet more of myself for her scan.

Beth frowned. "Undoubtedly. I'll run the report up through the native sciences section, flag it to check out." She closed the scanner. "All clean, but I'd like to review details of the incident with you." Her eyes met mine. "Maybe...over dinner later this week, if you're free? It would be good to talk to another Generational."

My heart lurched at the invitation. Daved died shortly after we landed, one of the first victims of the biomass. We'd planned to have a life together on the surface, but then I was left with a small child, in a newly built apartment meant for three. I'd thrown myself into Alpha and Beta radian construction. I told myself I'd meet someone to spend time with after they were finished, but Admin had immediately pushed for Gamma radian, then Delta, and Epsilon...With the extra burden of caring for a child, even one who'd left me without a backward glance as soon as he was of age, over twenty-five years had passed. It was still just me, working on Zeta. I worked around Grounders all day, every day, my children in all but blood. So with a simple sentence, Beth's words made a little sliver of hope lodge in my heart like shrapnel from the explosion.

"That would be nice," I said, and was rewarded with a radiant smile.

* * *

I met up with Beth two days later at a new diner in Zeta offering Ship Food. Some of the crops and livestock from the ships made the transition to the ground, but not all. For example, I hadn't eaten a pineapple since a month after landing. Since we'd found how to sterilize the biomass, the vast majority of restaurants used fungal printers to deliver food that was almost, but not quite, a repulsive and twisted mirror of the food Generationals remembered.

That meant those who'd adapted to the local gravity well largely tended their own gardens, ate in when possible, went to Ship Food restaurants when they could, and tried not to vomit when a Grounder forced us to eat biomass-printed dinners.

"Glad you made it," Beth said as she pulled a chair out for me. I almost commented on the archaic gesture, but decided to enjoy it as she tucked me into my seat. "My intern turned me on to this place when he said the food was too spicy."

"Oh thank all the stars," I said. "I've been poking down bland mushroom patties at crew lunch for years." I looked at the menu, suddenly second guessing my reaction. We'd had funerals for four crew members the day before, and I'd spent not enough time comforting the families because my crew had to get back to work, and Admin granted leave requests very grudgingly. We'd lost too many to the biomass.

I looked up to take back my complaints about the food, but found Beth studying me.

"Anything look good?"

I swallowed my grief over my crew. Beth wasn't interested in my feelings of guilt, and she didn't know my crew like I did. For her, these deaths were a matter of course for the colony. And right now, she *did* seem quite interested in me. Could I let myself have this one thing? Forget being mother hen to a group of Grounders for an evening?

Maybe it was the recent trauma, but I found I could.

"Everything looks great," I answered, keeping eye contact. "Nothing here has been spit out of a printer."

Beth laughed, and I enjoyed the wrinkles at the corners of her eyes as she did. The server came then, and we ordered. I followed Beth's lead to choose a selection of hydroponically-grown greens, veggies, and fruits—the house specialty—and a very small cut of pork. Pigs had no trouble adapting to Lida's environment.

"Tell me about yourself," I said after a few delicious bites. I slowed before I chowed through the whole plate. "Any family here? Partners?"

"A couple long-term relationships back on UGS Khonsu that fizzled out, but after we landed?" Beth shook her head. "A few meetups with other Generationals. Nothing serious."

It was a common story for Generationals. Most of us put so much of our life into building the arcopolis for the Grounders, we hadn't taken the time for families. Now the end of the construction was in sight, many of us were unsure of our futures.

"Don't the Grounders seem younger every year?" I asked. Beth rolled her eyes and chuckled.

"I force myself to let my interns go after they complete their rotations, but I'm always suspicious how much information they've retained. So many disregard what we did on the ships because we don't have the same resources, though I tell them the processes are still sound."

Now it was my turn to laugh, and we fell into competing stories about how incompetent the Grounders were. That was unfair. A lot of very competent workers had rotated through my crew, but it made both of us feel better. I squashed the part of me saying I shouldn't be happy on account of my injured crew. I closed my wounded hand gently to remind myself of the blood and flesh I'd put into the radians over the megaseconds since we'd landed on Lida.

As we left the restaurant, we traded addresses.

"Can I see you again?" Beth asked.

"Definitely," I answered. She leaned in a little and I took her hint, meeting her for a quick kiss. She smelled sweet, like one of those long-lost fruits. Must have been a perfume.

* * *

I swore at the communique I'd received that morning from Admin. Harie, walking slowly, one hand on the bandages I knew covered his chest under his bright orange vest, craned his neck. He'd recovered fast over the past week. I tried not to think of how much he resembled my son.

"New orders come in?"

"Yes, and they're just what I expect from those assclowns," I grumbled, rotating the clear screen so he could see.

"We're being held to the same schedule?" Harie's voice pegged up half an octave. "We still haven't filled that giant shaft and we're down seven crewmembers. Four of them *died*. We haven't even finished all the reports yet. We only just had the funerals."

"Admin is compensating the families twice as much as normal, but insists the radian has to be finished by the original date, due to 'mounting pressures' by the increasing population. They say the grand opening has to take place on schedule." The compensation was a minor win, more than they usually conceded, though that didn't make up for more Grounders dying. They *were* worried. "They also say there are some strange rumblings in the nearby biomass. They're trying to finish before the biomass develops yet another new and unexpected thing."

"Strange rumblings like giant pits filled with exploding spore casings?" Harie grimaced and put a hand to his chest again. "We're going to lose more crew if we don't study the new mutation."

"And there *will* be more. Likely things we aren't prepared for." I kicked the mat of spiky hyphal nets stretched over the ground like angry cheesecloth. There was a reason I still wore the heavily-repaired nanotanium-toe boots I'd fabricated when we first landed. The spines went right through ordinary clothing, even dense denim, and had been known to puncture the pigskin leather the colony used for new boots.

"So what do we do?" Harie asked.

I clenched my unhurt hand, and stretched my chin toward my foreman. "Up to you. Time to step up, kid. You're in charge today. I'm going downtown to fight this." I waved the screen like I might hit someone with it. Maybe I would.

The rest of the day was an exercise in futility. I talked my way through five levels of bureaucracy, working my way up to Administrator Brighton herself, though I'd never met her, even back when the ships were still on approach to Lida. She'd commanded the UGS St. Chris, whereas my ship was the UGS Abeona. My old administrator was a lot more relaxed than Brighton, but he now ran the arcopolis' food production. Brighton was City Planner, Lead Admin, and Alpha Bitch. And also the one determining my build schedule.

I finally gave up as the sun was setting, having only gotten the promise that city planning would 'look into my concerns' and 'determine the best timeline based on all available information.' Assholes.

I had to do something. My crew's lives were in danger because Admin wouldn't delay the opening schedule even faced with a fungus that grew like it was on steroids. I made a detour to the biomedical complex on the way back to Zeta, since I'd already spent the time credits to get to the middle of Alpha radian, halfway across the arcopolis.

Frank Silver was an old curmudgeon, but he was also one the best biomed scientists from the fleet. I knocked on the door with 'Dr. Silver' on the glass. I knew he was still working because he'd done the same thing back on the ships, and because I could see his outline through the frosted window.

Frank answered the door with a bag of air fried veggie chips in one hand. His eyes narrowed, no doubt trying to place me.

"Agetha," I supplied. "I was married to Daved back on the ship. We used to play tabletop on restdays?"

His eyes widened. "Oh yeah!" He stepped back. "Come in. What can I do you for? Haven't seen you in—what, almost four hundred megaseconds?"

"Ah, yes, I think it's been a little over twelve years," I said, automatically converting. The Grounders were getting me out of the habit of using megaseconds, and Admin wanted us to switch over to local time. "I've been busy with Zeta construction. And before that Epsilon, and Delta..."

"Hmmpf. Inaccurate measurement," Frank grumbled. "Interesting soil samples coming out of Zeta though. Some strange hybridization there." He waved a hand back into the lab. A couple large and mysterious contraptions clanked and whirled, and behind that I could see a futon with clothes draped around it. Typical Generational. More comfortable surrounded by machinery than the fungus houses of Lida. "So why are you here after so long?"

Frank was practical to the point of rudeness. I liked that about him. It took me back to the ship days, and away from the crew I'd so recently failed. I could at least make the deaths more meaningful if I figured out how to finish our city in time.

"Those soil samples you mentioned. Have you learned anything about how to subdue the biomass?" I squeezed my injured hand. Just a little. Enough to remind myself I'd gotten off easy. "Admin won't budge on their schedule despite me burying four of my crew from 'fungal encounters' last week. Is there any way to get Zeta up and running?"

"Eesh. Those are the worst, and sorry about your folks. Let's see what we can do to slow the mushrooms and avoid Brighton's evil eye." Frank ambled to a seat, plopping down in front of a bank of screens, each showing graphs and data I presumed dealt with the biomass. I recognized main chemical sequences we'd identified in the spores, but there was much deeper stuff going on than I had experience with.

Frank pointed at the chemical readouts on the screen. "Compounds from this world, from Earth, and weird mixes in between. Some I don't even recognize. Little bits of everything, from pigs to humans to the original animals that must have lived here. This is like looking at a sample of a comet that's passed through several inhabited star systems. This isn't evolution, it's consumption. Digestion. Which I suppose makes sense, seeing as how the biomass covers the entire surface of the planet." He swung the chair back to me.

"This is why we've had such a hard time clearing it out. Every time we develop an effective counter, we use it on a small section and then find the next one is resistant. Half the time we have to burn it all out, including destroying property, or dig out each individual hyphal strand. It isn't just the spores that are mutating. The whole mass is mutating. Consuming whatever it can, and changing. Adapting."

I held up my patched hand. The regrowth kit was doing a good job, but there was still a messy hole in the middle of my hand, visible through the translucent covering. "Fire didn't work so well this time. We came across a new type of fruiting body down a shaft that mass-ejects spores like bullets when it's heated. But the rest of the body acts like an ascomycete. We don't know how it's spreading so fast or how it tunneled under the construction site in less than a week."

Frank peered at my hand. "So it mass-releases like a basidocarp, but the rest of the body develops ascii? We keep trying to match records of this stuff to mycelium from old Earth, but it acts like a weird chimera of the recognized phylums. And most of the fungus on Earth was tiny in comparison."

"These aren't tiny," I said. "They took out four of my crew, and Admin has my nose to the exhaust to get this radian's construction completed on time. Can you recommend a solution?"

Frank peered meditatively into his bag of veggie chips, then shook his head. "We could freeze them, but I doubt the entire colony has enough dry ice to knock it back enough to finish the radian. We could try the usual chemical compounds, but there's nothing to say they won't set off the spores just like the heat. If you get me samples of this particular strain, I can tell you more in a few days."

"I'll do that," I said. Results in a few days were better than banging my head against the wall until we completed the radian. "Anything to help in the meantime?"

Frank started to shake his head again, then stopped. "Actually, there's another Generational, working in the biomed section developing some excellent solutions for defense. She might have something. Name's Doctor Elizabeth Harley."

"Beth?" I asked. Frank raised an eyebrow and I cleared my throat. "I've, uh, met Doctor Harley already, but I thought she was just a medical doctor."

Frank shook his head. "She was one of the best biologists in the fleet, but she's butted heads with Admin for as long as I can remember. They finally 'transferred' her to one of the hospitals in the newer radians to get her out of their hair. Had too many controversial ideas about the biomass. Damn shame, if you ask me."

"No wonder she didn't bring it up when we last talked," I said. "Though maybe we have more in common than I thought."

Frank grunted. "I think every Generational has a problem with those cryosleep popsicles. The unthawing must muddle their heads."

I laughed and turned for the door. "I'll make sure one of the Grounders runs over some samples. You can have as many as you want while we dig out the growth in this shaft."

* * *

I rang Beth the next morning, juggling the screen in one hand while directing my crew—dressed in full containment suits—to remove broken earth and cracked limestone now too fragile to hold the weight of a building. The spores were *everywhere* and growths were springing up like, well, mushrooms. Nasty, nightmare-inducing mushrooms. A patch close to the original shaft was developing what looked suspiciously like pale replicas of femurs and humeri, as if a prankster planted a crop of rubbery fake skeletons as a joke. I had Cindie drive over that part first.

Sections of limestone looked like slices of fluffy bread rather than solid rock, riddled with the spore's trajectories. From what we could tell, the projectiles used a caustic acid to ease their flight, and I'd sent two more of my crew to the hospital with second-degree burns.

I shook a patch of wet, clinging, orange goop off my boot, as the phone pinged. Before building, we'd have to cleanse the entire site to a depth of three meters and sterilize it, lest the fungus grow right back. As we worked, my crew pulled samples of the various growths to send to Frank. Around the shaft, we cleaned even deeper, though now we didn't have enough crushed and purified limestone to fill it. We were coming up on two weeks behind schedule.

Beth answered on the fourth ping. "Agetha! How's the hand? Ready to take me up on that offer of another meal?"

"Healing nicely and...yes, actually," I said, surprised by how much I wanted to see her again. "But I'm calling because Frank Silver recommended you. He thought you were hiding some fancy new technique to kick this biomass in the ass. Why didn't you say something when we had dinner?"

Beth's chuckle was warm even through the limited wireless on Lida, and I smiled in response. Video still took up too much bandwidth for everyday calls. "Frank's not afraid to buck Admin, is he?"

My smile slipped. "Meaning?"

I heard her quiet sigh, though the audio was muffled because I was listening through a full protective helmet. "It's true I've had a side project in the works for a while. About five years after we landed, I've theorized I could develop a mycophage for the fungus, but it never went anywhere. Only when we cracked the method to sterilize the biomass sludge for printing structural materials, was I able to sequence the inactive phage sequences."

"Then what's the problem?" I asked. "Sounds effective."

"Too effective. In the small tests I've run, it's completely rotted the biomass specimens, but *also* any biomass-derived materials it touches. I'm afraid to run larger tests because we all know how well the biomass adapts to new countermeasures. There's potential that if a sample gets absorbed into a resistant strain, the biomass could rot biomass-derived particulates by touch."

I thought through the catalog of building materials, tools, clothing, medicine, and even food based on the biomass. "That's...almost everything." My sigh fogged the containment suit plastic.

"Right." Beth sounded frustrated. "The formula needs to be iterated to a final solution, but Admin refused more testing because one of the PR folks decided it would turn into some sort of nano-sludge and take out the entire city."

"But...it won't, right?" I asked. I squished through a field of knee-height hanging pods growing from a suspension of goo the consistency of grape jelly.

"Uh...probably...not," Beth said. I hadn't heard her sound so uncertain before. "It reacts strongly because it's supposed to completely wipe out the biomass. To do that, the process has to be so quick and powerful that it can't adapt."

I trudged through the destroyed worksite. How much extra risk could I take? How many lives? Beth's solution might save us all, or damn us all.

"How about we have dinner in two days," Beth suggested, not nearly so jolly as when I'd called. "I'll tell you all about the compound. We can discuss risks and benefits. I'll even pay."

I watched the excavator stall out while lifting a section of limestone riddled with fungus tunnels, limp root growth clinging to the bottom. There was no way we were meeting Admin's deadline, and we'd have gape-jawed Grounders swamping us if we didn't finish in time for the grand opening of the radian.

"You had me at risks and benefits," I said. "But if you're paying, well, just tell me where."

* * *

Our second date was in the Alpha radian.

"You booked us a table at Maertin's?" I asked as Beth led me down the street to the unmistakable glittering profile of the arcopolis' premier Ship Food restaurant. Rooftop gardens dangled over the sides, tempting bystanders with fresh tomatoes, cucumbers, and strawberries. The owner had been a botanist, back on the ships. I wondered how often they incinerated a bed that the biomass hybridized. There was a constant battle against airborne spores with gardens far above ground level.

"Don't worry about it." Beth brushed my incredulity away with a quick squeeze of my arm. She was wearing a color-shifting nail polish that must have been the new Galaxy Gloss out of Alpha radian. 'Starshower Red,' if I wasn't mistaken. It moved between the colors of the sunset, like her fingertips were dipped in reflective clouds. "I treated the head server last year for free. He owes me a favor." She wagged a multihued finger at me. "And everything's on me. Whatever you want."

I opened my mouth to argue, but Beth shot me a glare with raised eyebrows. I closed my mouth and shrugged.

The food was as good as the hype. Fresh vegetables, fruits and cheeses, the finest cuts of meat, and no fungus in sight. Not even a portabella.

With a desert of fresh strawberries and cream—a delicacy—Beth got to the other reason we were meeting. "I can show you the compound and give you a sample, if you want. It's back at my place."

"Is that a pickup line?" I asked through a mouthful of strawberry.

"Is it working?" Beth returned.

"Yes," I said.

Beth's apartment was in one of the better blocks of Delta radian. She probably made good money, even working in Zeta hospital.

Fortunately the front door recognized her, as we'd both had a bit too much pear brandy, and Beth might have lost her fob on the way. We collapsed into the open door, her hand on my ass, pushing me inside.

I got to know the details of her couch very well over the next hour. She found the mole on my lower back, then the other one on my left thigh. It was not low on my thigh. I found out her hands were extremely soft.

Then I got to know the details of her bed. Turns out Beth liked real bamboo sheets, rather than the ones printed as standard from the default house options. She liked the way the corners rolled up. They were easier to tie around my hands.

Beth, like me, had sagged with the higher gravity on Lida, as the megaseconds rolled by. But it was a comfortable sagging—the kind where, after our initial rush to remove our clothes and explore each other, we could sit on the bed naked for half the night, talking while our hands roamed over each other, with occasional brief pauses for higher-pitched conversation.

Thankfully, I had the next day off, as it gave us time to address the second reason for our date, which we hadn't gotten to the night before—for some reason. Beth kissed my nose just before my mouth opened in a massive yawn. I plopped down in a chair as she served me a breakfast of cantaloupe from her garden. It smelled divine—sweet and fragrant.

As she sat, she placed a little vial on the table near my chair. I stared at it like it might explode.

"So how exactly does this work?"

"A little goes a long way," Beth said, taking a bite of cantaloupe. "It uses the biomass' replication rate against it. If you place a drop on a fungus, the organic mat will try to assimilate the substance. But in doing so, it replicates the mycophage through the local structure. It will break down the mass in seconds. The problem is, it also has to incite a replication explosion in order to combat the biomass' natural resistance. Any other native connected fungus will start the process again. You have to make sure to isolate the sample completely, otherwise the reaction will keep growing."

I frowned. "But the whole planet is covered. Why not tape this to a drone and fly it out into the wilds? Let it decimate the whole biomass so we can move in?"

Beth gestured with her spoon. "That's what Admin asked. My concoction would take out a large swatch, maybe even a continent, but the fungus would eventually fight back. It adapts. That's what it's good at. However, our biomass building and printed materials are made of dead and sterilized material. They can't react like the biomass. If this got loose, it would dissolve right through them, and might even invoke the same spore ejection protocol in the dead material. We never got that process completely turned off."

I stared at Beth, then at the vial. "That would bring down the whole arcopolis except for Alpha and parts of Beta radians."

"Which is why Admin rejected it, forbade me to use it, and sent me to the worst-supplied hospital in Zeta." Beth caught my eyes and held them. "I was a well-respected scientist in the bioorganic division before my compound. Now I'm just a Grounder band-aid with legs.

Brighton would have my head if she knew I was even talking to you about it."

I swallowed. Had I gotten myself into a relationship I would regret? "Then why did Frank recommend you if this is so risky? Why are you even working on this?"

Beth leaned over the table. "You know exactly how invasive the biomass is. The original burnoff from the ships killed it to dozens of meters within the planet. We erected nanotanium walls to keep all but the most persistent fungus out of those sections. Admin and those living in Alpha and Beta are isolated from the true biomass replication rate. You work with it every day. If we want to expand on this planet, we need to be aggressive. Admin's pussy-foot approach is going to get us all killed sooner rather than later."

"Aggressive, yes, but not at the cost of what we've already built," I answered. "We're at risk, but our population is sustainable. We will need to expand eventually. What do the other bioorganic experts say about your formula?"

"They say it's too risky, just like Admin," Beth sneered. She'd stopped eating her cantaloupe, hands in fists on the table. I heard the resinplast creak in a moment of silence. "They voted to send me out here and bar me from all but the dregs of their research. Is that what you think too?"

I blinked at her intense gaze. I wasn't completely sure I disagreed with the other scientists' assessment. There was being behind schedule, and there was putting the entire colony at risk.

"I'm...just not sure it's a good idea to test this in an uncontrolled environment." I pushed the rest of my cantaloupe away. Suddenly, it tasted rancid. "If I used this, rather than being days behind schedule, I could reverse nearly twenty years of construction, put thousands of people out of homes."

Beth frowned. "You were the one who asked me for a solution. Yes, it needs to be carefully contained, but it *is* a solution. As long as you're careful—"

"Have you seen a construction site?" I broke in. "It's anything but contained. This isn't a sterile lab I can clean out when something goes wrong. Any sliver of biomass material could turn this into a disaster."

The thought of the progress we'd made in Zeta crumbling to dust made me shiver.

"But you *can* use it," Beth insisted. Both her hands were flat on the table, fingers going white with pressure. "I promise it will work. And it will show Admin and the other bioorganic scientists I know what I'm doing. Get them out of their self-satisfied rut. Maybe it will even get me out of Zeta hospital."

I knew it was unfair, but I wondered how much of last night was real, and how much was Beth seeing a way out of her exile. Had she been thinking about this scenario ever since our first dinner? Since the hospital when I came in with a new type of fungus?

"Is that all this is for you?" I asked, gesturing to my unfinished cantaloupe. "A chance to improve your compound after Admin rejected it, with good reason? Is Zeta radian not good enough for you? You want to get back to the security of Alpha?" I'd thought Beth understood me. Now I wasn't sure. I stood up.

"I should get going," I said.

"I thought you had the day off?" Beth's eyes held that same feral light like when she'd explained how her mycophage worked. "Sit down. We can talk this out."

"That was when I thought there was a chance to cut down our backlog. I see I need to get this radian finished with good old hard work. Thanks for last night. I'll see you around, Beth."

I ignored her protests. I had to get back to the site.

* * *

With little urging from me, my crew worked over the next few days, even though they were off-shift days. They knew Admin would come down on them as hard as on me if we fell so far behind we couldn't make up the time. I was determined to catch up, now I knew Beth's magical solution came with a high price.

The shaft was nearly filled in, finally. We'd vacated the site one day and dropped enough firebombs down the shaft to sterilize several square kilometers of biomass. From all scans it looked clear. Now, our incinerators were working full time and we called in favors to borrow additional ones from other crews, just to process all the limestone we dug out. After running through the crusher, it went into the incinerators, and then back into the ground. It felt like we weren't making any progress at all.

I swiveled at a deep *thump* reverberating through the ground. "What was that?" I asked Harie. He shrugged. Then someone started screaming.

We spent the rest of the afternoon dealing with two workers who had been in range when an incinerator exploded.

This time, Harie went to the hospital, while I stayed at the site. As much as I wanted to be with them, the shaft had to be filled by the end of the day. We absolutely had to start on foundation tomorrow.

From what anyone could tell, a hypha from the original mass burrowed into a slice of limestone through a tiny pinhole to escape our bombing attempts, then fruited with explosive spores. It made it all the way into the incinerator undetected. Now we had to check the rest of the remaining limestone to make sure no more fruit grew while we weren't looking. I gritted my teeth at the delay.

Harie called me two hours later. "Jones had three fingers amputated and half the muscle in his right shoulder cauterized to get rid of the embedded spore shards. Michela..."

"What about her?" I clutched the screen in my hand, the hard edges grinding against the joints of my fingers.

"Agetha...a spore went through her chest. She's stabilized, but barely. She won't be working on the site in the near future, if ever. Admin's quality checkers are already swarming around the hospital. I heard rumors they might audit the site."

I very carefully didn't throw the screen, and tamped down the scream threatening to shred my throat. These were *my* Grounders. Closer to me than my biological son. At least one was likely disabled for life. And Admin had the gall to think they could stick a site audit in the works at the same time? I glared at the extra incinerators. We'd have to ship them back to their original crews today. Beth's words came back to me. 'A self-satisfied rut.' Was that where we were? Were the long-lived Admins, with their Vagal super soldiers and gene mods, so long-sighted they would kill the colony off before we had a chance to thrive? For all they professed to care for this first generation of Grounders, it was the same situation as back on the ships. The

Generationals had been the force that maintained the ship. But those in Admin remembered old Earth. They survived through cryosleep, and had genetic enhancements to slow their aging, the process impossible to replicate once the colony ships departed. They had lived past hundreds of years of Generationals on the ships, just as they would live past this generation of Grounders, and the next, and the next. Their drive was to build a successful colony, but would they kill it before that happened?

"Still there? Why don't you take tomorrow off," Harie's tinny voice finally suggested, probably responding to my extended pause. "I can handle the site for a day."

I shook my head before remembering it was only a voice call. My ship instincts never quite left me. "No. I'll be here. If you want to—"

"I'll be there too," Harie said.

* * *

I glared, bleary-eyed, at the banging at my door. I usually got up early to get to the work site, but this banging had woken *me* up.

Frank Silver looked pale—paler than normal—when I opened the door.

"It's The Flowering," he said without preamble.

I hadn't made what passed for my coffee nowadays—the coffee beans almost instantly hybridized with the biomass and what we brewed here was closer to mud than coffee. But it still had caffeine.

"What are you doing here, Frank?"

"Those samples you sent," he said, pushing his way inside. I fell back at his charge, rubbing my eyes. "I found something in them last night—or maybe this morning. Just confirmed it with Doctor Harley. The local fungus is evolving quicker, starting with that explosive shaft you found."

I tried to wrap my head around what he was saying. Beth had warned me the biomass was going into overdrive to colonize a new area. "You think the biomass is having a mass spore event? That would track with what we're seeing, but why—"

Frank was shaking his head. "Not just a spore event. This is more. Much more. New. Unheard of. I never thought the hybridization would go the other way."

I was slowly waking up, at Frank's drawn face and shaking hands. "So—the fungus is mimicking something new? What, like multiple ascocarps at a time? Even on parts that don't support them? We usually only see one or two, right?"

"No. Not ascocarps." Frank's hands came together, then his fingers splayed out, opening like he would make a dove appear. "Goddam, stars-above, genuine-as-fuck flowers. The biomass reverse-engineered *our flowers*. Some of its spores are now compatible with pollen. They've got double the ways to reproduce. The mass will explode like a field of cucumbers in a hydroponic garden. Like a tomato in full sunlight. Like green beans on the best fertilizer we can find."

I stared. Then I took out my phone.

"We've got to get the site contained. How long do we have?"

"Days," Frank said. "If that. The shaft was just the beginning. The biomass around Zeta will grow faster than you can cut it back. You're going to see all sorts of weird shit."

Harie answered on the second ring. He sounded annoyingly awake.

"What's up, boss?"

"More bad news. I've got reliable info that the biomass will go fucking nuts in no time. We've got to get back on schedule."

"I...wish we could do that," Harie said. "I was up early, calculating our new finish rate. We're three weeks out at the very least, and that's if the site audit goes smoothly. They're coming out today. If you've got any ideas, I'm willing to entertain them..."

If Frank was right, the biomass would rip through our construction site, and the others, and might even grow into the parts we'd already built. We'd be cleaning it out of existing buildings while falling farther behind. Admin would see their colony overgrown before they reacted to the situation.

"Harie. What if there was a solution to clear out—"

"Take it," Harie interrupted.

"But what if it had a risk associated—one so big it could endanger the whole arcopolis?"

"Take it, Agetha." Harie's voice was as serious as I'd ever heard him. He'd always been a good foreman, following directions, questioning, but never contradicting. "I don't know what you know or where it comes from, but we can't keep going like this. I'm guessing it's some Generational whiz-bang someone's come up with. Anything is better than what we're doing. We'll just have to be careful."

His last words echoed in my head. Was I the unreasonable one, not taking Beth's compound? Could we be careful enough with it?

"Thank you," I told Harie.

"Are you coming to the site?" I heard his confusion.

I looked to Frank, mouthing thanks. He nodded. "I'll be there soon," I said. "Make sure the site is as clean as possible when I get back. I want to be able to lick the ground."

* * *

I waited in Beth's office at Zeta hospital until she finished with her latest patient. She stopped in the doorway when she saw me.

"Didn't think you'd be back here," she said. Hope lit in her eyes.

"You were right," I said. "It's worth the risk." The audit had been a disaster, as suspected. Swarms of Admin-related idiots with no idea how to handle themselves near biomass. Not a Generational among them. We handed out containment suits to three inspectors, and I barely saved one from toppling into an acidic defensive growth. We'd gotten a passing rating only by promising to implement stronger security measures 'to stop any future incursion-related injuries.' As usual, the safety precautions were so overbearing my crew would be at greater risk simply because they'd have to get closer to the biomass to record more data. Harie rolled his eyes and told everyone to ignore the new procedures as soon as Admin left. They would never follow up, in the tradition of self-assured bureaucrats everywhere.

Beth's face fell. "So you're here for my invention, not for me."

I raised my chin. Was I? "Did you ask me to your house for me or to use what Admin wouldn't let you?"

Beth winced, but nodded. "A little of both."

That, oddly, made me feel better. "Then I'm here because I was stupid about taking risks. What that means for us...I don't know."

"Then let's take this in small steps," Beth said. She crossed to a compact safe built into the office wall, opened it, and turned back with a small vial of liquid.

"You kept it here?" I asked.

"I had a feeling after two of your crew arrived a few days ago riddled with biomass." She passed the vial to me. "You only need a drop for the fungus to absorb the mycophage."

"How isolated does the biomass need to be?" I asked.

Beth looked uncertain. "I've done controlled trials in a lab, but never on the surface. Be very careful."

Was I making another mistake? No. Jones had survived, but couldn't lift anything with his left arm. Michela might never work again. She had a two-year-old daughter. Their livelihoods should have been worth more than a building, or finishing late, but the biomass would never stop. The first generation Grounders would use themselves up to build the colony, to see their children grow. They—and their way of life—now outnumbered the Generationals. We were on our last bit of fuel to create the life our ancestors dreamed of. If I could keep others from dying by using this compound, it was worth it.

"Thank you," I said and turned to leave.

"Stay safe. And...if this works, would you be interested in another dinner?" Beth's words came out in a rush, one hand outstretched toward me. I stopped. "I'd like to see you again. I've...I've felt more connection to you than I have to anyone else in years. Let me make it up to you. My place. I'll cook. Fresh veggies from my personal garden."

Generationals were protective of their personal gardens. To ask someone to share your crops was an invitation of intimacy. She was serious about putting our differences behind us.

I wanted to say yes. Not since Daved died had I felt such a connection. But I was also old enough to know not every relationship succeeded. I sighed, then held up the vial. "First, the test. I'll let you know if it works."

I left her without an answer.

* * *

"So how does this work?" Harie asked, the vial held up to one eye. The biomass in this section had grown unchecked in a rolling, waving, conglomeration of hyphae, ranging from tendrils on the ground to dense formations reaching far overhead.

Here, I could see Frank's Flowering. Petals—the wrong colors or twisted into corkscrews—peeked from crevices and jutted from tendrils. Stamens dripped with oozy pollen.

No, not pollen. I watched in horror as a small, slug-like ambulatory fungus dripped from a flower and dragged itself along a branch. It rubbed up against other flowers, pollinating them before settling itself on the branch. It shivered, then its head spread and split into another grotesque flower. The biomass was using spores and pollen interchangeably.

I shuddered. We had to stop this quickly. "Place a drop on a tendril, according to Beth—Doctor Harley," I told Harie. "We'll have to contain the reaction so it doesn't spread far. If the biomass becomes resistant to this, we have no other options."

I directed Cindie to separate a section of fungus to test with. Tiny creatures that hadn't been there before buzzed and whined overhead. One splatted against the face shield of my containment suit, and I recoiled, pulling away a wriggling thing with wings. I threw it to the ground, and it nestled in, roots already searching for new soil.

The Z22 paved a pathway through a thick mat, nearly as tall as I was. It its wake, slug-like things oozed toward cleared land, thick-petaled flowers opening where they planted themselves. Ribbed spines, bark-like tendrils, and strange, fleshy growths, bent and shrieked as the excavator worked. A glop of slimy pollen splashed onto the cab and I saw Cindie gag and cover her mouth, even through her containment suit filters. A moment later, the stench hit me, five meters away. I choked at the smell of putrefying meat, looking away.

A flower slug oozed near my feet. I couldn't tell whether it was truly fungus, or still had animal parts. Things like this might once have been a separate species, but now they served the greater fungus spanning the planet. Tiny spores glistened in its oozing wake, vibrating so fast tendrils of smoke rose from them. In seconds, one of the seeds cracked open, a slimy hypha crawling into the ground.

I brought my boot down on the slug with a squelch.

"Hurry that Z22 up!" I called. Taking the vial had been the right decision.

The excavator broke the last tendrils of fungus free from the biomass with a whistling tearing, almost like a faint scream. I shivered at the noise, but Cindie plopped the plug of fungus on bare earth. We'd separated it from the concentration of biomass by more than ten meters, which had to be safe enough. Cindie gave me a thumbs-up, her eyes watering at the stench.

"Here goes," I told Harie. The plug sat at eye height, wheezing and gasping as air pockets deflated. A mockery of a human hand with long burgundy petals instead of fingers grabbed for me, two orange stamens like long tongues drooping from the palm. I danced back, but a red succulent stalk crossed with something like an insect antennae swiveled toward me, stabbing down. I turned so it missed me by millimeters, opened the vial, tipped one viscous drop on the stalk, and jumped back.

The stalk flared with an inner light, then collapsed into ash, the light flaring into the body of the plug. Flashes and sparks made me shield my eyes as the biomass shrieked like freezing ice and folded in on itself.

Hesitantly, I stepped closer. Of the original head-height mass, larger in diameter than the length of my body, nothing remained but a thin layer of ash covering the ground. The air around me was noticeably hotter. One of the slug fungi crawled a few centimeters from the wreckage before sizzling into a gooey mess. No flowers sprouted from it.

Harie let out a whoop, followed by the rest of my crew.

"I guess it works," I said. I gestured up to Cindie and she revved the excavator. "Shame we can't do the whole thing at once. Cut out a larger plug. We'll flatten this biomass and its new flowers one piece at a time."

* * *

Over the next day, despite Frank's dire warning, we made good progress for the first time in weeks. Cindie carved out chunks of biomass and I applied one drop of Beth's mycophage to each to dissolve them. We held a constant watch for the flower slugs, using flamethrowers where needed to incinerate them before they could take root. I passed the information to other construction crews around the radian, though ours was the farthest out in the pie-shaped wedge. We were the first line of defense. If the critters got into the completed housing, we'd have to destroy the structures to get biomass out of the crevices.

That night, I went to Beth's house in Delta to apologize, to take her up on her offer of dinner, and to get another vial of mycophage. I was already running low. I was armed with a square of chocolate I'd traded for a few months back and had been saving for a special occasion. Only two of the Generationals managed to get cacao trees to grow in their private gardens. They were both wealthy people with lots of friends.

"Come on in," Beth said as she opened the door. "I've got steamed broccoli and green beans along with what could be considered a squash casserole if you don't look at the cheese too closely."

She'd gone all out on the vegetables, and I wished I'd brought some of the carrots I'd been growing rather than the chocolate, but her eyes lit up when she saw the foil-wrapped square.

"Is that what I think it is?" I nodded and she wrapped a hand protectively around my waist. "This is going to be a fine dinner."

It was. Beth was an excellent cook and she'd squirreled away something that was not wine, because grapes had severe problems with the fungus on this planet, but in the same class. I told of the biomass' trick with the flower slugs, how we'd isolated sections of the biomass, and how the compound worked. She asked detailed questions about the mycophage's process and about the flowers.

"We've focused on building the arcopolis so long, we know almost nothing about the larger biomass on the rest of the planet," I said as I helped her carry plates to the kitchen. That had been the best meal I'd eaten in a long time. "I'm worried about the flower slugs, and more new tricks. I set some of my crew to watch for slugs overnight, but we don't have resources to keep that up forever. Frank warned we would see even stranger things. Yesterday I saw what looked like a palm tree in the middle of a section we dug out. Except the leaves were all fleshy petals with stamens that released clouds of spores and slugs. That was a fun decontamination."

"Hopefully it killed all the reproductive cells," Beth said. "We've conserved drones for low flybys, or we would have known about The

Flowering before now. The biomass is changing all the time." She gestured to me. "With these flower slug mutations, I'm certain the compound will only work for a limited time. Is the reaction slowing?" We sat beside each other on the couch in her living room.

I cocked my head as I split the chocolate slab in two and handed Beth half. "That's funny. I was just going to mention it. The first reaction was so fast I couldn't follow it, but the ones after took longer. I can really notice it now. How can the biomass adapt when the part we're destroying has been separated?"

Beth shook her head. "No idea. There may be enough genetic diversity between sections so the same solution doesn't always work. But then, I couldn't have guessed it would replicate our flora. Fungi are already better at reproducing than flowers. Is the incremental boost in reproduction worth it? There's so much we don't know, and we're only starting to venture out to parts that haven't regrown over the ships' landing exhaust. It's simply too dangerous to go too far. This is one reason I created the compound. We can make inroads into the biomass to learn more about it." She took a tiny nibble of chocolate and moaned. "Oh wow. It's been *years* since I've had chocolate."

I took a small bite of my own piece and let my eyes roll back. The creamy sweetness dissolved in my mouth. Chocolate took on the flavor of where the beans were grown, and this was even better than the chocolate from the ships. Those beans grew in a sterile environment. This chocolate had a musty, rich taste, surely the effect of the biomass.

"I was lucky to get even this much," I said, letting the conversation flow away from the biomass, though it still churned through my subconscious. "The choice was between this square of chocolate and a basket of fresh pears."

"Good choice." Beth took another nibble, her head falling back, her braids washing over her shoulders as she did. The metal bands in her hair caught the overhead light.

She must have felt me watching her, and tilted her head back up, eyes narrowed and watching me. "I wonder if maybe we could continue where we left off last time."

My cheeks heated at how I'd run off after I'd learned about the compound. "Look. I'm sorry," I said. "I overreacted. Yes, you wanted to see your compound used, but I should know people can have more than one objective. I shouldn't have left like that."

Beth was shaking her head. "No, I let my ambition get ahead of me. It's a flaw. I pushed to get the assignment in Zeta, though I live in Delta. With the Grounders becoming proficient in the workforce, it's getting harder for us Generationals to find worthwhile jobs. We're being phased out."

"Tell me about it," I said. "The Admins, with their lifespans, don't know why the Generationals have so many problems. They don't remember how it feels to get old." I stretched out an arm and felt my elbow pop.

"I heard that," Beth said. "I've got something I can rub on it later, if you want." Her eyes promised she'd massage a lot more than my elbow.

"You know, Doctor, I've got a lot of other joints that need attention," I said, and popped the last bite of chocolate in my mouth. A slow smile crept over her face.

"Hmm. Well, I've trained in techniques to reduce tension and stress." She licked the last chocolate off her fingers and slid closer, leaning in until I met her lips with mine. She tasted of chocolate and wine, and her tongue pressed hard against my lips. I relaxed into the kiss.

We broke apart and I took in her scent, so close. It was sweet and familiar, reminding me of rain in the hydroponic garden. And something else. Like one of the fruits that no longer grew on Lida. I breathed her in.

One of her fingers trailed over my shoulder and up my neck, gently pulling at my ear. I leaned into her other hand, which cupped my breast. She pushed me back, fingers walking along my collarbone. They trailed the curve of my chest, flicking at my hardening nipples. Then she moved back up and outward, trailing fingers down my arms. She rotated my elbow, surrounding the joint and tense muscles. A tightness I didn't know was there flowed away.

"How did you—" I started, but she stopped me with a kiss.

"I'm a doctor as well as a bio-organicist, remember? I know how the body works." She sat back up. "Come on, the bed is much more comfortable. I'll give you a *full* massage. Get rid of all those little aches and pains."

I felt extremely relaxed when she finished.

Later, when I asked to learn some of her techniques, she straddled me, pinning me to the bed with her hips.

"So you want to steal all my secrets, do you?"

"I'm a quick learner," I answered. "After all, isn't it about time for a little payback for all you've given me?" I rocked her off me, grinning as her eyes widened. I hadn't forgotten all of my Judo training.

Now I was the one to straddle her. I leaned over her, catching her hands, and gave a wicked smile. "Now, where does it hurt? You can let me know what to do."

Beth was smiling. "Maybe I can give up a few secrets."

By the time we fell asleep next to each other, I felt better than I had in months.

* * *

"You're in a good mood today," Harie said as he caught me humming for the second time.

"Had a good date with Beth," I said as the Z22 dug around another clump of biomass. The night crew reported the slug exodus died down once it was dark, but they'd incinerated every one they'd seen. I watched what looked like a pink sunflower with hundreds of tiny tentacles instead of seeds turn to follow my movements.

We had completed most of an apartment complex and some of the storefronts that would occupy the same street. I patted the new vial from Beth clipped to my belt. She had promised me more—adjusted to combat the slowdown. She didn't have anything for the flowers yet, but I thought we could handle that for the moment.

"I hope it lasts," Harie said. "The average height of the fungus is increasing, and we're getting into deeper layers of the biomass if our surveys are correct. The land is flat here." He pointed out across the slope of tendrils and frills lifting above the brown and green of the continent-encompassing organism. My mood darkened as I saw a bulb spiral open in the distance. A flock of what might have been winged seeds spewed forth, attaching to nearby branches and sending out shoots. With the biomass' adaptive skills, the slugs would not be the only animal-like creatures we saw.

Cutting sections of the mat with the Z22 became more time consuming. I asked if the firesquads were available to burn away the top layer, but they were busy with an outbreak of a new kind of wind-propelled spores over the top of the Alpha and Beta radian nanotanium walls. Was The Flowering happening all around the arcopolis? The other construction teams in Zeta were reporting strange growths popping up in places where there was no biomass activity. They were moving even slower than us.

Admin asked for metrics on how we were making better progress, but I'd forbidden my Grounders to share news of Beth's compound, for fear it would draw Admin's ire. Once Beth removed the risk of the compound destroying the arcopolis, then we would share.

A couple days later, I stared up at the section of mat Cindie dragged to the disintegration area. This mat was almost four times my height—the tallest section we'd excavated. The Z22 had stalled three times while towing it.

"Something weird about this one, boss," Cindie yelled down. "The balance feels off when I move it around." She'd taken to wearing a mask inside her containment suit while operating, to filter the stench of the flower pollen ooze. It smelled even worse than the normal biomass emanations.

As I pondered where to apply the mycophage, the tower of organic material wobbled, a nearby frond spasming and curling toward me. Without thinking, I opened the vial and poured a drop on the frond, then stepped back.

The liquid was definitely working slower. I watched the reaction eat through the center of the mass, revealing...what was that?

"Agetha, get away!" Harie yelled, and I ran as the top of the mat buckled and tore, spraying dissolving tissue.

I looked over my shoulder to see a *thing* climb free of the biomass. It looked like the torso, neck, and head of a giraffe attached to the shell of a giant crab. Flowers replaced its eyes and tongue, dripping slimy pollen. Openings along its flanks spilled flower slugs. It rushed on multiple segmented legs down the side of the mat, as if there was no difference between a vertical and horizontal surface. This thing could spread flower slugs far and wide, except it was already dissolving from the compound. Had we interrupted one of the biomass' new mutations?

My gaze locked on where the creature was heading—one of the new bioengineered walls. The ones that used sterilized biomass-derived material.

Beth warned me our building material had no protection from her compound. My eyes shifted to the rest of the arcopolis as the flowering creature galloped past, its back end already dissolving.

"Out! Out!" I screamed at Cindie, who unbuckled and dove out of the Z22. I got in as the giraffe/crab impacted the nearest wall, exploding in a messy burst of slugs and seeds, splattering over the resinous surface of the building. As I got the excavator turned around, the wall dissolved, the chemical reaction unstoppable. Slugs sizzled and burned.

I revved the excavator down the road. How far would I need to go? The third house? Fourth?

I stopped and swung the bucket at the freshly completed apartment, ripping the front wall away. I swung again, concentrating while the line of fizzling, dissolving light rushed toward me.

I used the Z22 like a bulldozer, barreling through our construction, tearing apart the building. We might fix the construction *if* I could stop the compound in time.

I exited the rear of the line of apartments in a cloud of broken building materials as the reaction reached my treads. I rolled back and forth, crushing disintegrating vines and flower material into bits, trying to halt the reaction. To my left, half the apartments we'd just finished were gone, like they'd been vaporized by a ship's exhaust.

I rolled across the line of wreckage again and again, searching for spots where the reaction hadn't died out, for slugs still moving. I started as the communicator buzzed beside my head, then reached for it.

"You got it, Agetha," came Harie's shaky voice. I picked him out, half a block away, waving. "What was that thing?"

I pried my other hand off the control and looked around at the destruction. "No idea. The next evolution of the flower slug? Whatever it was, tell the other crews to watch out for them."

I closed my hands to stop them trembling. Were there more of those creatures hidden in the biomass? What else would it throw at us before the radian was complete?

Weeks of construction, gone. At least Admin wouldn't wonder why we were ahead any longer.

* * *

Two days later, I sat in front of the oversight board on radian construction. Maimed crew, scheduling setbacks, an audit, and new biomass mutations hadn't brought me here, but property destruction had gotten Admin Brighton's attention. Three mid-level bureaucrats sat ready to rake me over the coals.

"It's obvious our suggested safety measures weren't enough. We'll assign your crew to a supervisor we feel will make better use of their skills," one said to me. I nodded numbly. He looked half my age, though if he was the son of some Admin as I guessed, he might be older than me. "We advise you to take some time to get over the stress of recent events."

Without pay was left unsaid. Just another aging Generational, whose judgment could no longer be trusted. Only one of the people pivotal in constructing this city from nothing. They'd bring up one of the Grounders to take my place. Hopefully Harie. He'd make a decent supervisor, even if I hadn't finished training him.

I made to get up, but the balding asshat in charge wasn't finished. "This incident has fortunate timing in any case," he said, and I looked up, unable to control my disbelief. He didn't seem to notice. The other two members—a man and a woman so nondescript I wouldn't be able to pick them out of a crowd—nodded along, as if this was all some sort of misunderstanding. Not as if I'd personally destroyed the last two weeks of construction.

"With many who served on the ships hitting a natural slowdown in their lives, we are letting those who were born on the surface try their hands at key job areas. Ones who are aging out of natural skill areas are instead being offered exclusive opportunities in the newer construction areas. With this change in your employment, you'll be one of the first with an opportunity to pick out a new place."

He made it sound like he was offering me a prize, but I knew how to interpret Admin bullshit. They were shipping Generationals off to the newer, less secure portions of the arcopolis to make room for more Grounders. And for Admins, their children, and Vagal soldiers, of course. *They* weren't hitting a 'natural slowdown.' *They* weren't moving away from Alpha radian with its nanotanium walls.

I stood. "Are we done?"

"We'll be sure to send you the first batch of pamphlets," the woman said. "We think this will be an exciting opportunity for you. Take all the time you need to look them over." I think she actually meant that kindly.

I walked out, shaking my head, my hand squeezing the healing wound hard enough to remind me what I put into the radian construction.

The next afternoon, someone banged on my door. I'd been staring at the pamphlets I'd received. The new apartments were a nightmare for Generationals, with open, bare ceilings and walls, obviously designed by Admins and Grounders, neither of whom had any concept of living in zero-G. *We'd* designed the areas we lived in, and allowed Grounders to design theirs, when they were old enough. Now Admin was forcing us away from the colorful Generational houses, with decorations on all surfaces, and into the floor-facing concepts they and the Grounders liked.

The knock came again and I sighed on my way to the door.

Beth waved her package of papers at me as soon as I opened the door, her eyes wide, braids almost vibrating as she spoke. "Can you believe this? They've already forced me out of bioorganics. I have to work in Zeta. *Now* they want me out of my house in Delta *next month*. I *built* that house, and they're going to give it to some Grounder family before I—" She stopped and took in my state. "What happened? Did you get pamphlets too? Your foreman told me you were here, taking a day off."

"The biomass is evolving its critters to better propagate. One made a run for it as we were dissolving a plug," I said. "I destroyed half a block of apartments to keep the compound from taking out the whole radian. They let me go. Said I'm entering a 'natural slowdown.'"

Beth sagged against a wall. "Those bastards! I'm so sorry. And so glad you stopped the reaction in time." She put a hand to her forehead. "You're right. Maybe the solution is too strong. But no wonder they're forcing me out. Who all knows about the compound I made?"

I quashed the spark of anger that she thought I would tell. Beth was ambitious, but I liked that about her. She simply thought others would act the way she did.

"No one knows except for my crew," I told her, and watched the fear drain from her face. "I knew the risks when I got it from you. I didn't tell them, and my crew didn't either. They labeled it an 'accidental structural collapse,' based on not following their new procedures after the site audit. There have been other collapses with the biomass propagating more rapidly. Just none this bad."

Beth lowered her hand. "You didn't tell them? Why not?"

I shook my head. "It would have just led to both of us getting fired."

"Then why did...?" Beth raised the bunch of papers.

"This is happy timing for them," I guessed. "They must have been planning to move us out of the original radians for a while. The Generationals are getting older, not able to contribute as effectively as the Grounders. They got to start with me as a fortunate accident."

"No longer useful, my ass! What about the radian construction?"

I shrugged. "Harie won't move any faster than me. The Flowering isn't going to go away. The incursions will get worse until Admin finally takes notice. I just hope it won't be too late." I wanted to take my crew back, but what could I do?

"And the Generationals will look even worse for failing to train the Grounders," Beth agreed. "Yes, the Grounders will eventually take over. They're already more populous than we are. But we can still make a difference, Agetha. We're the last generation of ship-born, the first to live on the surface of Lida." Beth shook her head, dropping the pamphlets on the table with a *thump*. "No matter how far Admin pushes us, this is *our* colony. We won't let the biomass win."

"How long can we fight this fungus, Beth?" I asked, holding up a hand. I had spots and wrinkles that hadn't been there five years ago. "The Generationals are past our prime. We were already wrung-out when the ships landed, but that's when the real work started. How many of us have seen our children take direction from Admin and leave us without looking back?" My son's face drifted through my mind. What was he doing now? Had he found his place in the colony?

"The Generationals will always know what we've put into this colony," Beth said.

"But is it enough? Can we keep the biomass from reclaiming the planet? We were never supposed to land here in the first place. Perhaps we *should* let the next generation take over the fight." If I had been younger, maybe I could have stopped the creature before it ran into the apartment wall.

"While the Admins live for centuries with their Earth gene manipulations, then pass that gift on to their children," Beth grumbled. "We won't see the eventual result. We're fodder to build this planet for the Grounders, which I don't resent, and to let the Admins live in style, which I *do*. If we're dying out, I say we impede the biomass growth as much as we can."

"How?" I asked.

"We're going to stop The Flowering so the biomass can't propagate as fast," Beth said. "The Generationals laid the foundations for the arcopolis, and we'll help the Grounders complete it, no matter how inept Admin is."

* * *

More of Beth's pounding awoke me the next morning, her braids jingling in righteous anger outside my door. I hadn't gone out. I wasn't even certain I'd changed my clothes. Behind her was a string of Generationals armed with hammers, axes, saws, neural-linked workbots, and even what looked like a small mech. Many had flamethrowers—a standard defense against the biomass. I recognized several crew from the UGS Abeona.

"What...?" I didn't quite know how to finish my question.

"I said I knew some people. They got the same pamphlets and they're all mad as hell, like us. If we're getting shuttled to new homes, we might as well build and protect them ourselves. We're going to destroy the biomass flowers and slugs so it will have to grow the old way."

"What about the construction crews?" I protested. "What about Admin?" We couldn't indiscriminately mob the Zeta construction sites. That would put us even farther behind, and the flower slugs might slip through cracks in the chaos.

"We're forming a new crew, with you in charge," Beth said. There were answering cries from the others behind her. They were all looking at me.

Beth held up another vial of her compound. "I've got this to clear the biomass. The Generationals will do what we've always done—pave the way for the next generation. We'll push the biomass back to let the Grounders build. While we do, we can collect samples of The Flowering, the slugs, and any other tricks the biomass pulls. With the number of biologists, engineers, and material scientists here, we're going to science the *shit* out of this fungus."

I straightened. Frank caught my eye from the crowd and gave me a thumbs-up. I wondered if he'd helped Beth make the new compound. She couldn't have done all that in one night.

"I'll get dressed."

* * *

Over the next week, the 'senior crew' turned our work into a competition. Generationals were competent and multi-talented by nature. Growing up on a generational ship meant if something went wrong, it had to be fixed correctly—the first time—or the entire colony would die. We were used to getting jobs done against overwhelming odds. Since Admin was forcing us out here, that attitude was focused on protecting Zeta construction.

Generationals came from jobs all over the arcopolis, some taking leaves of absence, others getting laid off with little explanation. I hoped Admin was taking notice of what they'd done. Alienating mentors teaching the next generation survival skills on a colony world was a bad idea, but ultimately, Admin, Generational, and Grounder all wanted the colony to survive. We'd do what we had to.

Beth worked by my side, taking samples with Frank while we blazed through the biomass—the largest direct offensive since the fleet glassed the landing site. She said nothing about her job at the hospital. She might have been let go or might be taking an extended leave of absence. We Generationals had more vacation time than we knew what to do with. 'Vacation' was implemented by Admin. Generationals didn't stop working.

We raced against Harie and my former crew to burn out biomass, sterilize the ground, incinerate flowers and slugs, and search out new types of critters, expunging them with extreme prejudice. We found five more of the giraffe crabs and sent them galloping back into the fungus and away from Zeta, their flowery hides ablaze.

Our 'senior crew' swelled in number until I wondered how many were left in our old jobs. How were the logistics of the arcopolis faring? We all had apprentices among the Grounders. That was our directive on landing—train our replacements. If nothing else, this would be a crash course in the Grounders running the city after we were gone.

Beth, Frank, and the bioorganically-oriented scientists set up a lab in a shell of a new building, bringing flowers and slugs, the remains of a giraffe crab, and multitudes of fungus, analyzing the hybridization of our flora in the evenings. They had enough equipment squirreled away to rival some of the setups in Alpha.

It was the fifth day when Beth came up to me in a rush, gesturing with a vial. I wiped a spray of pollen ooze from the faceplate of my containment suit. Even while protected, Xian had gotten a face-full of acidic pollen and the doctors removed half of his jaw to get rid of the flower infestation.

"I think I've got it," Beth said in a rush over the intercom. "Frank and I were up all night. That budding polyp you found yesterday was the clue. We isolated the Earth-based portion of The Flowering. Completely rewrote the mycophage to focus solely on the modified Earth proteins. I wanted you to be the first to see it."

I took a last swing at a segmented tendril trying to hook in my direction. It fell to the mat of wriggling fungus.

"What about the resinplast printed from the biomass?"

"Think I've solved that problem too. The floral hybridization is such a small percentage of the biomass, this solution shouldn't harm the construction materials. Just needed focused time working on the mycophage to get it sorted out."

"And test subjects." I moved away from the latest nest of flowers I was working on. They looked like squash flowers, but hissed as I moved. I knew from experience the insides of petals were coated in an adhesive that could support more than the weight of a person.

"Here goes." Beth raised the vial and poured two drops on the nearest flower, then pulled her glove back before it snapped at her.

The reaction was slower, but much more focused. The flowers wilted, then disintegrated into a smoking mess. However, the standard biomass the flowers were connected to didn't. Tendrils paused in their lazy movement in a growing circle around us, as if a wave passed through the biomass. I saw another clump of flowers farther away wither and turn to dust, then another farther out. I heard a cheer from several other Generationals working nearby. We started to draw a crowd.

I let out a breath I didn't know I'd been holding. "Is it working? What about the rest of the biomass?"

"According to lab simulations, it should slow the growth by up to sixty percent," Beth said, raising her chin inside the helmet. "A little something new I cooked up. Much harder for the biomass to become resistant."

I felt a small well of hope for the first time in weeks. "And you can replicate enough of this compound for Zeta?"

"Even better," Beth said. "I have one more test to administer."

She led our little group to one of the newly constructed buildings, where Harie and the rest of my old crew were working. We traded updates, and I pointed out a few corrections in private to Harie.

"Thanks, boss." His eyes had large bags under them. "I don't know how you kept us all in line for so many years. It's only been days and I'm about ready to jump in one of those shafts and hope for the best."

I chuckled. "Wait until they promote you." Harie would be a good crew leader.

I turned as Beth dragged a large sheet of resinplast from a nearby building to open ground.

"Last test," she said, and dripped a single drop of her compound on the resinplast.

Nothing happened.

"You fixed it!" I said.

"Even better than that." Beth gestured me closer, then pointed to the drop of liquid on the sheet of resinplast where it had beaded up.

"Not only does it not affect the resinplast, it isn't even absorbed. We can coat the outside of our buildings with this and it will keep the biomass away."

Realization washed over me. "You're talking about a permanent method of protection. We can keep the biomass out forever."

Beth held up a finger. "Not forever. The biomass adapts too fast. It will get around this solution eventually, but the mycophage might let us finish Zeta radian. If we're lucky, Eta and Theta radians, too."

"Good enough for me," Harie said, then turned back to my—no, *his* crew. "Let's finish these apartments!"

* * *

Two weeks later, there was a riot of motion as the crews—including the 'senior crew'—cleaned the last construction detritus from Zeta to prepare for the opening ceremony.

Although Zeta had technically been lived in for several months, there were a lot of incoming inhabitants. Grounders who had grown up in Alpha, Beta, and Gamma were moving out from family homes, while Generationals forced out of all radians were arriving at our little village. I had a hand in updating Harie's plans for a certain series of apartments, and we even got Admin to approve, since they needed to be completely reconstructed. They now included amenities for Generationals used to seeing pictures and plants on all six walls of a room.

Beth brought the last of her furniture to join mine in the apartment I'd picked. It was the one through which I'd driven the excavator. If I was forced to move here, I'd pick a place with meaning to it. After my changes, the space had hanging plants on all surfaces, and bright colors marking lines between rooms based on function. I'd adjusted the floorplan to a more reasonable hub design, with one common social room and utilities and sleeping closets located on the perimeter. Just like back on the UGS Abeona.

Beth and I watched the opening ceremony from the top of our new apartment. We weren't invited, naturally, and neither were the crews who had constructed the radian. It was all bigwigs from Alpha and Beta, Admins, and Vagal super soldiers. They congratulated each other on getting the radian complete on schedule, and on the new chemical compound submitted anonymously from a construction crew. Turned out it slowed the biomass growth *and* got rid of those pesky new flowers.

The tallest stalks rose above the reinforced perimeter wall. It wouldn't keep the biomass out forever, but Beth's compound would slow the growth while she worked on further adjustments.

"You alright?" she asked as we watched Admin Brighton's speech on a shared screen.

"Yep," I said. "I'm not even angry about it anymore. I think I knew subconsciously that Admin would pull some trick like this. Harie's a good kid, and he'll keep my crew in line. I'm just happy the radian's complete." I looked out over the arcopolis, where six of eight slices of a giant pie left a wedge of biomass between Zeta and Epsilon, on the other side. Back toward the center, Alpha and Beta were nestled behind their nanotanium walls.

I pointed toward the wedge. "Only Eta and Theta radians to go and our first city will be complete. It's a triumph of the Generational fleet no matter what Admin says. We can survive on a planet where we weren't supposed to land, and beat back this ever present fungus. It gives me hope we can truly flourish here. Perhaps one day we'll even learn to live in harmony with the biomass."

Beth put an arm around me. "We'll have to eventually, unless we manage to burn down the entire planet. Seems a waste. But no telling if we'll survive to see it completed."

"We're not *that* old," I said, thumping her shoulder. "Older than the Grounders, sure, and without the genetic fixing of the Admins, but I find I suddenly have free time for the first time in...forever. Time to learn more about this world. I plan to live as long as I can in this wilderness. Maybe it won't be as long as we would live on the ships, but then," I gave her a squeeze, "I wouldn't have found you."

Beth leaned in for a long kiss, and I smelled her sweet perfume I'd never been able to place. "Want to skip the rest of the ceremony?" she asked after we separated. "I have a present. I made a trade for medical supplies with one of the other Generationals. She was already living in Epsilon radian, and didn't have to move. She has an overflowing garden, and you'll never guess what she's gotten to grow."

"Apples? Peaches?" I guessed. Both were susceptible to fungal infestations, and no one had grown a tree to maturity yet.

Beth shook her head. "Even better. She has *pineapple* bushes—a whole row of them. Saved a cutting from the UGS Hina."

Something clicked into place. "Your perfume—it smells like pineapple! I thought they all perished the first year on Lida."

"All except hers," Beth said. "Up till now, I've only bought the fragrance she makes from the juice, but for this celebration, I splurged. I have a whole ripe one downstairs."

My mouth started watering. "How did I ever end up with you?"

"Getting shot by an exploding fungus, as I recall," Beth said, and I laughed.

"Completely worth it," I said, holding up my hand. The hole was almost gone, with a tiny pucker on the back where the seed had exited.

"I'm always around if you need another examination." Beth waggled her eyebrows.

"Maybe after the pineapple," I said. "Or was that the plan?"

Beth gave me an innocent look, her eyes wide. "What plan?"

I snorted, and hugged her close again. We stood on the apartment roof for another few moments, staring out across Lida, then went downstairs to celebrate. There was an entire world to explore, and we had seen only small sections. Once this arcopolis was complete, we would establish another one. But Beth and I would be here. We'd leave that job to the Grounders. Perhaps the Admins were right and it was time for the Generationals to retire, tend our crops, and watch what our descendants could achieve.

It would be something spectacular.

Want to read more of William C. Tracy's writings?

He has a full trilogy planned in this universe, so stay up to date by joining his mailing list at **www.williamctracy.com/newsletter-signup** and get a free story at the same time!

If you want to read along with the trilogy as it is written, check out William's Patreon at **www.patreon.com/wctracy**.

The Bibliothek Betrayal

A Quirk and Moth Debacle

Robin C.M. Duncan

Sapphic Representation: Lesbian, Bi/Pan
Heat Level: Medium
Content Warnings: Coarse Language, Violence, Gore

Author's note: This story takes place seventeen days after events in Yellowknife, NWT, during which Quirk confronted a past he thought he'd left behind. He travelled to Europe wanting nothing more than a pleasant jaunt around the Old World in intellectually stimulating company, and a week's break from his continually challenging assistant, Moth.

1

Tuesday, 08-DECEMBER-2099

AutoCafé, Brümmerstrasse, Berlin, Germany, Euro Bloc Nord

Cassie sipped her eiskaffee, the dusting of bitter cocoa matching her mood perfectly. Beyond the AutoCafé's plass window, snow fell thickly on Brümmerstrasse, but made no impact on the road's heated techmac. Customers chattered, spoons and forks clinked, handys pinged, the café charging each patron as they served themselves. And Karla was gone, leaving Cassie feeling desperate, hollow.

Her teaching assistants, sitting around the table, watched her, expectant. Fearing one of Professor Streich's infamous outbursts, no doubt. She scowled. It would be a long few days, travelling around Europe, 'collecting' seminal volumes of feminist literature. One volume was bought and paid for; others would be less legitimately acquired from four European libraries. Texts once considered heretical for championing alternatives to the pale, male establishment, now destined for a place of honour at Berlin *Freie Universität's* new Department of Human Realities. Her department. Her work. Collecting them all might even get her tenure, if it didn't get her shunned.

The books weren't her main goal, however, just a cover. Her second task was personal. A promise made during those lost hours facing Karla through the monitor, when she'd been present in spirit and in time, more than just a memory. This task was Cassie's heart's directive, a humanist imperative, a call to arms. Tenure took a backseat to Karla. Everything did. Cassie would reveal the heinous environmental crimes of the multi-planetary C Corp, exposing them to justice. She'd get justice for...no. She failed again not to think about her confidante, her lover, the woman she had never met. The woman on a screen, who had inhabited Cassie's nights, her life. Gone. Locked away, maybe dead, because of that verdammt C Corp dome.

"I take the 15:10 from Hauptbahnhof. Rome, Paris, Brussels. I'll be gone six days. *You* must sail the ship. Helm, engine, anchor," she pointed at each of them in turn, knowing she would never see them again, that she would go from Brussels to the Isle of Skye, break in with the unique biometric key comprising components sourced around Europe (she had the first already, from a drop at Staatsbibliothek zu Berlin), and retrieve the damning evidence. Samples of a twisted, ruined ecosystem. Enabled by Karla's underground eco-warrior contacts.

Of her assistants, Gunther was too eager. Taller even than her, blond like her, probably still harboured wet dreams about her, doomed to be unfulfilled. He went where told, however, kept classes in line. Uwe—thin, dark, delicate; as gay as she, and more feminine. Competent at simple tasks. Sabine was the clever, promising, knowing one. Pretty hair hacked short, dyed black. Sabine abjured cosmetics, despised attention. Unlike Cassie herself, for whom appearance was critical, her style was a weapon to deflect prejudice. Both believed in achievement as resistance to societal norms. Sabine would have her job one day, maybe soon, since Cassie would not return. Karla was gone. Nothing else mattered, nothing but finding and publishing the evidence to destroy C Corp—

Cassandra, this is Paperclip, her implant chirped.

Cassie stood, ignoring her assistants' questioning looks. *The conspiracy coordinator calls.* Karla's controller, now hers. No escape. CC would dominate her thoughts until she knocked them down.

"Excuse me."

She walked to the toilet, thumbed the pad. The AutoCafé checked her sign-in and admitted her. She sat on the unopened seat, pinched her earlobe to activate her implant, her subvocalisation relayed through her handy, subcutaneous neck sensors translating muscle movement and skin tension into words, preserving the silence.

<What?>

You're brusque this morning.

Cassie's mouth moved soundlessly, like a fish out of water. Ironic, since an academic undertaking espionage was hardly unprecedented.

<I'm brusque every morning. People are uniformly stupid, thoughtless and selfish. Brusqueness is the only appropriate response. What do you want?>

This is your two-hour notification. All systems go. Quinton Kirby is on a train from Forties Spaceport, arriving in Berlin in fifty-three minutes.

<Calls himself Quirk, I gather. My research suggests this assistant you hired for me is a dandy, blowhard, and womaniser.>

His reputation is...exaggerated. He's an able private investigator with a good track record of retrieving 'misplaced' artwork, pets, and people.

<You make him sound like a psychic.>

He's not, but he's a big fan of yours. His taste in women runs to the...authoritarian.

<I can't be fending him off all week. Arguments attract attention.>

He has other uses. He worked for C Corp, appeared in Yellowknife recently when...KABOOM.

<He's a saboteur?>

No. A simple contractor, a fixer with experience of CC.

<Can't he assemble the key then? Get onto Skye, find the evidence of their eco-crimes? He'd be less conspicuous.>

Au contraire. His departure from C Corp was messy. He bears a grudge, has a taste for CC's corporate wolves. He used to be one. He's motivated. And when you're done, we'll throw him to those wolves. As for him pestering you, surveillance suggests he's an unconfirmed pansexual. Think of him as a fanboy, slap him down, he'll stay slapped. Or don't, if you need some entertainment. Aren't you lonely, Cassie?

<My emotional state is not a factor.> Her jaw clenched. Subvocalised shouting was a pale imitation of the real thing.

I'm sorry. I didn't... Paperclip out.

2

Forties Express, North Sea, 137km North of the Netherlands UK
Protectorate

Quirk stirred his café noir though he'd added neither cream nor sugar. A galaxy of foam swirled, spun, expanded, slowing towards stasis. He steepled his fingers and watched the bubbles die. 2099 was ending badly, and he was doing all he could to usher in the new century as painlessly as possible.

'All'—presently—encompassed hurtling through the maglev tube from Forties Spaceport to Berlin; sipping coffee; watching the steward walking away; anticipating a week of R&R; and trying not to think about C Corp.

'All'—after the Yellowknife debacle—centred on this nursemaid job with renowned scholar, literary evangelist and paragon of androgynous beauty, Fräulein Professor Cassandra Streich of the *Freie Universität, Berlin*. Tootling around Europe liberating heretical tomes from fusty libraries and their fusty librarians. A week to look forward to. The evening receptions bedecked in Old World grandeur; the solidity of history; a stimulating if severe companion. No shrinking violet himself, he harboured the hope that sparks would fly.

A leaden sky hunkered beyond the walldow, low enough that the Deutsche Bahn Shinkansen seemed to scythe through the clouds. On a fair day, the rapidly disappearing view would be disconcerting, but today wasn't fair, it was foul. No vista to engage him, and the steward had sashayed through to the cheap seats in the next carriage.

Sweeping imaginary dust from the knee of his indigo and olive pinstriped Merrion suit, Quirk sat back, seeking the glow of anticipation at meeting Professor Streich. The tap of light footsteps drew his attention, and a figure appeared from behind his shoulder. She placed a valise on one seat opposite then sat facing him.

This offered possibilities. "Wrong carriage?"

"No," said the woman, brushing shoulder-length, auburn strands from her forehead. "I need to talk to you."

Her gaze was cool, professional. To know he was on this train she had resources. Police? Some security service? UN inspector? Intriguing. He leaned forward, hands on the PseudoWood table between them. "I'm all ears."

"That's not what I heard. All thumbs according to reports from Yellowknife."

This again. He deployed an easy smile—*Getting to know you, getting to know all about you, Act 1*—hoping for some stimulating conversation, and tapped the walldow. Numbers brightened into being, overwriting his view of the clouds. Forty-three minutes to Berlin; average speed, 498 kilometres per hour. "CC is under investigation after Yellowknife. Has someone grassed me up, as they say in my hometown?"

"No, Mister Kirby. Your activities have been noisy enough to render an informant unnecessary."

"Well, let's have a drink while you're pumping me for information." He raised a hand, hailing the steward via the cabin cameras. "But show me your ID first. I don't want to be arrested procuring alcohol for a minor."

She rolled her eyes. The steward appeared in his improbably tight trousers.

"Nothing for me," said the woman. All business. He held her gaze a little longer. It was practically a staring match, but he'd never been shy in that respect.

"Monkey 23, rose-hip tonic, merçi, garçon," he winked, meaning to imply that a decent gratuity was forthcoming before the train settled his account on arrival. The steward suppressed a smile, nodded, and departed.

"We have—" Quirk tapped "—forty-one minutes. What's this all about?"

She leaned over, brought up the compartment controls, opaqued the walldow, and activated the privacy bubble. The lady had ridden the Shinkansen before. Passenger murmurs, and the five-hundred kph background hiss faded away. She brushed her hair back again, produced a real leather card wallet from her suit jacket, and opened it on the table.

Rhea Navarro, Special Agent, UN Environment Control, Stockholm.

He nodded and smiled—*This is a genuine copy*—his expression as fake as he suspected her ID was. "Go on." He'd pay out some line; see if he could land the truth.

"You've heard of the Skye Ecosystem Protection Zone, of course."

"Of course." May as well ask if he'd heard of Near Light Speed travel, and the UN's philanthropic 'windfall' patent freeing Humankind to roam the stars at low, low prices.

The Skye Bridge (technically two bridges) opened over a hundred years ago, and they charged people to use it. An unpopular move with locals, who protested—firmly, vociferously—but to no avail. This was as a drop in Loch Alsh compared to the 2080 protests when C Corp purchased the island for the kingly sum of six hundred billion dollars, or £165B, under the UN's Earth ecosystem reclamation initiative, levied against use of NLS drives. Governments fell, one in Edinburgh, one in London, another in Edinburgh. In the end, money talked, the UK's eye-watering national debt was reduced: average disbursement to each of Skye's forty thousand population, one million pounds. Enough for a decent three-bed bungalow on the mainland, with something left over. CC demolished the bridge in 2082, citing the need to maintain ecological integrity.

The 'accident' happened on March, 15th 2085. Folk in the West of Scotland woke to the western sky ablaze. The Earth itself howled—a dull roar heard as far away as Stirling. Waters boiled, mountains rent and scattered, the sky blackened with fleeing birds.

C Corp's short statement admitted to an explosion in an ecospheric processing plant. Nobody believed that but, by then, CC had installed a massive electrified wall around the coast, and thrown an energy dome over the whole island. Containment measures to protect against the very unlikely event of future incidents.

Nobody believed that either: various governments; all the news outlets; the UN; INTERPOL; NASA; the WHO; the WWF; MI5; MI6; SI1; SI2; the BBC; the CIA; the CAA; CNN; CBBC; the MCS; SEPA; the RNLI; SNH; even GSFWC—all demanded access to the island to bear witness. Those demands and a hundred others were denied in the interests of maintaining ecological integrity, which nobody believed. Finally, CC permitted a journalist from the Argyll & Bute Herald to take photographs from just inside the barrier. Images were published. Everything looked fine. The end.

"UNEC suspect CC carried out terraforming experiments on Skye—"

"Let me stop you there, Rhea, if that's your name. I've locked horns with the UN before. You seem a mite too direct. Let's cut the carpaccio. If you're CC, admit it. Let's have a proper conversation."

The redhead's expression soured. "Fine, we'll do it your way. I'm CC, and—"

His handset rang, loud in the privacy bubble's dead air. He winced, but Navarro sat back, motioning him to proceed. He nodded thanks, withdrew the sleek cLife from his top pocket.

"Hey, Sparky, how's it hanging?"

He covered his handset, "My assistant, sorry," turned to the opaque walldow, hissing, "Not a good time, Moth."

"You're supposed *to say, 'Hey, Sparkle, free and easy. How're you?'"*

"Well, I'm not going to say that. I'm on a train. I'm speaking with someone."

"Ooooh. Is he cute?"

"I'm conversing with a lady."

"Uh-oh. You know that doesn't turn out well for you. What are you up to?"

He scowled, lips compressing. "I am not *up to* anything, I haven't had time. Now, back to your studies, and put Bea on."

"You want to speak to my syRen® nursemaid, S-17834?"

"Put her on, Moth."

"No way! I just called to say I've joined the Hygiea Marine Scouts and to get parental permission to go light sailing tomorrow out of Beta Port thanks so much love-you-and-you-can't-stop-me, bye-ee!"

"Moth, you are *not—*" She'd hung up.

"Kids," Navarro deadpanned, leaned forward, jacket swinging open, black palm-reader grip of a slate-grey pistol nestling beside her left breast where she knew he would see it. *Yes, CC for sure.*

"So," he said before she could speak, "you think I'm up to something, still have it in for C Corp? You're here to lean on me?" *I escape from CC's clutches in Yellowknife, and* this *is my reward? I'm giving up irony.*

"Seems you have me all figured out." She sat back, slowly. "Well, no. CC thinks your *client* is up to something."

Oh, damn. So, this is not a straightforward book liberating trip then? Doubtless Navarro wanted him to rat on Streich, and whatever she was up to. This was becoming a very irritating pattern.

"Don't think I wouldn't enjoy taking the time to figure you out, Rhea. But for now, just tell me your heart's desire. It'll save time."

She stood, lifted her bag, burst the privacy bubble then bent down, putting her lips to his ear: scent of bergamot, orange blossom, hint of ginger. "I need eyes on Cassie Streich. You call me if she does anything contra to CC's interests. You know I can make your life *very* uncomfortable. You don't want UN Revenue up inside your taxes, and it would be tragic if UN Families challenged your guardianship of Moth. You work for CC now. You work for me."

Navarro straightened, and walked away. The steward—arriving with Quirk's gin-and-tonic—turned to let her pass.

"Will there be anything else, sir?"

Quirk shook his head more sharply than intended, sipped his drink, forgetting to watch the steward's departure. His tax affairs were...confused after his trip to Milan, true, but threatening him with Moth was low, lower even than Navarro could know. And yet she seemed too fervent under that ugly CC veneer. *Was* Streich planning something involving CC and Skye? Would she come clean about it, and why hire him anyway—for his CC history?

Whatever the case, Navarro clearly meant business. Bringing a firearm onto the Forties Shinkansen was a vulgar display of influence. His enjoyable sojourn was over before it had begun.

3

Forecourt outside the Neues Museum, Bodestrasse, Berlin

'Meet me by the Spree,' Cassie had subvocalised, responding to Quirk's message. She stood in the cold, shadowed by the blonde stone splendour of the Neues Museum on her right, the Alte Nationalgalerie—temple to the history of art—louring on her left. Thankfully, a force-field prevented the winter rain sweeping across the plaza. She hugged her vintage black Extè overcoat around her.

The equestrian statue of Friedrich Wilhelm IV towered paternalistically atop the Nationalgalerie's sweeping steps, his horse high-stepping, tail erect. Cassie had specified Louis Tuaillon's bronze *Amazon on Horseback* for the rendezvous, rider and horse standing calm and determined in the corner of the plaza, shadowed by the king, but ready to fight. It was a test for Quinton Kirby. Paperclip's briefing insisted he was sensitive and insightful. That remained to be seen.

She saw him, one man among the strolling, circling tourists. Paperclip had linked his image on the Worlds Wide Web. He walked towards her, not the statue, raincoat swirling around an efficient frame, holdall in one hand. And that suit, a classic cut, but the colour, so...forward.

"Cassie Streich, I presume?"

Tone confident, accent the muddy burr of a well-travelled citizen of the system. She considered activating her handy's privacy pod, but a bubble in a public place was a flag in itself.

"No," she made a cutting gesture. "Address me as Professor Streich."

"What if you smile at me?"

She adopted an expression that said that was unlikely.

"That suit, the raincoat...such a detective cliché."

"In keeping with Berlin, itself an espionage cliché. I should have worn a gardenia."

He smiled, lopsided. She disliked his easy bonhomie, the engaging air she'd never mastered in years battling through the tiers of education and academia. Always the awkward misfit, struggling to understand herself, never mind those around her. Then she found Karla, who understood her, saw her, *knew* her. Karla had empathised, beguiled, unfurled her, undressed her, unwrapped her inhibitions, unclenched her restraint. Karla freed her. She knew it then. It hadn't just been kinky, unashamed online sex. Existing without Karla was too hard. Cassie loved her, but Karla was gone, ripped out of her life.

She scowled. "You're late."

"I'm sorry. Higher than forecast air pressure around the maglev." His gaze drifted over her head. "*Amazone zu Pferde*, very appropriate."

So, he passed. It didn't mean anything. A childish game, she supposed. Still, good that he was confident, knowledgeable. Perhaps she would succeed once he was embroiled too far to retreat. And what then if she did? What did it matter without Karla?

He made a curt bow. "I accept you as my fearless leader, bending the pins that restrain you, shattering the hard mould academia has cast you in."

She rolled her eyes. "I hope you understand the task as well as you seem to know the bronzing process."

"I read the proposal. Four European libraries, collecting controversial texts, etcetera. Wilhelm will turn in his crypt."

"Good." The more he embraced the public-facing task, the better her chances of maintaining the illusion, assembling the key's components, and unlocking Skye. "Just remember we will not be friends. You are my employee—"

"Contractor. But I'm here for the companionship, not the payoff."

"This is *not* a junket, Quirk."

He scanned the plaza, gaze slipping past the museum's glass door. Unhurried, yet searching, but for what, or who? "Expecting trouble?"

Her jaw clenched. "No, are you?"

"Always. Let's just say I've got a nose for deceit."

She sniffed, lifted her travel bag, and strode away towards the plaza's edge, and the rank of waiting Autocabs.

Time to go collect.

4

Berlin Hauptbahnhof, Europaplatz

Berlin's Central Station still looked like an upturned red wok. Long gone, the historic smoked glass boxes with their steel exoskeleton, the old cladding stripped and replaced with lightweight, super-strong plass, the big translucent red dome thrown over everything like some almighty entity was trying to trap creepy-crawlies for disposal.

Quirk had not spoken since they boarded the Autocar on Museum Island, but he smiled, glancing from the one-way window to her and back as the vehicle threaded through the streets of her city. His eye held a glint that she hoped was just flirting. *That* she could handle, with cutting words or long-practised jujitsu. What she feared was that the gleam · betrayed suspicion, or some knowledge of her true mission—Karla's dream, Paperclip's plan.

She strutted through the station's AirScreen—the temperature-regulating, weatherproofing energy curtain also scanning for contraband and checking their tickets—making for their platform as quickly as the crowds permitted. Screens, sound bubbles, scent clouds aimed to entice them to the latest SVR story, song and perfume. DB androids stood at strategic points, inactive; no assistance needed today, no one 'misguided.' They monitored the concourse, travellator and platform, watching them all the way to the sleek, yellow Shinkansen.

Quirk stretched out across the seats opposite, closed his eyes. She tried to roll the tension from her shoulders, failed, and called for a syRen®. The violet-eyed android enquired after the source of her pain. She snorted, activating her privacy bubble. Carriage noise faded, supple synthetic fingers began to work at the knots in her shoulders.

Silence.

Sound seeping into a hiss of nothing.

Eyes closed...soft glow...dreaming now.

Lying on her bed, ceiling screen displaying another room where Karla reclined, naked under a clear sekondskin bodysuit, auburn hair spilling across her pillow, hanging above her like a dirty, lovely fallen angel. The transparent suit revealed Karla's dark nipples, the drift of russet hair dusting her pubic mound, flattened by the pressure of Karla's fingers, breasts tightening the connected suit's fabric. Her room lit only by the screen, while Karla bathed in golden West Coast sunlight. Karla's hands traced her own curves and—over thousands of miles—Cassie felt that touch through her suit, stroking, rubbing, pressing, probing...

Bad idea—

Cassie opened her eyes, waved the android away, and stared at the window without seeing.

If just one of her drunken clicks after the faculty Christmas Party—buzzing, horny, naked in her bedroom's dim lamplight—had been different, she would not have found rosebudroom.sex, would not have found the 'Willing partners' thread, would not have met Karla. Ex-LA favela teenage hooker, former mule, courier, gardener, mentor, turned eco-guerrilla on a quest. Would never have been seduced by Karla's look, her voice, her ideas—ideas that were radical, intoxicating. Professor Cassandra Streich was once labelled an agitator, a campaigner for universal equality within a plascrete establishment, a maverick intellectual. But Karla was a firebrand. She came from outside the establishment, and she wanted to tear it apart, rebuild it, starting with C Corp.

"Feeling better?" Quirk inquired.

Cassie defeated the urge to scowl. A positive demeanour was important to maintaining his effectiveness as a tool, and prospective patsy.

"Much. Despite my frostiness, please know that I appreciate your assistance."

Did his eyes narrow by microns?

"That's nice."

"In Rome, I'm invited to the chancellor's reception at the Pontifical University. My contact is there. You will be my plus-one. My assistant has arranged evening dress for us."

"I thought this wasn't a pleasure trip?"

"A concession to the cardinal necessary to secure library access, and retrieve the book." And there was the matter of the second of four key components. After Rome, she would be halfway into Skye. "The Vatican is keen to be rid of it. Unofficially, of course, since they disavow its existence."

"Delightful." Quirk nodded, smiled, and took out his handy, began swiping and tapping.

The raid on Skye would be deadly serious. How would he react when she told him, when he realised he was committed without his knowledge? She'd promised Karla, made her peace with the possibility she would not survive the island, but CC, their horrendous abuses of nature and community, *would* be exposed. Quirk had opposed them before, surely he would buy-in. And if she should survive, and escape, she would find Karla, free her—somehow—after striking the blow they had dreamt of in the sticky afterglow, together yet alone in their shadowed rooms.

Oh, Karla, what have you made of me, love?

5

Piazzale dei Cinquecento, Rome, Italy, Med-Bloc

They were followed immediately on arrival, or so Quirk assumed. He would have done that, in Navarro's place. From the bright, white concourse of the Stazione Termini (advertising banned by Papal dictate), to the line of whispering AutoCabs (also white), and among the Eternal City's epic, millennia-old architectural facades.

These days, detecting surveillance was virtually impossible. Anyone with an expense account could track someone from their desktop, and there was next to nothing Joe/Joanne/Joh Blow could do about it. Few intelligence agencies bothered with boots on the ground anymore. Thorough to a fault however, Quirk faced backwards, and cleared a window in their taxi's OLED shell. Another white cab dogged their tracks.

They arrived at the hotel within sight of the floodlit Colosseo, checked into adjoining rooms, and freshened up without interruption. Quirk traded the Merrion for a tuxedo in the darkest of blues. When in Rome, it would be a crime to look anything less than fabulous.

He scanned the room with his Bug_Out app—more from habit than expectation. Nothing, but for the usual emergency sensors, because if dark (or light) forces really wanted to watch you they would, and his Weekend Warrior spy kit would be none the wiser.

Stepping into the hall at the appointed time, he was faced by Streich in a dinner suit of matching cut, hers midnight green, nails painted black, he thought, until her hands moved and the colour drifted from indigo through burnt Sienna to bronze. GG No.9, waggishly named Novae Nouveau. Cassie was severely stylish, all elegant angles, chic lines, features so full of mystery she would take someone a lifetime to decode. It irked him somewhat that he would not be that someone.

She nodded. "I approve."

He read the cypher of her lips as a smile, and made his own rules. "Thank you, Cassandra."

Those pale lips twitched. She made for the elevator.

Navarro, irritating CC agent and train stalker, was waiting in the foyer.

Damn.

"Don't you two look nice."

"Who is this?" Streich demanded, eyes narrowing.

"Agent Navarro, UNEC," she flicked her handset screen, and the handy in Streich's pocket pinged.

"I'm sure you are. We have an engagement." Streich made to brush past, but Navarro gripped Cassie's forearm.

"No need to be so brusque, Professor. I just wanted to check in; I've been watching you so long."

If possible, Streich's visage paled. Navarro had spooked her. Could they *know* each other? Either way, clearly Cassie was hiding something, supporting Navarro's theory from the train.

Streich's blue eyes narrowed. "I said we don't have time. Come back later if you must. Better yet, leave me alone." She stormed out between the twin, copper-potted aspidistras flanking the hotel's street entrance.

Navarro's narrowed eyes followed Streich's departure.

"Well played," Quirk said, "but why bother with mind games? Don't you just pop a cap in us poor schmucks these days?"

She turned on him, and snapped, "Just do what you're told, when you're told."

The Pontifical University was a Baroque confection, the main hall as opulent a setting for a reception as Cassie had ever seen. All in the pursuance of exalting the Holy Trinity. With this much shock and awe, could faith be far behind? The chamber was chock-full of cassocks, cocktail dresses and tuxedos. Warm candlelight supplemented smartEDs. Hubbub proliferated, servers glided through the throng (did this qualify as a flock?), proffering wine and canapés.

She had regained her calm after their encounter—Navarro grabbing her arm, exerting pressure like Karla had done once, urging her onto her back... She took a deep breath, offered Quirk her elbow, but he declined, clapping her on the shoulder before they descended the carpeted stairs to the edge of the crowd.

"Don't offend anyone," she instructed. "Speak when spoken to. In fact, don't speak at all. Stay by me and smile. Your principal skill, it seems. Let's get the book then be on our way."

Quirk? It's Navarro.

<Playing it cool not really your style, is it? A suspicious person might think you're not just following Streich, you're running her.>

Don't be ridiculous, I'm CC, I don't run people.

<Just torment them. What is your history?>

What is it that you want, Quirk?

<Why thank you for asking, Agent Navarro. I'd like to collect some antique books, and earn the respect of someone I admire. How do my chances look?>

Navarro's pause was too long.

Just remember what's at stake for you. Call me with anything suspect.

<Bite me.>

He hung up. Resistance felt good, but likely was useless. If they wanted Cassie, they would get her. Navarro would tail their every step, swoop in once Cassie had incriminated herself, prevent her ever reaching Skye. Assuming that was, in fact, her goal. What would he do then? Was he up for another battle with CC so soon?

She moved away from Monsignor Conte, fixing his directions and passcode in her mind. The second part of the key to Skye was close, and yet she was angry. First that UNEC agent, and now Quirk stood with two doe-eyed noviciates—one male, one female—guzzling prosecco while they hung on his words. Yet, intoxicated or not, he appeared beside her when she left the hall, smiling too much, but alert. She hated that his confidence helped.

The darkened library illuminated for them—sEDs warming wood and ancient vaulted brickwork, oak shelves and plass partitions, a dichotomy: antiquity vying with modernity around row upon row of real books. It was beautiful; smelled like nothing she'd ever encountered.

She had anticipated needing to park Quirk somewhere, but he took station by the door, looking out while she conducted her business. He may be a poseur, but he was effective. Almost as if he knew the books were a cover. But, how could he? Maybe she would challenge him on it, but not yet. It was too soon.

The book that the church would not admit to owning had been left out for her on a bright white table, in a space enclosed by bookshelves, ranked spines presenting a chaotic spectrum encompassing two millennia of learning. It was Johnina Smith's 2029 paean, *Transemancipation*, which the US government had destroyed all five thousand copies of, minus one, she supposed. She left with it under her arm. The Skye key component—found in a different book, per Paperclip's instructions—nestled in her breast pocket. Quirk pulled the heavy door shut behind them.

They reappeared on the edge of the throng, Quirk with an easy smile. Her expression felt tight and awkward. This time he took her elbow, and they walked to the stairs.

"You get it then."

"I did. On to Paris."

6

Quai de Conti, 6th Arrondissement, Paris, France, Euro Bloc Nord

Her head spun, Rome still a blur in her mind's eye. Slipping the wafer-thin component into the blocky sequencer key had elicited three beeps and four flashes of a pink LED on the matt black oblong's side. That was it.

She spent the hyperloop ride failing to sleep, pondering her next step, and contending with Quirk's artless inanities. The UNEC agent—Navarro—had used the word 'brusque.' Not a common word, but hardly obscure. Yet could she have spoken to Paperclip? Ridiculous. A coincidence. *Yet what do I know of Paperclip? An effective handler, yes, and another seeker after truth and justice, Karla had insisted. But who are they? Where does their knowledge originate? And why do they care about my mission?*

"CASSIE'S TRAIN DREAM"

FADE IN:

INT. BERLIN - BEDROOM - DAY - FLASHBACK

Professor Cassandra Streich sits on her bed, wearing a skin-tight transparent bodysuit, facing a wall screen displaying a similarly clad Latina woman sitting cross-legged in a candlelit bedroom. Cassandra wipes sweat from around her eyes.

CASSANDRA

Karla, you are amazing. Where did you learn that...thing with your thumbs?

KARLA

You inspire me, mi amor. I wanna make you sweat, and moan, and beg. Wish I could touch you.

CASSANDRA

At least I can feel your touch through the wonder of this uncomfortable technology.

KARLA

I love the way it squeezes you...

(Onscreen, Karla looks over her shoulder then back.)

CASSANDRA

Are you okay, love? We should recap Skye again. I leave in three days, and you said there was something bothering you?

KARLA

Thought I heard something. Just Señora Torres slapping her ol' man.

(pause)

Estúpido bastardo.

On the screen, Karla flinches, turns. Black shadows slip across the walls, dark shapes block the screen, grab Karla's hands and feet, twist her flat. Cassie the tugging, the torsion through her suit. Big, blocky yellow letters splash over the screen. LAPD, FBI, UNEC. They cuff Karla's hands, her feet. People are shouting, but a police ECM kills the audio (to prevent later incrimination). Karla yells mutely. A figure blocks the image.

FADE OUT

Quirk slept in the seat opposite. Her dream remained vivid. Her last words with Karla. But something was different. An idea formed, a terrifying, tantalising idea.

<Paperclip?>

Here. What can I do?

<Can you access my aether drive?>

With an authorisation from your handy.

Cassie did that: left thumb and retina scan.

<Use lipreading software on my last call from Karla. What did she say, at the end?>

That'll take a while.

<Why?>

I can't now. Being watched. Later. Paperclip out.

Walking across the Pont des Arts in the clear, chill air of wintertime Paris, feet clumping on wide wooden beams, the Seine's frigid waters below, she had two of four pieces that she needed to unlock Skye, and expose C Corp's malfeasance to all humanity. Berlin and Rome brought her halfway there. Karla's fervent wish—*her* wish— would be satisfied. She would free Karla by proving CC's guilt, of eco- crimes and more besides.

Ahead, at the bridge's end—across a road busy with autonomous cars, buses, vans and lorries—was the dome of the Institut de France. And, through heavy doors central in the left-hand of two curving terraces sweeping out from the dome, a cobbled courtyard, and the grand entrance to Le Bibliothèque Mazarine.

As they reached the road—Cassie glancing left and right—Quirk's pocket vibrated.

It's Navarro. You're having this too easy. I need to work you a bit. Agents inbound. Better hustle.

Streich flinched. "What's happening?"

Don't panic, Quirk. You'll be fine.

"Move, now."

He gripped her elbow, hustled her across the street, vehicles jerking to a stop.

To the right, three grey-coated figures closed on them through parting tourists, commuters, pet-walkers, androids. To the left three more.

Behind them, more slate-grey coats advanced over the bridge. The only way out was through. He pulled Cassie into a jog across the plaza to the library's heavy doors.

Their IDs scanned clear, they hurried in, across a corridor, out through a stone arch, across a courtyard. Scanned again at the grand library entrance. The ancient building's cool, low-lit interior welcomed them.

"We're done," Cassie spat.

"No," he growled. But dammit, Navarro's C Corp goons closing them down already? And yet, CC wouldn't have been seen if they hadn't wanted to be, wouldn't sport standard goon uniform and stir up the pedestrians if they really wanted to catch them. Not when a surreptitious needle in the arm from a passer-by would lay you out quickly and quietly.

"It's like they herded us in here. Maybe just trying to scare us," he said. Streich looked doubtful. "Let's get your book. Then, we need to talk."

She dashed about her task, Quirk shadowing her. He watched her sign for the book, but made no move to leave. So be it. She strode further into the palatial reading room, to a spot between the busts of Barack Obama and Aimé Césaire on their marble plinths, located the relevant tome, and retrieved a thin, vacuum-sealed envelope from between its ancient pages. Quirk stared knowingly, but had no chance to challenge her. Raised voices echoed from the long, columnated room's entrance.

They did the only sensible thing: they ran.

Flight took them to marble stairs. They scuffed up—shouts echoing around them—climbed narrower marble treads, then hollow, thumping wooden steps. At the top of the building, plaster walls, and the odour of ages past. Quirk picked a door. Locked. Another. Locked. Prepared to break the next one, but it opened. He pulled her in and closed the door gently. She bent to listen, but he gripped her upper arm, pulled her to the window, a dormer on the angle of a sloping, flaking ceiling. The rickety old window was alarmed. He worked the catch, pushed it open.

All hell broke loose. A buzzer rattled achingly loud in the room. Somewhere below, a klaxon wailed. Quirk stuck his head outside then pulled back.

"Out."

"Quirk, there's nowhere..."

"Raus! Raus!" He urged her up onto the sill. The tiles sloped steeply to a short rail and a wide gutter, beyond which was nothing. Her coat's collar choked tight, Quirk gripping it as she found her balance. "It really does help if you don't look down."

"You do this a lot?"

"More than I'd like. Go left. The river's behind us."

Boots in the hall, doors opening.

Cassie swung her legs out, stepped down, faced along the gutter and didn't look down. Quirk pushed the window closed behind him. To her amazement, the alarm stopped.

It was a short shuffle to an angle where two buildings met at the corner of the quadrangle below. Quirk boosted her up the sixty-degree roof by her rear then her heels. She scrambled up, straddled the peak.

The window was flung open and alarms blared again, filling the courtyard below.

She looked down at Quirk as he reached up for her hand, saw doubt in his eyes.

"I won't abandon you," she said.

"C Corp security. Don't move!"

A big lug with florid features hung from the window, determined but uncomfortable. A blonde crew cut poked her round face out, hauled Lug in by the shoulder then pointed a gun at Quirk.

"Desist, now."

"Or you'll murder me?"

"Dummy rounds. Shame if you fell resisting a legitimate corporate stop-and-search though, splattering your brains all over the ground."

Quirk sighed. "Where's Moth when I need her? She'd have a pithy rejoinder for this, something like, 'Fuck you, toilet brush.'"

A calm, polite voice spoke from behind her. "Corporate intellectual jurisdiction does not apply within historical landmarks." She risked a glance. A syRen® walked towards her atop the half-metre wide roof coping. "Please withdraw. Your actions generate unacceptable risks."

"You're not the boss of me, bolt-in-the-neck," Blondie snapped.

"I have contacted the police."

"Well, shit." Blondie withdrew.

The android grasped a handhold, reached down to Quirk, wind plucking at its Paris Historique wind-cheater. Cassie helped it haul him up to sit on the peak.

"Risk assessment dictates remaining here until rescued."

"No chance," said Quirk. "Please escort us down, to avoid further peril."

7

Forty-three minutes from Brussels, Flemish UK Protectorate

Leaving Paris was easier than she'd expected. Quirk repaid his fee with ten minutes of sweet-talking La PP—their blue lights waiting at the foot of the escape ladder. They could not resist his charm. A misunderstanding; a panic attack; his poor, pregnant fiancé (she'd started breathing heavily then, not entirely faked); what stunning eyes the officer-in-charge had; and somehow, they were dispatched with a warning.

Now they whistled towards Brussels in an AirShuttle one kilometre up, the piloting android sealed in the cockpit, oblivious to their conversation.

"The beans, Cassie. Spill them, or I walk the instant we land." She glared at him. "I don't need the money, and I stopped having fun after Rome."

She closed her eyes, tilted her head forward and back, side-to-side, neck cracking. "You have been useful thus far. What kind of confidentiality does our contract afford me?"

"The same kind as you asking me to keep a secret," he said, unblinking.

She nodded, sighed. "My...friend and I developed a plan to expose C Corp. Karla's contact in CC is helping us get onto Skye, the rest is up to me. To us."

"The envelope?"

She nodded. "Part of a biometric key to the island's barrier. Karla and I were to meet, go in together, retrieve the evidence to destroy CC. Then Karla was arrested."

"And my role?" His voice flat, dark green eyes searching.

She was exposed now, there was nothing else for it. In for a penny, as the British said.

"I have a controller..."

"Navarro?"

"What? No." But that word, 'brusque,' shared by Navarro and Paperclip. "Why would you think that?"

"Shot in the dark. She approached me on the train, 'asked' me to monitor you. She's CC."

Her breath caught. "Did she mention Karla?"

"No, but she's very interested in our activities. She told me about Skye."

"I'm tired, Quirk. How do you cope with this cloak-and-dagger nonsense?" She closed her eyes, rubbed her face. Yellow letters bobbed in her mind. Still no response from Paperclip to her request, and she needed *answers*. "Do you have someone who can perform detailed video analysis?"

He indicated the android pilot.

"Seriously?"

"Even if CC somehow managed to hack that android, I doubt they'd do it before we had an answer, and does it matter if they do?"

"Probably not."

She made the request, snipped the scene of interest, and sent it with a flick.

"Task complete," said the android. "There is dialogue in English, Spanish and German."

"German?" Why...? "Play transcript."

Officer #1, in English: LAPD. Freeze that pretty little ass,
(in Spanish) bitch. You're going downtown.
Karla, in Spanish: Fuck you. I ain't done nothin', pigs.
Agent #1: I'm arresting you...
Karla, in German: Ow, my fucking ankle, Shüller!
Dialogue ends.

Cassie's eyes met Quirk's. She knew she was gaping. "She was in Germany."

He nodded. "A staged scene. Germans posing as NAF officials to 'kidnap' your lover. It's possible. And very motivating, it would seem. You're still on her mission, aren't you?"

"I...She lives in LA. Why would she lie about her location? Why would she lie to *me*?"

"It looks like a setup."

"But I *love* her."

"I know for certain lies and love are not mutually exclusive."

Silence. The AirShuttle moved smoothly—the syRen® compensating for pressure pockets and air flows—but her mind was in turmoil. Karla was a part of her, ripped out, and now...had it all been fabricated? To what end? How much of their relationship was a lie? Verdammt, they'd talked about Cassie moving to that LA favela, surrendering everything, writing her novel. And now...had Karla used her? Used her to do the dirty work in taking down C Corp?

She snorted.

"I'm a romantic cliché, lifeless until I met Karla. You're the expert. What does this mean?"

Quirk tapped his lips. "Maybe a simple sell-out, maybe they blackmailed her. Maybe she was a plant, but that doesn't explain her speaking German. Does it change your goals?"

"I...no. There could be any number of reasons for the lie. Karla was fervent about punishing CC for their crimes on Skye, the destruction we believe they've caused, and still cause. It's a noble goal, and one lie doesn't destroy a relationship. I'll finish this for her, and damn the consequences, but I need your help, all the way to the bitter end, if you will."

His lips moved into that skewed smile, but his eyes were hard. "I will, Professor."

She nodded. "You're too amenable, Quirk."

"So the ladies tell me."

The android pilot—inexhaustibly patient—insisted they'd passed untracked through Flemish airspace, one in a million specs in the humming personal aviation band. Cassie barely heard Quirk's conversation with the automaton. Her mind whirled. What if Karla had betrayed her? Could Agent Navarro be her informant? Paperclip? Did the video prove that Karla had been working for CC, maybe she *couldn't* do the job herself, and so needed a patsy, and their relationship was a setup? Emotions aside, what did that mean? Would CC kill her and Quirk with impunity on the wasted beaches of Skye, or before they even got inside? Why had they been allowed to get this far?

Where does Karla's allegiance lie now?

In the end it hardly mattered. She couldn't go back to Berlin, or teaching. She'd be lucky to reach prison if CC agents took them. Karla's vision of tearing down Skye's dome sustained her resolve. That, and more personal, intimate memories. Memories of connecting, of sharing, of trusting—trusting completely. That had to be real. Blurred imagined outline; sinuous, urgent fingers; hot, wet longing to remain on the edge of ecstasy forever, because to orgasm was to surrender, and Cassie had always fought surrender, before.

Had her lover groomed her then betrayed her, or was Karla betrayed too? Had Navarro/Paperclip played them both for fools?

Or, what if…?

No.

Karla couldn't *be*…

Oh, no.

Whatever had happened in the process of Karla recalibrating Cassie's heart, whether out of love, lust, or a quest for justice, her lover had ruined her. Nothing else mattered but to do Karla's will or die trying. But maybe, maybe there was the slightest hope, a mote in the galactic ocean, that she could save Karla, and that mote was everything.

Hissing, rumbling tyres of cars, bikes, scooters and taxis filled Cassie's head as she surveyed the Koninklijke Bibliotheek van België, clinging to its national identity despite Belgium's fracturing into its constituent parts, and the UK's generous assistance as the NW Atlantic region's preeminent military power. Predictably, Britain wore the sobriquet 'Police-officer of Northern Europe' with post-colonial pomposity.

The rumbling ceased, and they started across Keizerslaan to the library. Cassie's handy rang. Local ordinance forbade phoning on a crosswalk, but…

Cassie! It's Paperclip. They're coming. Hurry!

Too late. Already too late.

Four CC agents moved to intercept them. Quirk moved in front of her, facing them down.

Navarro stepped from the building, dark raincoat despite the domed City Centre's controlled climate. Maybe it made her feel like a spy. Her expression was as sour as Cassie felt. Why was *she* unhappy? Everything was going her way. Suddenly angry, Cassie stepped forward, confronting Navarro.

She'd…been crying. A barely detectable shine to Navarro's eyes, slight pinkness in the sclera. How unprofessional. Why would she…?

There was no uncertainty now.

"Who are you?" Cassie came right out and asked, because it didn't matter anymore.

"Agent Rhea Nav—"

"You're CC. Are you Paperclip?"

"Cassie—" Quirk gripped her elbow.

"Answer me!" People should just speak their minds and damn the torpedoes. "Karla..." proud that her voice didn't catch. The name hanging in the air like a knife poised to strike. "Is it you?"

Anger twisted Navarro's features. Cassie held her breath. Quirk tensed. The goons moved forward. Navarro spoke.

"Yes."

Cassie was on the ground, hard cobbles under skinned knees. Blood and grit and pain.

What happened? Crying? Hands on her, raising her up. Stared at Navarro. At Paperclip. At Karla. Weight in the centre of her chest. Those dark, red-rimmed eyes, shining. Yearning? Would they shoot her if she touched...Karla?

The woman's gaze slid sideways, perhaps marking the location of her grey companions, or just avoiding Cassie's anger.

"Talk to me, Karla. Tell me I'm wrong. Explain why I'm still here, what I'm to do now, because I do *not* understand."

"Cassandra—" Navarro choked. Was there hope? What did the video mean? Agents began smoothing their suits, patting their pockets.

"I loved you, Karla. Tell me what to do."

"Cassie..." The goons' gazes searched the street, feet shifting.

Quirk's hand was in his jacket pocket, something narrow pointed at Navarro. "Let's keep calm," he said. "Go inside, get what we need while you two figure out if you're going or coming."

Was she to die in a gunfight on the steps of a Belgian library, slip away in her lover's arms? They all walked inside, Quirk with his hidden weapon, guiding Cassie by the elbow as if she would faint. Every step felt like wading through waist-deep water. Surely he couldn't get them through this with some pocket gun.

She found the appointed place, details provided by Paperclip who was Navarro who was Karla, wasting no time on the pretence of collecting the Freie Universität's book, since she would never go back. Her academic career was over. She found the envelope, slipped out the component, fed it into the key. Beep, flash, done. Lights cycled red, yellow, green. The key was complete.

Navarro/Paperclip/Karla led their tense little troupe back to the foyer. What a farcical performance for the library's occupants. The goons looked increasingly edgy.

"You have twenty-four hours before the genetic components degrade beyond use," her once-lover said to Quirk, not looking at her. The synthetic breeze—designed to prevent 'user' disorientation—plucked open Karla's superfluous raincoat, and Cassie's eyes recounted her curves, seeing the match now, looking past the sharp, charcoal business suit, the subtly different face, imagining white cotton underwear, warm, light sepia skin.

"Why, Karla? You lied to me, led me on, used me. And it cost you nothing, because lust is like credit—cheap for some. And love? I gave you that, and you discarded it. You threw it away. For what? Explain it to me."

Karla nodded, lips compressed, jaw tight. "I was told to plan a raid on Skye using outsiders, so we—CC—could swoop in for a PR coup: criminals break in, attempt to contaminate the environment. I needed a patsy, so I went online. I found you, Cassie. It's a huge cliché, but...you changed me, made me believe I could have more than a life of shadows." Karla leaned in, whispered, "Your trust, your commitment to what started as a fake goal. You changed my mind. I know you loved me, and I hope you can again, if you get through this. If I do."

The goons edged closer. Quirk kept his pocket pointing at Karla. Library visitors passed through the foyer, unknowing. Karla slipped a hand into one raincoat pocket.

"You were a tool to begin with, to CC, to me," she reached out, palm to Cassie's cheek. "But now..."

The feeling of another's skin, warm, smooth. Cassie leaned into the touch. It was Karla, undoubtedly, the caress as familiar as touching herself. Sad eyes met hers, as if etching a memory for later recall. "Such plans only ever have a slim chance of success, I'm afraid. It's time to finish this."

Karla's pocketed hand reached around her own waist, pulling the raincoat across her stomach. The back of the garment twitched. Blondie slumped to her knees. Twitched again, with a whipping sound, and Lug staggered. Karla barely moved as she shot the other two agents, who twisted, fell to the hard floor, convulsing then still.

Karla shrugged out of the now-ripped coat, gun clattering on the marble. She peeled off a sekondskin glove, let it fall.

"Good-bye, love." She managed a strained smile. "You can do this. Bring out evidence of CC's crimes. I just wish I could do more."

"I'd say you did plenty," said Quirk.

"Shut up, Quirk," Cassie mumbled as she turned, and walked away.

8

Kyle of Lochalsh, Independent Queendom of Scotland

Quirk closed his handset, looking up at the island's blocky, unnatural profile—immense pale monolith, glowing dully in early morning light. A twenty-second century White Cliffs of Dover. The boat's movement brought on a whiff of nausea. He placed a finger to his lips.

Cassie noted Quirk's discomfort. She felt fine, glanced at their skipper, a grizzled man the shape of a lifebuoy, who ended his sentences with 'ken?' She'd searched it. "He's saying, 'Know what I mean?'"

"I know," said Quirk.

The looming opaque barrier dwarfed them, no speck of land visible through its lambent surface.

The boat bumped the wooden jetty that ran straight to the only door in that rippling expanse. They lifted their packs, boots thudding hollow on planks greyed by decades of wind and rain.

"Thank you." She smiled, her sudden warmth mystifying. Perhaps Karla's betrayal made everyone seem more human. Perhaps she was reaching out to forestall crumbling into her own hollow core. *You...bitch. I loved you, hate you, want you.* Had CC hunted Karla down yet, cauterised the wound of her betrayal? Did it matter that Karla did, in fact, love her?

"Nae worries, doll," said the boatman. "Gang warily, ken?" He nodded up at them then gunned the ancient engine, turned for home, leaving a V of white turmoil on the dark waters.

"Disce pati," said Quirk, watching the vessel recede.

"Learn to endure?"

"Close enough." He started along the jetty towards the door.

Cassie followed, regarding the sheer surface, forty, fifty metres high, neck stiffening. She looked down, swallowed, dug out the key, a matt black lump in her palm.

"We have no protection," she said. "What if we're contaminated?" Because she needed to get out, publish the evidence they collected.

Quirk laughed. "You don't believe the CC PR then? If suits are needed they'll be racked up inside. CC are organised, if nothing else. Honestly? I'm more worried about them shooting us. We should leave some insurance."

He took out his handset, dialled Moth. Her image appeared eventually, laggy, but adequate for the purpose. She was wearing a purple envsuit, complete with helmet ring. She hadn't been bluffing about the Marine Scouts.

"Shut up, Clyde!" she hollered at someone offscreen, waving them away. Irritation transformed into the sweetest smile. *"Hey, Quirk. You balled the agent yet?"*

"Certainly not."

"Is that the Isle of Skye? Shit, Quirk, that's charged! Clyde! I swear to fuck I'm gonna airlock you, you an-DUH-roid!! Sorry, Clyde's being a fuck-tart."

He badly needed to find Moth's off switch when he got home, but was gladdened to see her coping with her recent trauma, externally at least.

He moved beside Cassie, putting the island in its glowing plastext shroud square behind them, leaning in, bringing Streich in-shot. "Smile, Cassie, you're on Damn-kid Camera."

"Moth, honey, focus, please." That always got her attention, sometimes triggering a stream of fresh vitriol, but stemming the flow of teenage angst for a moment. "Please have Bea record this. We need a GPS stamp. In case something happens."

"What do you mean 'happens'? Clarify 'something'! We've had this fight before, and you agreed always to come back. No take-backs."

"Yes, Moth dear, but I'm in a prime spot to do CC some real damage, which I owe them. Right now, I need the recording, okay?"

Silence stretched across 350 million kilometres. *"Okay, Bea's got it."*

"Pass the stress." He'd learned a little teen-speak in the last year. "We're locked."

"*Quirk, you're so lame.*" Pause. "*Yeah, so, be careful.*" Pause. "*I...like you. G'bye.*" Click.

"Are you having doubts, Quirk? I'm surprised you're still here. After everything. I lied to you."

"I don't care, and we don't have time. The stupidly short version—CC took my child from me, and experimented on him. So, can we get on?"

She nodded. *For the love I had, and just once to strike back against all those unseen, untouchable manipulators.* She placed the key in the door's reader.

A low tone. The door's magnolia glow became mint. A hollow, sanitary click. Quirk pushed the door inwards.

A bright corridor stretched ahead, walls, ceiling and floor radiating cool light. Cassie stepped inside, absently brushing the surface, smooth under her fingertips.

"You enter this facility at your own risk," said a formless, automaton voice. "C Corp declines all responsibility for injury or damage sustained on the property. C Corp disavows pre-knowledge of any risks present within this unstaffed facility."

The door clicked shut behind them.

Cassie looked at Quirk, who shared the glance. He seemed controlled, unperturbed by the emotions she'd sensed in his conversation with the girl. He'd been cool during the Brussels confrontation, and in Paris, but would her own nerve hold? What lay beyond this passageway, and could she handle it?

Quirk's thoughts drifted with the metronomic clunk of his Jeni Choo Outlanders along the acetic corridor. Laboratory smells, Arctic cold, braying animal voices: the nightmares of Yellowknife—his last bio-monstrosity event—remained close.

They stopped before another door, a featureless twin of the first. There were pale pink envsuits—transparent, PLaper wrapped—on hooks beside the door. They discarded their outer clothes in silence, ripped the wrappers open. Cassie shivered; her skin's tingling not from the corridor's chill, but the eerie echo of the sekondskin suit she'd used with Karla. Her heart ached. *Found her; lost her; touched by her; hate her. Love her. Karla.*

She smoothed the breathable, filtering plastext mask over the contours of her face, feeling a rush of panic at the momentary sense of suffocation, then breathed. So what if Karla had turned away from CC? People who lied always lied. She could never trust her again...could she? She straightened, reached for the handle, and opened the second door.

They stepped out into a scene of urban wreckage.

Boxy, broken-down two-storey terraced houses lined the street, smothered in ivy, windows smashed, tiles vibrant with moss. Privet hedges, wildly overgrown, prevented access to the buildings. Cars filthy with rain-spattered dirt sat dutifully at the kerb, windows green with mould. All except one.

Quirk turned.

Through the last crack in the closing door he saw four figures jogging towards them. Camo-suits reflected the corridor's pale walls. Black tactical sets made their heads beady-eyed, insect-like. Boot-mounted acoustic dampers silenced their movement. The door clicked shut.

"Run!" He waved at the clean vehicle.

Cassie ran.

Quirk dashed after her to that single maintained vehicle, a CC logo-ed, all-terrain rover with big run-flat tyres. He hauled the door open—movement flickered at the edge of sight—jumped in, Cassie landing in the seat beside him, tried to slam the door but the dampers declined, sucking it closed with maddening air-cushioned slowness.

"Start."

"Access code, please."

"Fucking start!"

"That code is not approved."

"Paperclip," spoke Cassie.

The dashboard illuminated as bullets rattled the bodywork. Belts snaked down from their shoulders.

Karla was still with them, or her groundwork was.

Could there be room for forgiveness?

Quirk jammed the pedal down, launching them forward, shooting across the road, flattening a signpost with a red triangle around an adult-and-child-holding-hands symbol. The ATR's fat tyres bounced over the kerb, across the footway, into an overgrown lot. Vegetation whipped the windscreen. They burst out of weeds and grasses onto a gravel track. He pulled hard on the wheel, wrestling them onto the path as a drone whined overhead.

"Where are we going?" he asked.

"There," she pointed ahead. "We need to get around the hill." A gap in the vegetation showed a patch of sky and trees flowing over a rise a kilometre away.

Another drone shot passed them, jerked to a halt in the sky. Red light sparkled and the windscreen fractured.

"Damnation!" Quirk yelled.

He tried to keep the power on, but the vehicle's alarm began pinging, and they decelerated.

"Handle above your head," he shouted. She saw it, pulled the red catch as he did the same on his side. The windscreen fell flat on the bonnet, and they accelerated at the next corner, a half-collapsed fence, and beyond, trees and undergrowth. All was overgrown, abandoned, but not morphed into otherworldly aberration, not here.

The bend came up quickly.

She realised Quirk had no intention of cornering.

"Excessive speed. Brake now. Brake now," the system insisted.

"I have some experience with this sort of thing," said Quirk, bent his knee up to his chin, and started ramming his heel into the dashboard.

"Illegal tampering. You are committing a violation of the Road Traffic (Scotland) Ac-ac-act, 2043. Desist nownow, or faccce prosec...ec...ec...ec, uuuuuuuujbbbbbrrrrrrrrr—"

In the chaos, she kept her eyes glued to the road, saw two drones in the air, three, four then the sky disappeared, fence and trees came up, too fast, too fast. She crossed her arms over her head. They crashed through the fence, smashed into the undergrowth. Quirk jerked the wheel, throwing them against their restraints, somehow steering between the trees. The ground sloped up, steep then steeper, gravity hauling her back hard into the seat. The rear-view mirror shook as the vehicle bucked and slewed. The red laser light of drones winked across the bonnet. Bullets thwacked into metal. Without warning they levelled out and plunged down a bank. She screamed. They tipped back upwards. Daylight under the canopy. Hit something—

Bounced, spun, tipped...too far, too far. And rolled.

Cassie. Cassie, love, wake up. Cassie!

Spitting dust and debris, she pulled Quirk from the ATR's crumpled carcass. As he coughed and groaned on his knees, drones purred in the air around them. Cassie contemplated dying, shot by a machine at the hands of a limitlessly avaricious corporation. But the drones just whirred and watched. Could Karla/Navarro still have such influence? She hoped so. They would need it.

"Move, Quirk. Aufstehen!"

She hauled him up, supported him, staggering upslope towards the sky.

They emerged onto the clearcut ridge of the hill. Except it wasn't clearcut. The old trees had been blasted flat, prostrated among fields of bright orange saplings, that fell away from them into the valley below. The far hills were white. Snow, she thought, before instinct told her it was ash. They were right. This place had been blasted.

Quirk coughed, hands on knees, choked out, "This looks...wrong."

"Exactly." She dug out his handset. "Moth, are you getting this?" Long pause. Of course not. The dome blocked all signals, all energy bar the sun. She hefted her pack, sample trays and bottles clunking.

The drones whirred. Back down the wooded hill, dark, human shapes flickered into being.

"Come on," she pushed him forward and he straightened. They started downslope, clambering over fallen trees, sticky orange saplings whipping their pink envsuits, thorns grasping and tearing, drawing blood that ran between skin and transparent fabric.

Cassie, get all the samples you can.

"Paperclip? Navarro? Karla?"

It's hard to hear you.

"Running...for my...life. If you're going to...disappoint me again...by not being dead...make yourself...useful."

I can't stop the agents, but I've hacked the drones. Cassie, I'm—

"Not...now. Pleased you're not dead. So...I can...murder you."

They needed liquids, soil, vegetation, creatures, if anything still crept or crawled here. Fruit, leaves, seeds. Samples that would paint a picture of the devastation CC had wrought on Earth then lied about.

The more she glanced around her, near and far, she saw the twisting, the unmaking, the reforming of this place. To her left, long, sickly yellow grass twitched and rustled as something hurried away from her. She veered away, but jerked back at the sound of a guttural keening, shivered, and hurried on.

The big, flattened trees thinned out, making progress easier at first, sick grass and grey ash underfoot, and saplings snagging them. Further downhill the saplings packed denser, taller, impossible to avoid. The thicker ones glistened with sap, seemed to reach for them. Her arm whipped out straight, and she yanked it away from a bending sapling, red spraying into the air. Her sleeve tore away, arm tingling now.

Quirk groaned, pointed up to the right. As she watched, something leapt above the ground cover, tried to flap threadbare wings, pumped rabbit's haunches and fell back down, squealing—confused and afraid as she was. Bile rose in her throat.

The way ahead ran crimson. Thickets of orange bark dripping red gunk. It coated their suits. She stumbled, hauled her leg free, ripping half the suit leg away.

Quirk was struggling too. He pulled away from a clutch of bleeding saplings that strained to hold him, tears all over his suit, his skin pale, eyes haunted. "This is worse than Yellowknife."

The bleeding saplings crowded them, tore away patches of their envsuits. Drones dogged them, but didn't fire. A bottle fell from a rent in her pack. She scooped it up, scraped sap, thorns and bark into it before stowing it.

The land flattened out, saplings too thick to see beyond. Her suit was ripped away, the red sap trying to peel her skin, thorns tearing, but Cassie fought onward. The horrid goo—in such high concentration—smelled like raw meat, her skin aflame now, but she heard the sound of running water and would not stop.

She burst from the last line of saplings onto the stony floodplain of a slow river maybe ten metres across. Quirk—naked and bleeding—

staggered out behind her, skin scraped pink, starting to bruise, red sap trickling down his arms and legs. Only her bra and the tatters of sekondskin round her chest and shoulders remained. Her plastext facemask hung loose. She tore it away, threw it down.

Eight drones circled them. She snatched a rock and threw it, amazed when it hit.

"Nice shot." Quirk was puffing—looked like he'd been mauled by a bear.

The wounded drone buzzed, popped, dropped to the beach with a crack. Quirk started towards it as the saplings began to sway. Eight figures emerged, dark agents sliding from the bloody forest, bright red slicking their now-black tactical suits. She and Quirk faced them, naked, wounded, slathered in burning, stinking sap, but unbowed.

"Don't move." Guns were levelled. "Surrender those packs." Two agents moved forward. One stripped Quirk's pack away, another wrenched the straps from Cassie's shoulders.

<Seeing this, Karla? I'll get you samples somehow, damn you. I'll get you all the fucking samples you could ask for. These bastards will pay.>

I'm proud of you.

<Geh und fick dich, Liebling.>

She started walking towards the river.

"Cassie," said Quirk. "Cassie, stay still."

"For your own safety, we cannot allow—"

She glanced over her shoulder, saw Quirk standing between her and the advancing troops, his arms outstretched like Da Vinci's Vitruvian Man, as if he could bar their way.

"Don't shoot. You've got us," Quirk said.

"Do not enter the river. Desist, now!"

The agents raised their weapons. The drones descended, forming a loose curtain, shielding her from the guns.

Cassie walked into the water, its chill creeping up her legs, saw as it lapped on her thighs that the water was a sickly green-yellow colour. It crept up, causing a shiver as it covered her crotch, backside, hips, waist, chest.

Gunshots rent the air, bullets sprayed spouts in the water, drawing broken lines either side of her. She was absurdly proud that she didn't start, just sank down, let the water carry her away.

She held her breath as long as she could, pushing into the channel's centre. Gravel scraped her skin, and she knew she must breathe or gulp the foul liquid enclosing her. She surfaced, gasped, half swimming, half floating. When water did splash into her mouth she spat it out, but was left with a taste almost sweet then burning in her throat and mouth.

The channel narrowed and straightened. Knowing it must be deeper, she chanced rolling onto her back, spread her arms for stability to search the sky, wondered why she never went swimming in Berlin's Tegeler See anymore.

No drones marred the high dome's even brightness. She had some time, but what was she doing? Her pack was lost. How could she bring samples out when likely they would shoot her dead as they must have done Quirk? She could not control that, but must proceed as if there was a way, do everything she could, and leave the rest to...luck? Fate? Karla? She snorted, and took a mouthful of sweet, burning water. Maybe an autopsy would bring C Corp down.

The water burned her mouth, but her stomach no more than ached, so far, at least.

Cassie, what are you doing?

She turned forward again, ignoring the voice in her ear. Great black trees overhung the river. Not silhouetted trees. The bark was black, leaves black, not burnt, but a glossy sable that troubled her, made her cast around for threats. Under the tree shadows ahead, great clots of blue algae scummed the river's surface. How did they remain stationary in the flow?

She struck out for the bank, already passing through the first cloudy, cobalt patches. They stung! A stabbing tingle struck her left arm, her chest, her left leg. She gasped. Ropes of slimy vegetation beneath the surface slipped against her stomach, thighs, legs as they pumped. The ropes coiled as if sentient, dragging her back, dragging her down. She gasped and slipped under.

The river turned her over, toyed with her as she bent double, rasping at cords around her ankle then thigh then calf, her wrist, her waist. Burning assaulted her throat, weight crushing her chest. She struggled another cinch loose, arms leaden. A snaking stem wound round her neck, dragged her down, her shoulder bumped hard gravel, scraped a boulder. She grabbed it, planted her feet and heaved with all remaining strength. The tendril stretched tight, choking her at the limit of her straining legs. She could see the light, see it fading.

Then she was free, burst from the water like a salmon, fell back thrashing, stroking hard with the energy of desperation. Then she was clawing mud, dragging her cold, near-naked, aching body onto a beach. She lay on her back on patchy, dark green ground cover, heaving gouts of air in and out like her chest would explode in a fan of splintered ribs. She breathed and breathed and breathed.

Cassie, wake up!

She woke, unaware of passing out. Buzzing in the sky heralded drones. Karla's drones? She twisted, vertigo assaulting her. She couldn't turn, couldn't move her legs. Dark-green-blue ivy snaked around her shins and thighs, dozens of aerial rootlets puncturing her skin.

Shock stilled her struggling. Were these the worlds that CC created, filled with horror? What had they done to this place that the very vegetation attacked her? How many more horrors were there to discover? Would she die here? Shot like Quirk, strangled or eaten by plants? How much had sweet, manipulating Karla known about this place?

"Fuck you!" she screamed at the drones. C Corp agents must be descending on her. Verdammt, but she would not surrender. Her defiance was all she had left, her defiance, her wits, her body, and she would use them as best she could, because to give up was to fail. She would make them stop her.

She bucked and rolled, screaming, tearing the rootlets from her legs, ripping, blood streaming across her soiled skin, glistening, her once-white bra now completely crimson. She rolled over to hands and knees, pulled her limbs free even as the ivy's tendrils turned, seeking her flesh, creeping after her. Finally, she stood on the muddy bank, free, verdant rot in her nostrils. She stooped to grasp clusters of black-blue ivy berries, avoiding the sickly orange-yellow, the bright red, the green. She stepped back to the water, sat in the shallows to hide her activity. Anything. She must do anything to bring out as many samples as she could, whatever they did to her. For the truth, for justice.

Cassie...stop. No more. It's enough.

<You don't get to tell me what to do anymore.>

She swallowed several berries, crushed and smeared them over her skin, sank her hands below the water, slipped berries into her vagina, her rectum. Her aching stomach spasmed. Perhaps the ivy had left a marker in her blood. The foul-sweet water, these choking, grasping plants, they were sick, unnatural. Was this what the inhabitants of humanity's far flung settlements must battle? The landscape of their new homes scoured clean by incandescent chemicals then salted with twisted, Earth-spawned DNA?

The growing staccato thwack of heavy rotors intruded on her thoughts, drowning out the drone whine. Two dark shapes hove into view above the blackened trees. In minutes, downdraft whipped strands of grasping ivy, chopped the sweet water, buffeted her dirty, bloody, punctured skin; chilling her as they descended.

"Trespasser, do not resist! You will be removed from C Corp property. For your own safety, lie face down, hands clasped behind your back."

She complied, lay down on the beach, straining to keep her face out of the cloying mud despite the pain that grew within her. All she had now was hope, the potential that chance would smile on her just once. Just once more.

She thought of Karla.

<I told you I'd do it,> she subvocalised, as viciously as possible.

9

Biella Spaceport, Piedmont, Italy

Quirk strode through the vast, airy arches of Biella Spaceport.

Strode was an overstatement, actually. He carried a significant limp from the Skye debacle. On the plus side, CC's goons hadn't shot him, so that was nice. He patted his pinstriped Merrion suit absently, lurching into the McStarbucks near the turbine train platform.

"Espresso, doppio, per favore." The violet-eyed syRen®nodded. Quirk slipped into a booth, triggered the privacy bubble, and sat, staring out at nothing.

He really had thought, even after everything he'd gone through working there, the lows he'd sunk to, that CC was going to kill him. The reality was worse. That chillingly familiar voice. *I've got a job for you, Quinton. One you can't refuse. Come see me when you're done with Streich.*

His cLife pinged. The time was nigh. He called Cassie.

She sat in a nondescript room, calm colours, simple furnishings—the last of Berlin's sunlight dashed golden across the wall.

"I wasn't sure you'd call."

"Cassie," he pressed a hand to his heart. "You wound me. We're a team. How are you?" He could see improvement. Now, she only looked awful. CC doctors had saved her life. Why? Because death demanded explanation. But CC must know Streich would get something out. They must be planning something, a media counterattack of some sort, a suppression campaign. Still, if Cassie could strike a blow, perhaps the truth could gain a foothold; secure a beachhead against the corporate behemoth. "Are you ready?"

"I am. Original, peer-reviewed reporting, omega-encrypted data packets including original sample analysis going to all universities, global newsrooms, soc-med platforms, fact-streams and the Earth settlements fast relay. All via the university's network. A fitting epitaph to my career. This material will spread so far through independent systems that CC cannot interdict it. Not all of it."

At least she was realistic about the countermeasures they faced. The android brought his coffee, slipping in and out of his bubble. Quirk took a sip, fervently hoping that CC was about to get a seriously bloody nose.

Cassie began. Her Teutonic blonde hair had grown back after CC's medics completely depilated her in their decontamination. Other things had stayed changed. Her eyes had lost their haughty glint. She looked tired.

"Package away." She met his gaze.

His handset pinged politely then dinged, donged, pipped, hummed and buzzed, as his message board, Cluster soc-med hub, Famebook,

Twit-woot nest, Clarion, Claxon, Myspace and Mail all received the report.

He waited for CC's counter strike, neutralising thousands of independent accounts, but the message—all they'd fought for—stared back. He clicked it, sipped superior espresso as text, infographics, images spooled across the screen. Technical, but many recipients would understand it, and the summary was crystal clear. CC was lying, had been lying for years. Maybe this, on top of the Yellowknife investigation. Maybe...

"You did it, Cassie."

"Putting a target on my forehead."

"Perhaps not. Erasing you, even by crude 'accident,' would attract a lot of attention. They did let us go."

She read something on-screen. *"I've just been fired. Very efficient."* She sighed. *"The university site is down. My soc-med profile. I've been locked out."*

"Mine too. The messages are disappearing—" CC had them covered after all.

"Some of them must have stuck!" She stabbed her virtual keyboard, eyes darting left and right. *"I can resend— No, the file is gone. My...aether drive is wiped."*

Her eyes glistened, thick with tears. Then, a grin broke Streich's sharp features.

News alerts pinged Quirk's rolling banner.

DAMNING REPORT INDITES CC.

CC FACES NEW ACCUSATIONS.

FIRST YELLOWKNIFE, NOW SKYE.

UNEC OPENS SECOND FRONT IN CORPORATE WAR.

CC TRADING SUSPENDED.

"Quirk. Quirk, I'm forwarding something."

New mail: *Prof. Streich? Just saw em landing. WHOA! Pinged to the student body. It'll go everywhere. Call me for* eiskaffee. *Sabine x.*

"We did it, Quirk." She smiled warmly, wiped tears from her eyes. *"Thank you. Now, go home. And don't keep in touch."*

10

89 Eppinger Strasse, Berlin

Cassie blinked, eyes tired from another hour of aimless browsing. The CC investigation in The Hague rumbled on. She should be glad it had even started. Three months in, CC now claimed the Yellowknife case was prejudicing the Skye proceedings. She flipped back to her manuscript, reread the previous page, searching for motivation, but it was far too late. Early, in fact. This chapter of her ordeal could wait another day.

She leaned back, chair flexing, contouring to nestle her, closed her eyes, knowing what waited. Words echoed softly in her mind, the voice from Skye, Karla's voice, and with it, flickering images last seen on the bedroom ceiling screen, dark for long months.

The ice in her glass was water now, diluting the little whisky that remained. So engrossing was clicking through pages of nothing that even strong spirits could not distract her. She snorted, brought the crystal to her lips, swallowing watery Dalmore.

The doorbell chimed.

1:34 a.m.

She sighed as the alert windowed on her screen, the image of a hooded figure standing at her front door. She cycled through the garden, deck, garage, roof, and boundary cameras. Nothing fancy, a standard domestic security bundle.

The bell chimed again.

If C Corp wanted to kill her they would have done it weeks ago. She kept this in mind as she went to the door, activating the two-way screen.

"Cassie." It was Karla. "I'm not asking to come in, just listen, please."

If C Corp wanted to kill her, would they send Karla? Cassie trusted her emotions implicitly. Ironic, since most assumed she had none. Not the case. She just knew when to dispense with them.

She thumbed the deadlock, deactivating the panic alarm, leaving the bioscan active. No weapons. She opened the door, stepped out into the cascade of soft light that held the darkness back. Karla lowered her hood. Her auburn hair was buzzed short. Cassie slapped her hard across the face. Karla gasped, but turned back, cheek pink. Cassie slapped her again.

"Liar."

Karla nodded. "Hit me again, I deserve it, but would you have believed a triple bluff? That I was CC, but suddenly rediscovered my conscience, hated what they had made of me—seducer, liar, killer—in five short years?"

"And you are so adept at those things." Cassie imbued her voice with the chill in her chest. "Especially seduction. The frigid academic, an easy mark. Seething with suppressed emotions. 'A couple of fucks will make her do my bidding.'"

Cassie swung once more, but Karla caught her wrist.

"If you do that again, don't slap my face. I'm out, and I want you back."

Cassie thought of all the online hours, the virtual sex, the remote talking, the encrypted plotting. How ironic the one thing she thought had been real—the love—also had been fake. At first. Karla's touch in Brussels—their first real contact—so soft. That had been true, but was Karla ready to change? Could she? Had she already?

Cassie stepped aside, waved Karla in, followed then secured the door.

"Is Karla your name?" she asked, raising the decanter as Karla sat on her actual sofa, in her actual house, the bed they'd never shared only steps away.

Auburn hair fell across dark eyes. "I don't drink. And it is. CC is old-fashioned that way. It's a pension thing. Cassandra, I...need you. This is our one chance to work this out."

So hopeful. So urgent. There was emotion there. Cassie poured herself another Dalmore, neat, the heat in her mouth, her throat, her belly reminding her of Skye.

"You'd better maximise it then."

Karla nodded. She knew her trial had started. "Espionage isn't about the truth, it's about survival. With you, I realised surviving wasn't enough anymore. I saw redemption, Cassie. And we did achieve something, but I can do more, and I want to do it with you."

Karla stood, faced her. "Run away with me, Cassie."

Cassie swallowed her Scotch, put the glass down, and turned; keeping cool, although she'd already decided.

"Show me what it will be like, Karla. Win me back."

The lying seductress moved behind her. One arm circled her waist; one hand smoothed her sweater, finding one breast then the other—naked beneath thin wool. Karla pulled Cassie against her body, melting into yielding contact. Karla's lips found her ear, tongue flicking her lobe. Hands on Cassie's hips turned her, pulled her in.

"Only if you want it. Send me away. I'll go."

Cassie pulled Karla's mouth onto hers, tasting her above the hot undertow of whisky.

Cassie fell on the sofa, sweater pushed up, Karla's mouth on her breasts, jeans ruched below her knees, Karla's tongue on her stomach, in her navel, tugging at her panties, teasing them aside.

"Did you...come here to...finish me?" she gasped.

"Cassie, darling," Karla whispered, "we're only getting started."

This is Robin's first foray into publication, but there is more in the pipeline, and hopefully the first Quirk & Moth novel will be available soon. You can catch up with RCMD at **www.robincmduncan.com** or **@ROBINSKI**, and find him on Goodreads from time to time. Check out some of the story behind the anthology at Mary Robinette Kowal's "My Favorite Bit," August 5th, 2021.

Rings
An Ardulan Tale

J.S. Fields

Sapphic Representation: Lesbian, Pansexual
Heat Level: Medium
Content Warnings: Coarse Language

Author's note: The following story takes place approximately three years after the events in Tales from Ardulum's final chapter. Atalant (species: Neek, bipeds with eight fingers per hand who secrete empathic mucous from their fingertips) and Emn (a genetically modified Ardulan known as a 'flare', standard biped form) currently live on the sentient, traveling planet Ardulum. The Neek are genetic cousins of the Ardulans. Both Ardulans and Neek are capable of telepathy, and Atalant in particular, being one of the ruling classes of Ardulum, can talk to the andal trees—Ardulum's native and dominant tree species. Ardulum is ruled by a triarchy government called the 'Eld,' made up of one man, one woman, and one third gender known as 'gatoi.'

Atalant and Emn spent three whole books trying to get together, only sharing their first kiss at the end of book two. Hence, with all the war and spaceships and firefights and Deep Lesbian Emotions, it's about time the two found a happy ending.

There were two distinct ways to wear gold robes, Atalant decided, as she stepped from the dais in the throne of the Eld Palace, and shuffled her way to the Talent Chamber. The first involved ironing and starching and some sort of tree-derived spray she didn't understand, but which made her hungry every time she smelled it. So that was out. Type two had approximately three variations, which were iterations of tossing said robe on the floor in a heap and hoping the worst of the wrinkles ended up near the hem. The variations were in where you tied your sash, or if your girlfriend let you get away with not wearing one at all.

Today, Emn had slept in. Which was fair, they'd had a long night that had started with trying to hang an antique Earth light fixture from the ceiling and ended up with the cord rather firmly around Emn's wrists. Atalant still wasn't entirely certain how it had gotten there, but by the time she'd noticed, she'd had other things on her mind.

The point was that, today, Atalant had managed to escape their shared chambers in the Eld Palace without critical inspection, which meant she wore a crumpled and slightly stained gold robe, no sash, and her strawberry blonde hair was in the kind of messy braid that her former captain would not have tolerated. Her copper skin was smudged with dirt, and she was certain there was a hickey near her collarbone.

She felt *great.*

Which was why she was now standing in the middle of the Talent Chamber of the Eld Palace—*her* palace—right beside her 'throne,' attempting to listen while Eld Ekimet and Eld Arik babbled about immigration. Normally she'd have begged off, or found some other god-level task that needed attention. Today, she felt prepared to tackle mundane bullshit. *Today* was going to be a very good day...once she got out of this meeting.

In the five years since the whole flare debacle, Ardulum had settled into the Eiean System, which boasted a host of sentient fungi who tolerated their presence. She and the other two leaders of Ardulum had done a lot of traveling and apologizing and attempting to repair broken ecosystems, but what everyone seemed to want, it turned out, was access to Ardulum proper. Arik had suggested they repeal the law dictating that only Ardulans could purchase land on the planet, and since doing that, well...Boom. Everyone and their eight-fingered uncle wanted a piece of the mystical, traveling planet.

"All I'm saying is we need limits. We can't get housing up fast enough, and Ardulum can only grow trees so fast." Ekimet rubbed at zir temples as zie slouched on zir throne. "How many Mmnnuggls did you say just filed? Ardulum isn't designed for spherical species. Their anatomy is too different from our own."

"Thirty-eight. But we have plenty of space in Mmnnugga-Ville. But," Arik paused, tucked a lock of black hair behind his ear, then tapped on the thin bioplastic held in his hand, "only seven live in said residential sphere we built for them on the capital's outskirts. Nicholas petitioned for 'Mmnnugga-Ville' to be recognized as its own city. We have to vote on that sometime soon. What do you think, Eld Atalant?"

"Huh?" Atalant shrugged out of a partial daydream that involved increasingly creative uses of the light fixture cord.

"Mmnnugga-Ville," Arik repeated, sounding exasperated. "City or not?"

"Sure. I like cities. Can I ask you two a question?"

Ekimet raised an eyebrow but Arik put his bioplastic sheet on the armrest of his throne and crossed his arms. "Yeah. What's going on?"

"How do you all do ceremonies here? You know, familial binding ceremonies."

Arik and Ekimet exchanged a long, knowing look.

"You haven't bound yourself to Emn yet?" Ekimet asked. "Even talked about it?"

Warmth rose in Atalant's cheeks. "Well, I mean we've talked about it but, you know." She shrugged. "There were Mmnnuggls. Then reparations. Then that vacation with Yorden, Nicholas and Salice where we found that other seeded world refugee, and we've been fixing *that* mess for the last three years. And now we have all these immigrants and yeah. Where's the time?"

"Atalant," Arik began, "Ardulans do not have very long lifespans, even the eld. *You* may be a subspecies and thereby gain a few extra decades, but Emn is Ardulan through and through. She will have forty years perhaps, at most. If you two are even thinking of reproducing without medical intervention you'll need a third gender gatoi and a license to start a household, at the very least. That'll go a lot smoother if you can show a history of commitment."

"Emn's only twenty-six," Atalant argued. "She has plenty of time. And I never said I wanted to reproduce."

"She's four years from her third don and our gestation periods are twice the length of a Neek's. We generally only reproduce during our second don," Ekimet's eyes narrowed. "You'd better get on this. Do you at least have a gatoi in mind? Have you been dating?"

"No." Atalant took a step back and shoved her hands into her pockets. "I...have feelings about the whole third party issue."

"Have you even *talked* about it?" Arik asked.

They'd talked, yes. And had the one gatoi Atalant might consider—August—to dinner the last time zie'd brought a group of delegates from Rithorununun. That had ended with some passably decent conversation and *maybe* a little light flirting. But everything with Emn felt too new. Too fragile. August had invited them to zir orbital station three times since and, though Emn had been game to go, Atalant always declined. She didn't want to share this. She didn't want to share *Emn.*

"I'm fine with using a medical center," Atalant muttered.

"Yes, and the gatoi deeply love being superfluous." Ekimet frowned at her. "You're an eld, Atalant. The Eld of Ardulum take two partners when they commit. A three-person family is an ideal. The goal. The eld must set an example."

"Yeah, well I'm a Neek and I don't like rules." Her daydream evaporated. "I'm going to start with the basics. One woman. One promise. Maybe a few candles." She grabbed the biofilm from Arik's throne, rolled it, and shoved it into her back pocket. "I'll look this over in my apartment. Comm me if something explodes."

She stalked from the Talent Chamber, past the tapestries of Ardulan seeding events (which normally put her in a *very* good mood), and stomped up the nearest staircase. Gatois. Bah. What she *needed* was some well-seasoned andal shoots, clothes that had been washed sometime in the last week, and a really spectacular gift.

* * *

Atalant flopped, face down, onto her sleeping pad. It was a bad idea—the Eld Palace was all about tradition and tradition was all about itchy, woven bark mats with very little padding. Nicholas had built them a wide version of an Earth bed and Yorden had cobbled together something called a 'mattress', which was a cloth bag stuffed with titha fur. And it *was* marginally softer, but it was lumpy, and Atalant always felt just a little uncomfortable doing anything intimate with Emn on a structure that creaked when they moved.

"Long day?" Emn called from the kitchen.

"Ehhhh," Atalant puffed into the mattress. She heard Emn walk into the bedroom, the sound of her bare feet on the polished andal heartwood soothing Atalant's nerves. Emn had vacated the 'Eld Advisor' position last year in favor of spending more time in the palace archives, but she always seemed to be around when Atalant was in need of support. In part that was down to their telepathy, but sometimes—to Atalant—it felt like magic.

Emn knelt next to her and long, delicate fingers stroked the back of Atalant's neck. Atalant could smell fresh lacquer on her nails and resigned herself to the inevitable glitter transfer. *Backrub?* she asked, the word tickling Atalant's mind and mingling with the whispers of the live andal trees.

"Yes," Atalant groaned. She stretched her arms up and turned her face to Emn. Her black hair still held the barest hints of red, and she'd allowed her hair to grow out since her flare-identity-crisis during the Mmnnuggl war. Her skin looked healthier than Atalant had ever seen it—still a pale, near-translucent white—but the black, geometric markings that ran over Emn's body were growing thicker, the lines now prominently raised. When they'd first met she'd looked like a young, tattooed Terran child. Now she was clearly an Ardulan, clearly a second don, clearly an independent woman who didn't put up with muddy gold robes on the floor and knew *exactly* how backrubs should be administered.

Atalant sat up long enough to peel off her robe—the fabric heavy with the natural *stuk* secretion of her people. Emn tugged Atalant's cotton shirt over her head and laid it across the mat, then gently pushed her shoulder until she was back on her stomach, pillowed into the mattress.

Emn's hands traced her muscle groups, fingers alternately stroking and rubbing, busy unwinding a day's tension. When Emn's thumbs pressed into the base of her spine Atalant groaned and turned to her side, capturing one of Emn's hands in hers.

"Hey uh, Emn," Atalant began. Her body flushed and her *stuk* thinned. Maybe she didn't need anything fancy. Maybe a moment like this—she *was* naked after all—was enough to make her case? "I was wondering if you—"

Eld Atalant. Ekimet's voice cut through her head, decimating every ounce of arousal and romance with it. *We just had another immigration request come through, or what looks like an immigration request. The ship just replays the same message and no one is answering the comm. Port Control is overloaded with immigrants and Arik went to Thannon to help a group of Terrans with a boating problem. They want houseboats. Boats. As houses.* A snort rumbled through zir mind. *Only Terrans.*

Atalant? Emn's voice joined Ekimet's and Atalant immediately felt a headache forming at the base of her skull.

"Hold on just a minute, Emn." She kissed Emn's palm, sat up, and scooted until her back was against the wall. *Why can't you go?*

Ekimet's tone dripped exasperation. *Because I am gatoi and by eld dictate we aren't allowed to make first contact with ships. They have to sit in quarantine for at least a week and the passengers have to prove full vaccination.*

That's—

Ridiculous. I don't need a lecture on it. But I can't go.

Atalant growled. *You're an eld now. Change the law.*

It would take all three of us voting in a full council meeting. Arik is already on his way to Thannon.

We have telepathy. Atalant smacked her hand into her forehead and ground her palm down. Emn took Atalant's hand in hers, kissing the knuckles.

Atalant, would you please just go. We can change laws tomorrow.

"Fine!" Atalant yelled the words, both out loud and in her mind. Emn flinched and Atalant turned away, apologetic. "More eld stuff. I'm sure you heard. I have to go."

She didn't like the way Emn's lips pursed to the side, or the crease between her eyebrows. "How soon will you be back? If not for a while, I'll head back to the archive. I'm about to finish my work on the seeding chronology of Rithorununun." Her face brightened. "Did you know that you can read Ardulum's history in the rings of the andal trees, too? Nicholas has been helping me prepare some slabs from fallen andal. There's a grove in Thannon that needs to be taken down because they've started producing fruit." Emn's eyebrow raised and she leaned in. "That's not normal, by the way. Ardulan andal trees don't fruit in any form. It's very weird. You should probably check it out at some point."

Atalant blew at a strand of hair tickling her nose. "Okay wait, one thing at a time. Fruit is low on my priority list. Will I be back tonight? Probably not. I'll see you in the morning but..." She lifted her shirt, yanking it on roughly, and turned her nose up at her robe. It was sticky with *stuk* and dirty at the hem from the mud of the new palace gardens. It smelled like sweat. The robe was toast. "The fruit sounds like an issue that should be brought to the council, not just me. I'll put it on our agenda." She stood, picked the robe up, and tossed it into the sonic washer.

"I've been to the grove. Only you would need to come. It's small. We couldn't fit all three eld in it anyway. Please just come? It's a small task and we can use it for a little personal time. We don't get much anymore. Also, want me to get another robe?" She stood and clasped her hands behind her back, the long sleeves of her rayon shirt falling below her wrists. Her pants were a slate purple, thick and baggy, and Atalant *really* wanted to tug them off and bury her face in something besides politics and immigration.

Her stomach rumbled, a distant reminder of forgotten lunch. "Nah. I'll have them print me a cheap one when I get there. No sense in sweating the whole way."

"Okay. Atalant..." Emn trailed off, her eyes suddenly very intent.

Atalant couldn't help the smile as her body went into full alert. Her *stuk* turned silky. "Emn?"

"What do you think? Will you stop by?" Atalant swore the air around her sparked.

Emn stepped in close. Atalant took a deep breath, inhaling the nutty, bark smell of Emn's andal soap. Emn's hand wrapped around her waist, the other buried itself in her braid. "Please, Atalant?" Emn whispered. She brought her mouth just shy of Atalant's and her breath was soft and wet across Atalant's lips.

"Definitely." Atalant managed to gasp the word right before Emn kissed her. Andal help her, *why* did politics have to be so time consuming? Hadn't they fought one, no, *several* wars just for the opportunity to do exactly this? Emn's lips were so soft but her hand on the back of Atalant's head was demanding, pulling Atalant to her. Emn's lips parted and Atalant's tongue darted in, salvaging some control of the situation.

Emn giggled and the hand on Atalant's waist danced lower, cupping her ass. Atalant covered Emn's hand with her own, *stuk* smooth and light, and placed it firmly in the hollow of her hipbone before releasing. Then, in a deliberate, telegraphed move—because if Emn was giggling there had to be a rebuttal—Atalant pushed both her hands under Emn's long shirt and cupped her breasts.

Emn's gasp was swallowed as they melded into each other. Atalant's tongue traced Emn's jawline and she whimpered when *stuk*-coated fingers found her nipples. Atalant stroked and gently pinched, fueled by the taste of Emn's skin and the pressure on her hip bones.

"The grove," Emn whispered when Atalant nipped at the soft skin of her neck.

Atalant pulled her hands, slowly, from Emn's shirt and backed away. "I just want it noted for the record that I'm not the one ending this perfectly wonderful make-out session." She smirked at the bright red blush across Emn's cheeks.

"I have a meeting with Nicholas soon," Emn said, "but let's plan on meeting at the grove for lunch."

It'd been far too long since they'd snuck away to the forest and been alone. Well, alone without clothes. Atalant grinned as she brushed her fingertips on her pants, wiping away the quickly congealing *stuk*. "That sounds like a great lunch date, sweetheart. I'll see you there."

* * *

"But what *are* they?!" Atalant stood on the exact same triangular landing pad at the exact port her ship, the *Scarlet Lucidity*, had arrived at some six years ago. Back when Ardulum had been a dream-turned-nightmare-turned-horrible-reality. Back when she hadn't been able to even *kiss* Emn without an existential crisis.

Back before she'd become a god.

She felt very ungodlike now, in the stained flightsuit she'd chosen over her robes—because gods could make their own wardrobe choices—while hundreds of...*creatures* sat around her, looking dazed. They were gray-ish, mostly, with shapely black noses, beady eyes, and ears that looked like they belonged on a child's toy. Their claws looked like those of a Keft—black, curved, deadly. She simultaneously wanted to pick one up and cuddle it, and shoot them all before they mutated.

"Fourth shipment we've gotten in the last month," the port operator said. "They keep coming in like this, on Terran shuttles on autopilot, with only a recorded message for explanation. We've tried four times to contact Earth *and* Mars and no one wants to admit it's their screw up." He stood well away from the shuttle the things had come in on, its shape too close to the *Mercy's Pledge* buran style for Atalant's liking. He, too, wore a stained flightsuit in muted green. His hair was a wispy orange the color of an autumn sunset on Neek, his skin a deep umber brown. Atalant couldn't make out his Talent markings but suspected Mind, since Mind talents tended to be involved in flying-related occupations. As an eld she got two Talents, Mind and Aggression. As a Neek she should have had none.

Fate was fucking ridiculous sometimes.

"What did you do with the others?" she asked. The closest creature looked up at her, round little eyes looking drugged and sleepy.

"So. That." The man looked at the ground and hunched his shoulders. "We've been trying to get an eld on this since the first ship arrived. We had nowhere to put them and our quarantine facilities just aren't equipped. They came with their own trees," he pointed inside the shuttle, where Atalant could see eucalyptuses in giant pots, all tipped over on their side, the soil scattered across the floor. She *knew* they were eucalyptus trees because Yorden and Nicholas had given her a tree identification guide from Earth on her last birthday as a joke. But there were a *lot* of ceremonies and a *lot* of council meetings, and learning the difference between sugar maple and red maple was a lot more entertaining than what design they should manufacture for this year's synthetic *stuk* storage. So, the joke was on them.

"Where did you *put* them?" Atalant prodded.

"Nowhere. That's the thing. They're called *koalas* and they're all cute and cuddly when they are eating their tree leaves. But sober them up and they get mean. We didn't know that, of course, so we just sort of...rounded them up and had them piled in the west shed. They got out. They climb trees. Ardulum is mostly trees. You can see how the issue started."

The man continued to look sheepish. He stood near Atalant, hunched and grimacing. If he went much lower he'd be in danger of impersonating a Mmnnuggl.

"They're in our forests?!" Atalant spun and scanned the canopy. This small town with its import post housed only a few thousand Ardulans. Well, Ardulans and now recent settlers. The andal forests were never far from any Ardulan town but here the trees started, thick-stemmed and densely packed, not fifty meters from the edge of the landing pad. Weirdly artificial looking, as often occurred when sentient trees were in the picture.

Atalant searched the closest tree, from its knobby roots to its curly bark leaking latex, to its branches, curling slightly upward.

In those branches she saw gray tufts. Cute little ears. Stumpy tails. The *koalas* were busy defoliating the tree—ripping the andal leaves off and shoving them into their mouths.

Atalant would have expected to hear the trees complaining about this. She was their conduit, more or less. It wasn't like they'd ever failed to give her a piece of their collective mind when there'd been too much rain, or a Minoran brought in an invasive beetle, or that one time when Nicholas had thought to tap them for something called 'maple syrup' and half the fucking andal on the planet had called for his immediate banishment.

She reached out and mentally poked the nearest tree. It had at least four *koalas* in it, and that was just those visible in the lower branches. *Are they bothering you?*

In that exact moment, in the most ridiculously unbelievable set of actions Atalant had ever seen from a tree (and she had seen a *lot*), four white flowers, each with eight heart-shaped petals, blossomed on the very tip of the lowest branch.

Arik. Atalant sent. She took a step back, trod on a *koala* paw, then had to hop out of the way when it lazily swiped at her ankle. *ARIK!*

She broadcast too loudly.

Atalant? Emn responded. *Are you alright?*

Arik answered next. *Eld Atalant? What's wrong?*

Then at least a hundred andal trees sent pinpricks of consciousness into the back of her brain, making her see black spots.

I just need to speak to Arik. If everyone else could hold on a minute…

In the time it took Atalant to project that thought, three more trees produced the exact same number and type of flowers, all on their lower branches. A *koala* from the first andal tree patted the flowers, swung/hopped to the next one, patted *those* flowers, and continued on. They were…pollinating?

Emn pulled back from their mental connection but the trees and Arik stayed firmly in her head.

We have a koala *problem,* Atalant said. It was really hard not to laugh at how ridiculous that both sounded and looked, especially while half the local forest listened in. *Invasive species got out. We need a mechanism of control. It's causing flowering and I didn't think andal did that. Can you ask the trees how badly they've been...*

The petals fell from the flowers and the whole aperture swelled. Atalant blinked several times as Emn's words came back to her and she realized what she was seeing.

Fruit.

The andal trees were *fruiting*. Just like Emn had said. Fruiting because *koalas* had defoliated enough for the trees to flower, and then *had pollinated the flowers*. Andal trees didn't flower. Andal trees didn't fruit. And if they did, there certainly wasn't a place for *koalas* in the pollination picture. What in Ardulum was happening?

The andal aren't talking to me right now, Eld Atalant, Arik returned. *They seem...very preoccupied. Have you thought of asking Ardulum itself? You're the only one the planet talks to.*

The situation was weird, but it didn't feel like 'wake a sentient planet and ask it for advice' level weird. Emn had said the fruit was a problem, so maybe that problem had just spread beyond Thannon. Though she'd never mentioned *koalas. Or are the andal maybe just taking care of it themselves?* Atalant asked. *Maybe the fruit is for the* koalas *so they stop eating the leaves? Maybe any defoliation works, and the Ardulans just got rid of all natural pests generations ago?*

You're assuming the fruit is edible by these koalas. Have you picked any? Arik asked.

Solid point. Atalant hopped between the scattered *koalas*, who were quickly becoming more alert. Five took swats at her boots and a sixth very clearly snarled at her. When she got to the nearest tree she reached up, hoping to knock down a golden fruit that dangled just out of reach.

The tree shook its branch, and the fruit dropped into her hand.

She almost didn't catch it. The thing was roughly the size of her head, perfectly circular, with just a pock the size of her thumbnail where the stem had detached. It was the gold of sunrise, the kind that had hints of orange and pink in it. The rind felt tough, almost woody. Atalant took a large pocket knife from her boot and dug into the skin, hacking the thing in half.

She really shouldn't have been as shocked as she was when inside—instead of, well, *fruit*—there was some light pulpy mass smelling vaguely of oil, and a ring.

A ring. Made by a tree. A tree ring.

Atalant didn't laugh, but she did groan as she separated the band from the rind and then wiped the juice on her flightsuit. The wood was the same color as andal heartwood—a brown so deep it was almost black, the grain wavy and distinct. It was about the size of her palm, the edges curled ever so slightly down, the inside smooth.

Atalant had absolutely no idea what she was supposed to do with it.

I'm heading to the grove now, Atalant, Emn said, breaking back into Atalant's mind. *Meet you there in a bit?*

Atalant sent an abrupt affirmative, then returned to the massive fruit and *koala* problem before her. She could deal with the fruit problem here, and the animals, then go to Thannon and...

"Do you think it's a collar?" The port authority man stepped up next to her, then pointed to the swell of ripening fruit above them. "That's uh, a lot of fruit. We have at least a thousand *koalas* on Ardulum at this point. Maybe the trees have solved the issue? We collar them and then...leash them? Use them as pets?"

One of the fruits fell just to his left. It split upon impact, halved itself, and another identical ring poked from the flesh.

"How far have they spread?" Atalant asked. She ran sticky fingers over the wood in her hand, listening for the low thrum of 'voice' that all andal wood products emitted. It was there, distinct, if a little muted.

"Within a month, probably across the continent. It's a small continent, and it's mostly unbroken forests."

A weight dropped in the pit of Atalant's stomach. "Do you think they've made it to Thannon?"

Emn, Atalant sent. *Any unusual furry things in the trees out there?*

Emn didn't respond.

Atalant panicked. Not *rationally*, of course, because a *rational* being would note that Emn had *brought people back from the dead* on multiple occasions, including Atalant herself, and had moved planets, and all kinds of outrageous impossible things, so a *koala* animal was not a concern. Atalant, however, chose to ignore the rational part of her brain, because overreaction had been part of her genetic makeup since birth.

The man's face moved from gloomy to thoughtful. "Well, that's clear on the other coast but yes, I suppose it's possible they made it that far."

"And what are they like when they're not high on eucalyptus?"

"Scratch your eyes out," the man returned. He hauled up his right sleeve and showed her three long, angry red lines that stretched from wrist to elbow. "Almost bled out before a healer got here. And that was just one of them, on the first shipment. And it was still half asleep!"

"I have to go," Atalant said. She thrust the ring at the man and took off running, dodging *koalas* as she went.

You don't need to rush that *much, Atalant. They're just* koalas, Emn sent.

"What am I supposed to do, Eld?" the man called after her.

"Collar them if you can!" she yelled back, though she had no clue how he would fit the collars over their heads. "I have to go. Emn is..." She felt silly saying 'in danger,' but if you couldn't protect your girlfriend from rabid *koalas*, really, what good were you as a partner? "I just have to go. I'll send a few more from port control over to help. Keep away if they get too aggressive. I'll catch up with you tomorrow!"

* * *

Atalant did not, as a rule, enjoy the forests of Ardulum. The monocultures were everything that was wrong with the forests of her homeworld, except thriving instead of dying. Monoculture. The same damn genus *everywhere*, occasionally broken up by a few liana and—far too often—harboring vicious ants. Yes, the planet was alive and yes, the trees connected to the planet and they were all sentient and whatever. Monocultures were stupid, Ardulan forestry practices were archaic, and Atalant just *really* didn't like ants.

And now, now they had *koalas*. And fruit.

Fuck.

She took the *Lucidity* back from the town whose name she could never remember, flew directly over the capital without bothering to swap out for an official flyer because she did not have time for bureaucratic bullshit, and landed in the middle of Thannon, a medium-sized fishing village that sat next to a deep ravine. At least it had been a small fishing village before the last move, but since Ardulum had settled in its new solar system and opened immigration, it'd become a favorite settler destination for the Quinns of Crodeque, who were blobs of gelatinous zooplankton. Hence, you never knew whether the puddle on the road was rain, tide, or a Quinn.

Hence, Atalant hopped out of the square, past clusters of curious Ardulans, two Mmnnuggls, a Yishin, and seventeen suspicious-looking puddles. Once she'd made it past the market and into the old Ardulan residential area she broke into a run and stopped looking at the ground.

Emn! she yelled, not for the first time. *Talk to me, sweetheart.*

A mildly exasperated voice responded. *Atalant. You don't need to rush. You're going to fall and crack your head and then the andal of Ardulum will be very upset. The fruits have nothing to do with the koala infestation, I told you!*

But how do you know!? Atalant slowed as the ground became steeper and the wood pavement more splintered. She needed to climb this hill, to the very top of the settlement, before she'd permit herself a breather. *You're sure you haven't seen any* koalas?

Not today, Atalant. There are no ferocious, tiny Terran animals currently attacking the gazebo.

They're probably in the trees! Did you look at the canopy?

Atalant didn't know what the emotional imprint of an eye roll was, but she was pretty certain Emn had just sent her one. She crested the top of the hill, houses behind her, and ran along a ravine perimeter, searching the ground. *I'm almost there,* Atalant thought. *Ah! Just found the rope ladder down the side of the ravine.* She paused, then added, *Why is this still here? We don't imprison flares anymore, therefore have no need of a secret flare rendezvous point in the middle of a ravine.*

This time, the tone was chiding. *There's a history there, Atalant, that shouldn't be forgotten.*

Atalant's boot slipped on one of the woven rungs and she scrambled, fingers digging into the liana that made up the ladder, *stuk* mercifully turning tacky enough for a decent grip. "Solid point," she murmured as she found her footing.

She slowed after that, trying to tell her heart to stop hammering. Emn wasn't in imminent danger because Atalant would *know*, and if she didn't know then Ardulum would definitely tell her, because the planet knew very well the only reason she'd accepted this damn god-leadership role was because Emn wanted to stay on her homeworld.

She reached the bottom and hopped down into a thick flush of waist-high red ferns. "Ugh," she breathed and kicked at the ferns as she stomped forward. Five minutes. She was five minutes away, max, from getting Emn out of this whole mess. What was the use of being a god if you couldn't be a bit overprotective of your girlfriend?

Except the undergrowth had grown thick onto the path that had once been routinely worn clear by flare escapees. No one came to the hidden gazebo anymore, it seemed, now that the flares weren't sequestered from society. The area was pretty, in that leafy, damp way that new undergrowth was, and the height of the ferns forced her to slow to more of a trot.

It'd be a nice place for a picnic. A nice place for a romantic interlude of the naked kind, steeped as it was in history and hope. Atalant made a mental note to remember the patchy canopy and the faint, sweet smell of andal sap for the next time she got more than five minutes of free time.

"Hey." Emn appeared from absolutely nowhere, startling Atalant out of her half-daydream. They almost ran into each other, but Atalant managed to stop herself by slipping on wet, broken fronds and landing on her backside.

"Hey," Atalant returned, her voice tighter than she'd intended. She stood, rubbing her rear, noting the wet patch near her tailbone. "Emn, I asked you to stay in the—"

Emn was in a dress. No, not just *a* dress, but the gray, strapped dress with the flare at the hip that she'd worn that first time they'd really talked after her metamorphosis into second don. In the bright light of morning Atalant could see the red highlights that persisted in her short, black hair, the subtle glint of silver thread in the bottom hem of her dress. She was barefoot, as was fashionable in the Charted Systems, where Neek was from, but not in the Alliance, where Ardulum had last been stationed.

"I, um," Atalant looked down at her stained and rumpled flightsuit. She smelled vaguely of oil and sweat. "Uh. I wasn't aware there was a dress code. For rescuing."

"Rescuing?" Emn laughed. "Oh, Atalant. What do you think I need rescuing from?"

"Uh..." Atalant pointed up. Trees had not yet closed over the path, and the nearest mature andal was at least twenty meters away. "There's, uh, *koalas*, in the trees..."

Emn smiled at her, in that sweet, near-mischievous way that meant Atalant was either in trouble, or they were about to get naked. Sometimes both. "I will survive the *koala* infestation. Would you come to the gazebo, please? I have sweetened andal."

She offered Atalant her hand. Atalant took it, admiring, not for the first time, the black veins that circled Emn's fingers, the pentagon on her palm. All flare markings, and all so uniquely Emn.

They walked to the gazebo in silence, Emn occasionally looking back over her shoulder, grinning, biting her lower lip. Above Atalant could hear andal leaves rustling, but was startled when she saw trees forming flowers, the petals dropping, and fat, round fruits swelling in the sunlight.

There were a lot of petals on the ground, now that she thought to look. White, yellow, orange, and a few red, but all the same shape. That didn't make sense, because there were no andal trees above them, and the wind barely ruffled her hair.

"Emn, what...?"

They reached the gazebo and Atalant lost her words. It was still an andal wood structure, round, made from hand-hewn boards with a latticed roof that had a big circular hole in the center of it. Andal trees still partially shaded the gazebo but flower petals—*andal* flower petals—covered the floor. There'd been petals in N'lln, Neek, when she'd arrived home after her exile. The air had been heavy with perfume then, too, of trillium flowers.

Atalant took a long, deep breath. She'd forgotten to breathe, it felt like, for an eternity. Emn's hand squeezed hers and Atalant turned, conscious that her mouth was slightly agape and that she didn't have a single coherent thought.

Andal fruit had been very deliberately placed in a circle in the middle of the gazebo, just big enough for two people to stand in. Fruit also circled the gazebo, and the air carried a heavy perfume.

"The *koalas*," Atalant managed to stutter, ridiculously. "And the fruit."

"Did you know—" Emn said as she let go of Atalant's hand and stepped into the gazebo. Her half-smile turned into a smirk worthy of Nicholas. "That while modern Ardulans hand carve the ceremonial wooden bracelets that the adults in a family wear, traditionally, Ardulum provided them, through the andal?"

Bracelets? Atalant went into full blown panic mode, her *stuk* thinning and forming droplets on her fingertips. How big had the rings been they'd pulled from the fruit at the landing pad? Too small to go over a *koala* head but looked like they might fit around the neck or...over the hand of a grown, adult Ardulan. But there were *thousands* of fruits which meant there were *thousands* of bracelets.

"How, uh, how many people were you planning to have in this family?" Panic continued to bloom inside her. Shit, she could barely conceptualize adding a gatoi, even much, *much* later in their lives. She didn't have to, say, bond with all of Ardulum did she? Oh, andal help her, if there was some eld requirement that she had to take on an entire planet's population, she was ready to hang up her golden robe *right now.*

Emn definitely rolled her eyes this time. "Oh, Atalant." Again, she offered her hand and again, Atalant took it, stepping into the gazebo. Here, the fruit smell was all-encompassing, and sweeter, somehow, intermingled with the smell from the petals.

Really, it just made the panic that much worse.

Emn led her to the circle, and stepped in. Atalant followed. Emn reached down and picked up one of the fruits, expertly tore it in two halves with absolutely no juice running, which was a miracle of eld-like proportions, and removed the wooden bracelet inside.

"The andal was a little out of practice, turns out." Emn took a square of cloth from one of her dress pockets and rubbed it over the bracelet, clearing away the juice. Fuck, Atalant loved her in that dress. Loved the way it clung to her hips and breasts, the way it showed the shadow of her belly button. "Would you believe even Ardulum itself got involved?" Emn shivered, her skin goosebumping. "You never told me the planet's voice was so…"

"Terrifying?" Atalant supplied, the word at the forefront of her thoughts.

Emn kissed her on the cheek. "Yes. The trees had been practicing here, in the grove, where no one was likely to see. But the trees, it turns out, are about as impatient as you are, Atalant." One of Emn's eyebrows angled. "Can't imagine how that happened."

Warmth rose in Atalant's cheeks. Again.

"So, while this was all supposed to be a *surprise*," Emn directed the last word at the nearest andal, "some of the trees got a little excited and thought they'd start producing on the other side of the continent, where you were so worked up this morning. The solitary trees themselves aren't the best at sorting emotions apart."

"And…and this?" Her words came out choked, strangled, utterly devoid of breath.

Emn brought Atalant's right arm up, straightened her wrist, and placed the tips of her fingers just inside the opening of the bracelet. "This, Atalant, is a proposal."

It was deadly quiet. There should have been wind blowing through the ravine. There should have been bird calls. There should have been a million fucking trees gently whispering to her all their stray thoughts. She heard a whooshing sound, moving in time with her erratic heartbeat, but other than that, absolutely nothing else.

Would it be all right if I continued? Emn asked, her eyes wide, the faintest hint of a smile on her face.

Atalant barely managed a nod.

"I've spent a lot of time thinking about this, Atalant." Emn leaned in and brushed her lips across Atalant's cheek.

"About how to get andal trees to produce ancient ceremonial jewelry?" Atalant said before she could stop herself. She clapped a hand over her mouth the second the sentence was out. "Sorry," she said, her voice muffled. "I didn't mean—"

Emn cut her off with another kiss. This one enfolded Atalant like a tsunami, sweeping her emotions up and bashing them around until the world spun. There was Emn's tongue in her mouth, the tip dancing across her own. There was a hand on her breast—insistent and warm—

then the same hand gliding down her flightsuit, cupping her possessively between the legs.

As quickly as it started, Emn pulled away. Her lips had swollen red, her face blushed almost the same color under her pale skin. "No more talking, Eld," Emn whispered.

Atalant nodded and clasped her hands behind her back.

"The crew of the *Pledge*, the *Lucidity*, are my family. I'd never want to replace any of them. But I like the idea of promises. I never knew my father, or my gatoi parent, if I had one. My mother never showed me images of either."

An image of a baby flashed through Atalant's mind before she could tamp it down, closely followed by a feeling of horror.

"No, Atalant." Emn chuckled. "I'm talking about having a bonded family. You and me, to start. Maybe to end, I don't know. We can talk about gatois and kids later. This isn't about that." She pushed the bracelet onto Atalant's wrist. The wood felt warm from Emn's hands, slightly sticky from the fruit juice, but it fit all the same. "I want to begin a familial bond with you, Atalant. A formal, traditional one, with all the rights and privileges associated therein."

The last part was in the book I read, Emn added. *The andal went to a lot of trouble for tradition, so I thought I'd better follow suit.*

"What...am I supposed to do?" Atalant didn't want to take the bracelet off, that much she knew. It had just enough weight to remind her it was there, not enough to impede daily life. She liked how it looked—a deep brown against olive skin. She liked how it made her feel—surprisingly calm—though nothing had fundamentally changed between them.

"Is it something you want too?"

Atalant's eyes went wide. "Of course! I, well," she got to her knees, more awkwardly than necessary, and grabbed one of the fruits. It slipped out of her shaking hands and she scooted after it, the fabric of her flightsuit catching on the rough wood of the gazebo and tearing through at her left knee. She grabbed the fruit before it rolled off the edge, smashed it against the endgrain of the wood there, tore the skin off, and fished the bracelet out from inside. It glinted weirdly in the light so Atalant wiped it hastily on her flightsuit before standing and moving back to Emn.

"It's not that I haven't been thinking about it. I have. Maybe not as much as you because I hadn't really worked out mechanics or—" She held the bracelet out as she babbled, paying more attention to the smile creeping over Emn's face than anything else, when she got the glint again. What she'd at first assumed was a trick of the filtered sunlight was not. Of course not.

The bracelet Atalant held wasn't brown. It was gold. As gold as her robes, as gold as the inlay on the Talent Chamber thrones. As gold as the tacky cutlery that had come in the mess of the *Lucidity*.

"Why are they not all brown?" Atalant asked, deadpan, more to the andal than to Emn.

"You're an eld, Atalant." Emn slipped into Atalant's free arm. Atalant reflexively tightened it around Emn's waist. She pressed her fingers into the fabric of Emn's dress, feeling for the raised veins underneath. Grounding herself. Remembering. *Ask me the question.*

Do they use the word 'wife' on Ardulum? Atalant asked. The panic rose again, filling her throat with the light taste of acid. *Is that just a Terran Common adaptation?*

"Atalant." Emn's left eyebrow arched.

"Sorry. Right, sorry." Atalant chewed on her lower lip for a moment, trying to pull words both smooth and sexy into some semblance of order.

She promptly failed.

"I'm really glad they're not *koala* collars and honestly I don't know how we'd get them on anyway and the gold would look real bad on that sort of buffed silver fur but for a bracelet it's fine so I'd really like it if you'd be my wife if you wanted to but only if you wanted to." She fumbled the bracelet onto Emn's wrist. Her face, she was certain, was as red as the inside of a *janu* fruit.

Emn clasped her forearm, their bracelets hitting each other with a soft clunk of hardwood. *Yes, Atalant,* Emn whispered into Atalant's mind.

There was kissing then. So much kissing. Atalant didn't know who started it and it didn't matter because her flightsuit was down around her waist one minute, pooled at her ankles the next. Emn's dress lasted half a minute, at most. They made it to one of the gazebo's benches— scratchy, the fibers lifting enough to tear skin if the friction wasn't managed just right—before Atalant remembered what had brought her to Thannon in the first place.

She turned her head, reluctantly, from the very flushed and very naked Emn, her short, dark hair fanned around her head, slightly curled, completely enticing. She poked her head out from under the gazebo roof. The days were short in their new solar system, where Ardulum had positioned itself, and the sun had already gone down behind the forest canopy. Light filtered through the leaves and reflected off eyes...hundreds of pairs of beady black eyes nestled in the upper boughs.

Watching.

"Atalant," Emn said with a slight emphasis on the last syllable.

"Huh?" Atalant turned back. "Sorry. We still have a—"

Emn pulled her head back down, moved Atalant's hand between her legs, and gasped. "You're too easily distracted," she said in between gulps of air. "A wife needs to focus."

Atalant pressed her fingers down, in a very specific place that elicited a very specific reaction. "Don't we need to do something in public now, to make it official? Isn't that how this usually goes?"

Emn's hand snaked between Atalant's legs as well, tickling its way across the sensitive skin of Atalant's inner thighs, teasing, before mimicking the exact movement Atalant had performed on her. "Have we ever followed what's usual?'"

Words, Atalant realized, were superfluous and she sucked at them anyway. She decided to focus on the way it felt as her fingers slid inside Emn, the noises Emn made that became truncated when Atalant resumed kissing her, taking the lead.

Maybe there would be more talk, someday, about a gatoi partner, or children, or maybe leaving Ardulum. She wouldn't mind shedding the gold robes. But right now, despite the *koalas*, and the excess wooden jewelry, and the soon-to-be rotting fruit, or the likelihood that immigration would go to hell, or Ardulum would move, or some *real* crisis would pry her from this spot, this moment, these sensations...

Atalant was just really, really happy that Emn was going to be there, with her, through it all. *Emn, I—*

Kiss me, Atalant. You can fail at words later.

Atalant, quite happily, shut up.

Interested in the story before the engagement? Want to learn more about the Ardulum universe? You can get the entire Ardulum series in print, eBook, and audio at all major retailers. For special behind the scenes snippets, bonus stories, and new works by J.S. Fields, join the patreon: **www.patreon.com/jsfields.**

You can also stay up to date at **www.jsfieldsbooks.com.**

Please take a moment to review this book at your favorite retailer's website, Goodreads, or simply tell your friends!

ABOUT THE AUTHORS

N.L. Bates is an author of science fiction, fantasy, and slipstream stories, and is the moderator of the long-running critique group Reading Excuses. When not writing stories, she enjoys biking, dancing, and tabletop RPGs. She also writes and performs music as her alter ego, Natalie Lynn and filks occasionally, usually by accident. Connect with her on Twitter (@nlbateswrites) or find her at her website, www.nlbates.com.

J.S. Fields (@Galactoglucoman) is a scientist who has perhaps spent too much time around organic solvents. They enjoy roller derby, woodturning, making chainmail by hand, and cultivating fungi in the backs of minivans. Nonbinary, and yes, it matters.
Fields has lived in Thailand, Ireland, Canada, USA, and spent extensive time in many more places. Their current research takes them to the Peruvian Amazon rainforest each summer, where they traumatize students with machetes and tangarana ants while looking for rare pigmenting fungi. They live with their partner and child, and a very fabulous lionhead rabbit named Merlin. You can find their books at www.jsfieldsbooks.com.

William C. Tracy writes tales of the Dissolutionverse: a science fantasy series about planets connected by music-based magic instead of spaceflight. He also has an epic fantasy available about a land where magic comes from seasonal fruit, and two sisters plot to take down a corrupt government. He will be starting a space colony trilogy based on the universe in *Down Among the Mushrooms*.
William is a North Carolina native with a master's in mechanical engineering, and has both designed and operated heavy construction machinery. He has also trained in Wado-Ryu karate since 2003, and runs his own dojo in Raleigh NC. In his spare time, he cosplays with his

wife and they enjoy putting their pets in cute little costumes and making them pose for the annual Christmas card. Follow him on Twitter (@tracywc) for writing updates, cat pictures, and thoughts on martial arts. You can also visit him online at www.williamctracy.com or www.patreon.com/wctracy.

Robin C.M. Duncan is a Scot born and living in Glasgow. A Civil Engineer by profession, he has been writing for decades, but seriously only for the last ten years. In addition to being a member of READ, and a senior member of Reading Excuses, he belongs to the Glasgow Science Fiction Writers' Circle (GSFWC). His claim to 'fame' before the publication of Distant Gardens was the long-listing of his story The NEU Oblivion for the 2019 James White Award. 'Robinski' can be found on Facebook (crawford.duncan.12), Twitter (@ROBINSKI), Goodreads (Robin C.M. Duncan), and at www.robincmduncan.com, complaining about stuff. Please feel free to say 'Hello', and to ask if he shouldn't be writing instead.

Sara Codair is a community college English professor and author of speculative short stories and novels, including The Evanstar Chronicles and Earth Reclaimed. They partially owe their success to their faithful feline writing partner, Goose the Meowditor-In-Chief, who likes to "edit" their work by deleting entire pages. You can follow Sara and Goose's writing journey on Twitter and Instagram (@shatteredsmooth). You can also learn more about Sara on their website, www.saracodair.com.